MW00623020

Sealed Orders

Alaric Bond

Sealed Orders
Copyright © 2018 by Alaric Bond
Published by Old Salt Press LLC

ISBN: 978-1-943404-21-6 e.book
978-1-943404-22-3 paperback

All rights reserved. No part of this book may be reproduced or transmitted in any form or by any means, electronic or mechanical, including photocopying, recording or by any information storage and retrieval system, without written permission from the author, except for the inclusion of brief quotations in a review.

The cover shows a detail from View of Cape Town, Table Bay, Cape of Good Hope, with a seventy-four gun ship lying-to for convoy, by Thomas Whitcombe (1763 – 1824)

Publisher's Note: This is a work of historical fiction. Certain characters and their actions may have been inspired by historical individuals and events. The characters in the novel, however, represent the work of the author's imagination. Any resemblance to actual persons, living or dead, is entirely coincidental. Published by Old Salt Press. Old Salt Press, LLC is based in Jersey City, New Jersey with an affiliate in New Zealand. For more information about our titles go to www.oldsaltpress.com

For Raymond and Tessa

By the same author

The Fighting Sail Series:

His Majesty's Ship

The Jackass Frigate

True Colours

Cut and Run

The Patriot's Fate

The Torrid Zone

The Scent of Corruption

HMS Prometheus

The Blackstrap Station

Honour Bound

and

Turn a Blind Eye

The Guinea Boat

CONTENTS

Sealed Orders

Part One

1.

The winter sun streaming through the scuttle gave Tom King a twinge of guilt. He must have slept from darkness to daylight and totally missed dawn; the most dangerous time for any minor warship. Such a thing had not happened since taking command of HMS *Hare* and he was suitably ashamed. He rose slightly in his cot and looked about. The sleeping cabin was a small space partitioned off from his main quarters and seemed unnaturally still with none of the pitching that was usual. There were also fewer shipboard sounds; the rumble of bare feet as men moved about the deck above, a more constant whine of wind blowing through taut lines or the regular thump of waves battering the brig's frail hull. Then realisation dawned and he remembered that, rather than being at sea, *Hare* had made harbour more than two days before and now lay safe amid the protection of one of Britain's largest naval bases.

Better than that, the despatches King had so carefully carried for several hundred miles were now on their way to the Admiralty; indeed, they might even have been delivered. Meanwhile, his own verbal report to the Port Admiral had begun to find its way around the clubs and coffee houses; soon all Plymouth would be abuzz with details of Admiral Strachan's action. It was a success that seemed to put the final seal on Nelson's victory off Cape Trafalgar and King could finally rest knowing all responsibility for transmitting the news was at an end.

However, *Hare* remained attached to the triumphant squadron and had been a witness, albeit a mute one, to the battle, so King's company had been much in demand. Only a few hours before, he had dined in the wardroom of a neighbouring seventy-four, which probably explained the dry mouth and his oversleeping. The news had arrived barely days after that of Trafalgar and the death of a national hero, so his audience were already high in emotion and extremely receptive, although King felt he had reminisced enough and was in need of some time to attend to his own affairs.

But then his returns were up to date and with all other journals finished he supposed there was nothing actually pressing. Croft, his first lieutenant, had been worrying like a mother hen over the various repairs *Hare* required, yet both knew he was more than capable of attending to the majority without reference to his captain. And Foil, the purser, was equally experienced and could be relied upon to indent for what stores they needed. All King truly had to do was ensure both carried out their duties correctly and that was more than enough for the quiet day he was envisaging.

The recollection allowed him to relax back into his cot for a moment although, now he was fully awake, King knew it would be impossible to return to sleep and soon he was clambering up and calling for McNamara, his steward.

The man, a slender specimen who had proved useless as a seaman but was an excellent servant, appeared almost at once carrying a large, steaming pewter jug that he placed on the deck.

"Good morning, sir." McNamara spoke with a soft Irish accent that often reminded King of a long-missed friend. "Shall I lay out your full dress uniform once more?"

"No," King told him firmly as he dismissed the memories and took a step towards his washstand. "Duck trousers and my second plain coat if you please. I shall shave directly."

"Very good, sir." McNamara departed only to return with King's shaving bowl, brush and razor. These were placed on the stand and the servant left once more. King splashed a little of the hot water into the bowl and, holding it awkwardly against the stump of his left arm, proceeded to work up a lather. He had worn his full dress frock coat for the last two days and should preserve it for truly special occasions; plain, undress, tunics carried less gold braid and were more for general use. But then the first of these already had a couple of small repairs to the elbows and, with little money to buy another before the next quarter, that should also be conserved. The second had yet more patches and shoulders that were bleached from the sun but, as he had no intention of receiving visitors or going ashore, would suffice. "And I should like the leather waistcoat," he added loud enough for McNamara to hear through the thin partition. November in England was never a comfortable month and far colder than the southern climes he was used to.

"The leather waistcoat, very good, sir," McNamara repeated as he returned with a large enamelled bowl which he half filled with hot water. The thing just fitted alongside everything else on the washstand, although was inclined to fall off when there was any kind of sea running. King reached for the razor and felt at the blade with his thumb. It had already been stropped, an act he found particularly awkward, although the fact that another man must do such work for him was equally frustrating. Then, replacing the razor and collecting the brush once more, he addressed himself to lathering his face.

"A frigate made harbour during the night and has signalled for victuals," McNamara informed him softly.

"Is she from Sir Richard's squadron?" King asked as he dipped the razor; the Irishman shook his head.

"No, sir. She's the *Devon*, thirty-six; Captain Brewster. I understand she were on an independent commission."

King made no response; in all probability the unknown Brewster had returned from a cruise – probably a couple of months, maybe more. A time when he would have been free to roam pretty much at will, preying on enemy commerce and probably clocking up a decent pile for himself in the process. And even if not, even if it had simply been a coastal trip from the Downs, Portsmouth or London, Brewster still had a frigate to command; a true ship of war and one that could make far more of an impact than any sixteen-gun brig-sloop.

"And Mr Brehaut thinks there may be snow on the way," McNamara added cautiously.

Snow. King sighed softly; that was just what he needed. He had barely held command of *Hare* two months but she had been in commission for over three years before then, with most of the time spent at sea. There were now a number of areas that required dockyard attention and they could well be called in for a minor refit during the current stay. In which case, he would be lucky to take her to sea again before the summer and an early dose of snow would hardly help.

On top of that, there was an even chance he would no longer be in command when she did finally emerge. Victory or not, *Hare* had taken little part in the recent action and it was only a few months before that King faced court martial for the loss of *Kestrel*, his previous command. The whole matter was quickly dealt with; *Kestrel* had been little larger than *Hare* and was overwhelmed by a vastly superior force. The court's verdict was swift; King had been discharged without a stain on his record and appointed to *Hare* almost immediately. But even with the country desperate for shipping, commands were not exactly common. There were plenty of more favoured officers keen for the chance to show their worth and it only needed one such hopeful with a measure of interest to attract attention and he could find himself on the beach once more.

The thought depressed him further as he scrubbed more soap into the small amount of beard that had grown since the previous morning. If he were truly planning a restful day he might have dispensed with shaving, although he had no wish to sink quite so low. At sea, anything might happen and often did without notice, yet it was a ceremony King rarely missed and saw no reason to modify the habit when in harbour. Besides, should he need to smarten himself it was far easier to change a shirt or don a better tunic than shave. As if to prove the point, a knock came at the main cabin door and was quickly followed by the marine sentry announcing the midshipman of the watch.

"In the sleeping cabin, Mr Summers," King called as McNamara returned and handed over a steaming cup of what King hoped would be chocolate. The midshipman also squeezed himself into the small space and appeared momentarily awkward at finding his captain in such intimate circumstances.

"You have a message, Mr Summers?" King prompted.

"Yes sir, there is a boat approaching," the lad replied, and a smile began to form as he remembered. "A visitor," he continued. "I think I recognised the Captain."

"The Captain?" King questioned, the razor hovering away from his face.

"Beg pardon, sir, Captain Sir Richard Banks," Summers

hurriedly corrected himself, before adding, "Him what escaped with us from France."

King sighed again, placed his razor down on the washstand, and turned to his steward.

"The better uniform, sir?" McNamara asked, and King nodded.

* * *

"'Ere, are you sure about this?" Sayer questioned. "I mean, that it ain't too early?"

Russell studied his reflection carefully as he pulled the smart blue uniform into place. "Sure?" he asked. "I'm bleedin' positive. Now round up the others; tell them I'll be out shortly."

The seaman gave a doubtful snort and slumped from the room, leaving the door slightly ajar as he did.

Moving away from the mirror Russell turned to the bed where the bicorne hat lay next to a particularly worthy hanger. He collected the weapon and examined it for a moment; it had a bright steel scabbard that concealed a blued blade which carried a modicum of engraving. He had bought it the day before – well, perhaps bought was stretching matters slightly – acquired maybe? But ignoring semantics, once secured to his belt, the sword looked fine and was the perfect finishing touch. He supposed it might actually prove useful, even if Russell had no real idea how to handle the thing.

The hat fitted well enough and, as he placed it squarely on his head, there was time for one last glance into the mirror. He was barely out of his teens but that was hardly unusual for a naval lieutenant and, though it was not a handsome face, Russell felt his dark eyes and firm jaw gave him just the right air of authority. And there was no doubt he knew how to carry himself while he also had a quick mind as well as the knack of knowing exactly the right thing to say or do when the situation demanded. This, combined with an innate ability to judge his fellow man, had always seen him right while bringing him to the point where he could enjoy the respect due to a commissioned sea officer.

And never had there been a better time to wear a blue uniform;

with defeat ashore and victory afloat, the Navy were definitely in favour yet, despite Trafalgar, few could see an end to the current war. If his luck held, Russell might continue for years to come and even develop his career further allowing others to take on the physical aspects while he set his mind to more ambitious projects. But for now he was content as well as supremely confident that the day would turn out as successful as those that had preceded it. And it was with that slight trace of arrogance that he twitched the white-faced lapels into place, straightened his neck cloth and finally ducked out of the low door and into the passageway beyond.

A few steps and Russell was in the main parlour of the boarding house where all were busy with breakfast. In the corner he saw Sayer once more along with the three other members of his team; they weren't the best but had already proved able to work together which was all Russell required. He stepped confidently through the throng, conscious of the effect his uniform and presence was creating in the crowded room. Many would be seamen, and so view him with anything from mistrust to downright hostility, although that was something Russell had come to expect and secretly enjoy. He allowed himself a sidelong glance at what might become prey themselves in time, although he had paid for the next two nights in the boarding house and was not so foolish as to raid his own territory.

"You'll be ready then?" he asked, reaching the men.

"Ready in time," Sayer replied laconically, only deeming to glance up briefly from his porridge.

"I shall be outside," Russell informed them. "And will be moving off directly; anyone not with me is left behind. Is that clear?"

At the change of tone the four looked up while all, bar Sayer, muttered grudging affirmatives. Russell turned on his heel and walked out of the room without looking back.

Treating him with public disdain would not do at all; Sayer would have to change his ways and all four could do with smartening themselves up. If they weren't prepared to play the part, he would have to think about dismissing the lot and finding others. This was a dangerous business and no place for any not totally committed.

* * *

"Not too early for you, Tom?" Banks asked, as King shook the well remembered hand.

"Not at all, sir; it is good to see you. Won't you make yourself comfortable?"

As a Cruizer class brig-sloop, *Hare* was not the smallest vessel in the Navy, and King's quarters represented the most palatial accommodation on board. But still the deckhead was uncommonly low for a man of Banks' stature, and the senior captain gratefully took the seat King indicated.

"An eventful trip, or so I am hearing," he remarked when King had ordered coffee for his guest. "Ties up Admiral Nelson's victory rather neatly, I should say."

"Indeed," King agreed. "Though I had not expected the public to take recent events so much to heart."

"Aye, the mob would seem to be tired of this war," Banks reflected as he relaxed in his seat. "They wish to see Boney's hash settled as quickly as any of us."

"I was thinking more of Nelson," King remarked. "I hardly spoke with the man more than a dozen times and am saddened by his loss yet hear the entire country is in mourning, with many that have never seen the sea blubbing like toads."

"I have long since abandoned any attempt to understand civilians," Banks agreed before adding, "Indeed most service men remain a mystery to me."

King grinned. It was pleasant to be talking with Sir Richard in this manner. There was considerable difference in their ranks and for much of his career King had served directly under, and secretly rather feared, the man. Yet the years of shared experiences had recently culminated in a joint escape from Verdun, an act that had done much to destroy any remaining boundaries between the two. Besides, King, though only a commander by rank, was captain of *Hare* whereas Banks remained a visitor, so they were almost on equal terms.

"Can you be tempted to say more of Strachan's action?" Banks asked and King recognised the same eagerness he had so often encountered since reaching Plymouth.

"Not much to say," he replied. "I had only been with the squadron a matter of weeks."

"The Admiral is a rum cove, by all accounts."

"Not the most predictable for sure," King agreed cautiously.

"They say that when Sir Dicky swears he means no harm and, when he prays, no good," Banks chuckled.

King paused for a moment; he was not sure if he should be discussing his commander in such a way, but his guest, it seemed, had no such inhibitions. "And I also hears the men call him Mad Dick," Banks added with a snort, "though expect they say much the same of me. But I am interrupting; pray continue."

King drew breath, now grateful to return to his story. "I took over *Hare* from John Bodly, who has opted for parliament," he explained. "They let me bring a few followers, but there was little time to become accustomed before we were sent to Gib. with supplies and despatches. Once there I were hoping to be attached to the Med. Fleet, but much was in progress and little attention available for an uncommitted brig. Eventually I found myself in Admiral Strachan's squadron."

"And what was the brief; chasing those who had escaped Nelson?"

At that moment McNamara entered with a tray and proceeded to pour coffee for Banks and chocolate for his captain. Both men remained silent while the servant was in the room, something which might be considered an unnecessary precaution as, in a vessel such as *Hare*, sound would travel easily throughout the small hull. But if secrecy were not possible, it must at least be observed and no more was said until McNamara left.

"Not precisely," King continued once he had. "As you are probably aware, there are several French squadrons currently at sea and, when *Phoenix* appeared from the north signalling she had sighted a fleet, we assumed them to be from Rochefort."

"*Phoenix*?" Banks mused.

"Perseverance class – Tom Baker has her," King explained. "I spoke with him briefly after the action. It seemed he were cruising off the Isles of Scilly when news of the Frenchmen came through from a merchant. He gave up his patrol to rout them out. We only discovered them to be from Villeneuve's fleet when they'd been taken."

"Which you did, and magnificently."

"Oh, I had little to do with matters," King confessed as he collected his cup. "Much of the action were done by frigates far larger than this little tub." He glanced round the small cabin with what was almost affection. "But they performed well; in fact the French liners were finally brought to battle by a couple of our fifth rates."

"Frigates, eh?" Banks raised an eyebrow in surprise. "And taking on two-deckers!"

"Chased them for most of a morning," King confirmed. "*Santa Margarita* and Baker's *Phoenix* were snapping at their heels like hounds after stags. Then they met them beam to beam as equals."

"I understand no single-deckers were fired upon at Trafalgar," Banks pondered. "Though, in smaller actions, protocol is inclined to go by the board."

"That was more than made up for," King grinned as he sipped his chocolate. "Would that I had something larger myself, but the French were all liners and I could not expose a brig to such fire."

"Of course not; no one would expect you to," Banks agreed quickly as he noticed the faraway look in King's eye. "Was it a long action?" the older man prompted.

"Just over two days from first sight to our main force closing."

"And the butcher's bill?"

"Little more than a hundred," King replied. "Though the French lost many times as many. When they could find no alternative, they formed line of battle and Admiral Strachan made straight for their centre."

"He has *Caesar*, does he not?"

"Indeed, and she is an eighty, though he took on four third rates without a thought."

Banks accepted this with a nod.

"The leading Frenchman tacked and *Caesar* were soon in the thick of it though *Namur* came to her rescue. Next we knew our two-deckers were to one side of the enemy with frigates the other; it were pell-mell to be sure."

"And four prime liners taken, or so I hears."

"An eighty and three seventy-fours. All will make a fine addition to the fleet."

"The last of those we faced at Trafalgar."

"Pretty much," King agreed.

"You said casualties were light, was there much damage?"

Banks asked.

King shook his head. "Not amongst our ships; the enemy's tophamper is a little worse for wear and last I saw there was work needed to their hulls. But they should be heading here as we speak; I was sent on with despatches."

"I'd have given much to see such an action," Banks sighed as he sat back in his chair. Then, noticing the look on King's face, added, "Though it were doubtless disheartening not to take a more active part."

"Oh, *Hare* repeated signals, fished men from the water and lent a hand when it came to securing prizes," King agreed. "But you are correct; it was frustrating."

"And are you content to remain with Admiral Strachan?" Banks asked suddenly.

King swallowed; the question had taken him by surprise and he was conscious of a tension that had suddenly risen within the small cabin. "I have little choice, providing my services are required," he replied. "Despite Nelson's efforts, there remain Frenchmen at sea. *Hare* is in want of a refit, though I think the larger vessels have more call on the dockyard, and she can probably serve a while longer..."

"But do you feel a commitment to Sir Richard Strachan?" Banks persisted.

King said nothing for a moment; the only Sir Richard he felt any loyalty to was the one sitting opposite him, although it would hardly do to say so. Besides, as far as King knew, Banks was still awaiting court martial for the loss of *Prometheus*. That he was here now, aboard a commissioned warship and in uniform, said much, but he may not have a command himself. Indeed he was nearing the age when many retired from the sea.

In truth there was nothing King would have liked better than to serve alongside his old commander but if he was about to be offered a shore posting – some regulating position, the chance to assist in supervising a shipyard or charge of a section of Sea Fencibles – he would not be interested.

"Would that be at sea, sir?" King asked hesitantly.

"Oh yes," Banks confirmed before adding, "and you would retain the command of this brig." The older man was now positively beaming. "You see, Tom, my name is strangely in favour at present: I have been given charge of a small squadron with a heavy frigate to lead it. And, as much as it can be, the choice of ships and officers is in my hands. So what say you join me?

2.

"I am a King's officer," Russell announced while holding up a much thumbed piece of paper. "By Act of Parliament I am empowered to search these premises in the pursuit of those who have deserted their ship, or might wish to serve His Majesty at sea."

The landlord stepped back from the door and scratched his head in surprise. "It's a touch early for this ain't it, Lieutenant?"

"We are at war," Russell informed him sternly as he stepped inside. "Now I would see your register; do you have any known seamen amongst those staying?"

His men were following close behind and there was no opposition. The dark room was crowded with tables but the only other person present was a young girl who immediately fled through a back door.

"Follow her," Russell directed but Sayer was already off in pursuit. The landlord heaved a deep sigh which Russell ignored. Experience had taught him that speed was essential; unless they acted quickly, every suitable man would be gone faster than rats down a drain and only a single word of warning was needed to clear an entire building. "Better go as well," Russell added to Wood, who was considerably beefier than Sayer; the extra weight might be needed if there were more than one to deal with.

"We were only visited by you people the night afore last," the landlord complained as he brought down a large book from its shelf. "Come round here so often and I'll have no trade left."

"I serve the King and am on his business," Russell reminded him curtly as he took hold of the ledger and began to pore over the yellowed pages. "Now, these men in room four, they are sailors?"

"One might have been, afore he lost his leg," the landlord told him flatly. "I cannot speak for his grandfather."

"I've one!" Sayer announced, appearing at the door with a

youth in tow. "Calls his-self an apprentice, but then they all do," he added with a sneer.

"It's true," the young man confirmed, before being propelled into the room by a firm push from Wood, close behind. The lad crashed straight into one of the tables, knocking over a chair and then, on recovering, turned on Russell as the natural target for his protest. "Tailor and cutter – an' I won't be free of indentures till December next. You've no right in taking me!"

"He has a point," the landlord agreed wiping his hands on his apron. "Apprentices are not for the press, ain't that the case Lieutenant?"

"We'll see – outside with him," Russell directed. The still protesting boy was forced through the front door while Russell turned to Fisher and Cross, his remaining men. "You two search the remaining rooms and bring any you find outside," he ordered.

"You'll be wasting your time," the landlord told him. "Apart from the pair in room four we've no one else a stayin' and neither will we if you folk don't leave us alone."

"Is that so?" Russell asked, apparently concerned.

"You have my word on it," the landlord confirmed. "Business is bad enough without the Navy messin' with our lives like you do."

"Then you'll soon be awanting a job yourself," Russell told him with a wicked leer. "And I might know the very thing..."

* * *

"A board?" Summers exclaimed. "When did you hear this?"

Adams unbuttoned his collar and rubbed at his neck. "Captain informed me," he replied with what he hoped would come over as indifference although his insides had not settled since.

"When would it be?" the youngster persisted.

Adams glanced about. They were in the cockpit: a small, dark berth set deep in the bowels of the brig. The place was home to most of *Hare*'s junior warrant officers yet, unusually, the pair were alone. If he were to confide in anyone it could only be Summers, someone he had known for most of his time in the service, and there may never be a better opportunity than this.

"Tomorrow at nine," he replied. "And honestly, Michael, the

prospect appals me."

Summers made no response; to his mind sitting a board – the examination that magically turned midshipmen into lieutenants – could not be so very terrible. The worst that might happen was failure and that did not mean having to leave the Navy, just a six-month wait before trying again. But if successful, if the right questions came up, or the examining captains were in a particularly genial mood, the future would be golden indeed. Adams could then apply for commissioned posts, maybe in a larger ship with greater possibilities of further promotion and certainly more money. And he would have the reassurance of a guinea a week should there be any break in employment; hardly a substantial income, but considerably more than a midshipman's half pay of precisely nothing.

Of late it had also become the habit to promote lieutenants to the rank of commander upon retirement; something that almost guaranteed a respectable old age, both financially and in terms of prestige. Really his friend had a lot to gain and very little to lose, so why was he so troubled?

"Is it your wound?" Summers asked and Adams glanced down at his scarred wrist, the memento of an earlier action.

"No, the arm is fine," he said. "I barely notice it and I am hoping our escape from France will count in my favour."

"I should say," Summers agreed. "So why the Friday face?"

"Because I have failed in the past," Adams admitted quietly, "and do not present well in such circumstances. Place me on deck with a duty to perform and I usually manage," he continued bitterly, "but when facing a line of lemon-sucking captains, my brain simply fails to function."

"It might not be so bad," Summers replied airily, even if he was starting to share his friend's doubts. Now that he had a chance to consider the matter, Adams might have a point; it was generally accepted that the only captains willing to present themselves for examination duty were those currently stewing on the beach. If they did have a command it was probably a guard ship, or some hulk that had spent the last ten years laid up in ordinary. And they would be of the old school; more akin to Hawke or Rodney than more recent commanders. It may be the same service but the Royal Navy had progressed much in the last few years, yet such stalwarts were liable to centre on obscure techniques and antiquated technology that a modern officer would know little of.

"You think not?" Adams asked with a hint of hope.

Summers shrugged. "Some must get through, else there wouldn't be no lieutenants – nor commanders or captains, if it comes to it," he added as his thoughts ran on.

"But there are always those with fathers," Adams sighed. "Or friends in high places."

"You have a good record," Summers continued, choosing to ignore the last remark. "And yes, not many have escaped from the French; that really should count for something."

"It should indeed," Adams agreed, rallying slightly.

"And there was that last action," Summers reminded him.

"With Strachan?" Adams questioned. "We hardly played a major part."

"Well if not that, then we took that Frenchman right enough."

"Aye, but when aboard a known smuggler," Adams reminded him with a sigh, and it seemed any impetus was lost. "No, Michael, you have to admit fellows like us are pretty much forgotten, and with all the talk still of Trafalgar, I can't see many remembering now."

* * *

"In truth, I should like nothing more than to join you, Sir Richard," King admitted, "Though, as we have already mentioned, I remain committed to Admiral Strachan."

"Of course, of course," Banks was quick to agree. "And I know you to be a loyal cove, Tom. Perhaps I spoke too soon; what say I simply tell more of my task, and the detached squadron I shall be commanding?"

"Detached?" King exclaimed with ill-concealed interest. So this would be no small part of a larger fleet but an independent command, free of an Admiral's apron strings.

"Indeed," Banks chuckled. "I have been fortunate in many ways; as you will doubtless know, my court martial went particularly well."

King did not; with the past few days having been filled with relating his own news there had been no time to catch up on any himself.

"And it seemed my favour stretched so far as to grant me promotion to Commodore."

"That is good news indeed," King remarked approvingly.

"Oh, it is only a temporary appointment, as is the nature of the rank," Banks added deprecatingly. "And it is of the second class so I shall still have to captain my own ship; ten shilling Commodores they call them, do they not? But I have been given a heavy frigate: *Relentless,* a razeed Ardent class."

"Similar to *Indefatigable*," King was even more impressed. "They are powerful ships."

"I shall also have a pair of fifth rates to back me up. Initially we will be convoying some John Company vessels to St Helena: I shall only discover our true purpose at ten degrees south."

"Ah, sealed orders..." Now King's tone held more than a tinge of envy, for this was something he could truly relate to. The concept of being despatched with a definite mission in mind, but one so secret that nothing could be divulged until many miles from England, was every fighting man's dream.

However, King found it hard to empathise further, for he remained under Admiral Strachan's flag and all he could look forward to was a refit. Quite who the captains of those fifth rates were he had no idea, but was already deeply jealous of them; a frigate was the ideal ship for any aspiring officer and serving with Sir Richard always meant action. But, even if he were released from *Hare*, such things were beyond him. As a mere commander he could only captain unrated vessels; frigates and above were the sole domain of those with post rank.

"Yes, and we shall be sailing under Admiralty Letter," Banks added. "So any prizes we take won't attract an Admiral's share."

King nodded politely; that was another attraction although he still could not see why Sir Richard should be telling him – not when there was no chance of being involved himself.

"I was also offered something smaller, if such a thing would be of use," Banks continued. "Which is when your name came up and why I am here..." he added thoughtfully. "Tell me, Thomas, are you absolutely dead set on staying with Strachan?"

King took a deep breath; what he had intended as being a quiet day had already been sufficiently filled with surprises, although this was by far the largest.

"As I have said, I should be delighted to join you of course, sir." They had been talking casually until that point, but now the honorific came naturally. "Though can see no way that I might in Admiral Strachan's absence."

"And he will know nothing of this of course," Banks agreed reluctantly. "But you said yourself, his ships shall require some degree of repair before taking to sea again, and with four line-of-battleships to his credit, I cannot imagine even Mad Dick quarrelling over the loss of a brig."

King could only concur, especially when that particular brig had hardly been a great deal of use to him so far.

"When is he due?" Banks demanded.

"I – I could not say exactly; I must only have been a few days ahead of the main force."

"Then might you not enquire upon his arrival?" Banks insisted.

"I might," King agreed more hesitantly.

"And I shall write to him also. There are no favours owing, but I think the man is sound enough to grant a favour. And if so, when might you be ready?"

"Three days," King replied instantly. Like any good captain, he knew the state of his command. "That is assuming all stores ordered are available and can be delivered. I also have no surgeon; *Phoenix* requested help, so I lent her my man, along with one of his loblolly boys."

"Then you may collect another at Spithead; I might arrange that in advance if you wish. Anything else?"

King shook his head – there was nothing of great importance he could think of. "Adams is standing his board tomorrow morn'," he replied vaguely. "You will remember him I am sure."

"I do indeed," Banks confirmed. "Though, you will forgive me, whether he passes or not shall make little difference."

King nodded; that was quite correct and in three days they could do much in the way of repairs, even if *Hare* would still not be quite up to scratch. For a moment he considered simply agreeing although it was important that Banks knew the full situation even if it meant the end of everything.

"I feel I should repeat, sir; *Hare* is in need of dockyard

attention," he reiterated cautiously. "Her hull leaked badly across Biscay and continues to weep steadily even while in harbour."

Banks scratched at his chin. "Frankly, Tom, I think every ship in my command to have defects of some nature and you are aware of the old adage I am sure; we refit when we can, not when we wish."

"Of course, sir," King agreed, but Banks had more to say.

"Right now every major slip is reserved for the victors of Trafalgar yet, despite the good they have done, there remains several powerful French squadrons at sea with the likelihood of more joining shortly."

"Because we cannot maintain a suitable blockade?" King suggested.

"Exactly; it were hard enough stopping up the French alone, now with Spanish ports also to be watched and many of our capital ships out of action, the Navy is spreading itself thin indeed."

"And you don't think we are to be used for blockade?"

"Three frigates and a brig-sloop?" Banks mused. "No, I do not. I think there is something far more interesting in line for us. But, whatever our task turns out, it must surely be an important one to warrant such haste."

And such secrecy, King pondered, glancing at the wooden walls of his cabin.

"Then what say we appeal to Admiral Strachan?" Banks asked again. "We have worked well in the past, and will doubtless do so again. In truth, Tom, I should like nothing better."

* * *

"I've me papers, in my room," the anxious young man declared as soon as Russell joined him in the street. "They'll show you."

"Tailor wasn't it?" Russell replied and the man nodded.

"With almost a year to serve," he added.

"Then I have good news for you," Russell beamed. "There are a deal of tailors in the Navy; you shall have company aplenty."

"But let me prove it!" the man pleaded. "I'm only down this way for a weddin', I live in Salisbury, this is the first time I ever seen the sea!"

"Wedding is it?" Sayer enquired with apparent interest.

"Sister," the tailor confirmed. "Marrying a bombardier – he'll speak for me!"

"Got a present for them have you?" Wood this time, and the tailor appeared confused.

"A present?"

"Something nice for them to start off their married life?" Sayer again.

"I was to give her a purse," the tailor admitted, fingering his pocket. "Since we lost father, money's been tight so I've been setting a bit by."

"And how much have you squirrelled?" Wood enquired with more purpose.

"Three guineas," the lad answered cautiously.

"Well, that should buy a measure of time," Russell assured him. "At least long enough for you to find your papers."

Sayer laughed. "Want us to help, do ya?"

Russell looked away as the two seamen dragged the youth back into the boarding house. The gang might have only been together a matter of days and they hardly showed him the respect his position deserved, but all were up to the mark when it came to carrying out their duties. Cross and Fisher might also have found a suitable candidate but even if not, the five of them would soon be three guineas up, and it was hardly gone nine.

3.

Breakfast was finished but Greenwood had yet to be summoned for duty so stood at the break of the forecastle gazing aimlessly at the small, grey houses that lay so tantalisingly close to *Hare*'s larboard beam. They ran in lines leading up to the dockyard at Hamoaze and several years before he had shared the attic room of one for nigh on nine months. It was while his first ship, an antiquated sixty-four, had been called in for refit. Throughout the time he had stood by the old girl, avoiding both the press and many more subtle attempts to lure him to different vessels. Once back in the water, Greenwood stayed with her a further two years until she finally gave up the ghost and was broken up. Since that time he had served aboard several others, all Royal Navy and varying in size from a mighty three-decked flagship to the tiny piss-pot of a brig-sloop that was his current home. Most won a degree of his affection in time, but none came close to the fondness he still held for his first love.

He moved away from the side rail and stretched his arms to heaven, luxuriating in the feeling of a full belly and tired limbs. As a topman, and one of the best, Greenwood was excused regular physical exercise on deck, his supple joints and limbs being too vital for the important work he carried out aloft to risk strain on more mundane tasks. But he did so enjoy a bit of a stretch and on that particular morning had joined a working party with holystones. For more than an hour they had scraped away at the sand-dusted forecastle until the strakes positivity glowed and Greenwood glanced at his own particular patch again now, feeling a wave of pride at the result. He was well aware that volunteering for such duties caused talk amongst his fellow topmen, most of whom failed to understand why he should lower himself so. But they only had eyes for their precious spars and line; Greenwood was a seaman through and through, and truly embraced every aspect of his craft.

A shadow signalled the approach of another and he looked round to see the ginger hair and cheeky grin of Parker, a fellow topman who berthed in his mess. Greenwood smiled in return; he liked the cove and would have done so even if they were simply shipmates. Parker was good company: he held his liquor, paid his debts and had helped him out on more than one occasion. Qualities that all but guaranteed friendship amongst regular Jacks. He was also all of thirty – a good five years older than Greenwood – and had been rated able for much of his time afloat although strangely never progressed further. Despite offers from both warrant and commissioned officers, Parker stubbornly rejected promotion to captain of a top, or any other position of mild authority reserved for more experienced hands. And, even though now considered old to be stationed aloft, he appeared content to carry out the duties of a regular topman without wishing for more.

Parker had also just eaten and felt the need to signal the fact by a generous belch that ended with the same brash grin. Greenwood raised his eyes to the heavens; his friend may not be seeking promotion, but there were some things he worked at with total commitment.

"Not been ashore at Plymouth these seven years," Parker told him as he leant on the top rail. "Yet there have been a few high times in the old Dock. Reckon we'll get any leave?"

"Doubt it," Greenwood replied. "Not unless they takes us in for refit, an' then we'll only be turned over."

"Which ain't out of the question," Parker conceded. "I hear we was making a foot each watch on the way back." Greenwood noticed he was concealing the business end of a clay pipe within one blackened palm; the stem ran up tight against his wrist and a faint wisp of smoke could be made out from the bowl before the light onshore breeze whipped it away. Noticing the other man's interest, Parker glanced towards the quarterdeck to check the master's mate who had the anchor watch was otherwise distracted. Then, with a wink at Greenwood, he brought the stem up to his lips and drew in a deep draught.

"Lovely, tell y'r muvver," Parker murmured with elaborate unconcern and amid a sudden cloud of dark smoke.

Greenwood smirked and was about to comment when something from the corner of his eye caught his attention. "Reckon that's the first of the lighters," he said instead, nodding towards a small vessel that had just set out from the victualler's wharf. "We'll be hard at it for the rest of the day, more'n like."

"*You* might," Parker corrected him importantly. "*I* has important work to do aloft for the bosun."

At Greenwood's glance, his friend elaborated.

"We needs to replace the mizzen tops'l slings along with two larboard shrouds. Could use an hand, that's if you ain't planning on joining the waisters like 'smorning."

"Oh, I've had my spell of deck drill for the day," Greenwood snorted. "And will happily join you, if Harridge allows."

Parker seemed pleased, and took another pull at the pipe. "I'll square it with him," he promised, adding, "It will be good to have a decent fellow to yarn with," before sauntering off.

Greenwood's gaze returned to the nearby dockyard. The lighter was making good progress, he had better get himself aft as well, or risk being chosen for another duty. He began to follow Parker along the waist. Greenwood was also looking forward to working aloft. He had only been aboard *Hare* a couple of months, but was already considering asking Parker to be his tie mate. There weren't many as level as him; a truly decent sort. Of course there were the obvious considerations to be made when dealing with one of his kind; he'd known many like Parker who were a nightmare to serve alongside. But even in the short time he had known him, Greenwood felt he understood the man well enough to know he would never make his particular condition an issue. In fact, he rather wished he'd stop trying so hard to conceal it.

* * *

Adams twitched at his stock for the third time in as many minutes and tried not to meet the eyes of the other midshipmen in the small, dark space. All five appeared older than him and far more confident than he felt. Everyone had arrived simultaneously on the dot of nine only to be shown straight into the little room where they had apparently been forgotten. Since that time there had been no conversation other than sighs and the occasional grimace. One, a fair-haired fellow, had a constant sniff while another, who was badly pockmarked, kept glancing at his watch as if there were something more important he should be doing. But however they managed the pain of waiting, it was a private anguish and not to be shared, especially amongst those presumed to be rivals.

From somewhere far off came the sound of a door slamming and all eyes rose up in expectation. But there were no subsequent footsteps and neither did anyone attempt to enter their stuffy domain. After a moment of tension the fair-haired man gave another dismissive sniff and there was the click of a watch being opened as the group returned to the same shared, but personal, agony.

And then, totally without warning, the door was flung wide and all jumped as the clerk who had accepted their journals entered.

"We shall be taking you alphabetically," he announced in a voice that seemed unnecessarily loud and Adams, guessing his would be first, felt his heart begin to race. For a moment he stood and attempted to brush the creases out of his shirt and britches, but the clerk had already gone and, suddenly fearful of being left behind, Adams hurried after him, leaving the door swinging open in his wake.

The sound of derisive laughter could be heard as he clumped and slipped along the marbled floor, but Adams was far too concerned with keeping up to care. The clerk, a small dark man with a shiny bald pate, was already turning towards a grand staircase which he proceeded to skip up with a practised ease that Adams, wearing a pair of oversized boots that had been rented from the purser, was unable to match. The man took pity and waited at the first landing then, together, they walked along another corridor. Thick carpet now muffled much of the sound, the scent of wax polish became very prominent and there was an undeniable air of importance about the place.

"The board will have examined your journals," the clerk told him as they repeatedly passed from day to night under a series of skylights set into the ceiling. "You may be questioned on them, so prepare yourself."

Adams made no response. He had been doing little else for much of the previous day, yet felt no better equipped for what was to come than when he started. Then his escort stopped suddenly, turned and knocked loudly on what might have been a random door. There was a gruff command from within, the clerk turned the brass knob and the next thing Adams knew he was standing in a well lit room and facing a large oak table. Behind this sat three post captains, each equal in age and the level of disinterest with which they viewed him.

"Well come forward and present yourself," the middle captain who was probably the president ordered and Adams obediently stepped deeper into the room. He forced himself to consider the faces in more detail; not one did he know on sight, but all must have been beyond fifty if they were a day and he swallowed dryly as his worst fears were realised.

"We have been reading your reports," the grey-haired captain to the president's right announced. He held up a pile of papers that Adams vaguely recognised.

"Indeed," the bald head on the opposite side agreed in a more kindly tone. "They have been taking much of our time, so it is perhaps fitting that you are the first to be seen."

Adams could not tell if any response was expected from him and swallowed once more.

"It would seem your former commanders speak highly of you, and one happens to be Sir Richard Banks, which is no bad thing in itself."

This came from the president and was a surprise. Adams had been one of the party who escaped from Verdun with Captain Banks, although he hardly expected so eminent a figure to bother giving a reference for a mere midshipman.

"Yes, he speaks heartily indeed," the president allowed grudgingly. "And well he might, as your actions say as much."

Now panic began to take hold and Adams felt his hands begin to shake. They had clearly confused him with another candidate: surely he could not be held responsible for such a mistake? But then he had been a midshipman long enough to know such a thing to be not only possible but actually quite likely.

"My name is John Adams," he found himself announcing, and noted the surprised looks of the three men opposite with increasing concern.

"So we understand," the more kindly of the three replied. "Though it is good of you to confirm it."

There was an awkward pause before the president continued.

"All we have read states your knowledge of seamanship to be exemplary and fully endorses your promotion. Consequently, and bearing in mind we have a lot to see this morn', I can find no reason to disagree. Gentlemen?" he asked, turning to his colleagues.

"Sir Richard's recommendation would say much," the bald man agreed, although his colleague to the other side was less convinced.

"Oh, I think we should set a small test," he sighed. "If only to show due process."

"As you will," the president allowed, before turning back to Adams. "But what say we make it a simple one? Tell me, young man, can you name three animals that eat grass?"

There was a pause, all Adams could hear was the slow ticking of a clock that might have been many rooms away. Was this some sort of trick, a ruse to encourage him to speak out of turn? He looked back at the elderly eyes that were now examining him with growing interest. His mouth opened but no sound emerged and it eventually closed with its task undone. Then finally the more kindly captain spoke.

"Come, Mr Adams, that is surely not so hard," he pointed out. "You have a commission all but in your pocket."

But Adams was in serious trouble. The question reverberated about his brain as he struggled for a sensible answer; one that would not place him into a whole heap of trouble. Once more his mouth opened, and this time it remained so, until he was fairly gaping at his inquisitors.

"Never encountered such a thing afore," the president declared. "Fellow knows his name but little else."

"Belike he is some form of imbecile," the man on his right confirmed as he made to collect Adams' papers.

"Come, come, sir," the bald captain tried for what felt like the last time. "Why, there are so many to choose from; horses eat grass, do they not? And cows – you need only name one other and we will all have done our duty."

Like a shaft of light, realisation dawned and Adams flushed. "Oh, 'animals'," he gasped with relief. "I thought you'd said 'Admirals'."

* * *

"What ship, sir?" The voice came from behind and cut into Russell's thoughts like a keen blade. But he had faced such incidents before and, as he turned back, was unperturbed.

"Good day to you," he replied, taking in the dark blue uniform that hung on a body considerably older than his own. "Though I do not believe we have been introduced."

"I enquired of your ship," the grey-haired officer insisted and Russell wondered if there might be a hint of the lower deck about him.

"John Russell, third of the *Anson*," he answered brusquely. "And yourself?"

"Croft, first of *Hare*."

Russell knew both the vessel and her captain; a worn-out brig with a one-armed man commanding her and, presumably, a superannuated first lieutenant; this would not be a problem.

"But why are you ashore?" Croft persisted. "*Anson* has been flying her peter for most of the morning."

"Indeed? Then you must not detain me further," Russell told him with sudden urgency and was about to make his escape when a firm hand grasped his wrist. Russell glanced down for a moment, then up and into the eyes of the older man.

"Unhand me, sir; I must away to my ship."

"You are going nowhere," Croft informed him with a strength in his voice that more than matched the grip. "Where are the others?"

"The others?" Russell questioned as the doubts finally began to rise.

"Your little set." The words were spoken with disgust. "Taking men for the Navy, or so I am informed."

"It is perhaps regrettable but a necessary evil." Russell spoke slowly, while keeping his eyes fixed on Croft's. The officer was alone, yet he had four stout fellows who would return at any moment; there was still no need for concern.

"Except you have not been so very successful, have you, *Mister* Russell?" Croft's eyes met his stare and, despite being slightly rheumy, were every bit as strong.

"This morning? Perhaps not," Russell admitted lightly. "But the chance of a stout hand must never be left untaken; now, if you will excuse me, I must away." From the corner of his eye he could see the welcome sight of Sayer and Wood, who were leading a group of men. If this troublesome officer was determined to be obstructive, he would simply have them deal with him. Once more he made to go, but the grip on his forearm remained.

"Wood, Sayer; here with you!" Russell called finally. If the old fool were truly seeking trouble, he would simply have to provide it.

But all his cry evoked was sudden laughter, and it was with a cold shock that Russell realised several in the street had stopped to watch and were clearly enjoying the spectacle. Even the wrinkled face of the officer that still held him was now smiling.

"Your men will not help," he stated calmly. "They are just as deeply in the mire."

Russell finally drew his eyes away and looked directly at Sayer and Wood. Both had their hands tied and were obviously under the charge of the group of seamen behind them.

"I'd heard there were a bunch of tricksters working these

parts," the elderly lieutenant continued. "And no doubt giving the press an even blacker name than it already possesses."

Russell looked away; there was no sign of Fisher or Cross although, even if they were to appear, little good could come of it.

"But at least some have been found for the Navy," Croft conceded as a grinning seaman took Russell's other arm and proceeded to bind the two together. "And we are especially fortunate in that you would appear to have some knowledge of the sea," he added, eyeing Russell's broadcloth tunic. "Though you may find the uniform you chose to wear to be somewhat superfluous."

4.

King stood on the quarterdeck openly enjoying the wind and spray as it stung his already chilled face. The fact that he had not expected to put to sea again so soon added extra spice to his pleasure. Less than a week ago he had been worrying about *Hare* being taken in for repair and whether he would retain her command, yet here he was rounding Little Mewstone, and would soon be setting course for Spithead and a whole new raft of adventures.

Less than two days after his meeting with Banks, Strachan had appeared with the first of his prizes and, rather than King having to go through the torment of choosing the right time to request an interview, the Admiral had actually summoned him. It seemed Sir Richard had been as good as his word and a message had been waiting on the senior man's arrival. As for keeping King under his command, he clearly could not have cared less, and *Hare* was swiftly removed from his flag. King was vaguely concerned that, in requesting a transfer, he might have delayed his rights to prize money, but preferred not to pursue that particular path. All that truly mattered was *Hare* would be joining a squadron under the command of his former captain, a man he trusted more than any other, and the future looked bright.

There were downsides, of course; the first being the next few months would be spent shepherding a bunch of Indiamen to the South Atlantic. After so long in the Navy he should have grown used to an Admiralty that never wasted warships if their journey could include protecting a convoy of merchants, but the duty did seem an unnecessary check on what was clearly intended to be a fast moving squadron. And it was equally galling that they must accompany them most of the way to St Helena. Ten years before, King had been a midshipman aboard a sixty-four sent on just such a mission. That voyage had ended prematurely when the convoy was raided by a superior French force and, although he survived to tell the tale, some close to him had not. But with Cape Town now in the hands of the Dutch, St Helena had become even more important to Britain's eastern trade and he supposed it inevitable that the outpost should be the current convoy's goal, although King had more reason than mere superstition to wish to avoid the place.

A later trip to the same island, aboard a different ship and before the loss of his arm, had left an equally deep impression as well as memories he had no wish to revive. But then Sir Richard would be reading his secret orders before they reached the outpost, so it was possible his ships would leave the convoy to its own devices before making for their true destination.

And that might be India, China, New South Wales, the West Indies or the East, if it came to it – there was action aplenty in every station and guaranteed employment for a fast and powerful squadron. Perhaps they were to be given a cruise along the South American coast; Spain was now firmly in the war and there would be rich pickings indeed while, with Banks in command, King had no fears of being badly led.

He might even earn some serious prize money. King had not exactly been neglected in that department; several times a considerable sum had come his way but never quite enough to make a tangible difference to his life. Like any sailor, he found the spending of money far easier than its earning, although others of his rank had made true fortunes of late; sums so vast they could not be lost quite as easily. Even when he finally benefited from the recent action, with so many other British ships present his share would not be substantial and nothing to what might be earned if Sir Richard had really been blessed with a cruise. With merchants as their prey, he might come back with literally thousands; certainly enough to set up as a gentleman for the rest of his life.

Aimée would like that. When last seen she had been establishing their modest home in Alton, a village several miles inland from Portsmouth. It was a small rural community as might be found in any part of southern England although, despite her French heritage, Aimée had been readily accepted and seemed comfortable. Their house was barely more than a worker's cottage set amid a line of similar buildings with a washerwoman to one side and an ostler the other, but it was theirs for the next two years at least and if he truly came into funds King could make a more positive move towards securing her happiness for longer. A larger place with servants to run it and horses for her to ride – not that she had expressed a wish for either. But along with an ability to spend, King also shared the average sailor's belief that there was little money could not provide.

When last heard of, the convoy had almost assembled but, being as he was heading so close to his new home, it would be strange if King failed to spend a couple of days there. He had not seen Aimée for several months and it would be a while longer before *Hare* was finally paid off. By then King sensed he should have made a name for himself although whether it would be as a skilled commander or an outright failure he dared not guess. Should it be the former, he may be offered another command: a larger one that came with promotion to post rank. Of course King could then decide whether to accept such an offer, and the amount of prize money earned to that point would be a significant factor in his decision. And if not, if the worst happened and he came back poor and possibly with further wounds, he would be perfectly happy to resign his commission, retire from the sea, and spend the rest of his life in quiet isolation with Aimée.

Or so he told himself.

"All fair, Mr Brehaut?" King asked. The sailing master had appeared on deck and was studying the traverse board.

"Very good, sir," Brehaut replied, stepping away from the binnacle and across to King on the windward side of the quarterdeck. "We should be past Great Mewstone and into the Channel proper in no time, then might add the t'gallants and possibly royals if you so wish," he added.

"I do indeed," King confirmed with a grin. With the extra sail and in such a wind, they should make Spithead in good time and so might still catch the convoy unprepared, in which case the chances of seeing Aimée and their home was almost guaranteed.

* * *

“So you two knows each other,” Greenwood, who had overall charge of the mess, asked.

“In a manner of speaking,” Sayer confirmed. “Russell here used to run a set, but it weren't all that successful was it, old cock?” he added, with a sneer at his former boss.

“It worked right enough,” Russell insisted while fiddling with the wooden platter that lay on the table before him. “We was just unlucky in falling in with that bastard of a lieutenant.”

“That bastard of a lieutenant is an officer aboard this ship,” Greenwood informed him levelly before glancing at the others seated at the table for confirmation. His mess had been light by two for a while and he was glad to have received fresh men. But the pair had hardly been aboard long enough to become shipmates let alone part of his personal domain and he wasn't going to let a couple of sham crimps run down the brig's second in command.

“And you're gonna be directly under his care, matey,” another seaman added. “Likely you'll come to realise our Mr Croft ain't quite the knave you paints him.”

There was a murmur of agreement from the rest and Russell quickly abandoned any thoughts of further comment and contented himself with playing with his recent acquisition. The platter had been issued to him along with the clothes he currently wore, while more lay crammed into a ditty bag under the table. He also now owned two hammocks, two blankets, a pillow and a mattress. Only the bedding had been free, with the rest paid for by his signature on the purser's ledger. All appeared to be of a reasonable quality, however, and Russell was content; he had no intention of staying long enough for the debt to be honoured and a good deal would be going with him when he went.

Still, it was amazing the difference that wearing an ordinary seaman's rig made after the splendour of an officer's uniform. Much of his dignity had been lost with that broadcloth; those he had led while ashore were behaving with even less respect while this current crowd seemed to view him with something close to contempt. And there was no doubt that a King's ship was one of the last places he wanted to be, although Russell was not downhearted, for he knew himself to have come off lightly. The amount swindled from that apprentice was enough to make him eligible for the gallows and, even if he had avoided that, a brief time aboard a man-of-war was surely better than seven years' labour in New South Wales. Besides, he had been working Plymouth and the surrounding area for several weeks so it was time to move on and that tarpot of a lieutenant might even have done him a favour.

For they were heading for Portsmouth; a place Russell had actually been considering as the next location for his operation. He would need to get hold of another uniform but that should be relatively easy in such a large naval base and, being as it was busier than Plymouth, he might remain undetected for longer. Of course, the first problem to overcome would be actually leaving the ship, but Russell was not unduly concerned about that. For he was nothing if not an optimist; should even the slightest opportunity present itself he would grab it, as he had done on countless occasions in the past. What some regarded as obstacles he viewed as opportunities and was very able to make his own luck.

"Served afore, have you?" a slightly-built seaman asked and Russell considered him for a moment. He seemed cheerful enough, with ginger hair and prominent freckles that gave him a mildly juvenile appearance, although Russell had noticed something else far more significant.

"While back," he admitted cautiously, "though that were in a collier and only one trip. Never in the RN."

"What about you?" Greenwood asked, turning to Sayer.

"Several times; they've judged me ordinary, which is a might better than chummy here," he added nodding at Russell, who had been rated as landsman.

"I hears there were five of your lot originally," Parker, the ginger-haired seaman added.

"The other three went to Benson's mess," Greenwood replied before Russell could. "They're on the larboard watch, while we're starboard, so you won't be seeing so much of 'em."

"Don't want you getting back with your old maties, now, do we?" Parker grinned.

"There ain't no fear of that," Greenwood stated firmly. "The King might have chosen to forget your past, but I surely won't.

And neither will any aboard; if either of you tries any flash games with a regular Jack you'll be awishin' you was back on land and waiting to be lagged – or worse."

Russell held Greenwood's gaze for a moment, then looked away, his eyes returning to the ginger-haired seaman. His new mess captain was clearly made of stern stuff and not to be trifled with, although that would hardly alter any of his plans. He looked destined to spend the next few days at sea but that did not mean there were no benefits to be drawn from the situation. And there was something about the freckled seaman that intrigued him. As one who survived on various forms of deception, Russell was quick to notice a fellow practitioner and was certain something could be gained from this one. He just had to work out how.

5.

The gunroom aboard *Hare* was the equivalent of a wardroom in larger vessels and had never been a particularly crowded place. As a brig-sloop, she only warranted one lieutenant and her meagre military complement was entirely directed by NCOs, so no space was taken up by Royal Marine officers. Added to that, King had managed to sail without chaplain or schoolmaster and their surgeon was currently on loan to another ship. So when Lieutenant Croft entered the small space he was not surprised to find it empty.

And this was in no way a disappointment. The brief time they had spent at Plymouth had been fraught enough, with much accomplished that would normally have taken several weeks. And before then there had been the mad rush to deliver Admiral Strachan's despatches, a journey that had strained *Hare*'s hull and tophamper. But now she had been re-victualled and with some of her more urgent repairs addressed, Croft supposed he should be able to relax and definitely felt the need for a measure of peace. Such luxury is rarely granted executive officers however and, even when he had slumped down in his usual chair at the head of the gunroom table, his mind continued to race. The work already carried out had definitely been essential; *Hare* was in danger of losing something vital aloft although much remained to do in that department that was almost as urgent. But the tophamper was not his chief concern; what truly caused him worry was the brig's hull.

It was an area far harder to reach and repair than any mast or spar, while being even more intrinsic to the safety of the vessel. Croft had been with the brig for the last three years and cared for her as any first lieutenant should. Yet Anderson, their young Scottish carpenter, was a relatively new addition and, though he should know her at least as well, Croft wondered if he really did.

The position of carpenter was a sensitive one aboard any ship, but probably more so in lighter vessels, when a correspondingly smaller workforce made each man that much more important. Anderson had taken over from Pope, the brig's original carpenter, who had seen her from the laying of her keel to final launch. A combination of old age and ill health had forced Pope to retire and, even if the new man was as skilled in his duties, Croft doubted Anderson would ever show the same concern as his predecessor. And in a frail craft like *Hare*, the difference could mean much.

He had no firm evidence on which to base these feelings and Croft grudgingly admitted that Pope had not been quite as attentive towards the end of his time, while all Anderson's work appeared to have been carried out competently enough. But still the doubts remained and would only be eased when *Hare* was finally taken out of the water.

In fact the refit was something Croft had been secretly looking forward to; he had joined *Hare* just after her last time in dock and was concerned then that nothing had been done to her hull. But Pope was sure the brig was sound and, up until the last few months, she certainly appeared so. Now, though, she was taking in far more than a vessel of her size should and further investigation was definitely required.

But, before that could happen, Commander King, *Hare*'s new young captain, had committed them to a long, deep-sea voyage. It was one that would take them far into the Southern Hemisphere and Croft could not help but be concerned. On making Spithead they might be given time to continue minor repairs, although these would mainly be confined to topside, spars and rigging. They might add filler and splash a bit of paint about lower down, but little serious work could be carried out and there was scant chance of a proper inspection.

At that point his musings were interrupted by the sudden

opening of the gunroom door and Croft visibly jumped. He tried to hide the reaction by clearing his throat, but privately admitted such things had become far more common of late. And there was little consolation when the steward who had entered seemed equally surprised to see him.

"Beg pardon, sir, I believed you to be on deck. Would you be requiring dinner?"

Croft blinked for a moment. He had not eaten breakfast that morning, nor a reasonable meal the day before so he supposed he must be hungry.

"If you would be so kind," he told him, and the man disappeared into the pantry with less noise.

But when he was alone once more, Croft's thoughts were not of food, they had returned to the problem of the brig's hull. He told himself he was worrying unnecessarily and it was a common trait amongst first officers as much as old men. He had mentioned his concerns to the captain who ordered a detailed report when they were in Plymouth. And Anderson had done his best, although little could be revealed while the brig remained afloat. Commander King appeared satisfied, however, and now there was little Croft could do to force the issue. But still he could not shake off the lingering doubts and, if he were entirely honest, did not feel the matter had been given enough importance.

* * *

"What cheer, matey?" Parker grinned. "How's your luck?"

They were on the berth deck, just forward of the officers' quarters, and both were officially off duty. However, Parker had needed to replace several lengths of line during his time on watch and some of the old might yet be reclaimed. The work was not exactly arduous and he was as happy attending to it then as later.

"Well enough," Russell admitted gruffly. "Though I can't say I cares for being here."

Parker shrugged and returned to his work. "The old barky's straight enough once you get used to her," he said. "I been aboard worse."

"I was thinking more of the company," Russell's voice now carried an extra edge that made Parker look up. "I can see what you are," he told the topman bluntly, "even if everyone else is blind."

Parker set aside his splicing and gave Russell a considered stare. "And?" he asked cautiously.

"And you'd better be careful," Russell warned, standing over the man and extending himself as much as the deckhead allowed. "A secret like that ain't something you want spread about."

"You can tell all you care to," Parker replied. His tone had lost all trace of bonhomie, and was now uncommonly cold. "And see how far it takes you."

"Once word gets 'round, you might not be so cocky," Russell countered quickly, even if the first seeds of doubt had already been sown. "You want that, do you?"

"Worse has happened," Parker assured him. "I don't bother anyone else, so why should they me?"

Russell was now starting to worry and his concern increased as Parker returned to the work before him. "But that's not how it is," he insisted. "I only needs to report you, and the heavens will open – you see if they don't."

"But I ain't done nothing, not to you, nor no one," Parker remained annoyingly calm. "And don't intend to."

"And you'd better not," Russell agreed. "But that don't mean I can't report you anyways. I can say what I likes."

"And you'd lie about such a thing?" Parker asked, pausing for a moment.

"I might," Russell replied, coyly. "It all depends on you, an' how much you want your secret kept."

There was a pause as Parker considered this, then he collected his fid once more and returned to work. "Go ahead," he said, not deigning to look up. "Everyone knows about me; you might say I'm common knowledge, though neither do they care."

"Don't care?" Russell exclaimed before lowering his voice and adding, "But you'll be thrown off the ship – after they finish punishing you, that is."

"I've told you, they know already," Parker assured him after pausing again. "Just as they know I'm a sound hand – able, they calls it," he permitted Russell one contemptuous glance. "Whereas you are merely a landsman."

"But a man, none the less," Russell responded instantly. "That must account for something."

"Not with me," Parker was adamant. "I'm long past caring about men – or women," he continued. "Never truly have, if it comes to it – most folk respect that."

Now Russell's deflation was turning to interest, and he lowered himself to Parker's level.

"But you can't mean it," he insisted. "You're a Molly, you must..."

"Think womanly thoughts?" Parker snorted. "Well I don't, and never have. Besides, you might find I'm not alone; there are a number of us currently serving His Majesty, and several more aboard the brig, if you did but know it. Most of us keep to ourselves and do right enough," he added. "You see there ain't no crime in being who you are, trouble only comes when you do something on account of it."

Russell looked his confusion and Parker sighed.

"You pay better attention to the Articles of War next time they're read," he told him. "They're the rules we work by – break any and you know what to expect. But there's the rub, see? You have to commit the crime."

"How do you mean?"

"I mean, as you have so cleverly observed, I don't care so much for the fairer sex, but that don't mean I'm gonna start leaping on every man that passes. If I did I'd be for it, though, as it happens, I don't care to. You'll find most accept that, so you may as well pipe down and leave me to work in peace."

The topman's speech had come as a revelation although, as he considered it more carefully, Russell was not so very surprised. Even ignoring the penalties that could be inflicted on one such as Parker, Russell had met a few of his type on land so it was probably natural to encounter them at sea as well. With the shortage of men suitable for the Navy such things were bound to happen – he had even heard tales of women, bearded or otherwise, claiming to have served before the mast.

"Well, all I can say is, you wants to be careful," he blustered.

"And why would that be?" the topman asked. "I've told you, I am a sound hand; that's what matters with the officers and you'll find your regular Jack just as easy. Share a mess for any length of time and you'll discover everyone's secrets and there are a good few worse than not wanting to spend your coin on doxies."

"But if you care for men more than women..."

"I told you, I don't care for either!" Parker interrupted. "At least, not in the way you mean. Give me a sound ship, decent messmates and a fair captain and I'm happy; all else can go hang."

"But there'll be those aboard who are yet to cotton on," Russell insisted as a fresh angle occurred. "I mean, some ain't so bright. Were I to tip the wink there's a Molly aboard they might be more'n interested."

"I've already said, try trumping up a charge and I know who'll be believed," Parker countered.

"I'm not talking about reporting you," Russell's confidence was returning now; he sensed he had found the topman's weak spot and only needed to strike. "This would be far more unofficial and not exactly pleasant; some of them waisters are hefty coves and a shrimp like you might keep them amused for hours."

Russell smirked as he waited for the reaction although Parker remained unconcerned and, even when he placed the fid down and paused for a moment, his attention was apparently elsewhere. But when he did move, it was swiftly and with a grace that caught Russell totally unawares.

The topman's supple body shot up from the seat and, though his frame was light, it carried a strength that was more than able to pin Russell against the solid oak of a nearby hanging knee. Then, with a skill born of many years' work aloft, Parker whipped the line he had been working about the landsman's neck. At a twist of his wrist, the stiff fibres dug deep into Russell's throat and there was a brief gurgling sound as he winced with both pain and shock.

"You do your worst, Mister," Parker's face was now close and the words carried true menace. "There ain't nothing that hasn't been tried on me that would come as a surprise and I have dealt with every one, just as I can you."

Russell attempted to nod, but the action was misinterpreted and Parker increased the pressure further.

"How I were born, or how I chooses to live, is no concern of yours. And before you come to any other ideas, consider how the other Jacks treats me. I think you'll find I'm respected, both for what I do, an' for who I am, while you are nothing more than a newbie what knows nothing of ships nor how to sail 'em."

Russell raised a hand in supplication but the pressure remained and his face began to glow red. Then, with a far louder hiss from the landsman, Parker released the line, returned to his seat, and picked up the fid once more. Russell stepped away and stood rubbing at his throat while his mind reassessed the situation. Parker was clearly able to look after himself, another thing that had come as a surprise, and was best left alone, at least for the time being.

But some confusion remained. In the world he had previously inhabited things had been far more clean cut: men were either straight or bent, and women either gave or charged. There were no half measures. And someone like Parker, someone mildly different, would be especially nervous of the fact being discovered, so was surely the perfect subject for extortion. Yet, rather than play by the rules, the topman openly confessed and still seemed accepted by his peers; it really made no sense at all. Then, as he turned to go, Parker looked up once more.

"I were at fault," Russell told him automatically; he was happy to give the impression of climbing down as it could only help his cause. "I had not come across one such as you and did not truly understand."

Parker nodded and there was a softening in his expression.

"Well now you do," he said, "and can think yourself lucky I chose your neck."

6.

Despite the initial fair wind, their passage from Plymouth Dock was not quick. The bluff-bowed *Hare* fared especially badly against the south, south-westerly they met in the Channel and King began to wonder quite how long he would be able to spend ashore with Aimée. Then all such plans were totally dashed when an anchored East India convoy came into view as soon as they entered St Helen's Road. With no sign of other HEIC shipping, King sensed these to be their future charges. It was clear they were intending to leave almost immediately and may even have been awaiting *Hare*'s arrival; all bar one had topmasts raised and yards crossed, with the last actually performing the evolution as they watched.

There was no evidence of the escorting warships, although that was not unusual. The East India Company offered better wages and conditions so was a popular berth with many seamen while such a fleet would also provide a degree of anonymity to any from the Royal Navy who chose to desert. Consequently, it had become customary to place such temptation well away from government vessels; Banks' forces were likely to be anchored elsewhere and might still be victualling. But he was certain they would not be delayed for long and, as *Hare* had already been fully provided for, there would be no excuse for him to linger further. If only out of courtesy, King should report to the Port Admiral, and they had an injured man – a holder who had managed to rupture himself whilst shifting stores – to transfer ashore, but no more. Croft was still rumbling on about checking the hull, but with no identifiable leak and both time and dockyard space at a premium, any attention in that area would simply have to wait. It was a shame as King had all but promised himself a spell in Alton but there was no helping it.

Thoughts of the injured man brought his mind back to the problem of needing a surgeon. He would apply for one and his request was bound to be granted, but King would have preferred a little more time to select for such an important post. The last incumbent, a middle-aged Welshman with a passion for sea birds, had been something of a disappointment. Although capable enough professionally, Jones always gave the impression his first love was creating the remarkably detailed ornithological drawings that covered his small cabin and had started to appear in the gunroom. *Hare* had sailed before the return of *Phoenix* so there was no chance of him continuing in post; a fact that King had initially welcomed. But with little time to choose and the standard of naval surgeons varying greatly, it seemed possible that they would be lumbered with someone far worse.

And there were other matters to consider; Adams had passed his board so would probably wish to seek a position as a lieutenant. It was not something King could offer on a vessel the size of *Hare* so he may find himself having to seek out a new senior midshipman as well. Then there would be the problem of pay; the hands had not received anything for several months and were starting to grow restless. There was no possibility of shore leave at

Portsmouth, but still the bumboats would come calling and the lower deck were always more content with coin in their pocket, even with no easy way of spending it. Such were the concerns of every captain and King knew most would be solved in due course, but at the back of his mind one remained that was far more personal and not so easy to settle.

Of course, he was delighted to have retained command of *Hare* and, even more so, that he would be taking her to sea under Sir Richard Banks. But still a part of him wished things could have been different; that *Hare* had been called for refit, or another sent to replace him as her captain. It might have signalled the end of his active career and, should such a thing have happened, he would obviously be devastated. But even such a dreadful turn of events would have had one saving factor; he could spend time ashore with Aimée, and, after several days with the coast of England so tantalisingly close, part of him wanted nothing else.

* * *

"Passed midshipman," Summers said, savouring the words. "Sounds fine, don't it?"

"Lieutenant has a better ring," Adams muttered in reply while applying a further dab of blacking to his boot. He had long since forgotten the exact details of his board which, from the description given to his young friend, might have been an entirely different occasion. But one incontrovertible fact remained: he had indeed passed. Now all he needed was for a suitable position to become available and he would be a commissioned officer.

"Will you try for a posting in Portsmouth?" Summers asked. *Hare* was too small to warrant two lieutenants and the downside to Adams' success was the pair were bound to be separated.

"I surely shall," Adams confirmed. "This is a worthy little brig and I enjoyed my time aboard *Kestrel*, but have a hankering for larger vessels. A frigate at least, or perhaps a two-decker?" he added with the air of one able to choose.

Summers made no response. They were in their tiny cockpit and, apart from a modicum of privacy, the conditions were not so very different to those of any regular hand in a mess. That alone was hardly an enticement to remain when bigger ships offered far better accommodation. Once Adams secured a posting as lieutenant, he may gain his own cabin; one within the prestigious environment of at least a gunroom, while officers' quarters within a first rate's wardroom could be better than those enjoyed by passengers aboard an Indiaman. The position would also entitle him to a considerable increase in salary as well as a greater share in any prize, or head, money. But still, the pair had gone through much together and it seemed a pity to break up what had been a fine team.

"I suppose I might follow," Summers spoke doubtfully.

Adams looked up from his polishing. "Follow? Why, you would be more than welcome, Michael, though we have to consider Commander King." He took another dab of polish and applied it to the boot. "Losing one midshipman might be an inconvenience; two would definitely cause him distress. I'd say he more or less relies upon you."

Summers nodded: that was undoubtedly true.

"But we have yet to hear if shore leave is to be granted," Adams continued. He would be sorry to go, although had far more to gain from the move. "Sure, I may not be allowed off at all and then it is doubtful a position can be found so very quickly."

"It is two years or more before I will even be given sight of a board," Summers sighed.

"The time will soon go," Adams assured him.

"But even then, there are the questions," the younger man continued dolefully. "I'm not sure I am up to being tested so."

"Ah yes, the questions," Adams agreed, pausing for a moment in his work. "They can be the hardest part."

* * *

HMS *Relentless* was indeed a cut down liner; that much was obvious at first sight. Originally a fourteen-hundred ton, Ardent class two-decker, her upper deck had been removed a few years before, making a far sleeker craft, although one whose girth was slightly too wide for her new lines. Such a beam would make for some interesting handling in rough weather, King decided as his gig brought him nearer, while the gun deck was also closer to the waterline than was usual in heavy frigates. But there could be no doubting the firepower from her main battery of twenty-four pounders. Including the carronades to forecastle and quarterdeck, she would have a broadside weight of nearly a quarter of a ton. And much of the load would be fired from Bloomfield long guns, superb pieces famed for their accuracy and range while timbers originally intended to support the bulk of a line-of-battleship must make for an unusually solid frame.

He supposed that, in effect, she was the ideal command for one such as Banks. A fast ship, soundly built and one that could pack a true punch. In addition, she would have the accommodation to support a Commodore, when the chances of entertaining other senior officers or the occasional diplomat were so much higher. But there was one facet that did not endear her to him. However carefully she had been adapted to her new role, *Relentless*' starboard entry port remained inordinately high and would necessitate one such as him being swung aboard from a whip like so much dunnage.

There were times when King could almost ignore the loss of his left arm. After the initial shock and a reasonable time to convalesce, he had adapted to the different lifestyle and could now carry out a surprising number of tasks quite well. In addition, with promotion and being placed in the position of captain, some duties that would previously have bothered him no longer fell within his remit although annoyances still remained. He could not go aloft with any degree of safety and neither was he able to fight, or take part in any operation where agility or dexterity were required. And though he might have found ways to care for himself and had mastered a multitude of smaller chores that seemed impossible at first, he still could not clamber up the side of even the steepest tumble-home, making a dignified entrance into most warships impossible.

"Avast there – await a bowlin'!" the call of a master's mate rang out for all to hear as soon as his coxswain answered the frigate's hail. Clearly those aboard *Relentless* were aware of his disability and happy to share the information with the rest of the anchorage. Even as he watched, the canvas straps of an improvised hoist could be seen as they were raised aloft in preparation for being lowered into his gig, and the knowledge that such a thing had been considered, discussed and presumably prepared beforehand, only made King's indignity that much worse.

But there was no getting round the necessity. Even with the help of Bryant, his coxswain, King found it hard to clamber forward then had to stand awkwardly in the small boat while being threaded into the darned contraption. And then the men at *Relentless'* halyards made matters worse. Perhaps it was the novelty of having a commanding officer at their mercy or, more likely, simply the boundless enthusiasm of lower deck men carrying out an unusual task, but King was plucked from the gig like a rabbit caught by an eagle, then swung high up into the air until the frigate*'s* top rail was cleared by a good twenty feet. They lowered him as briskly and he was finally deposited on the starboard gangway with a jolt that made the soles of his feet sting. No sooner had King started to struggle free of his harness, than the squeal of pipes signalled the traditional greeting given to any senior officer upon boarding a ship; the noise made him jump, probably visibly, and was almost the last straw.

But as soon as he had gathered his wits, matters began to improve. There was Banks waiting to greet him with the well remembered grin on his face. The man seemed genuinely pleased and, once more, King felt they were meeting as friends and near equals. And then as he stood, still slightly dishevelled and amid the debris of the improvised lift, another sight caught his eye. It was Robert Manning, the surgeon King had shipped with for most of his professional life. When last seen he had been heading off to meet with Kate, his wife, who had recently given birth to their second child. Manning's last letter had been so filled with intricate details of family life that King had discounted ever seeing the cove again, but there he was, back aboard ship and wearing the dark tunic of a naval surgeon.

It was surprising that Banks had been able to entice him aboard *Relentless*; the two had also served together in the past though neither had ever been entirely happy in the other's company. But presumably the lure of a newly commissioned frigate together with her mission, which was intriguing in the extreme, had proved too great a temptation.

"Good to see you, Bob," King said with genuine feeling as he stepped forward to shake his friend's hand. And then came the biggest surprise of all.

Thinking about it later, King could not imagine how he had failed to notice immediately; perhaps the combination of his ungainly arrival, coupled with the surprise of meeting with Manning had been enough. But when the surgeon moved towards him, the figure standing behind was brought fully into view and King was taken aback.

Brushing his grinning friend to one side, and tripping slightly on the canvas straps that still clung about his ankles, he staggered towards her and, muttering a brief gasp of pleasure, fell into Aimée's arms.

* * *

An unusually high proportion of *Hare*'s crew had spent that morning pumping. Despite being in harbour, the brig required both chain pumps to be worked for up to an hour each watch to clear her bilges. Such a mindless task usually fell to minor defaulters although, with a fair captain and a generally contented crew, these were few enough so waisters and members of the afterguard were called in to assist. Then, just as they were finished with their work below, the same men had found themselves drafted aboard a visiting water lighter to carry out a similar task.

The first lieutenant had not ordered additional water, *Hare* having taken seventeen tons aboard at Plymouth which was sufficient to last them all of three months. But it remained a vital commodity and even more essential to any vessel planning deep sea travel, so the prospect of an additional supply from wells on the nearby Isle of Wight was welcome. After all, they might not be calling at Funchal and all other friendly ports would be several hundred miles away, so it made sense to stock up with a supply that was reckoned to be the best in England. And so Croft had ordered every available cask to be rousted out and filled which meant a busy morning for the men concerned.

Russell, who had been included in the working party, was not so very troubled by this. He had been lucky in being on the second team called to clear the bilges; the pumps had sucked dry after less than ten minutes, while the modern machines on the lighter turned out to be incredibly efficient. They needed considerably less effort, and men, to send streams of clear spring water up their brand new canvas hoses to *Hare*'s main deck, which allowed him time to stroll about the small craft's unfamiliar deck.

But he was not relaxing; his senses, honed during a life of petty crime, were razor sharp and being used to good effect. For this was just the break from routine Russell had been seeking; when such things occurred, they usually brought opportunities and the one he craved most was the chance to escape.

The lighter contained many hundred gallons of water and would probably be calling on each ship in the Commodore's command. But she would run dry eventually and, even if not, must surely return to the shore by the end of the day. And Russell was in no particular rush.

Much of the vessel was taken up by the three hefty iron tanks that emerged from her hull to stand proud above the main deck, but there were also two stubby masts as well as rowing positions for eight men for when sweeps were used. Russell glanced about the usual shipboard appointments of channels, fife rails and bitts; there was no chance of investigating the accommodation below as each hatch was securely locked, presumably to discourage any with similar ideas. Nevertheless, there remained one small area to the stern that definitely required investigation.

When he did he discovered it to be a place for the craft's crew to shelter from the weather and possibly take their meals; something four seamen were doing when he poked his head beneath the makeshift covering.

"What's about, matey?" one asked, looking up from the small table where he and the others sat.

"Just takin' a look," Russell explained hurriedly.

"Well you don't want to spend too long," a second warned. "Our skipper's not the most accommodating. Hates the Navy with a vengeance, even though it feathers his nest."

"Aye," another agreed, eyeing Russell pointedly. "If he thinks you've a mind to use us to do a runner, he won't take it kindly."

"Have you over the side before you can say knife," the first confirmed. "Seen it happen often, so we have, though it's a better prospect than finding yourself at the end of a rope," he added to the obvious amusement of the others.

Russell nodded quickly and withdrew although those brief seconds had been enough. The lighter's hands were only used for managing the craft, all pumping being carried out by the crews of the vessels they supplied. But when under way they would attend the sails or man the sweeps as necessary. So, despite what he had been told, when the time came to leave they would be fully occupied, leaving the area empty and, however much of a tyrant their captain might think he was, Russell remained confident of getting the better of him.

Sadly there hadn't been a great deal in the area to help; in his brief inspection he had noticed the one table with two benches and a couple of casks that might contain anything, but the far larger coffer set to one side had true possibilities. It was almost time for him to return and take his place at the pumps and, as he nonchalantly made his way forward once more, his mind was working fast. He had no way of knowing if the chest held anything but the lid had been open and there looked to be nothing inside. And, though it might be a tight squeeze, he reckoned it would accommodate someone of his size perfectly.

The chances of being spotted would be high, of course, and the lighter's crew weren't the first to warn him of what a captured deserter might face, although Russell was not convinced by such tales; if the Navy were so desperately short of men they would hardly hang those already in their possession. Besides, he had spent his life taking risks; they were almost the air he breathed, and even a slender chance was better than none at all.

7.

It had taken a good half hour for Banks to be rid of all distractions and speak to King privately but, even when they were both safely ensconced in *Relentless*' great cabin, it was clear the man's attention lay elsewhere. Banks supposed the French woman who had come on board with Manning was to blame. She and King first met while they were being held prisoner in Verdun and there was obviously some form of relationship as she accompanied them on their escape – much of which, he reluctantly allowed, had only been possible due to her family's assistance. But all that was surely in the past, yet it seemed King had set her up in a house and was still apparently infatuated by the wench. Privately, Banks failed to understand why she dominated his attention so – it wasn't as if they were married. Besides, he was reasonably sure King still had a perfectly serviceable wife elsewhere.

But, now he finally had the young officer to himself and presumably back in the real world, Banks was determined to make good use of him. There had been so much he had been wanting to discuss and although Granger and Bruce, who captained the two other frigates in his squadron, were undoubtedly fine fellows and more senior in rank to King, neither had the understanding or perception of the commander who now sat before him.

"So you have no further clues as to our eventual destination?" King asked and Banks was pleased to note the somewhat faraway look in his eye was starting to fade.

"None whatsoever," he confirmed. "Which makes drawing the correct provisions difficult. We are heading south, assuredly, but for how far? I am currently instructed up to ten degrees into the southern hemisphere; it is then that the sealed orders can be broached."

"And after that?"

"After that I assume we may abandon the convoy," Banks supposed, "and could be diverted back to the North Atlantic, or ordered further on to New South Wales, the Americas, somewhere in the Pacific – it is truly anyone's guess. Yet many of the options require differing supplies and all the time I have the sneaking suspicion that Faulks knows a good deal more."

"Faulks?" King questioned.

"The India Company Johnnie who commands their merchants," Banks replied with a dismissive wave of his hand. "Fellow carries a constant smirk on his face and, I own, it is starting to annoy."

King was about to ask more but thought better of it; if Banks were not getting on with the merchants' Commodore anything he said would only make matters worse. "I should think us to remain in the south, sir," he suggested instead. "Otherwise they would surely never have lumbered us with a convoy to escort so far; especially considering the haste in which all is being undertaken."

"And that means provisions for the height of summer," Banks agreed. "But how far will we be going? Beyond the Cape it starts to chill once more and may leave us needing cold weather stores again. Really, Tom, such a lack of information is insufferable."

King gave a grimace of sympathy but said nothing. In fact, he was feeling more than a little guilty. With all the rush of lading, then their temporary repairs at Plymouth followed by six frustrating days beating along the coast to Spithead, he had given little thought to the squadron's eventual destination, or even when they might expect to be free of the merchants.

"And the convoy is another matter," Banks continued, unintentionally picking up on King's train of thought. "It ain't unheard of for East Indiamen to head south in November, though unusual, and most water at Funchal, which is being denied. And they are all of the larger classes," he added despondently. "Usually you can expect at least as many independent traders, but every vessel is a copper-bottomed John Company liner of at least eight-hundred tons."

Banks paused and considered what he had said. So far Tom had made no real contribution to the discussion yet his presence was already proving beneficial. There were few other men he trusted as much and the simple act of stating his concerns to him had breached a dam in his own thoughts. Now that he was able to think more clearly, the convoy's make up seemed even more at odds; as was the fact that their bills of lading were yet to be presented. As senior officer in charge of the escort, it was essential that he knew exactly what each ship carried, yet, despite being so close to their departure date, the HEIC had failed to provide even the most basic of manifests. But the annoyance should not last for long; after ten degrees south, Faulks and his precious ships could continue to St Helena alone and, once they were at sea, he was unlikely to have to deal with the fellow face-to-face. Banks had long ago accepted that he lacked any skill in diplomacy so it was not surprising he found Faulks' brand of arrogance annoying. And it hardly helped that the Company insisted on styling him as Commodore, when the cull had no right to such a rank.

"To prevent our watering at Madeira would seem harsh," King mused. "Sure, there can be little need for secrecy once we are so far south. I doubt that our merchant cousins think much of the arrangement."

"Yet they have offered no objection," Banks agreed. "I tell you Tom, it is all deuced strange."

"Do we have a date for sailing?" King asked, and Banks brought his mind back to more immediate concerns.

"Friday," he replied.

"But that is tomorrow, sir," King exclaimed.

"We have already watered," Banks shrugged. "You will have time to do the same, and I hope you aren't one of those superstitious types."

"Absolutely not," King insisted. "One day is very much as another as far as I am concerned. And we took on water at Plymouth, though I noticed the lighter approaching on my way here so doubtless they are supplementing our supply."

"And the rest of your provisions?" Banks asked.

"They are sufficient," King confirmed. "Nevertheless I do have other matters that should be seen to," he added with less certainty.

"Other matters?" Banks was aware King's brig was not in top order materially, although all the vessels in his squadron could benefit from some degree of dockyard attention. If *Hare* were fully victualled there should be nothing else to detain him.

King went to reply but stopped; some things were not so easily explained, especially to a dry old stick like Sir Richard. He had not expected to see Aimée until he returned from wherever they were bound and the sudden and recent meeting, though wonderful, had woken feelings that should have remained suppressed. After being together, even publicly and for so short a time, it seemed unfair in the extreme to literally up anchor and be off with no further word.

"You said there was something else?" Banks was pressing now and King noticed his set expression. Doubtless the Commodore had spent sufficient time with his own family but even if not, he understood the man well enough to know it would take more than mere personal interests to delay him; not if there were service matters to consider.

"I was mistaken, there is nothing sir," he replied simply. "At least, nothing that will not wait."

* * *

It had been easier than he anticipated. As soon as the last cask aboard *Hare* was filled, Russell and his colleagues had begun retrieving the hoses. The lighter's captain then made his first appearance and turned out to be something of a tartar, at least when it came to Navy Jacks using his equipment.

Apparently the wet canvas should have been properly drained and then folded, rather than simply stuffed back into the lockers. Bryant, *Hare*'s coxswain, had intervened when one of his team was called a lubber and then it turned out that *Hare* was not due to be watered in the first place. The first lieutenant was called and there had been a right old tilt which even required the marine guard turning out. In the ensuing fracas, Russell had found it simple to make his way to the stern of the lighter and, once within the small and now empty shelter, clamber inside the empty chest.

He then discovered his earlier assessment had been slightly optimistic. The thing was indeed big enough but only just: his elbows needed to be wedged painfully against his sides and both legs packed so tightly it was hard to take full breaths. Then there was a problem with the lid; if closed, he would be hidden from view, but the amount of air entering the chest was minimal. It would do no good to reach the shore half dead through suffocation, although leaving the thing open made his presence far too obvious. Eventually he compromised, closing the lid upon himself, but slipping a finger into the gap so that it would not seal fully. That way no one would be any the wiser and he could also see something of his surroundings through the crack.

In time the argument on deck came to an end and the lighter squared away once more; Russell could feel the motion well enough but had no idea where they were bound. Then came the sound of voices and two of the sailors he had seen earlier appeared, together with a stout man wearing a round hat that he recognised as the lighter's captain.

Russell stayed perfectly still, hardly daring to breath. The two seamen seated themselves at the small table, but the captain had other ideas and made his way towards the chest. Noticing this, Russell found himself actually holding his breath, although he kept his finger in place and continued to peer through the small crack. For a moment there was no sign of the captain, then he caught sight of a portly leg immediately in front of his face. And the next thing he knew, the man had planted himself down heavily on the lid.

* * *

“So we are sailing almost immediately, sir?” Adams asked, his face falling.

“I believe so,” Croft confirmed as he sat back from the gunroom table. For most of the morning he had been trying to put the finishing touches to *Hare*'s watch and station bills but first Commander King had returned from meeting with the Commodore, then there had been the trouble with some fool of a lighter captain. The man had given them water only to then ask for it back so, when Adams appeared with some ridiculous request for shore leave, Croft felt he had more than enough to cope with. But such was the lot of a first lieutenant and he forced himself to appear receptive. “The captain says we should be ready on the morrow,” he told him. “Did you have specific plans ashore?”

Adams went to explain then thought better of it; even in his heightened state he realised that revealing he wished to seek employment aboard another vessel might not be diplomatic.

“We are in all respects ready,” Croft continued. “Most of the important repairs to the tophamper have been carried out: even our water is up to capacity,” he added with a hint of irony.

“Yes, sir,” Adams agreed, wondering if the first lieutenant's mind might be starting to wander.

“Was there anything else?” Croft regarded him not unkindly and Adams thought for a moment. He had been working up to this interview all morning and, as this was the first time he had caught Mr Croft alone, it seemed a shame to waste the opportunity.

“Might I ask, sir – do you have news of our final destination?”

“None whatsoever, I'm afraid,” Croft replied evenly. “The captain may know more and will doubtless make an announcement if he is able.” In reality, he feared Commander King might be just as uninformed but it would be wrong for him, as first officer, to say so. And it was strange that Adams should be so concerned; combined with his earlier enquiry, it convinced him there was more to the young man's request than the need for a simple spree ashore.

Actually Adams' assertiveness both in seeking leave and asking of the squadron had touched Croft on a sensitive spot. He wished he had shown similar spunk when dealing with senior officers in the past and was still cursing himself for not enquiring of their final destination when the captain returned from *Relentless*. But Commander King had brought a fresh surgeon with him, a man some aboard *Hare* appeared to already know, and Croft had not liked to appear too inquisitive in front of the newcomer. However, unless there was definite news before long, they would be setting off totally unprepared for what lay ahead; something that any conscientious first lieutenant would wish to avoid.

"I see, sir. Thank you."

Croft now started to rearrange the various items before him – an act Adams interpreted as signalling the interview was at an end and he prepared to leave.

"Though we shall doubtless be calling at a British port before long," the older man volunteered unexpectedly. "You may get the chance to go ashore then."

"Yes, sir," Adams confirmed politely, even if his expression remained as downcast. The most likely was St Helena and that was by no means guaranteed. Besides, the place might be an important outpost, but there would be scant chance of finding a sea-going lieutenant's berth there.

"After that I cannot say," Croft continued and once more went to return to his work. Adams prepared himself to go for the second time but, before he could turn away, Croft looked up and considered him sharply. "I wonder, John," he asked in a completely different tone, "would you permit a word of advice?"

The younger man was surprised to see Croft's expression had softened slightly and he could even have been smiling.

"Of course, sir."

"You have passed your board, which is commendable," the first lieutenant began when Adams had taken the chair he indicated. "And I fully understand your need for shore leave; the temptation to secure employment as a commissioned officer must be great indeed. But do not rush; take your time and choose carefully."

Adams stayed silent and his eyes remained fixed on the older man.

"As a midshipman, you may make mistakes; indeed some would consider them essential to your training. But once you walk a quarterdeck as a responsible officer, all that must end. With a commission in your pocket, every decision you make will be an important one. More than that, each will be examined by your peers as well as those beneath you, with every perceived flaw discussed in the greatest detail. And do not think that will change should you continue to progress; the higher you rise, the greater the number of those eager for a chance to knock you down. And there shall be no going back; the day you leave the midshipman's berth the cockpit door shall close firmly, while things may not be quite so comfortable on the other side."

Adams swallowed. His initial guilt at being found out was now turning to curiosity; Mr Croft was highlighting an aspect of promotion he had not considered, although it hardly quelled his desire for a lieutenant's post. Admittedly, with a position of authority he must expect to be held to account, but it was surely easier to give the right orders after sleeping in a private cabin and dining amongst gentlemen in the luxury of a wardroom.

"For now, be content to serve at your current post," Croft continued. "And do so knowing that another, a better one, shall surely come. But do not rush: that way lies trouble indeed."

"Trouble, sir?" Adams questioned.

Croft shrugged. "You may find yourself in a bad ship with a worse captain; one who is determined to blame every possible mistake on his most junior officer, which shall undoubtedly be you. And even if you break free of such a man, his report will follow like a bad smell making further employment the harder to secure. You may be forced to take increasingly inferior ships with captains to match until the career you had been dreaming of becomes more akin to a nightmare."

"Yes, sir," Adams agreed, although the first lieutenant wondered if the lad was merely paying lip service.

"Oh, I realise I come over as an old fool," Croft admitted suddenly and Adams immediately shook his head. He might be well beyond forty, but he had never considered Mr Croft to be a fool. "And I am not saying it would be the end," the senior man continued. "Luck and persistence may allow you to start again and you might recover your career in time. But by then it will be too late; you could conceivably become second or even first lieutenant of a smaller vessel though the chances of making commander would be slim indeed, and anything further must surely have gone by the board. Younger men, those who had not rushed, will have these, and you shall be deferring to them for the rest of your days. Is that what you truly wish?"

"No, sir," Adams replied more firmly. He had finally grasped what Croft was trying to tell him and for a moment both nodded in mutual understanding.

"Then go, John, but remember this meeting," Croft urged. "And you can be sure that, as soon as a suitable port presents, I shall do my utmost to see you are permitted shore leave."

The younger man thanked him and slipped quietly out of the gunroom. For a moment Croft was still, his mind some way in the past. And then he returned to the work before him and was about to begin again when the gunroom door began to vibrate to a frantic knocking.

Dilson, one of the younger volunteers, entered at Croft's summons, his face white with shock.

"Beggin' your pardon, sir, but there's a man what's fallen overboard."

"Very well," Croft replied, after closing his eyes for the briefest of moments. Then he rose from the table and left for more immediate matters.

* * *

The pain from his finger had been bad enough, but even that was soon forgotten as events took Russell over. Almost as soon as he emitted that single, echoing, yell, the chest had been opened and three faces peered down on him. Russell immediately went to clamber out but, before he could, the lid was slammed down hard, cutting out all light and much sound from what had become a very private world. Then the chest began to move and he realised it was being hoisted up and presumably carried away. There was also a deal of muffled laughter with one phrase, "never fails" repeated rather a lot, although Russell was more concerned about where he was being taken. And even that mystery was soon solved; the fresh bite of winter air was unmistakable as the lid opened once more. For a moment all he could see was blinding white cloud although that was replaced by the grey aspect of Spithead as the chest began to be tilted to one side. For a moment it seemed to totter and then, amid a roar of laughter, Russell found himself tumbling out and down into the dark sea's cold embrace.

8.

King closed the deck glass awkwardly and replaced it in the binnacle. They had left harbour without further incident and, as all traces of England disappeared over the horizon, the convoy was beginning to fall into the pattern agreed with Faulks, the HEIC Commodore. *Hare* had taken up position to leeward of the merchants, a station that befitted her lowly status, while *Athena*, a thirty-two gun frigate, was to windward with *Taurus*, another fifth rate, as back marker and Banks leading in *Relentless.* The whole affair looked almost picturesque in the rare sunlight, with the merchants' sails contrasting with their dark hulls, while the yellow chequer of the warships' sides added yet more colour to the vista. Turning from the sight, King caught the eye of Brehaut, the sailing master.

"That were relatively pain free," he remarked and the Jerseyman grinned.

"Aye, sir. The merchants seem a fair bunch of seamen, but then we should expect nothing less as they are all Company ships."

King nodded; that was true and, once more, it stood out as strange not to have at least a few independent traders amongst their charges.

It was mid-morning and the watch on deck had settled after what had been a busy few hours. Now *Hare* was keeping station adequately enough nothing more need be expected of them until Up Spirits was piped in a couple of hours. King had left harbour countless times before and, with a crew as experienced as this, knew it would take no more than a day before a routine became established and every man settled into place. With an escort force large enough to see off even the most determined privateer, there should be little to occupy them for many leagues, although he was too much of a realist to think such an outcome likely. Even ignoring the fact they were sailing in late November, a time known for gales and storms, for at least part of their journey there remained the very real threat of action from a powerful enemy.

Despite the recent victories off Ortegal and Trafalgar, there remained several French battle squadrons loose on the Atlantic and, with Britain's blockading forces currently depleted, the chances were high more would soon be joining them. All the Indiamen carried some degree of armament and could be expected to use it reasonably effectively but, were they to run across a force similar to that which Admiral Strachan had so recently defeated, King was willing to bet the outcome would not be so favourable.

He took a turn across *Hare*'s small quarterdeck as his thoughts continued to flow and, as captain, they naturally returned to his command. Here the news was certainly better, for they had a reliable surgeon once more. Robert Manning's appearance had come as a surprise almost on a par with that of seeing Aimée. King had written off any hope that the man could be tempted back to sea and been resigned to employing a series of jobbing medics similar to the recently departed Jones. However, it seemed his old friend was not so enamoured with family life as all expected.

By the time he reached home, his wife had one lively toddler and a demanding baby just starting to become active. But having been a Mother Midnight herself, little was required of Manning either as a surgeon or father, for in his absence Kate had become proficient at carrying out the role of both parents. Knowing the woman as he did, King could well imagine this and could also guess Robert must have initially been relieved at finding himself redundant. But it appeared the novelty soon wore off and, when Sir Richard offered the chance to return to sea, he had jumped at it.

King was still surprised Banks should have acted so; the Commodore and Manning had never been exactly happy shipmates, yet Sir Richard had known *Hare* lacked a surgeon and went out of his way to contact Manning as a favour to him – an unusually sensitive act from one not known for such things.

However, any pleasure in serving with Robert Manning again was more than offset by the frustratingly scant time he had been able to spend with Aimée. Despite everything, King still sensed she blamed him for not following her back to their Hampshire home for even the shortest of times. The brief hour they had spent on *Relentless*' crowded quarterdeck had not been sufficient to assure her to the contrary, nor did it allow them to talk in the way both would have preferred. Then there had been the final cut; the last memory when she had all but thrust that pile of letters at him, before stepping into the shore boat which took her away for what might be forever. Most turned out to be accounts and could certainly wait, but amongst them was a somewhat terse note from a legal firm in the City. It seemed his estranged wife was aware of his recent prize money as well as that which might be expected following Strachan's action and was determined to claim a share. She was not entitled to any of course, but the very act of lawyers writing to his Hampshire address led him to think she must also know of Aimée, all of which spelled a deal of problems for the future.

What he had already received was a reasonable sum, although most had been spent on the advance needed to secure their new home. Wife or no wife, Juliana could have no claim on anything he possessed, but if she wanted to make trouble on a more personal basis there would be little he could do about it while stuck out somewhere on the South Atlantic. Such a situation was beyond his control and totally unintended, yet still he could not help feeling he had behaved like a scoundrel. For, like it or not, he had effectively abandoned Aimée, and at a time when she needed him most.

* * *

Although officially off watch, Greenwood's mess had been called for duty when *Hare* left harbour and now, with little more than an hour before their main meal of the day, most had gravitated to the area near the forecastle where they berthed. The mess table was already rigged and Sennett, Brown and Jackson were playing a listless game of Crown and Anchor at it. Georgie, the boy, was munching on an onion and Russell and Sayer rested in the warmer positions next to the brig's side. Their brief call at Portsmouth had brought on an outbreak of head colds and, as Parker and Greenwood joined them, several were clutching at improvised handkerchiefs that showed various degrees of use.

"Well, that's the last we'll see of England for a spell," Greenwood muttered as Sayer made way for him to take his customary place at the table. "Bit of luck, it'll be summer by the time we's back."

"Aye, but what year?" Jackson asked disconsolately before

throwing the dice.

"Don't give a care about the time or the season," Swain, a heavily built hand, grumbled from the middle of the table. "I just want to shift this blighted cold." To demonstrate, he blew heartily on a square of waste cloth which was promptly wafted in the air to dry.

"You want to take a dash of burnt rum with butter," Parker, who had not been affected, advised as he settled himself next to the mess captain.

"Or brandy and ginger wine," Sennett added. "Might not shift the illness but you'll feel the better for it."

"Onions is good for coughs," Sayer volunteered. "Yon' lad's got the right idea," he added, nodding towards Georgie. "Eat plenty of onions and you never get sick."

"Never make any friends neither," Jackson added.

"It isn't the cough what carries you off, it's the coffin they carries you off-in!" Parker chanted cheerfully to a less than appreciative reception.

"Well, ain't that a rare jape?" Seldin wheezed. "Quite the little Joey Grimaldi, ain't we? Tell there ain't nothing amiss wi' you."

"It comes from being a topman," Parker assured them loftily. "I spends me time in the clean fresh air."

"Aye, an' with your head in the clouds," Jackson agreed.

"Everyone knows you catches a cold from being in the wind and rain," Swain grumbled thickly.

"Then how comes you got one?" Parker asked. "Rain hardly reaches your precious hold, and the only wind down there is what you makes yourself."

There was a ripple of token laughter, although few were feeling particularly merry.

"Ne'er mind, it will be Up Spirits in no time," Greenwood added in an effort to lighten the mood.

"Up Spirits? That's a laugh – it's been beer every day since we left Plymouth Dock," Brown, a former tin miner, pointed out.

"An' 'ardly the best neither," Sayer agreed.

"It will be beer again today an 'all," Swain assured them. "We just brought another hogshead up."

Sayer sighed. "So why all this talk of serving rum aboard Navy ships?"

"The rum will kick in once the beer runs out," Greenwood explained.

"Or goes off," Swain interrupted.

"Already has," Sayer snorted.

"Stingo's standard issue in home waters," Jackson announced.

"Gave us blackstrap in the Med.," Swain mused. "Went down lovely it did."

Sayer pulled a sour face. "Well it ain't what I were expectin'," he said.

Greenwood cast a covert look about the crowded table. The new hands had actually settled in rather better than he had hoped, although there was still something about Russell that vaguely worried him. But at least the mess had started to work as a group which, as their head, was all he wanted.

"Don't pay to hope for nothing," Jackson, who captained one of the carronades, told the newcomers firmly. "I learned that years back when I were a barber ashore. Always get your money first, 'cause if they don't pay up, you can't put it back."

There was more general laughter even though several must have heard the gunner's quip before.

"It's not as bad as that," Parker added quickly. "You can hope for all you wants, just don't expect it; that way no one'll be disappointed."

The banter continued although Russell, sitting next to the spirketing, made no contribution. But he caught every nuance of the men's conversation and his eyes were equally alert. Since being dragged from the sea the day before, his life had undergone a dramatic change. First there had been the shock of a near drowning; like most, Russell had no concept of swimming or even keeping himself afloat. And as those aboard the lighter had been happy to leave him in their wake, he would have drowned were it not for the intervention of the eclectic group of men that currently bickered about him. His messmates had gone on to help further; at the time of his dunking the marine guard called out to restore order aboard the lighter had yet to return to their posts, so no one was quite sure how he had come to be so far from the brig's side. But his new found friends had been as quick to invent a story as they were in reacting to his plight.

Rolled hammocks were thrown and, by the time he had caught

hold of two and was able to remain more or less buoyant, the jolly boat reached him. By then Greenwood must have guessed what had happened and invented the tale of him falling from the bowsprit. Russell had naturally gone along with the nonsense and was only too pleased to find himself being treated with rum and warm towels rather than placed in irons and sent below to await punishment for attempting to desert. *Hare*'s officers were content to let the matter rest and Russell returned to duty at the next watch, although to him the matter was by no means over.

For the experience of being supported by a group of friends was a new one to him. He had done nothing to deserve their assistance, while Parker at least had good reason to wish him gone. And yet not only was he saved from probable death, those before him now had gone out of their way to give their protection and see him safely back into the mess. It was almost as if he had found a home; a concept that Russell had often heard mentioned but never before experienced.

The riddle was yet to be fully solved, although Russell could hardly think of it as a problem and, despite what Parker had said about not entertaining hope, for the first time in his life he was starting to feel genuinely optimistic.

* * *

Robert Manning was finding it relatively easy to adapt to life afloat again, the more so as he now worried less about Kate and his growing family. Of course, he was still concerned for her – deeply so – but his brief stay ashore had taught him that not only was she content to look after the children on her own, she actually preferred to do so.

Besides, Manning remembered, she was not entirely alone. Poppy, Kate's former maid who had given birth to a baby boy a year or so previously, had moved in with her and was ostensibly carrying out the duties of a servant, although the women shared the upbringing of their two families equally. Manning totally approved of the arrangement; much could be saved by combining chores and he would rather see Kate supported than lonely. And he definitely had no objection to his wife reorganising her life in his absence – how could he when so much of his time was spent at sea? But, though he knew it to be wrong and would only admit it to himself, he had grown used to masculine company and to live in a house where women dominated and the wants and foibles of children were paramount was hard to acclimatise to.

He had some company in this in Seth Driver, a horse doctor's apprentice who, though not the father of her child, was engaged to Poppy. The lad was in pretty much the same position and it was no surprise to anyone that, when Manning announced he would be returning to sea, Driver elected to go with him.

And now he was safely installed in the sick berth and learning the duties of a loblolly boy. Being that they differed little from his former responsibilities, Manning felt Driver would soon become proficient, and it was good to have one in his department who knew something of his family, especially as the novelty of being back at sea again, though initially welcomed, was starting to wane. And though somehow he felt something valuable had been lost, he was coming to accept that the only one truly to blame was himself.

* * *

It was simply bad luck that the call for topmen and afterguard had come less than a bell before the change of watch, so all of Russell's mess had been deprived of almost half an hour's sleep. Such inconvenience was rare, however; *Hare*'s officers, being of a considerate nature, usually tried to time events such as reefing or tacking to the change of watch when all were expected to be on deck. But the wind had been growing for some while and, when the Indiamen were forced to reduce sail, King had no option other than to follow.

And it was all done simply enough; the topmen swarmed aloft in near darkness while those on deck handled the yards in perfect coordination. And, even though such an evolution performed on solid land and in broad daylight would have been beyond most landsmen, to *Hare*'s seasoned hands it was part of a normal day's work.

Russell had not been called to go aloft, of course. As a member of the afterguard his duties were on deck, hauling on braces, halyards and lifts but he had watched the vague smudges that represented his shipmates as they hung precariously above his head with an air of wonder. He had yet to be ordered aloft and the knowledge that only skill, confidence and a modicum of tired line kept them suspended so was hardly an encouragement. At the end of the evolution they had been stood down once more and a few of his mess were ordered to secure one of the boats, which was in danger of shaking free from its housing. Russell had not been amongst them; as a landsman he lacked the skills necessary for such work and was free instead to seek the shelter of the berth deck. Nevertheless, as he crept about in the dark underworld that was fast becoming familiar, he was unusually thoughtful.

For the short time he had been aboard *Hare* had taught him much. There was the revelation about Parker of course, as well as his rescue from the deep; both incidents had shown him seamen were not quite the fools he had first thought them. And, as he came to learn more of their craft, a modicum of respect was starting to form.

Respect was another concept Russell had rarely encountered. When moving in criminal circles there was something similar, although that had been founded on fear; a rival gang would either be stronger or weaker and must be treated accordingly. But what he was encountering now was a purer form of deference. Privately, and still from a landsman's point of view, he could see little ordinary in the average lower deck hand, while those rated able could almost be regarded as gifted. Yet such talents were freely shared and for the common good, which was definitely against the ethos of his old world.

A topman fastening a reef or a seasoned helmsman at the wheel worked not only for themselves but every soul aboard, while the artisans – the sailmakers, carpenters, caulkers and their like – seemed to toil as much for the pride found in their work and the good it would do the barky as for any monetary payment. They were also generous with their abilities; should Russell have chosen to, he could have learned any number of skills, from simple splicing to more complex ropework or any one of the countless talents many lower deck men possessed. And some were gifted in more domestic crafts; he might try his hand at needlework, crochet or discover the intricacies of scrimshaw from an old shellback while, such was the eclectic background of regular Jacks, even if he chose not to follow their particular speciality, he could still get his shoes repaired, hair cut or clothes mended by an expert. A small payment might be required for these or other services, although much could be achieved by barter and it was then that Russell realised that he was apparently talentless.

The only ability he possessed was bare-faced cheek and what he formerly considered a certain skill in judging human behaviour; nothing that would be marketable to his shipmates, many of whom had more than enough of both. There was little he actually needed, but still felt the lack of funds and was already in debt for his clothes; a few bob might make all the difference and allow him a little dignity in his new world.

And then his former instincts revived and alerted him to something previously missed. As it was still officially night, the hammocks remained slung and the open mouth of a ditty bag poked from one. Both bag and hammock belonged to Swain, the stocky and least intelligent member of his mess. The others were yet to return and it would take Russell no time to rifle through the bag. Swain had been aboard the brig a fair while and may well be keeping back a little coin, or something else suitably anonymous that could be traded for the same.

He glanced about; the berth deck was still strangely quiet and he had all the time in the world. But something made him stop, even when he had Swain's bag in his hand. It was the physical act that did it, actually touching the rough canvas. Russell swiftly dropped the thing back on the hammock as if suddenly burned and even glanced at his fingers for a moment, although they appeared little different. But something had come over him, and slowly he realised what it was.

It seemed foolish, ridiculous even, but there was a truth he could not deny: becoming accepted and a member of the mess was actually worth more to him than anything he might gain from theft.

Quickly he pressed the thing back firmly into the blankets of the hammock then hurried away before any returned. As far as revelations went it was probably not so great, though it meant a lot to Russell who was now eager to return to the deck and join the others in securing the cutter. And, in his haste he walked straight past Greenwood, the mess captain, who had been hidden in shadows at the opposite end of the berth deck for some while.

9.

They had known the storm was coming long before the first drops of rain began to fall. *Hare*'s motion had started to alter more than twelve hours earlier, with the sluggish roll all were accustomed to steadily increasing to a far deeper rocking that soon found out any item, or person, not properly secured. The very air also changed, with a heaviness that could be detected without resorting to one of the sailing master's devices while the growing breeze took on a stark, metallic scent that signalled danger to all but the rawest of hands.

And there were few of those aboard *Hare*, most were seasoned mariners who knew the area well and of the prevailing wind that currently pressed them to a credible heel as the brig battled to remain with the convoy. This need to keep pace was not one King had foreseen on discovering their charges to be exclusively East Indiamen, even if it was obvious as soon as he thought about it.

Company ships were made well, certainly on a par with government vessels, and maintained just as professionally – possibly better, following St Vincent's recent disastrous dockyard reforms. With none of their ships owned outright but merely leased, the HEIC could also afford to be selective; few were retained for more than four full trips to the East and each of those *Hare* currently shepherded was at least the size of a fifth rate. So with a complete absence of smaller, independent vessels, it was hardly surprising the convoy was travelling quickly. Having such professional charges also meant *Hare* and the other warships were relieved of one of the least popular aspects of escort duties: the constant chivvying and rounding up of stragglers. So far all had kept good station and responded correctly to every instruction while, when a pair of suspected privateers had been spotted off Finistere, the Indiamen had closed up to allow their guardians to see to the danger without indulging in foolish signals or letting off stray cannon seemingly on impulse. But, however practised the merchants might be, and however far they might have travelled in a relatively short time, they were still about to endure a storm and, if King's instincts were correct, a particularly hefty one.

"Reckon we'll be in for a bit of a blow, Master," he said,

turning to Brehaut who stood next to him on the quarterdeck in a watchcoat already darkened by the spotting rain.

"Indeed, sir," the sailing master agreed, raising his voice as he did. "One that will last a fair time I should say, though we have made good progress so far."

King nodded briefly. Brehaut was right; it was doubtful if *Hare* could have reached their current latitude any faster on her own. But the weather wasn't right for conversation and would definitely grow worse in the next few hours. The afternoon watch was barely started, yet already the sky had begun to grow dull. *Taurus*, the frigate currently on the windward station, was all but invisible although *Relentless,* in the van, still maintained good speed, just as King would have expected. Whatever Banks' sealed orders contained, they could only be broached once the convoy passed ten degrees south, and the Commodore had made it clear he wished to reach such a position as quickly as possible. But, however determined Sir Richard might be, he could not control the weather and, even as King watched, a line of bunting broke out aboard his ship.

"General from *Relentless*," Summers, the signals midshipman, announced. "Convoy order seventeen." There was a pause as the lad struggled with a second sheaf of papers. "Reduce sail commensurable with the weather."

Brehaut glanced briefly at King for confirmation, then bellowed, "Strike t'gallants!"

A line of topmen emerged from under the shelter of the forecastle and soon the windward shrouds were dark with bodies streaming up the ratlines. King watched them go; their work would be done within minutes but it would not be long, probably earlier than the next bell, before they were needed again to take a reef in the topsails with another likely to be required not long after.

King felt the motion beneath his feet increase slightly with the reduction of sail. He had not been blind to Croft's warnings about the hull, though still could see little point in pushing for investigations that would either have been refused, or possibly seen *Hare* withdrawn from service. Besides, with the carpenter confident all was as sound as it could be, there was no reason to take such a course, and the next few hours would tell them almost as much as a dockyard examination. The weather they were about to encounter was bound to flex the hull, straining her frames and timbers and testing any previous repairs while potentially creating the need for more. Still, Mr Anderson was well supported by his team and King did not think the storm would discover anything they could not handle; his main worry was that it might split the convoy.

For he knew well how bad weather lasting more than a day could separate even the most orderly group of shipping. Were it to stretch to three, four or even five days, it would be all but impossible to maintain the convoy, and a week or more might easily see all totally dispersed. If such a thing were allowed it would be a disaster for Banks. However well his duties were carried out later, he would always be remembered for losing an India convoy; something that might mean his first experience of commanding a squadron would also be his last.

And any failure on Sir Richard's part would also reflect badly on King. *Hare* was by no means the finest vessel in the Navy and having been granted command of her so soon after his court martial was still remarkable. Being transferred to Banks' squadron had been another incredible stroke of luck but such fortune could not last forever. If Banks did a good job, King could expect to rise with him, possibly to a better command and promotion, but without his influence the future looked bleak indeed.

Another figure appeared on the quarterdeck, whether drawn by the noise of shortening sail or the change in the ship's motion King did not know but Croft, his first lieutenant, had joined them and, after paying due respects to his captain, was now checking their course.

"We seem likely for bad weather, Mr Croft," King commented as the older man replaced the traverse board and approached.

"Aye, sir," Croft replied. "I had hoped we would raise St Helena without incident though really did not expect to at this time of year."

King was about to reply when he noticed the man was regarding him with a particularly significant look. It was as if he were eager to discuss something but unwilling to bring the subject up. In a flash of intuition King realised it must be the damned hull again and he had to check himself before his irritation became obvious.

For there was no doubt in his mind that Croft was a worrier; maybe such a thing came with age, or perhaps the position of first lieutenant encouraged it, in which case King was particularly pleased never to have been burdened with the post. But the older man must still be bothering about the brig's fabric and the fact annoyed him, the more so as it awoke a guilt he had been trying to suppress and one that was in danger of starting him on the same heading.

"Sail ho!"

The call interrupted anything Croft might have wanted to say and both men instinctively looked up at the masthead. The sky had darkened further and it didn't seem possible that anything of significance could have been spotted.

"Riding on our leeward quarter; a schooner or something similar," the lookout continued. "Can't make out much and I'm losing her by the minute."

"How far off?" Croft demanded and there was a pause while the man considered.

"Hull down," he finally announced, adding, "Though she looks to be closing."

"Maybe a runner?" Croft supposed. Particularly fast merchants were licensed to travel independently although few so frail would be expected this deep into the Atlantic.

"Maybe," King agreed. "Though even if a privateer she can do us little harm, and *Taurus* has our stern. In any case we have a common enemy in the coming storm."

The sighting had been enough to break their conversation however, and King was able to retreat to his side of the quarterdeck without causing offence. Croft continued to peer at the convoy and then seemed to be exchanging a word with Brehaut. Watching him, King supposed the man's concern for the ship was understandable, but nothing would be gained by raising the subject yet again and he really should know when to let alone. As captain, he had made the decision to sail and the responsibly remained with him. In King's experience nothing good ever came from unnecessary fretting and often a great deal of bad. But it was equally fortunate that he could avoid the subject if he chose. He had no idea what Croft and the sailing master were discussing but he was perfectly entitled to remain aloof. The position of overall command came with several disadvantages, many of which were not obvious, but at least it gave a measure of isolation when most needed.

* * *

"So, is it that you don't like women, or just want men more?" Russell asked, and Parker eyed him suspiciously.

"This harking back to our earlier conversation, is it?" the topman demanded and Russell hastily shook his head.

"I were out of order then," he allowed. "Not been to sea properly and didn't know the life. Didn't know as much as I thought in many ways, if I'm honest."

Parker nodded, satisfied with the explanation. "I don't dislike women," he admitted after a pause. "Nor especially like men. Truth is, I have little feeling either way."

"So you're not a Molly," Russell confirmed. "Not in the normal sense."

"Normal sense," Parker laughed. "Now there's a statement. I don't want to lie with either – if that's what you mean."

"But ain't that strange?" Russell insisted. It was coming to the end of the second dogwatch, the rest of the mess were still below but the two men had come on deck early and independently to check on the approaching storm.

"Don't seem so to me," Parker declared. The full force had yet to come but the wind was growing steadily and he lowered himself behind the protection of the weather bulwark.

"Well, don't you think of getting married?" Russell persisted as he joined him.

"Should I?"

"Ain't that what most of us wants?"

"Not me," Parker sighed, leaning back. "I chose this life, no one pressed me. And there ain't no one waiting for me ashore, neither man nor woman, which is just as I likes it."

"That's sad," Russell told him.

"Is it?" Parker asked, surprised. "Most Jacks on board spend their time dreaming of home – yet I'm already there. I don't call that sad."

"No, I suppose not," Russell conceded.

"There ain't no point in being where you don't belong. I know the pressed men weren't given a choice, but they won't be here forever. Mostly they'll get back to where they wants to be eventually. Then, if they've got any sense, they'll move inland and never come near the sea again. But I know when I'm well off and will be staying for as long as the sea will have me."

"So, what's the attraction?" Russell asked and Parker considered him more closely. The sun had set some time ago but enough light remained to show the men's features.

"Of being at sea? You tell me," Parker instructed.

"Me?" Russell shrugged. "I've not been aboard more than six weeks."

"Yet you've changed in that time," Parker insisted. "I seen it, and so have the others. Sayer, what joined with you, ain't stopped talking about getting away as soon as he can. He'll never make a proper seaman – but you will."

"Go on!" Russell scoffed.

"You're taking to it," Parker insisted. "And showing you can manage. Stick at what you're doing and they'll rate you ordinary in a year or so. Or you might make it to the quarterdeck before then."

"What, be an officer?" Now Russell was grinning openly although there might have been a hint of something else in his expression.

"They does that," Parker confirmed. "You can follow the gunner, or the bosun or any of the warranted men what started on the lower deck. Or try for the cockpit and become a volunteer."

"Is that right?"

"They got their eye on our youngster as it is."

"What Georgie?" Russell asked, amazed.

"Na, he's but a boy. Sennett, the Sussex lad. He'll be wearing a snotty's uniform before you knows it and we'll both be calling him mister – mark my words."

"Well who'd have thought..." Russell replied after a moment's pause. And then there was a further silence.

"You wants to do that," Parker continued eventually. "Think on it and look for the opportunity when it comes. That's if it's what you wish for, of course."

"So why didn't you?" Russell asked turning to the man again.

“What me? Be a middie?”

“Or bosun's mate,” Russell countered as Parker shook his head.

“It wouldn't suit,” he said. “Happy to be a topman, and when I gets too old for that, maybe join the fo'c's'le. But I don't want no promotion.”

“Or a woman – or a man,” Russell reminded him with a grin. “Sounds like you don't want nothing.”

“Well you're wrong there, matey,” Parker told him seriously. “I wants to stay as I is.”

* * *

The storm broke fully later that night and robbed most of those aboard *Hare* of any chance to sleep. As King predicted, Greenwood, Parker and the other topmen were called twice more, and that was just the start of their time aloft. Other journeys were made to both set and strike canvas and then, just as night was at its blackest, the lower foreyard sprung.

And this was no simple repair; first they had to turn *Hare* before the wind and clue up the fore topsail, while reducing canvas on the main to balance pressure from the driving weather. Then, using jeers, top-burtons, lifts and pendant-tackle, the yard was gingerly lowered to the deck, where it could be reinforced: a process known as fishing, using studding sail booms and spare capstan bars as splints.

Meanwhile, others were equally busy. In warship terms *Hare* was a lightweight but even she carried many tons of ordinance. Extra tackle was rigged to each carronade which, though less than a third of the weight of an equivalent carriage piece, were still heavy enough to puncture the brig's lee side if they came adrift.

Below deck, the holders were also at work. *Hare*'s mighty leaguers – containers that each held several hundred gallons of drinking water – were already snuggled down safe in their beds of gravel but the smaller casks, and those half emptied, were far more vulnerable and needed to be checked and secured. Much of this work was carried out in near darkness and often whilst wading ankle deep in surging water, but the men who managed it were soundly built with minds to match and did so without complaint.

The surgeon and his team were also busy. Newly returned to the sea and still in the process of organising his department, Manning found himself faced with a constant stream of minor injuries that ranged from cuts, sprains and bruised limbs to one man who had been knocked cold by a tumbling cask.

And all the while both main pumps needed to be kept in constant use. This last duty used every spare man and was not initially blamed on a deficiency in the hull, when even the soundest of vessels would leak if faced with such conditions. However, as the night wore on it became clear that *Hare* was taking in an inordinate amount of water.

Some came in from above: however firmly they battened down, a regular flow continued to seep in over companionway coamings or through the tightest of plugged hawse holes, not to mention the excess from overworked dales and scuppers; drains that could never have been large enough to deal with such a torrent. But there was more; despite the efforts of those at the pumps, the level in *Hare*'s well continued to rise and soon it became apparent that the excess could only come from one place.

The carpenter's regular checks revealed no specific leak so there was little anyone could actually do other than conclude the storm was a particularly bad one – that and pray for morning, although even the coming of daylight would not necessarily bring peace.

But, as the first lines of dawn began to show, there was a slight easing; the wind continued to blow hard but had shifted more to the south, there was less rain and, as the bland, metallic light grew, it gave them all hope. The full extent of *Hare*'s wounds were also revealed, however, and she was a mess.

Ignoring the tangle of line forward as the boatswain's team still struggled to re-rig the foreyard, there were other areas of damage. One of the cutters had been knocked asunder by an unusually large wave that also removed the galley chimney, while the jolly boat that hung from davits at the transom had been swamped with several planks burst from her frame. And there were other casualties; the binnacle had taken a battering that had deftly removed both traverse board and speaking trumpet while leaving several panes of glass cracked and the flag locker was all but demolished with much of its contents missing. But the most serious consequence of the storm was only revealed when what sun there was had fully risen, and it had nothing to do with the brig herself.

For it was then, when the light was at its feeble best and Brehaut, Croft and King had gathered on the quarterdeck, that the main lookout confirmed what each had been secretly fearing: the convoy was nowhere in sight.

* * *

King, determined to maintain his composure, remained silent. He knew they had lost both time and position by turning to ease the pressure on their foreyard, but it had only been a temporary diversion; unreeving the topsail sheets and making them fast on deck had seen their original course regained shortly afterwards and he had sincerely thought daylight would reveal at least some of their former charges in plain sight. Enough, at least, to give a bearing – an indication of where others might be found. And, now that the wind had changed, the convoy would have to beat into it to make what southerly progress they could, and even seasoned Company men would not be happy with constant changes of course. Consequently, King decided it more likely that they would be sailing on extended legs, each lasting several hours, in which time they would cover a fair distance – long boards, as they were known. But would these be to the west or east? King could not begin to guess, yet it was up to him to decide.

"Take us south, as close to the wind as she will lie," he ordered as soon as the lookout's words had been fully digested.

"What tack, sir?" Brehaut asked.

"Larboard," King replied, more out of instinct than anything else. The coast of Africa was a good way off and, even if the current breeze were to fail, the prevailing wind meant it was rarely a lee shore. But still the vastness of the Atlantic felt preferable to his sailor's instincts, just as he hoped it might have to Sir Richard's.

He watched as *Hare* was brought closer to the wind. It was

asking a lot: the foreyard should not be trusted with anything but the gentlest of sail, although King was equally aware of another undeniable fact. The longer they remained out of contact with the convoy, the less likely it became that they would ever find it again.

10.

As the daylight increased it brought further improvement in the weather. The constant deluge they had been enduring throughout the night finally died to be replaced by spasmodic showers that even allowed a modicum of drying time between outbursts. And as the morning wore on, their wind, still southerly, began to drop until they were in little more than a stiff breeze and sailing waters verging on the moderate. It was also possible to take a noon sighting which gave them a better indication of position, although there was still no sign of the convoy and King's concerns continued to grow.

"I can only estimate currents and have no clue as to when, or whether, the Commodore shortened sail," Brehaut murmured as the two of them examined the chart in the privacy of the great cabin. "Though would still predict them to be to the south."

"Which should place them off our larboard bow," King remarked.

"In an ideal situation," Brehaut sighed; as sailing master he was probably the best to appreciate the predicament his captain was in.

King pursed his lips as he stared at the chart. He could not fault Brehaut's reasoning as it was so close to his own. Both had allowed for Banks making for the west, while the recent midday sighting placed *Hare*'s latitude roughly in keeping with their dead reckoning. And they surely could not have fallen so very behind during the storm? The convoy should be there: all the evidence dictated it. But, however much logic was applied, one hard fact remained: no shipping of any variety was in sight, and they might still be heading in entirely the wrong direction.

It was then that a shout from the deck made both look up in anticipation and, moments later, a hurried tap on the cabin door followed by the marine sentry's announcement which heralded the arrival of the midshipman of the watch.

Cole, a volunteer and one of the youngsters who had joined them at Portsmouth, made a hesitant entry into the cabin. "Mr Croft's respects, sir," he said, his eyes round in wonder at this rare entry into the captain's quarters. "And there is a sail in sight."

A sail: perhaps the problem had been solved and one of the convoy had been spotted?

"Where away?" King demanded.

"I-I don't know sir," he confessed, blanching slightly. "Mr Croft gave a bearing but it escapes me."

"Come on," he grunted at Brehaut and, brushing past the unhappy child, made for the deck.

Once there it was clear something important had occurred, although the tension that had been present all morning was still evident.

"What of this sighting, Mr Croft?" King demanded as he returned the first lieutenant's salute.

"Masthead reported it a moment back, sir, but has since lost it in a squall. Hull down and off our windward bow," Croft added seriously, "and beating south – on the larboard tack as we are."

For a moment King's spirits rose; that was almost exactly where he had expected to find Banks' ships. But Croft had more to say.

"It seems unlikely to be part of the convoy, however."

"Unlikely? Pray, why?"

"It is but a light vessel," Croft replied. "Two masts; possibly a topsail schooner but certainly not one of Sir Richard's force."

King could think of nothing to say in reply and simply glanced about at the empty grey waters in frustration. He had so wanted this to be one of Banks' ships but Croft was right. Hull down, a lookout might mistake a brig for a snow or even a frigate for a ship-of-the-line, but with hefty East Indiamen making up the merchants' share and none of the other escorts being less than a fifth rate, the sighting was definitely something different.

"Do you think she may be a predator?" Croft asked, just as King was coming to the same conclusion.

"I think it highly likely, Mr Croft," he replied. "Was there not something similar sighted just afore the storm broke?"

"I believe you are right, sir," Croft agreed.

“Lay us on the starboard tack,” King ordered briskly. They had yet to confirm the mystery vessel's size although he had already guessed both her nationality and intentions.

“Starboard tack, aye aye, sir,” Croft repeated before turning away to bellow out the appropriate orders. King watched as *Hare*'s yards were braced round and her wheel put across. The change of course would make little difference; they would still be heading south though not quite so deeply into the Atlantic. However, if King's hunch was correct, they might have already found the convoy, or at least evidence of it. Changing tack would take no pressure off the damaged foreyard, but it would close the distance between them and the sighting and settle her identity for certain.

Hare soon settled on her new course and King took the opportunity to examine his command more carefully. They had achieved a lot in a short time. Already the brig appeared more orderly with much of the previous night's damage set to rights. The cutter was back in its former housing with a small repair made to her prow, while the jolly boat was currently lying on the main deck and being attended to. Thoughts of the carpenter led him to the inevitable question, and he moved forward. The chain pumps were still in operation with streams of white water flowing from both dales; something that did not bode well so late into the watch. He had already spoken to Anderson who remained as certain of no obvious leak in the hull, although, considering the recent improvement, little could now be blamed on the weather. And then there was this mystery sighting to contend with. Not so very long ago joining Banks' squadron had seemed the answer to everything; King would have guaranteed employment and be working under a man he particularly liked and respected. The prospect of sailing with sealed orders had added extra flavour to the brew but, with a mystery leak, a potential enemy in sight and no firm sign of the convoy, there could be little doubt the voyage was not panning out as he had hoped.

* * *

“Come to join the party, have we?” Parker asked, as Greenwood reached the mainmast crosstrees.

“It's six bells,” his messmate informed him as he eased himself onto the well worn timbers. “I'm your relief.”

“Well, we also has Mr Summers,” Parker indicated with a grin and a flick of his thumb. Greenwood glanced up to see the youngster clinging precariously to the topgallant mast.

“Told him he wouldn't learn much more from further up,” Parker added in a lower tone. “I lost the sighting in yonder squall, but it's clearing all the time, an' if she were visible from here before, she will be again. But you know these young gentlemen...”

Greenwood did indeed, except Summers was obviously prepared to put a bit of effort in, which was no bad thing.

“So, show us where she was then,” he directed.

“Fine on our larboard, though we have tacked since,” Parker replied, before pointing out over the starboard bow and adding, “I should say we can expect her thereabouts.”

There was no horizon in that direction, the grey sea simply merged with a dark sky amid the gloom of a storm that might hide anything from a singleton to a fleet. “I get it,” Greenwood spoke slowly as he looked.

“Well don't spend too long on that quarter,” Parker cautioned. “We don't want nothing nasty creeping up from behind now, do we?”

Greenwood had noticed before that Parker was particularly perky when aloft, as if he were truly at home, and it was pleasant to be with someone so comfortable in their element. Nevertheless, he gave his friend a particularly hard stare and was just returning to the original sector when a shout from above alerted them both.

“I have her!” Summers' voice rang out loud enough to be heard on deck, and both topmen drew breath as they peered out once more.

“That's clearer than last time,” Parker agreed as the ghostly outline of a topsail schooner gradually emerged from the gloom. “She's almost hull up.”

“And a warship right enough,” Greenwood agreed. “Wouldn't find no merchant sparred so.”

A squeal from above told them Summers was having difficulty keeping his position while focusing a glass and shortly afterwards the lad slid down the topgallant mast and joined them on the crowded crosstrees.

“Couldn't get a fix,” he explained briskly while levelling the telescope once more.

"She a Frenchie?" Parker asked, but there was no response.

"Masthead, what do you see there?" Croft's voice came from below; clearly all on the quarterdeck were expecting information and did not wish to be kept waiting.

"Sail in sight," Summers reported, still staring through his telescope. "Two-masted; probably a schooner, close-hauled on the opposite tack. She's hull down and fine on our starboard bow, though we looks to be gaining on her. And I'd say she were a pirate."

* * *

"A privateer, I have no doubt," Croft confirmed as he peered through the glass. It was some time since Summer's positive identification, *Hare* had drawn considerably closer and the sighting was now in clear view from the deck. "And not likely to be one of our own," the first lieutenant added.

Croft passed the telescope back to King who, resisting the temptation to look once more himself, handed it straight to Brehaut. They were grouped on the poop; a grand name for what was little more than a platform above and abaft of the wheel and a feature of Cruizer class brig-sloops. But it was the best place to view the mystery vessel and do so in relative privacy.

"Privateer for sure," Brehaut confirmed. Then, after considering for a moment longer added, "And I'd chance her to be the sail we spotted afore the storm."

"We thought her a letter of marque then," Croft agreed.

"The hull, or what we can see of it, would seem large for such a rig," Brehaut continued, "though she presents as sleek and fast."

"Cannon?" Croft asked and, though he had yet to make any contribution to the conversation, King listened intently. He had reckoned on at least a dozen carriage pieces but wished to hear other opinions.

"I would not care to guess," Brehaut admitted. "Such things are not in my line."

King stayed silent but glanced surreptitiously at Croft.

"Six- maybe nine-pounders," the first lieutenant supposed. "Unlikely to be anything heavier and I would judge no more than six a side."

"But from the sailing point of view, such a craft would give the old *Hare* a run for her money," Brehaut added. "Especially in her current state."

Again King could not dispute this and, still silent, collected the glass once more.

The schooner was still off their starboard bow and seemed content for the British to continue closing on her, despite having canvas in hand; something that added to his suspicions that she in turn had the convoy in sight and wanted no more than to keep pace with it. She was also in the perfect position to turn and bear down on them with the wind on her tail should she so choose. *Hare* was well armed and, in theory, should account for a heavy schooner although the opportunity might not come their way quite so easily. Apart from her two bow chasers, all the brig's cannon were carronades; heavy pieces but not known for accuracy over a long distance. A quick and nimble adversary such as the one that lay before them would have no difficultly in keeping her at a distance, while sniping with what were likely to be lighter, yet far more accurate, long guns. *Hare* had never been a particularly agile craft but with a weakened foreyard and water in the hull, it would be difficult to respond to such tactics. All it would take was for the brig's tophamper to be damaged further and they might easily find themselves taken.

"What crew do these Johnnies usually carry?" Brehaut was asking Croft who considered for a moment.

"Not more than seventy I'd say," the older man replied. "And possibly less, if she were well into a cruise."

Still King remained silent, although he was somewhat surprised at Brehaut posing such a question for he had never marked the sailing master out as a fighting man. But the information had been enough to set his mind racing; it was yet another factor to consider and one where they still held an advantage.

Hare carried nearer a hundred men, many of whom were trained fighters. And while her carronades were not particularly accurate over a distance, when loaded with canister and fired at close quarters little could match them. Even one carefully aimed broadside would sweep an enemy's deck clean and turn the odds firmly in their favour. But the effective range of canister fired from a carronade was even less than that of round shot, and he did not think an experienced privateer would be foolish enough to venture that close. Unless, of course, they had reason to...

"I wonder what they are making of us?" This was Brehaut again and, once more, King was surprised at both the question, and that the sailing master should ask it.

"Right now they won't know us from a merchant," Croft stated flatly. "Though will probably suspect us to be Royal Navy. There are storms about and no ill-manned trader would carry such canvas unless they had to. Besides, our netting is fair stuffed with hammocks and will be in sight afore long."

"Along with our ports," Brehaut agreed. "Though would we not be heading so and carrying the same sail were we a merchant trying to regain the safety of a convoy?"

Yet again it was a surprisingly perceptive comment from an officer charged only with sailing and navigation.

"But we are no merchant..." Croft began before King finally spoke.

"I believe I see what Mr Brehaut is striving for," he said, and both officers turned to him. "A trading brig could be as easily separated from the convoy as ourselves, perhaps more so. And, were that the case, would be trying just as hard to regain their former position of safety."

"So our damaged foreyard might even prove an asset," Brehaut added eagerly, but Croft shook his head.

"I fail to find any advantage in a wounded spar," he said. "And how our likening to a merchant vessel could be to our favour is equally beyond me. Why, if the fellow is a privateer, he will simply turn and snap us up the more readily."

"Which is surely what we want," Brehaut agreed with a grin. "In a close action we would have the advantage whereas, if they keeps their distance, a well armed schooner might prove a difficult nut to crack."

Croft shook his head in disbelief. Though older and more experienced than either of his fellow officers, he was decidedly old school in his outlook; the only form of combat he could envisage was where two ships slugged it out at an ever decreasing range. But King and Brehaut were of the same mind. "We might fit

Quaker sheets in reverse," the sailing master suggested. "Cover our guns and netting with sailcloth. Anything to lure the fellow closer."

"Indeed," King agreed as his pulse begin to race.

"Though we must act smart before we become any more visible," Brehaut added.

That was undoubtedly true, and King leant back to bellow at the heavens.

"Masthead there – strike the commissioning pennant!"

For a moment Greenwood, perched in *Hare*'s main crosstrees, paused although he could sense his captain's determination even from such a distance and soon the long, tapering flag that marked them as British man-of-war was gathered in.

"Mr Adams, ask the sailmaker to join me immediately." King's voice was now directed to the watch keepers by the binnacle below him. "Then send for the bosun," he added as his thoughts carried him further. His attention then returned to the two officers beside him; Croft still appeared mildly confused, although Brehaut carried the same look of excited anticipation that King had noticed on other men in the past.

"It is a worthy plan," King told him. "I have often heard of merchants disguising themselves as men-of-war, but rarely the other way about."

"But do you think it will answer?" Brehaut's voice was now less certain and he added an apologetic, "sir," as he realised the honorific had not been used for some time.

"I think it worth the try," King assured him.

11.

Hare cleared for action shortly afterwards and, once every preparation for battle had been made, the stirring sound of a marine's drum sent them all to quarters. Summers and Adams found themselves together at the break of the forecastle. Despite sharing a mess and, for as long as Adams remained unemployed as a lieutenant, being the same rank, the two stood different watches so were seldom on duty at the same time.

"We're still gaining on her, but only just," the younger man commented as they stared at the distant vessel that was stoically maintaining its course. “Why does the captain not set the foresail?”

“No wish to risk the spar,” Adams replied, glancing up to the repaired yard above their heads. “There's enough on her with supporting the topsail. And in any case, we have a measure of work yet to be done on the screens. Starboard side is mostly sorted, but it will take the best part of a glass to rig the larboard.”

The boatswain and his team had begun well with setting worn sections of canvas over their starboard top rail. When all were in place the impression should be of a plain hull although the areas around the chains were proving particularly hard to cover and they had yet to even start on the larboard side.

“Captain wants false ports painted on after,” Adams commented. “Though I cannot see that being achieved.”

“Not with only two hours until the start of the dogwatches,” Summers mused. “The Frenchie had better turn soon else it'll be dark.”

“That is assuming she is a Frenchie,” Adams reminded him.

“And that she is going to turn,” Summers agreed.

* * *

But they were not disappointed on either count. Long before the next bell, and when Harridge, the boatswain, had yet to make a proper start on the larboard side, the schooner wore sharply and was soon bearing down upon them with the wind comfortably on her quarter.

King, standing with his officers further aft, noticed this without comment. All knew their preparations were incomplete and when the enemy began to increase sail, adding topsails to her fore and aft rig, silently accepted that what they had achieved so far was about to be put to the test.

“Take her a point to larboard,” King ordered softly, and the brig's speed increased as she began to take the wind more on her beam. “They already have the weather gauge,” he added, peering out at his enemy, “and I think it worth the risk; certainly if we wish to try out our starboard disguise.”

“And at least we shall meet him in daylight,” Brehaut remarked. “I had feared we were to be ignored.”

King cast a sidelong glance at his sailing master; the man was behaving more like a fighting officer with every passing minute.

"You mean the Frenchman might choose a rich John Company convoy in preference to us?" Croft asked, as if wishing to confirm his position as second in command.

"There was always that chance," Brehaut maintained. "We must appear as little more than a tuppence-halfpenny brig, whereas a well found Indiaman can be worth many thousands."

"But a few hours of daylight still remain," King reminded them. "Perchance he thinks he can take us first, and still have all night to turn his attention to the convoy."

* * *

By the time the schooner was in plain sight from the deck, the preparations to their starboard side were complete and, from that angle at least, *Hare* must appear as nothing more than a damaged merchant brig battling hopelessly to regain the safety of a convoy. King's thought to disguise her further by the double ruse of painting false gun ports on the canvas screens had not been so easily accomplished. Without rigging stages it proved an awkward procedure and one that almost cost the life of the topman who volunteered for the task. And the end result was hardly convincing: an irregular line of misshapen squares crudely daubed in paint that had very obviously run. It might fool a cautious or naïve opponent and he hoped the Frenchman was anything but.

However, at least there was no doubt they were dealing with a French vessel; a tricolour had been hoisted as soon as the schooner began bearing down on them. And she was quite a sight; graceful and built for speed as much as fighting. With the wind on her quarter and a cloud of spray bursting from her stem she made an impressive opponent. King had no hesitation in answering the challenge by hoisting their own Royal Navy ensign, while the commissioning pennant had also been reset and was once more flying proudly from *Hare*'s mainmast. To those aboard the schooner both should appear as yet more subterfuge from a desperate merchant; an irony that was hugely appreciated by *Hare*'s lower deck.

But as the enemy craft swept closer all humour began to fade. It soon became clear she was large for her type and earlier estimates must be hurriedly reassessed. A schooner of such a size might hold upwards of one hundred men while if each of her ports, which all agreed amounted to twelve, hid a cannon they would be facing stiff firepower indeed. But King still sensed the privateer would not wish to draw close, not unless they could be certain their adversary could do them little harm. To that end, when clearing for action he had ordered greasy rags to be added to the galley stove's dying embers, and a pall of black smoke still issued from its patched-up chimney. And it was almost an advantage that a regular stream of bilge water continued to flow from the pump dales. That being ejected to leeward would be out of the enemy's sight, but the starboard flow was a useful addition to those precautions already taken. And then he thought of one more.

"Send for Mr Williams, if you please." Cole, the messenger, sped off, returning a few minutes later with *Hare*'s gunner. Rather than touching his hat in the usual manner, the grizzled old Welshman knuckled his forehead like the regular hand he had once been, although King's attention remained with the youngster.

"Mr Cole, have you fired a cannon in the past?"

The boy looked surprised at his captain's question. "Not fired, sir," he replied after a moment's hesitation. "Though I have seen a crew at exercise many a time and once was allowed to work the rammer."

"Very good," King grunted; he had expected little more. Cole was barely in his teens; a volunteer yet to even reach the position of midshipman. "Mr Williams, would you introduce Mr Cole to our bow chasers and instruct him on the fine art of gun laying?"

It was strange how closely the aged gunner mirrored the youngster's look of astonishment, although his expression soon changed and it was clear the order was not welcomed.

"And be sure to allow Mr Cole free rein," King added as the unlikely pair made their way past the amused servers sheltering in the lee of the starboard bulwark. The oncoming Frenchman was still a good three miles off and well out of range, but that did not mean the boy's education could not begin. And if he made poor practice at first, that could surely only aid their cause.

"Open fire when you are ready, Mr Cole," King ordered after the gunner had condensed many years of experience into less than a minute's instruction. Williams allowed himself one last rebellious look to the quarterdeck before reluctantly passing over the firing line and, amid a smattering of anticipatory laughter from all about the cannon, stood to one side.

After diligently peering through the weapon's sights, Cole called for the servers to aim the piece to starboard with their handspikes before stepping back and tugging hard at the firing line. The cannon erupted with a credible crack, but the shot fell predictably short as well as wide of the oncoming vessel. Ignoring the fact that he had obviously taken poor aim, Cole had also fired at the deepest point in *Hare*'s roll. The result would have shamed any hardened gun layer although the youngster was clearly enjoying himself and eagerly turned to the second cannon.

"No, we'll leave it at one, Mr Williams," King directed from the quarterdeck. It was conceivable – likely even – that a long distance trader might carry a single light cannon in the bows to see off the occasional pirate, but two was the mark of a warship.

The gunner knuckled his forehead once more and led the boy aside to allow his crew to serve the cannon. Then, when the weapon was loaded, the elderly man turned back to the quarterdeck.

"Very good, you may continue." King's voice cut through the murmur of ill-concealed laughter from those on deck.

"The French will consider us fools," Croft murmured under his breath.

"Then Mr Cole is doing us a service," King replied more forcibly. Croft must surely understand the game he was playing yet clearly did not approve. And he was possibly right; tempting the enemy so was certainly taking a big risk. Were they to have simply packed on more sail, *Hare* might have been identified as a warship and easily avoided by the more agile Frenchman, who would doubtless continue to stalk the convoy. As it was, should they fail – should the privateer realise their true identity and take full advantage of the longer reach of his own cannon – King's preparations would look foolish indeed. Another loud crack from forward told how the gun had been fired, with little improvement in Cole's aim and still no hope of even reaching the enemy. King pursed his lips; the Frenchman was creeping ever closer. Soon it would be time for all subterfuge to end and *Hare* could start behaving like a proper man-of-war again.

* * *

Russell was feeling decidedly uncomfortable. In the time he had spent aboard *Hare* he had learned much and was now relatively proficient for a landsman. Furthermore, and in addition to any seaman's skills, he had also become more adroit when dealing with his fellow man: a subject in which he had previously considered himself an expert. But, though he now felt thoroughly at home aboard the brig and actually more content than at any time in his life, being exposed so, with little to separate him from an unseen enemy, still did not sit easily.

His mess served two broadside carronades and actually tending to the guns was not so much of a problem. From the very beginning Russell had found the team work required during gun drill to be both stimulating and enjoyable, with the final firing of the piece the icing on the cake. But as to how he would fare in battle when others would be pointing their weapons at him was another matter entirely.

"Well this is a rare old fix, and no mistake," Brown murmured from his position in the lee of the starboard bulwark. All the servers had been ordered to shelter there some while before and it was not the most comfortable of stations.

"How comes we're not allowed to walk the deck?" Swain grumbled.

"Because they wants the Frog to think us a merchant," Greenwood replied patiently. "An' you don't find traders shipping with so many hands."

"Nor marines, neither," Sennett added, nodding towards where Sergeant Bates and his men were hidden further forward by the forecastle.

"Ask me, it's taking matters too far," Swain grunted. "We stay like this much longer, there won't be no point in closing with the Frog: we'll all be too stiff to move."

"If that Frenchie comes alongside you'll move right enough," Greenwood assured him. "And where men's lives are concerned, I don't reckon you can be too careful."

The discharge of one of their forward six-pounders punctuated Greenwood's sentence and this time there was a murmur of approval from those serving the piece.

"Sound's like the youngster's aim's improving," Jackson commented. He was captain of number four gun, the starboard carronade that his messmates were currently grouped about, and took his duties seriously. "That, or the Frog's getting closer, though I'm surprised he's still in the chaser's arc."

"Be easier if we could at least get a bearing," Swain grumbled.

"So why doesn't one of us take a look?" Russell suggested. To his mind the others were being far too casual; he felt as if he was the only one with any concept of what they were facing.

"Because we've been told otherwise," Greenwood replied firmly.

"Surely one little peep won't do no harm," Russell protested and made as if to stand.

"Stay where you are," Jackson snapped.

Russell stopped, but gave Jackson a challenging stare. He was aware his messmate captained that particular gun but some remnants of his old life were not so easily shaken and he still automatically rejected any authority that had not been properly established. "We ain't in action," he stated coolly.

"We're at action stations," Greenwood reminded him more gently. "And while we're at his gun, Jacko has the say; we all listens to him, even me."

Russell swallowed; he did not want trouble with Greenwood, especially as he was evidently speaking for the rest of the mess.

"We'll get the word as soon as we're needed," Parker added lightly. "Until then it won't make no difference how close the bugger is. And if he sees your ugly clock peering over the top rail, we'll be smoked for sure."

* * *

The Frenchman began to return fire when *Hare* was comfortably within range, and did so with far greater effect than Cole's amateurish efforts. The schooner also mounted twin bow chasers which, either through confidence or arrogance, were let off simultaneously, with both shots passing to either side of the brig's rigging.

"Reckon we were lucky there," Brehaut muttered when it was clear no damage had been done.

"Three points to larboard," King ordered. It would have been a reasonable enough command if he truly were captaining a merchant vessel; bringing the wind more firmly onto the beam would increase their speed, while lengthening the distance between them and the approaching enemy. But though it also meant the schooner was brought closer to their hidden broadside's effective arc, he remained concerned that *Hare*'s cannon would still not have the necessary range. In a rash moment he had ordered the gunners to add canister to the round shot already loaded; the tight bundles of scrap iron and musket balls would create merry hell on an enemy's crowded deck, although the additional load would lessen the guns' effective range still further.

But either the gods were on his side, or the Frenchman was especially confident for, no sooner had *Hare* made her turn than the schooner bore round and began to make straight for her. It was exactly the move King had hoped to encourage even if he now felt his mouth grow dry. For it was indeed a far larger vessel than any had estimated and he may have been wrong in thinking no such craft would willingly close with a Navy brig. Now more of the hull was being revealed he could judge her to be soundly built, while the grace of her lines told him she would handle beautifully. For a moment his mind wandered back to *Kestrel*, another French built vessel and his first true command, only to be roughly brought back to the job in hand. The schooner was considerably less than two miles off; if nothing altered dramatically they might eventually collide without the enemy's broadside guns being able to bear until the last moment. Only a fool would remain on such a heading, though; it would be far more reasonable for the schooner to fall off to larboard as she came up and so present her broadside to *Hare*'s stern. Such a move might even intimidate a true trader into striking without further delay; it just depended on how close the Frenchman came before making it.

Loaded as they were, King's guns would lose all accuracy after eight hundred yards. Beyond that all they could expect was a series of ill-aimed splashes while the schooner's carriage mounted pieces could do *Hare* significant damage at nearly twice that range. And she was coming up fast; both vessels were almost level now and need only hold the same course a little longer. Perhaps five or ten minutes would be enough for King to uncover his guns, yaw to starboard, and let loose with a true bellyful of a broadside that must surely shake the enemy to the quick. Then he should be in a position to tack, seize the windward gauge and close still further before taking the schooner by boarding. But it was then that he realised the precious time was not to be granted; his opponent clearly had no intention of waiting any longer for the schooner was turning once more – and turning hard – though not in the direction King had expected.

* * *

"She's coming round to starboard!" Brehaut exclaimed in a mixture of anger and disbelief. But there was no doubting it; even as they watched, the schooner's prow crept further until she was running on a near parallel course. The enemy had lost distance during the turn, but would soon make that up. And once they had, must be in a prime position to deliver a broadside on the British brig, while still remaining beyond anything *Hare* might send in reply.

"Lay us to starboard, Mr Brehaut," King ordered coldly. "Set stays'ls and bring her as near to the wind as she will hold!" Even in her wounded state, *Hare* was capable of being close-hauled and would make reasonable progress as long as the foreyard held firm. The sudden change must also shake the Frenchman's gunners, although it would not be long before the schooner had closed enough to release that broadside. Quite what the French captain would make of his manoeuvre was another matter. Until then, King had behaved like any cautious merchant commander; *Hare*'s turn could not be judged as a trader simply trying to avoid being fired upon and might sow the first seeds of doubt in his opponent's mind.

The deck pitched as *Hare* was brought round and King staggered slightly while trying to keep his eyes fixed on the enemy. Her ports were open with guns run out; he forced himself to count – there were indeed twelve – more than any of them had originally anticipated and again he cursed silently to himself.

But *Hare* was behaving well; despite ominous creaking from the fished spar, she held a reasonable line while battling on the very edge of a luff. And all the while the enemy was growing closer. The schooner's bow chasers fired once more, but this time the shots went wild and King noticed with relief that some of the much needed distance had already been gained.

"I have her!" Adams, in position next to the furthest broadside gun, had raised his arm in confirmation. So the Frenchman was finally within their firing arc, now all King had to do was bring them close enough for their shot to be effective. There was still a comfortable mile of grey water between them but, with the two vessels converging, it would not be long before *Hare* was in a position to strike with her own cannon.

That might be too much to wish for, however; King could see the enemy was catching up fast although what he actually noticed was those ports growing steadily nearer. He could now see them in minute detail, as he could the barrels that grinned out from within, and knew that each would soon be aimed directly at him.

* * *

"Starboard crews be ready," Adams ordered as he walked down the centre of the main deck, "but keep your heads down unless you wants to lose them."

Greenwood and the rest of his mess cautiously stretched their limbs, although all remained well below the shelter of the bulwark. The brig's broadside guns had been charged since the last exercise and now, with a cylinder of canister resting on a standard round shot, all they had to do was remove the canvas screen, then take aim and fire.

"Head down there I say – you, Swain!" Adams growled and the server who worked number four carronade's trails lowered himself once more. "Corporal, take that man's name!"

"I were only 'avin' a look," Swain grumbled to his mates.

"If you can see them, they can see you," Greenwood reminded him.

"We don't want no Frenchmen smoking us now do we?" Russell added pompously.

"Enemy is off our starboard quarter," Adams told them. "We can almost reach her as it is, though the captain wants to make it easier. Have your dirks to hand; when the order comes to strike that canvas I want it gone like it were never set." All regular seamen carried a pusser's dirk: the short clasp knife that was an essential tool of their trade. Greenwood and Parker wore theirs on lanyards about their necks in the accepted topman fashion.

Despite action being imminent, those at number four gun were growing increasingly uneasy. Jackson, the gun captain, glanced back to Adams standing barely ten feet away, but the officer was giving all his attention to the quarterdeck. For a moment he also wondered about taking a swift look; no more than a peek which he was sure would not be noticed. Last time he had laid eyes on the schooner she had been little more than a smudge, and he would shortly have to lay a gun on her. But that would mean falling into the same trap that had snared Swain, and Jackson, who was harbouring a secret wish for promotion to quarter gunner, had no wish to tarnish his immaculate record.

"All right, be ready," Adams once more. "Enemy's closing fast an' will be coming on our beam. Reckon we'll be needed shortly, boys." The last sentence was delivered in a lower tone and generated a ripple of appreciation from the servers nearby. And then, just as each man was preparing himself for action, Adams spoke again.

"The devil take her – she's turning once more!"

12.

King had also been anticipating opening fire when, almost within the space of a single breath, the enemy threw her helm across and began to steer for their counter. The evolution was clearly well practised and he realised in horror that, rather than opening fire on a near parallel course, the schooner would soon be in the perfect position to deliver a devastating broadside into their vulnerable stern.

"Lay us hard to larboard," he snapped. It was his only choice, they were already too close to the wind for anything else. He felt his face begin to redden as *Hare* rolled into the turn. Whatever had he been thinking of? Even the rawest midshipman should have expected such a move.

But *Hare* performed well and turned sharply enough, while the manoeuvre might even be to their advantage, or so King assured himself, for the schooner would soon be comfortably within striking distance. And this was definitely the end of any deception; if the savage turn had not been enough to reveal *Hare*'s true purpose, her larboard side was free of canvas screening. Soon the French would see the row of unconcealed ports and it would be time for a different kind of battle to begin.

* * *

"Larboard battery be ready!"

The main deck vibrated to the rumble of feet as those detailed to both pieces crossed to the opposite gun. And Jackson went with them, even though the larboard piece had an experienced gun captain in Seth Daines, he could not bear the prospect of standing idly by while other guns were being despatched.

"Steady there!" Adams was firmly in command and making sure no one fired without properly taking aim. He had drawn his sword in readiness and held the blade high for all to see. "Take your time, lads: make it count!"

Daines, a thick-set northerner with a broken nose, was doing exactly that. In no time he had the Frenchman firmly lined up and, conscious of the jealous eyes of Jackson watching him, was just turning the carronade's elevation screw when he had the first inklings that the enemy might have a similar idea. The schooner's broadside began with one of their forward guns and quickly rippled smoothly down the dark hull. Almost as the last cannon fired, the first shot was being received and *Hare* lurched slightly as the rest hammered against her side. But the Frenchmen had aimed low; damage might have been caused to the brig's nether regions but her gun crews remained unaffected and Daines continued to line up his piece with barely a pause. Then, when the enemy was comfortably within his sights, he stood back and raised his left hand. Adams had seen and knew him ready, although some were not so quick and still tending their weapons. Jackson felt his fingers itch – a simple tug from Daines would send one weighty ball and a generous dose of rough metal flying across the short gap and over the Frenchman's deck where it would cause true carnage. But he knew his place, as well as the importance of a timed broadside and, once more, accepted that they must wait.

"Very good, Mr Adams!"

Again this came from the quarterdeck and now all focussed on the young officer with the raised sword.

"Fire!"

The weapon descended with a dramatic sweep and *Hare*'s larboard guns were released with a simultaneous roar.

"Stop your vents!"

Daines gritted his teeth as the sound of the discharge echoed about the main deck. But there was no time to stop, or even witness the result of their work; the French had fired thirty seconds before and would be well into loading their own weapons. Blocking his mind to the shouts from all about, the Geordie wrenched the hammer back one notch, flipped the frizzen clear and rammed his thumb deep into the still smoking touch hole. The metal was hot, but years of practice had made the digit all but fireproof and he was far too centred on what he had to do to feel pain. Looking up he saw his servers were ready; a hiss of steam as Russell, one of the men from the opposite piece, plunged a length of sodden lambswool into the cannon's short barrel. A cartridge followed, then a wad before Sennett added the metal canister of small shot that had been ordered. Another wad to set all tight and that part was complete.

From further behind, Jackson was shouting but Daines paid no mind; whatever was going on about him, his only responsibility was to see his gun served.

Bending over the breach, he began to probe into the warm touch hole with his priming wire, his breath coming in short gasps as he punctured the cartridge several times, then added a dose of fine-milled powder and spirit from the horn that hung from his belt. Most gun captains had known times when a carronade had been so hot as to misfire at this stage, but that would have been well into an action. Stepping away he allowed Compton and Curtis to heave back on the tackle and, still keeping his mind fixed on the job in hand, watched as several hundredweight of warm metal slid forward on its slide. And only then, only when it was the next logical step, did he allow himself to bend down to the weapon's sights and view his opponent once more.

And when he did it was almost a disappointment; the Frenchman was sailing very much as before with the only discernible difference being a faint cloud of dust and smoke that continued to rise from the schooner's deck. Other than that, few would know a broadside had been received less than two minutes before. Daines grunted; little adjustment was needed, the image remained square in his sights, and he could crank the hammer back to the final notch before standing to one side with his hand raised.

"Beaten 'em to the reload," Sennett remarked with youthful glee, although Jackson only had eyes for Daines. The man was carrying out his duties adequately enough but that hardly compensated for not being able to fire a gun himself.

"Hit 'em again, lads!" It was a different voice and came from further aft – possibly the quarterdeck, although few took notice of that either. Adams, who had proper control of the guns, was standing close by and once more his sword was raised.

Some of the other teams were still attending to their weapons but they would soon be done and, ignoring the strange temptation to pee, all continued to wait. Then, catching a glint of meagre sun as it did, the sword descended; Daines gave a firm tug to his firing line and the gun discharged once more.

This time the warm piece leaped a few inches before crashing down on its slide with a hearty thump, but Daines was as quick to stop the vent and the rest of his crew a good deal smoother in serving the piece. The enemy might fire again at any moment; within seconds *Hare* could be doused by a truly effective broadside that wreaked destruction and carnage all about. But there was nothing any of the servers could do about that. The only thing in their power was to tend their gun as quickly and efficiently as possible. And they must continue to do so, no matter what the French threw at them.

* * *

"That's two broadsides to their one!" someone announced but King paid no attention. *Hare*'s guns had certainly been efficient. There might be little in the way of visible damage to her hull, but that last barrage had contained no round shot and even the frail sides of a schooner would hardly crumble to a dose of canister. Men were made of softer stuff however and King knew a good proportion of the Frenchman's crew must have fallen in the last few minutes. But there was no point in speculating further; he was still unsure what damage had been caused to his own hull and, with another hostile barrage overdue, needed to close up, and fast.

Even as he thought, the second French broadside began to roll out, and King forced himself not to wince as the shots rained down upon them. But once more the aim had been low and, though the brig vibrated to the thud of hot metal striking her vitals, there was little damage to her upper deck.

"Take her two points to larboard."

With the immediate danger passed, it made sense to make his move now; *Hare*'s guns would be even more devastating close up and King felt confident enough to force the issue.

"Mr Croft, I should be obliged if you would organise boarding parties."

The first lieutenant touched his hat briefly before moving forward and bellowing a series of orders. Within seconds the designated men from gun crews, afterguard and waisters were sent to collect small arms while Sergeant Bates' marine contingent, that had been stationed by the top rails, fixed bayonets and formed up for physical contact with the enemy. Soon two distinct groups emerged, with Adams in command of that by the forecastle while those aft, which included all the marines, were to be led by Bates with Midshipman Summers in support.

"I should go as well," Croft told King when he returned and it was proof of his concern that he omitted the courtesy a captain was entitled to on his own quarterdeck.

"Why so?" King questioned. On larger vessels, a commissioned officer would assume overall charge of a boarding party although, apart from himself, who was unqualified by reason of position as much as the lack of an arm, *Hare* only possessed one. And even if Croft's duties as second in command had not claimed his presence on the quarterdeck, King would never have ordered a man of his age into the carnage of hand-to-hand fighting. But he could tell Croft would need convincing; he had the same look of determination in his eye King had noticed before, and he sensed this would not be easy.

"We cannot lead a force of men with midshipmen and NCO's," Croft stated firmly.

"Mr Adams has passed his board," King reminded him.

"You will forgive me, sir – he remains a midshipman aboard

Hare."

That was undeniable but still no reason for the older man to go. There was no time for debate, preparations for boarding were well underway and, if Croft were really to lead, he must make it known immediately. "Very well, but it is your choice," King told him briskly. "Though none shall think the worse should you remain."

"I consider it my duty, sir," Croft replied almost sadly. Then, after touching his hat to King, he turned to join the nearest group waiting to board.

* * *

"Help yourselves lads," one of the ship's corporals urged while passing out pistols like hymn books in church. "All charged up – only needs a priming. Or there're cutlasses and half-pikes by the main if you prefer. Just make sure you brings 'em all back."

Brown, a former tin miner, was one of two designated boarders from Jackson's redundant cannon. He collected a pistol and sniffed at the barrel to be sure it was loaded, then wrenched back the hammer to half cock and snapped the frizzen fully open before collecting one of the powder horns provided for the purpose and liberally dosing the pan.

Swain joined him and was fingering a half-pike experimentally.

"You don't want a sword and pistol instead?" Brown asked. "Gives you a better chance."

"I has a better chance with one hand for me-self," Swain told him as they returned to their gun.

They arrived as Adams was preparing to despatch yet another broadside from the larboard battery and the pair joined the permanent members of the starboard battery in watching with critical interest.

From behind his gun, Daines looked round and caught the eye of Jackson.

"I've a mind to join the boarders, Jacko," he told him. "Never could resist a bit of ruck – if you'd care to take over here, I'd be greatly obliged."

Jackson's face split into a grin and he eagerly stepped forward and took the firing line while Daines hurried away to find himself a weapon.

"Fire!" The air was dry and acrid and Adams' voice cracked as he bellowed out the order. Once more, *Hare*'s cannon recoiled in a collective barrage. Grey, sulphurous fumes eddied about as the teams began the process of reloading while the air of expectation increased from all those preparing to board. But at one gun at least, the substitute gun captain was a happy man indeed.

* * *

"I'm ordered to go with Bates," Summers told Adams, his eyes smarting as he tried to waft away the smoke.

"So be it," his friend replied briskly. "You cannot follow me everywhere."

"But now Mr Croft is coming, I might stay with your party," Summers suggested.

"Croft is coming?" Adams exclaimed in surprise, then looked aft and noticed the first lieutenant was indeed standing in line with the other boarders. "Have you spoken with him?"

Summers shook his head.

"I'm sorry, Michael, but you'll have to remain with his party," he said.

"Very well," the lad sighed. "Though I'd rather be with your lot."

"You shall be fine," Adams told him with as much conviction as he could muster. "Be sure to stay on deck, even if she strikes, we can mop up any below later."

"An' what if she don't?" Summers questioned. Adams paused. He understood the lad well enough to know this was not a lack of courage: Summers was simply a cautious type and needed the full picture.

"You will have Mr Croft in command and must follow him," he replied. "But do not stand still whilst on the enemy's deck – a stationary target is always the more inviting. I have seen too many fall to such folly. And if you feel you cannot hold the deck, do not be afeared to return," the senior man added in a lower tone. "It is always better to fall back and try later."

Summers nodded seriously before making his way aft without another word.

Adams' attention returned to his guns; once more they were almost ready to fire, yet there had still only been two broadsides from the French. He glanced over the top rail; the schooner was very close now, less than a cable off, and he could see the damage they had already caused.

The enemy's hull was peppered with minor hits, while many of the lower shrouds and halyards were either frayed or missing and an ominous trickle of red showed at the scuppers. Yet a good number of the schooner's people must remain even if he could see little activity about her guns.

The reason for this became clear when *Hare* dropped another point and the gap narrowed further. By now the French could be in no doubt they were facing a British warship; cheers and insults were being hurled from either side and, just as the distance diminished to a matter of feet, Adams despatched the last broadside. Shouts instantly turned to screams as the deadly iron bit deep, although there was still a small crowd gathered about the enemy's top rails as the two hulls drew closer. And then the French released their third broadside.

There had been no attempt to use any form of anti-personnel shot; the schooner's cannon fired standard ball, but this time their aim was higher and a good many British fell. Half of those attending number three gun were taken out with a single shot and part of the beakhead exploded in a mass of chips and splinters. But Adams had no time to consider this or anything else; *Hare* was heading on a collision course. Even as he watched, the two hulls ground together with the squeals and groans of protesting timber. His job was now to board the enemy; something that must be done immediately if they were to make any impression.

It would seem the French had the same idea, however, for as Adams mounted *Hare*'s gangway he could see a positive wall of Frenchmen facing them. He looked to one side; Summers and the marines were having more luck further aft where there were already several red coats visible on the schooner's deck. A bullet whined past his right ear and he turned back in time to notice a stocky Frenchman with a black moustache attempting to clamber onto *Hare*'s bulwark. For a moment the brute stood tottering and it took no more than a gentle swipe from Adams' hanger to knock him down.

The action seemed to inspire those to either side; several pistols exploded close by, making small inroads in the mass they faced. Then Adams saw his chance and leaped. The schooner's deck was both lower and closer than anticipated and he cleared her bulwark easily, only stumbling slightly upon landing. And he was not alone; two seamen had jumped with him and one, Swain from Jackson's cannon, was armed with a half-pike. Brushing past, he nonchalantly plugged a Frenchman in the belly, before retrieving the weapon and moving on to strike again.

Adams took his lead from the hand and, dodging a blow from an ill-aimed hanger, struck out with his own sword. Daines, on his left, was cutting into the crowd using vicious swipes from a boarding cutlass while cheers from those behind urged them on. And it truly was amazing the impact a few positive moves could make. Adams took a moment to glance about: already they had cleared a good portion of the schooner's deck and yet more British continued to tumble across.

He raised his sword once more and bellowed, "Aft lads; join with the other party!"

Once more he could see flashes of red that could only be their marines but now they were considerably closer, barely yards away in fact. The enemy also appeared to have diminished while what French he did encounter must either be topmen or gun crew for few carried weapons. And suddenly there was Summers; he could see the lad as he battled valiantly against a heavily built opponent wielding an axe. Even as Adams watched, the slower man was neatly taken down by the midshipman's cutlass. For a moment both paused and their eyes met, then Summers gave a brief smile before setting off in search of further prey.

The incident reminded Adams of his own advice to keep moving and he continued to advance; two men tried to block his path with shouts and flailing fists but they were unarmed and he now felt unstoppable. A well aimed kick sent one spinning to the deck while the second crumpled to yet another lunge from Swain with his pike. A heavy object fell from above, probably a block or some similar piece of tophamper, but still Adams was invulnerable and powered on.

There was an enemy officer, resplendent in a dark and decorated uniform that seemed out of place in such a rough house. He was calling to his men but broke off to defend himself from a wild-eyed British seaman armed with a boarding axe. Adams barged in to join the fray, bringing his own sword down hard on the man and actually striking him on the head with the hilt of the weapon. That one blow was enough; the officer tumbled to the deck and was swiftly despatched by the hand.

"Secure the wheel!" This was a fresh voice and Adams was surprised to notice it belonged to Croft the first lieutenant. Standing next to the schooner's bulwark, he must only recently have made it across, although there was already blood on his britches.

"You heard the or-fi-cer, secure the wheel!" Sergeant Bates bellowed, taking up the cry like any good NCO. "Oats, Cartwright, Long – see to it!"

The marines snapped to with parade ground efficiency and were soon advancing with bayonets fixed and muskets at the charge. Seeing them approach, those by the binnacle fled, which set the tone for the next stage of the battle. Suddenly it seemed that any not actively seeking shelter below deck were surrendering and soon there was no fight left in the enemy. Adams glanced round in disbelief; the British faces appeared equally bewildered although there could be no mistaking that peace was steadily descending.

"Very good, Mr Adams." Adams turned to see the first lieutenant had sheathed his sword and was now wrapping a large white handkerchief about his left hand. "Mr Summers, you will oblige me by lowering the enemy's ensign," the older man ordered casually and watched as the midshipman scampered past with all the energy of youth.

"I give you joy of your victory, sir!" Adams told Croft formally as he took a step towards him. The older man looked up sharply.

"My victory?" he questioned, and Adams noticed his face was unnaturally pale.

"Indeed, sir. You are the senior officer present," the younger man explained.

Croft appeared doubtful for a moment, then cleared his throat and, abandoning his wound for a moment, accepted Adams' outstretched hand.

"Thank you, but it were a joint effort," he muttered gruffly before turning his attention to matters more immediate.

13.

"How goes it, Robert?" King asked. It was much later; night had fallen some hours before although every improvised sick bay King had ever known had been just as dark and cramped.

"Right enough thank you, sir." Manning used the title consciously; the pair had been friends long enough to make such things unnecessary but, despite the atrocious conditions, they were in a public place and a measure of formality was called for. "I am about done here," the surgeon added quietly as he stepped back from his current patient. The man's chest had been torn by a savage splinter, but the wound was now dressed and he seemed at peace. "What say we speak in my quarters?"

King nodded briefly; he had no wish to stay in what was usually *Hare*'s warrant officer's berth. The canvas covered deck was all but filled with the bodies of men; some asleep while others moaned gently although all had been attended to.

"We shall be aft," Manning told Driver, one of the loblolly boys. The man glanced up only briefly from adjusting the bandages of a marine with a head wound.

"Very good, sir."

Manning led the way and King willingly followed. The contrast from so recently being on deck in the cold night air only amplified the odour of injury and he was keen to be free of the place.

"There are seven dead, at least seven that made it down to me," Manning announced bluntly when they had squeezed into his tiny cabin. "Another fifteen are badly wounded but a further twelve have been returned to light duties."

There was nothing to be said to that – any comment King made would only sound crass and serve little purpose. But at least he now knew how many he had to work with. As it was, *Hare*'s men had secured the schooner and confined those of her crew that showed signs of resistance, which were in the minority as most had accepted their capture philosophically. No senior enemy officer had survived the action but a pair of civilians that were probably passengers were currently being held in King's own quarters.

"Are there any amongst the wounded I should see?" King asked as Manning removed his apron.

"No, all are relatively stable and we are expecting them to live," the surgeon replied. "Unless there is infection of course, and obviously I cannot speak for the French."

"I have just inspected the prize; their man appears acquainted with his duties and is well supported."

"He may approach me for supplies if any are needed," Manning said as he rolled the soiled apron into a ball and tossed it into the corner of the cabin. "So, what is the situation, Tom?" There was only one chair in the tiny room; the surgeon settled on his sea chest as he considered his friend. "Have you plans for our future?"

King paused. It was a subject recently discussed with the first lieutenant; a seasoned officer accustomed to the ways of a ship and the Navy in general. But somehow it was easier to think in the anonymity of the small cabin and, though he was coming to trust Croft, King had depended upon his old friend for many years. Besides, there was another advantage in confiding in the surgeon; Manning had little nautical knowledge, so he could speak freely with no risk of being judged professionally.

"The Frenchman can be made to sail," King began. "She needs a measure of repair aloft; enough to keep a bosun's party busy for a day or more but we could find no critical damage to the hull."

"And ourselves?" Manning persisted.

"We are a different matter," King rubbed at his forehead. "It is no secret we have been leaking steadily for some while, although Anderson is unable to find any definite cause. Until now I have had little choice other than to put it down to general strain and a lack of caulking, which is probably correct though the problem has increased greatly of late. Combined, our pumps can clear a ton of water every minute yet we are barely keeping pace."

"That does not sound healthy," Manning grunted.

"Perhaps it is not so bad," King admitted. "When a ship

settles, the ingress of water naturally reduces and a state of equilibrium is often reached. However, another storm might easily see us founder."

"Cannot the leaks be plugged?" Despite the relative privacy of the surgeon's cabin, both men were now barely whispering.

"The most recent damage is above the waterline," King replied. "In the main it can be reached and the motion is light. Anderson remains confident of having all sorted by the end of the morrow, but there remains the original problem. That would seem to have grown far worse and there is still a fair distance between us and St Helena."

"What of the convoy?"

"What indeed?" King allowed himself a faint smile. "They were last seen before the storm though I still believe them to have been barely beyond the horizon when we sighted the Frenchman. A lot has happened since and they may be many miles off with little to tell exactly where. Even if we were able to head south immediately it would be pure luck to fall in with them and I cannot see us making any movement immediately."

"So what are our options; can we turn back?"

"We could," King answered cautiously, "though I should be loath to. It would mean abandoning Sir Richard along with the convoy and the long trip northwards would be no easier."

"But if you could make *Hare* sound?"

"Then I must definitely continue south," King replied without hesitation. "The Commodore was setting a fast pace, though we might still catch up. And even if not, there is a chance the convoy may yet be at St Helena when we arrive."

"And the prize?"

"I might send her northwards alone."

Manning raised his eyebrows; it seemed a bold move.

"We have perhaps fifty prisoners," King explained, "and are nearer Gib. than any British port to the south. All might be placed aboard the schooner which should make it within two or three weeks, though any form of enemy would see her retaken."

"And if she did not make for a British port?"

"There is only truly Madeira," King sighed. "Anywhere else and we would lose her for sure while the prize agents at Funchal aren't renowned for their plain dealing."

"But surely it would be better to travel in company; could we not escort her to Gib. then perhaps return to find Sir Richard later?"

Again the smile; King had heard something similar from Croft. "Obviously if we are unable to secure *Hare* further I shall have to. Though we are a part of Sir Richard's squadron and my duty is to rejoin him as soon as possible; anything else would trigger official investigation and I have had my fill of such things for a spell."

Manning nodded; he did not totally understand the intricacies of Royal Navy protocol, but knew how seriously King's apparent abandonment of the squadron would be taken.

"So why not keep the prize in company and take her south also?"

"I believe I shall have to," King replied, apparently coming to a decision. "It would be a longer journey and there remain the prisoners to consider, but still seems the best choice." Now the smile had turned to a grin, "And I thank you for helping me reach it."

* * *

Russell was no stranger to bloodshed; in his previous life hardly a week had gone by without one of his associates involving themselves in some degree of violence and the sight of a dead body was nothing new to him. But never had he known such general carnage as the recent action, while the fact that it was legal and had been carried out by responsible men in the pay of the King, made it somehow more disturbing.

"Hammer," Newton, the carpenter's mate, demanded and Russell duly passed the tool across. He had been drafted in to assist the carpenter's team and was currently helping one of the more skilled workers as he patched up the brig's hull. The damage was remarkably consistent, with the entrance holes on the starboard side being mainly neat rounded affairs while any shot that passed through and exited to larboard caused far larger square openings. Newton worked quickly and well, using scrap timber, sheet lead, canvas and oakum to address each and, with Russell's assistance, the pair had already set most of the aft section of the berth deck to rights. And Russell had learned much; there was not the time for him to do anything other than take charge of the tools and be ready when particular material was called for but already he felt he might be trusted with basic caulking, or perhaps finishing the nailing-in of a patch. Whatever, it was a better task than the one set for him earlier that day, which was something he had no wish to repeat.

The cannon fire had not been so bad; Russell had seen the weapons in use before, if only in the more relaxed atmosphere of a general gun exercise, although being fired at in return came as a novel experience. He soon came to terms with it, along with witnessing those he knew being brutally injured or killed by the enemy's shot, but what had really made an impression was the boarding action.

Being a landsman and relatively new, he had not been directly involved. But once the two groups of boarders left, he and the other gunners were all but redundant and had a grandstand view of what took place.

In all the tap-house brawls or minor riots that had come his way until then there had always been a time factor; the maximum amount of damage would be caused as quickly as possible, with one ear constantly alert for the imminent arrival of authority. But the boarding action had been different; he had known from the start it would last for as long as was necessary and must contain all the horrors of a pitched battle to the death. As it was, Russell had only felt relief when the French flag was finally struck and all butchery ceased while, even now, the memories sent a chill throughout him.

To that point he had been coming to terms with his new life and vocation. Having been pressed into a warship, Russell was not so foolish as to expect never to hear a gun fired in anger and he was by no means an innocent in other areas. But if that were the only hand-to-hand combat he ever witnessed, he would not be sorry.

* * *

The following morning Croft felt quite encouraged, for a lot had been achieved during the night. All the prisoners were now secure and some, who claimed to be American, had opted for service in the Royal Navy. Croft suspected most of these to be Irish, and possibly deserters but, such was the need for competent hands, he preferred not to investigate further. The new men were drafted in to carry out any number of tasks ranging from caring for the wounded to repairing both vessels, the latter being of prime importance as they were many hundreds of miles from a friendly port. Throughout the darkest hours the work had continued and was now at a stage when the prospect of getting underway that day was not so fanciful. But, by the end of the middle watch – four in the morning in landsmen's terms – Croft had personally reached the point when exhaustion had started to take him over.

His hands had begun to shake and even such simple tasks as remembering individual names or the most basic of orders were starting to defeat him. He had realised then that rest was needed – either that or make what might be a disastrous mistake – and now, after three glorious hours of oblivion, knew it had been the correct decision. But as he dressed himself in the most basic of uniform and prepared to meet the new day, Croft also recognised he was suffering from something less easily cured. For there was no avoiding the fact that some activities were now beyond him.

And this went far deeper than simply working hard into the night. Even before the current emergency, Croft had become increasingly aware of the first worrying signs: some regular habits he had barely considered now must be avoided. These included rich or spicy food, an extra glass of port of an evening and brandy altogether. And there was much that concerned him beyond the sphere of his stomach; for some time he had not been able to sleep an entire watch without needing to wake at least once and what used to be a full head of sleek, dark hair was now grey and had to be carefully arranged if it were to cover his entire scalp. But his experiences in boarding an enemy the previous day confirmed yet another failing, and it was one of far greater magnitude.

Croft wasn't considering the ache from his strained limbs, a discomfort that would have been ignored in the past, nor the cut on the palm of his left hand caused when catching a splinter clambering over the Frenchman's bulwark. These were minor items that, if noticed at all, could be laughed away. There was something far more fundamental and, as he stepped from his cabin and made his way through the crowded gunroom, he had already decided he must never place himself in such a situation again.

From the moment he had launched himself from *Hare*'s quarterdeck, things had gone badly. The Frenchman's bulwark had been barely a yard off, yet he missed his footing and only by scrambling like a child unable to negotiate the simplest of obstacles had he avoided a potentially fatal dunking in the ocean. An unknown hand had helped him and he soon regained some composure although, even when he was finally astride the Frenchman's top rail, took far too long to heave himself over and gain the deck. Looking back on the incident, Croft knew he was lucky to have got away with little more than a scratch to his hand; had he been one of the first across, he would have been slaughtered for sure.

Of course, he need not worry greatly; such combat was relatively rare and every man must be allowed the occasional mistake, providing they do not die as a consequence. And it wasn't as if his naval career had been so terribly filled with hand-to-hand fighting to that point. Croft supposed a reasonable share of action had fallen his way and he was definitely no stranger to gunfire but, apart from one cutting out expedition when he had been second in command and a prime ketch was plucked from under the noses of enemy shore batteries, he had remained relatively inexperienced in physical combat.

That single occasion was many years ago, when Croft had been a senior midshipman; the incident was actually cited when he received his lieutenant's commission and, at the time, he had been hungry for more of the same. But the chance never came and those few terrible minutes aboard the schooner were enough to tell him it no longer should.

Not that the prospect was likely, he assured himself as he gained the brig's tattered quarterdeck and glowered about at the work in progress. His current position was relatively high considering the ill luck he had met as a commissioned officer and senior enough to keep him from such reckless undertakings. Besides, it had been his choice to join the boarders; the captain had not required him to go, so, on another occasion, he would simply make sure he remained. But still Croft could not dismiss a measure of regret, for he had discovered yet another entry for the lengthening list of activities he had once been capable of, but could carry out no longer.

14.

King did not have the time to spare for passengers but as the civilian couple collected from the prize had been installed in his own quarters he supposed he should grant them a moment or so. Besides, with no senior French officer having survived the action, they might shed some light on the schooner's recent activities. But when he finally entered his cabin, King's attention was initially taken up by the shambles that surrounded him.

The lack of cannon housed there meant his quarters need not be cleared for action, although McNamara had arranged for his private effects and much of the furniture to be removed. And the precautions had not been wasted: a round shot had punctured the side, spreading dust and splinters over the canvas covered deck before finally embedding itself in an opposite timber. All had been attended to in a very basic manner and the scent of marine glue still hung in the air. But as he turned away from the damage, King found the two civilians seated on the stern lockers to be almost as compelling.

One was an older man; plump and with a scalp barely covered by iron grey hair. He carried a sour expression on a red-veined face and sat forward on his seat as if reluctant to trust the deal lining of *Hare*'s spirketing. His dress was conventional enough: tan breeches with a white shirt and plain dark jacket with no hat or wig. Beside him was a slender, younger woman who appeared more composed and agreeable. She wore a printed chintz skirt, a simple half jacket and a modest white cap with woollen, fingerless gloves that reached up her lower arms. It was a style of dress common throughout Western Europe, although the patterned skirt was so similar to one regularly worn by his estranged wife that King was momentarily caught off guard.

"My name is Callahan, my wife and I were travelling aboard the *Spartiate,*" the man informed him briskly after standing and somewhat reluctantly extending a cold hand. "We are bound for the Cape and are in no position to delay; when do you expect to be underway once more?"

King absorbed the information without acknowledgement. Whether Callahan was truly a passenger or the schooner's owner was something that must be investigated, as would his exact reason for being in such a hurry.

The surname gave some clue to his place of birth although Callahan's accent was not strong enough to confirm him as an Irishman. That, combined with the man being captured aboard an enemy privateer, suggested he may be a renegade; one of those who chose to side with what should surely be a common enemy. It was a type King had encountered before and, privately, he was not without sympathy for their cause. Many English landowners had behaved abominably in the past, even if such problems must surely have ended with the Act of Union. So to continue what was now an old fight to the extent of siding with the French would seem at the least short-sighted; even if they were successful and England was defeated, Ireland would fall under Napoleon's control and the self-proclaimed emperor was hardly known for granting true independence to captured territories.

"You will no doubt have learned that your ship's master was killed," King said. "As well as what we presume to have been his officers, although there were but the two."

"I was aware," the man sniffed. "Though in truth the *Spartiate*'s crew had become depleted of late; a fact that had been giving my wife and myself increasing concern."

"Depleted, you say?" King questioned.

"Until meeting with your ship, Captain Savarez had been most successful in his undertakings," Callahan announced with unconcealed satisfaction. "Since leaving France he took three of your trading vessels, as well as a small warship that was immediately burnt."

"Burnt?"

"Oh, do not concern yourself; the vessel – a brig such as this – was captured fairly enough with those aboard being transferred to one of the prizes. They should be on their way to France as we speak."

"I see," King replied coldly. He supposed there was nothing to be surprised at; serious damage might have been caused in the action and, even if sound, manning another warship would have strained a privateer's resources. Besides, small men-of-war were ten a penny in France with most rotting at their moorings in blockaded ports. Financially it would have been far more prudent to see the valuable merchants safely home and privateers were men of business.

"When your ship was sighted, the captain was following a convoy of Indiamen," Callahan continued. "He had proposed to take one before continuing for the Cape but instead chose this vessel as an easier option."

That the schooner had been in contact with what was presumably Banks' force was not lost on King and he relaxed slightly. "Then I suppose we should be thankful he were so undermanned," he allowed. "Otherwise it might have been a harder fight."

But there was no sign of compromise in Callahan's expression. "Make no mistake, Mr King," he told him sternly: "Otherwise you would have been beaten."

There was a moment's silence as the two eyed each other. King had already decided there was little to like in the man, although nothing would be gained by falling out and arguing with a prisoner was hardly dignified.

"I presume Captain Savarez had papers," he continued.

"I am sure of it," Callahan stated. "He was an honourable man; indeed every French officer I have encountered has been so."

"A search will be made and I am sure they will be found," King continued evenly.

Appropriate government issued documents were required before any vessel could act as a privateer although it was a law more frequently recognised in its breach than observance.

"Did Captain Savarez make a habit of carrying passengers?" King asked.

"I have no idea," Callahan sighed. "Though my wife and I were eager for a passage to the Cape and it suited us to travel so."

"And where are you from, sir?"

"America."

That explained much, especially the man's faintly antagonistic attitude. England's former colony was prospering well, but there remained some ill feeling between the two countries and the place was a well known haven for those bearing a grudge against their former homeland. Men, it would seem, such as Callahan.

"Perhaps you would care to introduce me to your good lady?" King suggested.

"I was not thinking," Callahan admitted, although his face showed no trace of remorse as he gave a casual nod to the smaller figure on his left. "My wife, Anne."

"Your servant, madam," King muttered briefly. Even in the poor light of the cabin, the woman appeared considerably younger than her husband; her face still bore the freshness of youth with skin that was too pale for one who had been at sea for any length of time. The pair would more likely to have been judged father and daughter than a married couple.

"I regret there is little of any comfort in this ship, madam," King said, switching to the woman. "Though we shall be happy to provide anything in our power, should you require it."

"I need nothing, thank you Captain," the woman replied politely and once more King was taken aback. Her accent and manner of speech was so similar to his wife's that it might even have been her.

"Forgive me, madam, but are you from the Texel?" he found himself asking and for a moment the pale face came alive as she went to reply.

"My wife is American as well," Callahan interjected, adding a glare at his wife for good measure. She turned quickly towards her husband before lowering her eyes and said no more.

"I know the area well," King continued, purposefully ignoring the brief interaction. "During the last war I was held prisoner there for some while; a delightful place."

The woman's gaze rose briefly to meet his and there was the trace of a smile but she made no further comment.

"Tell me, Captain, when do you intend for us to be underway?" Callahan repeated, and King's attention returned to him.

"I could not rightly say, sir," he replied briskly. "There is much to attend to before we even make sail."

"As I have already mentioned, my wife and I are eager to reach the Cape."

"Well I doubt us to be venturing quite so far south. And, as you must know, the colony is held by our enemy, though we shall probably be calling at St Helena."

"Then we will have to find passage from there," the man grunted.

"Before that can happen we must investigate your background, sir," King cautioned.

"My background?" Callahan spluttered. "I am an American citizen, you have no right to detain me."

"An American citizen who was found aboard a private enemy warship," King reminded him more coldly. "And one that had been preying on British shipping. I am certain you will be able to show what you claim to be correct, in which case your status will be respected. Otherwise, I fear it will be some while before you reach the Cape, or any other French controlled territory."

* * *

"If you have done with that splicing you can swab up the mess," the first lieutenant told both seamen firmly. The morning was already half spent and Croft had been summoned to the gun room for a meeting which would probably prove a waste of time, but still his pathological need for a tidy ship was at the fore.

Sennett and Jackson exchanged glances; the pair had indeed finished their repairs to the larboard shrouds and the scattering of hemp fibres that littered the deck probably should not have been left as evidence. But when set against the carnage that still abounded elsewhere, their small amount of detritus seemed insignificant.

Jackson went to object, but the younger seaman nudged him in the ribs.

"Very good, sir," Sennett agreed with a philosophical knuckling of his forehead before reaching for a besom broom. Though younger than Jackson, he was wise enough to know first lieutenants needed to behave in such a way; it was almost expected. Mr Croft had also put himself forward to join the boarders when many of his age would have held back. And he appeared to have been wounded as a result, there being a makeshift bandage about his left hand and stale blood obvious on his white britches. Yes, the first lieutenant might be a bit of a tartar but that was the nature of the beast. Besides, he was as hard on himself as any man under him, and there were few regular Jacks who could resist giving such an officer respect.

* * *

"Gentlemen, we have much to occupy us, so I shall keep this as brief as possible." King glanced round as the small group assembled in the shambles that constituted *Hare*'s gunroom. Croft was there, along with Adams – who was the nearest they had to a second lieutenant – Brehaut and Summers, together with the brig's young volunteers, none of whom had served at sea for any length of time. As councils of war went, it was hardly impressive, but then King supposed he should judge it fortunate that all had escaped the recent action without serious injury. The bulkheads had been restored and the gunroom's dining table and chairs brought up from the hold so there was somewhere to sit, although little other furniture had reappeared. Consequently, rather than the elegant brass lanterns that had been provided by a previous set of officers and were now regarded with an element of pride, the place was lit by a pair of government issue lanthorns which were already smoking abominably.

"We have achieved much but further attention is still needed to topside and spars, while our hull is continuing to leak. However, it is the prize that I wished to speak of. I understand she is more seaworthy than ourselves, though still needs work from the bosun and his team. Our nearest port is Praia, which is over two hundred miles to the east," he glanced at Brehaut who gave a brief nod in confirmation. "A degree of support may be found there but I am reluctant to effectively turn our prize over to the Portuguese. To that end I intend to make a run for St Helena."

There was a murmur of comment amongst the more senior men as King gave the news, but it took no more than a glance from him to regain silence.

"Obviously any serious weather might mean the end for either vessel, but I feel there is little option. As it is, we will be benefiting from those of the enemy who have either joined our ranks or agreed to assist, though the latter must remain under close watch at all times. Consequently, I shall be moving them, as well as all prisoners, to their previous ship, and also detailing our entire marine force to that vessel to maintain order."

Taking account of the recent casualties, that amounted to a total of fifteen fit privates and one NCO, but King did not feel inclined to expand.

"When Mr Anderson is satisfied both hulls are as sound as we can make them and sufficient sail might be raised, we shall set off once more and make what speed we can. I think it unlikely we will beat the convoy to St Helena but shall surely try; otherwise there is the chance of meeting with the Commodore's force if his sealed orders have directed him north once more."

King felt it unlikely that Banks would have been sent so far south only to turn about but it was not the time to say so.

"When all is ready, Mr Adams will take command of the schooner. He will be supported by Mr Summers as well as Sergeant Bates' marines and as many hands as can be spared from *Hare.*"

There was perhaps a slight intake of breath from the first lieutenant, but King had been prepared for that and, as he offered to answer questions, already knew from where the first would come.

"Are you intending the passengers to accompany our prisoners in the prize, sir?" He was correct, except Croft was not asking the question King expected.

"I am," King confirmed. He found having Mrs Callahan about far too much of a distraction; she would be better off with Adams in the schooner. For a moment he wondered if Croft would ask another question, but the man appeared satisfied. Adams was next.

"Will we be sailing in company, sir?" the young man was understandably concerned about taking charge of a captured vessel, especially one that would be carrying enough prisoners to retake her several times over.

"We will stay in sight at all times, Mr Adams," King assured him. "Although I cannot guarantee to remain within hailing distance."

This induced a small amount of laughter, which is what he had intended. Then Croft did go to speak again and for a moment King's earlier concerns returned although he only wished to address a problem with victualling the French prisoners. Some, it appeared, had already objected to being fed British fare and it was agreed that, once both vessels were underway, the schooner's own provisions could be tapped.

"Well, if there is nothing more..." King said rising slightly, and the cue was enough for all to follow his example. Soon the majority had exited the gunroom; only Croft remained, just as King had expected he would.

"You do not wish me to command the prize, sir?" he began.

"No, I do not," King agreed, motioning the man to be seated once more. "Should you be sent I would have no other commissioned officer," he continued, taking a chair himself. "And that would simply not do."

"Adams has passed his board," Croft reminded him, and King wondered if it might be a warning sign. The command of a substantial prize would normally fall to the first lieutenant, and King had every sympathy with the older man. But lives were at stake and there could be no room for sentimentality.

"Adams is as raw as they come," he stated firmly. "I cannot I rely on him as my first officer."

Croft made no reply, although King could sense his disappointment. "James, you are not being passed over," he said, leaning forward in his seat. "I simply feel it better that Adams goes and you remain with me in *Hare*.

"He may fare well," he continued. "Indeed I expect him to, but should he not; should the prize be overtaken or otherwise lost..." King left the sentence unfinished and Croft seemed to understand.

"Do not think I am ignoring your talents," King added more gently. "Indeed, it is because you are valued that I am retaining you here."

The older man looked up and for a moment their eyes met.

"You do not consider me too old?" he asked.

"No, I do not," King stated firmly. "I value both your knowledge and experience; were it otherwise I should give you command of the schooner and gladly be rid of you."

For a moment Croft's expression turned to one of hurt confusion, then he noticed the look on his captain's face and smiled also.

"I do understand, sir," he said, realising King did as well. "And thank you."

15.

Being prize-master of a large armed schooner would be a new experience for Adams and he wasn't certain if he welcomed it. But since being passed by the board he was effectively a lieutenant, so it was not a position he could reasonably refuse. Something of Mr Croft's advice had taken root however and, though he remained just as keen to progress, he was also slightly more cautious. But then he could remember the same feeling of apprehension before standing a watch for the first time and had survived that, so didn't suppose the current trial would turn out any different.

Summers squirmed excitedly next to him as the pair were ferried across in *Hare*'s cutter. In the past, such an adventure would have been shared with adolescent chatter from the two of them, but even the temporary appointment had reminded Adams of his seniority and he felt it more professional to inspect his new command in a studied silence. She was an elegant craft to be sure; heavy for her type but still built for speed although, as they were to be travelling in company with *Hare*, he doubted there would be much opportunity to test that to the full.

The boat crossed the short distance in no time; soon it had been secured alongside the schooner and Adams was standing awkwardly, with one hand resting against her side as he prepared to board. He had visited the prize twice before but knowing this time he would not be returning to *Hare* put a slightly different slant on matters and, as he clambered up and onto her deck, his heart was pounding.

"They've made a fair job of that foremast," Summers remarked as he followed and Adams supposed the lad was right. Certainly a good deal of line had been replaced, as had two of the deadeyes and the catharpins; he was sure the spar would now carry sail without trouble. The work carried out to the main looked equally competent; in fact Harridge, the boatswain, had done wonders – the more so when Adams remembered what had also been necessary aboard *Hare*. And the carpenter had been no less busy; there were still several members of his crew working on the forebitts, but they would be gone shortly leaving him with just his prize crew to command. This consisted of two junior officers other than himself and fifteen prime Jacks plus a few landsmen, as well as all the marines that were fit to serve; not a vast number to sail the schooner and supervise forty-eight prisoners.

Forty-eight prisoners and two passengers, Adams corrected himself as he noticed the couple standing on the small quarterdeck next to a marine private. Adams was still relatively inexperienced when it came to dealing with civilians and his only meeting with Mr Callahan had not gone well. But there was little to be gained in prevarication and, after a brisk instruction to Summers to see to their dunnage, he made for the pair.

"I see you are here afore me," he said, extending a hand that was cautiously accepted by the man.

"Indeed," Callahan replied gruffly. "We were returned with some of your soldiers, one of which now seems reluctant to leave."

The marine private remained poker-faced although his eyes flashed from his charges to Adams and back again.

"Sergeant Bates was obeying orders in providing you with an escort," Adams explained. "Though I am sure we may dispense with such things now – providing you give me your word to cooperate."

"If that is all it takes then you most certainly have it," Callahan snorted. "It has been the very devil of an indisposition; my wife requires some time to herself below."

"Escort this lady to the great cabin," Adams ordered, addressing the marine. "They are the best quarters available," he said, returning to Callahan. "I trust you will be comfortable."

The marine snapped to attention before making crisply for the aft companionway with the woman following meekly behind.

"Such a thing is not necessary," Callahan stated. "We already have a cabin which is well provided for as far as feminine requirements are concerned."

"I shall have no need of the late captain's quarters," Adams replied as firmly, "and expect to spend much of my time on deck."

"Then it is good of you," the man grudgingly allowed.

Adams made no comment; he knew little of the American's history or even his exact status aboard the privateer, yet had already decided the man would not be easy to deal with, so if a small concession made their lives easier he was not averse to granting it. Besides, it was customary for a marine to stand sentry outside the great cabin and, despite receiving Callahan's word, he would feel more comfortable knowing the passengers were under constant supervision.

* * *

Aboard *Hare*, King had been listlessly watching the encounter with little knowledge of exactly what had taken place. But even at such a distance it was clear Adams had at least begun on amical terms with Callahan and in that he was relieved. For King found the man prickly at best, although that was not the only reason he was pleased to be rid of the couple.

A close examination of the schooner's papers had revealed nothing untoward; she had been sailing under a letter of marque right enough and there was nothing to suggest the American was even part owner. But he was clearly disaffected with the English, although King still had no idea how far this hatred went. He could have adopted the United States for any number of reasons many of which would have little bearing on any political situation, or he might be an ardent separatist, in which case he might yet be wanted in England or his country of birth. But it wasn't Callahan that concerned King; it would be up to others to prove him evil or otherwise and take the appropriate action. Instead, and despite her humble manner, it was his wife that troubled him more.

King had not spoken with Anne Callahan extensively; her husband's constant presence together with his own increasing reluctance had seen to that. But even during the few times they exchanged words, he had learned much that disturbed him. Not only was she from the Texel, but the same small village as Juliana, his estranged wife. Even if the two were not close friends, they must surely know of one another. Consequently, and considering his own delicate position, he wanted as little to do with the woman as possible.

Croft approached with a touch of his hat. "Bosun expects us to be ready to proceed later this afternoon, sir."

"Very good." King's reply had been automatic although the statement was correct; Harridge had done wonders in such a short time as had Anderson, the carpenter, despite the fact that *Hare* continued to take in water.

"Have you spoken to the carpenter, sir?" Croft was clearly following his train of thought and King swallowed. He had not done so since the previous evening and doubted anything had been learned since. But the first lieutenant was obviously just as worried about the hull and King would rather approach the man again than endure another redundant discussion with his executive officer.

"No, but I shall do so forthwith," he stated briskly, and promptly took his leave.

* * *

"So why have I been chosen?" Russell asked in surprise.

"It's not down to me, blame the captain," Greenwood told him.

"You're saying the captain said I should go?" Russell scoffed.

"Not exactly," Greenwood allowed. "But he wants men from the same mess where possible; figures those what live together are more likely to get on. It's why we all serve the same gun."

"But you and Parker are topmen," Russell reminded him, "and Sennett knows his way about, whereas I'm..."

"You're still a landsman," Greenwood agreed with an easy grin. "Though there'll be jobs for all. And if you've a mind to be rated ordinary, a spell aboard a captured ship won't do you no harm."

"Ordinary?" now Russell was truly surprised.

"It's the next step, matey," the older seaman assured him.

"Maybe, but I never thought..."

"I'm not saying straight away," Greenwood continued. "But you're learning fast."

"I'm getting better at splicing," Russell agreed cautiously.

"It ain't all about ropework; there's more needed if we're to turn you into a sailor." Greenwood was now considering him more carefully and Russell began to grow uncomfortable. "I'll not deny it, I had my doubts to begin with," the seaman continued. "But you've shown a deal of improvement and needs to be encouraged."

"Improvement?" Now Russell was definitely unsure. There was no doubting the work he had put into learning seamen's ways. And though some had not come easily, he had indeed made progress. But whether he was up to moving from the brig into an unknown vessel and working as part of a team of experienced men was not so certain.

"Improvement," Greenwood insisted. "If truth be told you've come on by a fair mark – and it ain't just your seamanship I'm thinking of."

* * *

"I'm not saying there's no leak, sir," the carpenter scratched his head as he spoke. "Otherwise we wid nae be taking in water so. But I still canna find an obvious cause."

"You have checked previous repairs?" King asked as he stared about in the darkness of *Hare*'s orlop.

"Oh aye, a dozen times," Anderson confirmed, indicating the small brass trumpet used for hull inspection. "A've listened long and hard an' there's no regular sound what might suggest a single leak, and neither is there any discernible stream. But will ye look a there?" The carpenter indicated the side of the ship and his mate shone a lanthorn at the dark planking. It was hard to see in the poor light but, as his eyes adjusted, King thought he could make out dark lines between the strakes.

"You'll notice what looks like rust," Anderson remarked. "It's as good an indication as any: shows yon caulkin' ha' failed. Like as not it weren't attended to last refit, though that were afore I were appointed."

King nodded; such a fault would only be revealed after several sheets of copper had been removed. Clearly Anderson's predecessor had not felt the need to request it and, with the pressure of having to turn ships around so quickly, the yard did not insist.

"We're blessed wi' a pair of the best pumps going," Anderson continued, indicating the two massive structures to either side of the main mast. "Though I'd ha' preferred it if they'd spent the money on the hull."

King inspected the pumps more closely. All four wooden tubes were square in profile and had been soundly built with heavy iron reinforcements every few inches. The constant rumble from within showed the unseen team stationed at the cranks above were working hard.

"They're a pair of Cole-Bentincks and the latest model, unless a'm very mistaken," Anderson continued. "They ha' the brass links, which are better than iron. I ha' spare chains for both wi' fresh leathers in case they're a wanted."

"How long, should one need to be changed?"

"Upwards of two hours, sir," Anderson replied. "That's if all goes well, though a'm hoping that won't be necessary. My mates ha' been takin to replacing the leathers during the time the pumps are not in use: we inspect the chains then and dose 'em well wi' tallow."

King nodded, he knew little about carpentry and less still of the workings of chain pumps so it was good to be dealing with a capable man. During the brief inspection, Anderson had risen greatly in his estimation, even though he was no nearer to finding a solution for the current problem.

"What about the damage caused in the recent action?"

"They hae bin sealed," the Scotsman replied with certainty. "Though were never a concern. In truth, sir, I dinnae like the strain that recent weather put upon us."

That was undeniable; damage caused by the schooner's cannon must have been obvious and reasonably easy to set to rights. But what the brig had endured during the storm was far worse and potentially a greater danger. No, King's earlier conclusion was correct; Anderson and his men had done extremely well, especially considering the carpenter's team was likely to be overworked after any action. And their repairs to the hull, many of which would have been carried out in total darkness, seemed good to King's inexperienced eye. Yet the fact remained that *Hare* still needed to be pumped for well over half a watch and, with no obvious way of curing the problem, that was worrying indeed.

"Frankly, y'r honour, I think the problem to be lower down," the carpenter continued, while staring accusingly at the boards beneath him. "An' that means a docking."

"There is no alternative?" King asked, even though he knew the answer well enough.

"No, sir," Anderson confirmed. "The best we might do is shift stuff about, but there comes a point when that is impossible; certainly whilst a' sea. Besides, I'm thinking there is not one leak but many and the entire hull is no longer sound."

"In which case?"

"She needs her copper off and a good seeing to. I'm not sayin' she's crank, sir, but they're not making 'ulls like they did; dinnae have the wood for a start. Even rats can chew through the strakes they're using now given time, and that's just what this old girl has had."

"Very well," King grunted. He had learned long ago that any problem could only be fixed, disregarded or accommodated. They were in the midst of the Atlantic and if their leaking hull could not be repaired, only a fool would ignore such a thing. But at least with two sound and working chain pumps they might keep matters at bay. It was only if something happened to one that things would become truly critical.

* * *

His first evening in command of the schooner was a tense one for Adams. They had squared away several hours before and his only true worry lay in holding what was clearly the faster vessel back to match *Hare*'s stodgy pace. But he could still invent others and, since getting underway, most of his time had been spent doing exactly that.

The first job had been to carry out a full inspection of his new command, something that involved all aboard, including the prisoners, who had to be moved from the forecastle where they were accommodated. But as evening came on and he returned to the quarterdeck he did begin to relax. The French had been fed and were now confined for the night; with luck he should have nothing more to do with them until morning. And if he only stayed close enough to the brig to keep her dim topmast lamp in sight he need not concern himself with any thoughts of navigation. Sennett had the wheel; though young, he was quite capable of keeping them on station in such mild weather. And there were six seasoned men dozing quietly in the lee of the forecastle, all of whom would be ready to do his bidding should the weather alter or a change of course be required. So it was probably the best time for the two figures to emerge from the aft companionway and stroll leisurely in his direction.

Noticing the passengers brought on a wave of guilt; in attending to his new command and the prisoners' security, Adams had all but ignored the couple's welfare. A lad had been allocated to look after them and the schooner's late captain had left a good supply of cabin stores. But still it might be polite to ensure all was well with the pair.

"I trust your quarters are to your liking," he asked after brief pleasantries had been dispensed with.

"We have no complaints, Captain," Callahan informed him thickly as he tapped cigar ash onto the deck.

"Our dinner was really very good and our boy extremely attentive," the woman confirmed.

"Though he might care to see it served hotter in future," Callahan added, with a strong scent of spirits on his breath.

Adams gave a nod of acknowledgement. He had taken his main meal prior to getting underway; it had consisted of cheese, a little dry biscuit and no alcohol.

"We are bound for St Helena, I understand," Callahan stated, before drawing heavily on his cigar.

"We are heading south," Adams confirmed cautiously, "and may be calling there."

"Well are we or are we not, sir?" the man demanded suddenly as he flicked ash once more. "Commander King seemed assured of it, yet you have doubts; do the pair of you not consult?"

Adams felt his face redden in the dying light. King had obviously avoided mentioning the Commodore's secret orders, so he should as well, yet avoiding the subject placed him in an awkward position.

"I understand that is the intention," he replied vaguely.

"The intention?" Callahan repeated loudly and with a slight slur. "Tell me, sir, do you know where this ship is bound or not?"

For a moment Adams was stumped and he actually took a step back when Callahan released a deep grunt of frustration.

"Forgive me, my dear; a spell on deck might indeed have been pleasant, though I think I will opt for an early night instead," he snorted, before tossing his cigar over the top rail. "Perhaps some sleep will make things clearer in the morning." So saying he turned on his heel and stumbled back towards the companionway.

"I am sorry, my husband can be awkward at times," the woman explained after a moment's pause.

"This is my first command," Adams replied miserably, "and I am not certain what matters can be discussed openly."

“Oh, it is of no matter,” the woman assured him. She spoke excellent English with only the hint of an accent that Adams thought made her voice sound all the more attractive. “I am sure David will understand in time. He certainly appreciates your treatment of us, though is not inclined to say so.”

“It is usual to care for passengers,” Adams explained. “After all, you had nothing to do with the privateer and are from a neutral country.”

“Indeed so,” she agreed, and there was silence for a while. The sun was falling fast and night would soon be upon them. Together they watched as the golden orb turned to white before quenching itself in the sea with a brief hint of green as it did. For several seconds there was darkness, then the first stars began to make themselves known. Soon the entire sky was filled with dazzling pinpoints that lit the small vessel and all about it as well as any moon. Adams' eyes quickly switched towards *Hare*; but even without the help of her topmast lamp, the brig was clearly visible.

“I wonder,” the woman said, breaking the moment, “do you know what will become of us?”

Adams shrugged. “I suppose you will be allowed off at the next British port.”

“But will it really be as simple as that?”

He looked at her sharply and for a moment felt a wave of doubt. “Is there any reason why not?” he asked.

16.

Eleven days later they had run just under a thousand nautical miles which, though not exceptional, King considered reasonable progress. There had been no sighting of the convoy, although that hardly surprised him; he had long since resigned himself to receiving no further news until they finally raised St Helena. However, the island still lay almost fifteen hundred miles over the horizon; they would be lucky to reach it in less than two weeks and, even then, could not be certain Banks would be there to meet them.

For King was equally aware that the tiny outpost lay five degrees south of the point where the Commodore could open his sealed orders and, unless they instructed Sir Richard to continue to Jamestown, he was unlikely to discover his ships there. The prospect did not concern him greatly though, for he had also learned not to worry over the distant future, especially when there were so many more immediate concerns to hand.

The first of these was the actual state of the brig. *Hare* continued to leak and, if anything, the problem was increasing. They now had to pump for nearly three out of every four hours, which was proving a strain on their diminished crew. Anderson was keeping an eye on matters and continuing to replace the pumps' leathers during the rare periods when they were not in use, but King still worried that more significant maintenance might be needed at any time. So far the elements had been kind but if their pumping capacity were suddenly halved, the brig might yet sink, however placid the ocean. From that unpleasant prospect his mind naturally ran on; they were now well into the doldrums and, in addition to the more common lengthy calms, it was an area where sudden storms were not unknown. The next few weeks could almost be expected to reveal such bad weather and *Hare* could easily founder, even if both pumps proved reliable.

However, the schooner was in a far more serviceable condition; the carpenter's team had done well to patch up the few areas of damage to her hull, while Harridge had brought her tophamper back to functioning order. If the worst happened, all aboard *Hare* might yet transfer to the prize which, being as they were now over five hundred miles from the nearest land, was a definite asset. But then it was less than a year since he had lost *Kestrel* and King had no intention of giving up his second command so easily. So when dawn began to break on the morning of the twelfth day and revealed the prize to be several miles off *Hare*'s starboard quarter, he was understandably annoyed. For many reasons both vessels should have remained in close company yet the schooner was considerably out of station.

"What the devil is Adams playing at?" he demanded crossly of the first lieutenant, who had the morning watch.

"I really could not say, sir," Croft replied primly. "Though the wind is remarkably fickle in these latitudes; why I would judge her becalmed even now."

"Did no one notice she were falling behind? Who had the deck

– no belay that!" King added quickly, remembering he had taken the first watch himself. He set his glass on the prize once more. Perhaps it was not so great a distance and *Hare* had a decent wind; once that was picked up by the schooner, Adams should be able to close in no time.

But the fact that the prize had been allowed to wander so kindled his temper, and when he realised Croft was right, she was undoubtedly becalmed, it rose up further. Her sails were hanging quite loose although that in no way excused her from being so far adrift. If Adams had kept a sound watch he would still have the brig's wind; instead both craft were endangered.

"Will a signal be read?" King asked, glancing about for the signals officer and finding only Dilson, the youngster who had been given the duty when Summers transferred to the prize.

"I'd not like to say, sir," Dilson answered cautiously. Despite his current mood, King could scarcely blame the lad; less than two weeks before he would not have known one flag from another yet was making excellent progress in learning the more basic messages.

He glanced across at Croft who shook his head.

"I doubt it, sir," the first lieutenant replied. "We would definitely not read a signal of theirs, though the light is hardly in our favour. Still, I'd credit Mr Adams with the sense to close up as soon as he is able."

King could only agree although the situation soon grew worse. As the sun continued to rise, not only did the schooner remain becalmed but, such were the vagaries of the area, *Hare* began to benefit from a steady northerly. Were the prize in close company they could both have added sail and logged a decent account for the day, but as it was, King had to order a reduction in canvas and all the while the brig's pumps continued to play their mournful tune.

"Take her two points to starboard," King finally ordered as the morning wore on and the schooner showed no sign of catching them. But despite her change of course, and while showing considerably less sail, *Hare* continued to draw ahead and the atmosphere on the quarterdeck grew increasingly tense. King was in no way repentant; it was almost a captain's prerogative to be bad tempered and he definitely had excuse on this occasion. No proper seaman willingly abuses a favourable wind, and his recent efforts to close up by standing to the west might even see both vessels becalmed.

But the day soon brought worse than the simple loss of a breeze. It was at seven bells in the morning watch, when the pumps had finally sucked dry and those on the lower deck were looking forward to their first issue of grog, that Benson, at the masthead, gave forth with the terrible news.

"Deck there, I've a sail fine on the larboard bow!"

King had been below but, such was the unnatural stillness, heard the call and came hurrying onto the quarterdeck as more information was given.

"One at least: hull down though I'd still chance her to be a warship. And she has our wind."

"What heading?" King demanded angrily, and there was a pause.

"She's close-hauled on the starboard tack," Benson continued. "I'd say she were steering to cut off both us and the prize."

* * *

Adams heard of the sighting shortly afterwards and it felt like the last straw. He had long ago decided that being a commanding officer had its drawbacks and, as he paced stiffly about the schooner's cramped quarterdeck, wondered why the prospect of promotion had ever appealed. There had been little rest for him since transferring to the prize and none at all after the wind began to fail the previous evening. And now, in clear daylight that also carried a heavy sun, his command was drifting listlessly while *Hare* lay spilling her wind in a steady breeze off their larboard bow. There was no one to blame, he assured himself, it was simply bad luck that had placed him in such a position, although he privately acknowledged that an impartial observer might judge differently.

The previous evening had run very much as any other; throughout the journey he and Summers had been standing watch and watch about, meaning one of them was at the conn while the other attended to other matters and grabbed what sleep they could. Adams had come up at the end of the second dogwatch just as dusk was starting to fall and was not surprised to find the two civilians also on the quarterdeck, as had become their habit. Summers retired below almost immediately and Adams had not been sorry to see Mr Callahan follow shortly afterwards. And then he supposed it was inevitable that he should fall into conversation with his wife.

Such a thing had happened often enough before; not every night but most. After a run of such hot days it was especially pleasant to talk in the cool of an evening. And there had been little harm in it: no flirting or even personal conversation. Despite the woman being only a few years older and undoubtedly attractive, Adams had remained the model of respectability throughout. The pair discussed trivial matters at first, starting with the night or what might be expected for the rest of the voyage and only going on to their various homes and how much they were missed after several evenings' discourse. Adams soon realised the woman welcomed speaking out of her husband's controlling presence while he enjoyed conversing with one of the opposite sex, as any young man might. And he had been attentive to his duties – at least for most of the time.

The lookouts were changed every hour, he listened for the call of, "All's well," from the marine sentries at each bell and, when the wind first began to falter, ordered extra canvas to catch what breeze remained. But it was two hours into his watch and only when a cautious enquiry from the helmsman drew his attention that Adams realised the cardinal error he had been making.

For no longer did the schooner nestle less than a mile off *Hare*'s quarter; the wind that had died for him remained strong for the brig and the faint masthead lamp was now barely visible.

Normally such a mistake could be quickly rectified; a wind might rise as easily as it fell and with the schooner's faster hull, only a gentle breeze and less than an hour of steady sailing would see them close with *Hare* once more. But, though he stayed on deck for the rest of the night, and even with every element in his body willing a change, the air about the small craft remained turgid and lifeless, while *Hare* continued to benefit from a firm wind and her topmast light grew gradually dimmer.

Mrs Callahan disappeared below as soon as she realised the position and, mercifully, neither of the passengers had appeared on deck since. But though she was in no way to blame, Adams knew her presence had been a contributing factor.

"Sighting appears to be a warship, sir," the lookout called, bringing Adams' attention back to the present problem. "I can see royals for sure, and there's what might be another comin' up from behind."

That was a further complication that surely could not be blamed on him, and one that may even be about to increase, unless Greenwood, at the masthead, was mistaken.

Adams glanced about; Summers was not on deck and he could easily imagine him resting peacefully below, blissfully unaware of this new danger. There was nothing the lad could do but still his presence was missed and the temptation to summon him strong. Forward, in the schooner's waist, Sergeant Bates and a detachment of marines were supervising a group of prisoners as they took the morning air and there was Henderson, the boatswain's mate, next to Sennett at the wheel as well as at least five other regular hands in clear sight. But still Adams could not rid himself of the feeling of loneliness and, when the masthead confirmed the second ship, it became stronger.

"I suppose they might be from Sir Richard's squadron?"

Adams jumped. So caught up was he in his own concerns that Summers had been able to emerge from the aft hatch and approach unawares. He disguised any relief in seeing his friend with a curt nod of acknowledgement.

"Maybe so," he grunted in a faint approximation of Commander King's quarterdeck attitude. "Though I fail to see why."

"They might be searching for *Hare*," Summers replied innocently and Adams could not suppress a sigh.

"The Commodore has more pressing matters," he snapped. "With ten Indiamen and two further escorts to consider, he is hardly likely to spend time seeking out a single wayward brig." Summers' face fell; something that made Adams' emotions turn from gratification to guilt, and finally wind up in regret. "Though they may yet be British," he added in a tone intended to appease.

"I can see them now!" That was a hand on the forecastle and Adams glanced forward. Sure enough there was the faintest flash of white that came and went whenever the sighting mounted the swell. And it had to be the sighting that was rising and falling;

there was precious little movement from the schooner.

"It seems strange that we should be so becalmed," Summers remarked as he glanced about at the leaden waters.

"It is the doldrums," Adams told him patiently. "They are to be expected within ten degrees of the equator."

"And what is the cause?"

Adams shrugged. "None can be certain, though there are various theories," he announced, drawing heavily on recent reading for the lieutenants' board. "Some say it is due to the meeting of the Trades, others have more fanciful ideas."

"But *Hare* has all the wind in the world," Summers protested.

"As we might also," Adams sighed, "were we a mile to the east. It is the way of these latitudes and little can be done about it."

"Is that so?" Summers questioned.

Adams sighed again and turned on the lad. "Do you have a proposal, Mr Summers?" he asked, his exasperation now evident.

"M-might we not send the men to the sweeps?" Summers suggested meekly. "We could probably reach *Hare* in an hour or so, or at least collect her wind."

Now Adams was starting to wish the lad had stayed abed. "We have less than twenty hands aboard, plus a few marines," he told him testily and was about to add more when the sight of the Frenchmen clustered forward on the main deck caught his eye. As if to a silent signal both young men turned to the other and uttered the same two words:

"The prisoners!"

* * *

"The prize appears to be rigging sweeps," Croft remarked a few minutes later. The first lieutenant had recently joined King and Brehaut on the quarterdeck, this was after taking a morning nap that had lasted far longer than he intended and he was still finding it hard to clear his head.

"She surely is," Brehaut agreed as he focussed his glass on the schooner. "Adams has done well to get the French to cooperate, especially as it would seem their fellow countrymen are bearing down on them."

"You are convinced the sightings to be French?" Croft

questioned.

"There seems little doubt," King confirmed, and all eyes now turned towards the hazy image of at least three ships sailing close-hauled off *Hare*'s bow. "Masthead cannot make out colours, but their sails are of a continental cut for sure, and the number and layout of spars would seem to confirm it," he continued dispassionately. "A single ship so rigged might be a capture, but when a squadron is set so, I'd say their nationality is incontrovertible."

Brehaut and Croft nodded wisely at their captain's words, with neither guessing at the turmoil his bald assessment concealed. For King was going through one of the deepest crises in his life and, however pragmatic the appraisal, it did reflect his true thoughts. He had no doubt that they had discovered a French force which vastly outnumbered his own; any one of the ships now facing them could snap up *Hare* and the prize without breaking sweat and, if what the lookout claimed was correct, there were more hidden from their view.

"Mr Adams is steering to reach us," Brehaut was viewing the prize through his glass once more, but King did not bother to look. He would have done exactly the same in Adams' position. Areas of catspaws seemed to be randomly distributed about the otherwise placid ocean; he might make for any one and collect a breeze. And *Hare*, for all her insignificance when compared to the enemy's size, must represent a degree of security to the young officer. Were Adams to close, he might also renounce at least some responsibility for handing back his command to the French, while King would take overall charge of all the captured British. It was an experience King remembered well from *Kestrel*'s capture and he wondered if he could face a repetition; especially when there was a viable alternative.

For though he had no wish to betray the young man's trust, and hated to even consider such a course of action, it now appeared obvious, if awful. As he glanced across to where the prize was struggling to keep steerage way, King knew it would take an hour at least for the schooner to come within hailing distance. And by then he had every intention of being many miles away.

17.

"Is that the best we can manage?" Adams demanded, his voice cracking slightly.

"It is the best for now, sir," Henderson, the boatswain's mate, confirmed. "We can only raise eight actual sweeps though if we had more, it's doubtful there would be enough fit to properly man them – not and tend to the ship and prisoners."

Adams glowered about at the scene on the main deck. The two rows of four oars were working well enough and the schooner now had steerage way, but every one of those pulling at them was British. With several of their own country's warships in sight, he supposed it hardly surprising the prisoners refused to help as they must sense imminent liberation. Of course, he could have ordered them to be encouraged – Henderson and Bates would be masters of the art. But however strong the persuasion, unwilling oarsmen could cause such trouble with irregular timing and general bloody-mindedness that the whole exercise would soon become pointless. And so he had little option other than to strike the prisoners below and draft in every available member of his prize crew although, even then, there were not enough spare to double bank two full teams.

"Keep her heading for *Hare*," he told the helmsman quite unnecessarily: the man was a seasoned hand who had been at sea before Adams was born.

"Very good, sir," Goodridge replied phlegmatically. "Though, if you'll pardon me sayin', I think we has a breeze comin'."

Adams turned his attention from the French shipping and looked to larboard. Goodridge was correct, a darker patch of rippling water could be seen, and the schooner would soon be in the midst of it.

"Mr Henderson, watch for that wind!"

The boatswain's mate gave a kindly smile and Adams realised most aboard the schooner had already noticed. "We's prepared, sir," Henderson confirmed, indicating those not committed to rowing were now standing by the braces.

Adams looked over the starboard bow once more, his eyes reluctantly falling on the oncoming French ships. He could now see each individually and identify four as heavy frigates although the one furthest away was possibly something larger. They could be outlying scouts for a fleet or, more likely, a battle squadron in their own right but, whatever the case, were certainly both able and likely to take him. Even if the enemy lost the wind, the sea remained passive and they would send boats in; a couple of decent sized cutters filled with men would be enough to overwhelm his meagre crew. Even if he tried to fight them off with the schooner's cannon, it would only be prolonging the agony. And if their wind held it would not be long before the leading ships opened fire with their bow chasers. His eye then swept to *Hare*, about six miles from his prow and still hove to, despite what was apparently a steady breeze. For all that he wanted to join up with Commander King, the brig was almost in as bad a position although at least they were sure of a wind and might yet make an escape, even if to do so would mean abandoning him.

Adams had spent much of the previous year in French hands and had only made his escape due to a combination of bold leadership and good fortune. The idea of being held once more did not appeal. Then he remembered Commander King had been with him and shared his captivity; he would be equally unwilling to become a prisoner again.

"French don't seem to be bothering with the old *Hare*." It was Summers, another who had been confined. Yet again the youngster had managed to creep up on him; something Adams would need to address when other matters did not demand his attention.

"So it would appear," he grunted.

"Though she has a wind; if we can reach her, we both might yet make an escape," the lad added. But Adams shook his head; it would not do to say so out loud, but even thinking such a thing was futile. King could not wait for them: why should he? It would serve no purpose. Better by far to make his own escape. And then, even as he watched, two of the French frigates broke away and began to steer directly for the brig.

* * *

"Blimey, we're for it now!" Swain groaned. *Hare* had not cleared for action, nor beaten to quarters and all that remained of

Greenwood's mess aboard the brig were officially below. But despite this they had gathered on the forecastle near to the guns they would man in action. From that position the sight of the French, still several miles off and close-hauled on the starboard tack, suddenly took on a greater significance as two of the leaders began to turn.

"What's about?" Sayer asked.

"The Frogs are splitting," Seldin replied with less emotion. "Appears two of 'em are tacking and will be headin' for us, that's if the cap'n don't do somethin' about it first."

"And fast," Swain agreed, in a tone uncharacteristically serious.

"But what about the prize?" Sayer persisted, glancing towards the schooner that was still battling to join them.

"She can look after herself," Swain stated firmly. "She'll have to: we can't do nothing to save her."

"An' just as she is getting a wind," Seldin commented.

All looked, and he was correct; sails that had been hanging dank and lifeless were now starting to billow: the schooner was also holding a straighter course and had withdrawn her sweeps.

"Much good that'll do her," Swain again.

"Might mean she joins us the quicker," Sayer suggested, only to receive a chorus of negative moans.

"If the wind is with her, the French will be able to get in close," Seldin corrected. "Not that it'll make much difference, she's almost in range of their chasers as it is."

"An' it won't take many shots from a frigate to see her brought to," Swain predicted. "I'd say she were done for."

"Just like we will be," Seldin agreed. "Unless we turns away sharpish."

* * *

King's thoughts were running on a similar course although to order the helm across and effectively abandon *Hare*'s prize, together with a good proportion of her crew, definitely went against his instincts. Croft and Brehaut had fewer doubts and were obviously waiting for the order, but still King remained reluctant to act. And it wasn't even a question of considering his options; there was no choice other than to square away immediately and put as much space as possible between themselves and the pursuing French. Even with her sodden hull and weakened tophamper, *Hare* should put up a reasonable chase for a pair of fifth rates and must at least stay safe until nightfall.

The two frigates had finished tacking now and were beating towards him; every minute he delayed brought *Hare*'s capture nearer and more likely. The only thing he could do was bear away for all he was worth. But even if the answer was obvious, it remained the hardest decision King had ever faced and he longed above everything for an alternative.

* * *

Aboard the prize, Adams and Summers could also see no other option although for them there were more immediate matters to consider. What had begun as a gentle, almost indiscernible, breeze had grown to something greater and, for the first time in hours, the schooner's sails were drawing tight and powering her through the still calm seas at a creditable rate. But though their situation had ostensibly improved, the same wind carried the Frenchmen into range; indeed, unless Adams did something quickly, their job would actually be made easier.

"We are gaining on *Hare*," Summers pointed out. "If she stays as she is we'll be up with her in no time!"

"Though I can hardly see Commander King remaining while a pair of frigates bear down on him," Adams answered without looking around. "And if we continue on our present heading all we shall do is draw the other three back together."

"Then turn about and make for the west," the midshipman suggested. "That way you will spit the enemy the more. Besides, we should be faster than any Frog frigate."

"We have come from the west," Adams reminded him. "And there was no wind, or had you forgotten?"

"Claw to windward?"

That was probably a better proposition, and Adams actually considered it, even though his eyes remained fixed on the enemy creeping ever closer.

"Come, John, you must do something," Summers was now

almost pleading. “The French will open fire at any moment.”

As if to prove him correct, a puff of smoke issued from the leading warship's bows and was quickly followed by the whine of shot passing overhead as the sharp retort of a six-pound long gun also reached them.

“That's the first,” Summers stated sadly.

“Very well,” Adams sighed. “Mr Henderson, we will be steering to larboard.”

To do so meant abandoning any hope of reaching *Hare*; instead the schooner would be taking the wind on her larboard bow, heading away from the brig and extending the chase for as long as possible. But though the order had been almost torn from him, now that he had reached a decision, Adams found everything else came more easily. The boatswain's mate touched his hat in acknowledgement and called for those who had abandoned their sweeps to attend the braces. Then, when all was as ready as they could wish, Goodridge spun the wheel across and the lithe hull turned savagely in the rising waters. The schooner's yards were brought round with commendable speed and soon all her canvas was drawing perfectly.

“So we are making a run for it,” Summer stated softly as their speed began to increase.

“Aye,” Adams agreed. “Let's see how well we make out on our own.”

* * *

At roughly the same time King was also coming to a decision and it was not so very different.

“Take her to larboard,” he ordered at last and as soon as the words left his lips, all about him began to react. Brehaut bellowed orders that set men at the braces hauling the yards round while the quartermaster turned the wheel.

“It is all we can do, sir,” the first lieutenant assured him. “It will hardly aid Mr Adams if we attempt to intervene.”

King said nothing. Croft was right of course, although that hardly eased the feelings of betrayal that were already starting to well up inside. He glanced over to the schooner and was surprised to see she had also turned and was currently beating into the wind, although far closer than *Hare* could ever achieve. King almost smiled; the manoeuvre was every bit as sensible as his own. Both vessels had effectively abandoned the other and he could only feel relief. Were she in proper trim with a seasoned crew who knew her ways, the schooner would have the heels of the heavier warships; as it was, Adams might keep the enemy at bay for a while although, even if they were able to escape, it was probably the last King would see of the prize. Darkness was not so very far off; once that fell there would be twelve hours in which each vessel would do what they could to put a distance between themselves and the pursuing ships. Come dawn, and providing both avoided capture, the French might still be in sight. But even if the ocean were totally free of enemy shipping, there would be little chance of the British craft finding each other. Locating a single vessel in the vast expanse of the Atlantic would be almost impossible, as King had already discovered. After all, he had already lost an entire convoy.

No, each must take their chance and, with luck, would make it to safely alone. But any thoughts of reprieve were short lived, as a shout from behind told him the leading Frenchman had opened fire on the schooner once more.

* * *

"It will be close," Adams' voice was brittle with tension, "but we should make it."

"Of course we will," Summers agreed enthusiastically.

Adams closed his eyes briefly; he had no doubt the lad was trying to be agreeable but his eternal optimism was starting to cloy. He longed for the days when his only area of responsibility had been for a group of boarders or a battery of guns, rather than the control of an entire vessel. The schooner had settled on her new course and was gathering speed although the three pursuing frigates were growing no smaller.

He switched his attention to *Hare*; the brig was also in the process of turning and her new course was very obviously several points from their own.

"The captain's heading away," Summers exclaimed, following his gaze.

"Of course," Adams replied levelly. "It would do little good for him to do otherwise; he has his own command to consider."

"But once we escape, he will be hard to find," the youngster protested. "We might spend days sailing about in search of them."

"Then we shall face that problem when it presents." At that moment Adams found the idea of an empty ocean extremely attractive, although it would do little good to say so. Instead, he looked away and up at their sails. "First let us see what can be done to increase our speed."

The whine of a shot passing directly overhead caused both to instinctively duck and, before they had straightened once more, there came a clattering from the tophamper. This was followed by a small yelp as a marine was struck on the shoulder by a piece of falling tackle.

"Main tops'l yard's parted!" the boatswain's mate cried from further forward. Adams cautiously raised himself to his full height and stared upwards. Henderson was right: the spar had been neatly struck close to the mast and both yardarms were dangling in a tangle of line and canvas.

He exchanged glances with Summers; even ignoring the loss of power from the sail, the rig would now be out of balance and their speed must undoubtedly decrease.

But Henderson was doing his job and had already ordered men aloft to sort the mess. Adams gratefully left him to it: in all his reading on jury rigs and running repairs, the one conclusion he had reached was such things were best left to intelligent boatswains and their mates. "It is no matter," he assured both Summers and himself. "We can still make closer to the wind than any square-rigger."

But Summers optimism had been sorely tried and he looked back at the pursuing enemy. "I believe one is about to yaw," he remarked cautiously.

Adams instantly switched his attention from the repairs; sure enough, an enemy frigate had fallen off the wind and would soon be presenting her broadside to them. The ship's hull was painted a dark brown that appeared black in the current light and made her ports almost impossible to distinguish. But there would be sufficient firepower to finish off a single schooner; Adams knew that for certain.

"It will be long range," he claimed, just as another shot from the leading frigate passed overhead to prove him wrong.

"But they'll be heavier pieces," Summers replied more slowly. "I mean, those bow chasers can only be six-pounders, yet broadside cannon..."

"Thank you, Mr Summers," Adams snapped. He was conscious of the lad staring at him in surprise and mild disappointment, but he had a vessel to command so could spend no further effort in reassuring a boy. And Summers was right, the enemy's broadside would undoubtedly be heavy – probably being made up of twelve- or even eighteen-pounders that would make short work of them, given half the chance. On the other hand the frigate was still to complete her turn and would be all but stationary while his craft drew further away with every breath. And though the lighter bow chasers were certainly proving a nuisance, they were being fired from the prow of a moving ship; so far only that one spar had been struck. So really they might still be at extreme range, at least for accurate shooting, although Adams was equally aware it would not take more than another hit to an important area for them to be brought to.

Another shot from the leading frigate's chaser passed by, and this one went very wide – proof indeed that they were starting to stretch the limit for accuracy. Adams drew a modicum of reassurance before turning his attention to the darker ship that was now broadside on. They seemed to be taking an age to size them up and he went to say as much to Summers when the first sign of smoke issued from the frigate's hull, and an erratic broadside followed.

The discharge being irregular might mean something or nothing; it was possible the enemy gunners were poorly trained or, more likely, greater attention had been paid to accuracy than timing. Adams supposed they would shortly find out which. It would take several seconds for the first shot to reach them and all those aboard the prize could do was wait. Then a series of white flashes showed how at least one round shot was skimming across the water in their direction.

It fell short but was soon joined by others pitched deeper and suddenly the schooner was in the midst of boiling water. They must have been on the very edge of the barrage, but the spray generated was more than enough to hide all else and Adams and his men might have been in their own, very private, storm. Gradually the waters subsided and they drew breath once more; despite all evidence to the contrary, it appeared they had weathered the onslaught and might even expect to make their escape. And then it happened.

It could only have been a fluke of gunnery, Adams decided later. One shot, perhaps slightly rounder than the rest; a particularly skilled gun captain, or maybe a modicum too much charge but, whatever the reason, a single ball made it as far as the schooner. Further more, either their luck was out or the enemy's in, but fortune also dictated the solid lump of hot iron carried enough force to strike them. And though there were several places where a practically spent round might have been weathered, the schooner's rudder was not one.

The crash of crushed timber was followed by a cry of disbelief from the helmsman as the wheel spun uselessly in his hands. The vessel's head immediately fell away, then there was the sound of flapping canvas as she wore round and seemed to dig her bows into the gentle sea as she lost momentum. But all Adams knew was that he had run out of options. They might attempt to rig a temporary rudder, but nothing could be achieved before the Frenchmen closed with him, and he knew then that they would be taken for sure.

* * *

All aboard *Hare* had witnessed it from the start: from the leading Frenchman sniping with her bow chasers while doggedly clinging to her prey, to that single broadside that finally did for the schooner's steering and the striking of her colours that followed almost immediately. And though they had problems of their own, and were forced to weather several long-range shots themselves before shaking off their own pursuers, there was little in the way of celebration when they had. For some time afterwards an air of loss seemed to hang over the brig and it was only several days later when a doubtful sighting from the masthead gradually grew into firm identification – first of a British warship, then the convoy they had so eagerly sought – that the depression began to lift.

On the quarterdeck, King lowered his glass and released a long-held sigh. It was *Athena*, there could be no doubt of that; she was holding the leeward station in *Hare*'s absence and even now standing towards them with the interrogative flying from her foretop yardarm.

"Make the private signal," he ordered and Dilson immediately called his signals team to attention. The appropriate flags had been ready to hoist for some while and raced up the halyard before breaking out in the stiff breeze. There was the briefest of pauses before Granger replied and then another flutter of bunting as he reported their arrival to Banks' flagship, which soon came dimly into view over the horizon.

"Convoy is maintaining the same formation, at least what we can see of it," Brehaut muttered as they drew closer. "And some would appear to have suffered same as we have."

That was also correct; as King looked he noted several of the merchants had jury spars rigged and one was completely missing a main topgallant mast. The damage had probably been caused during the recent storm and must account for their slower speed. But even if she was not alone in suffering from the elements, *Hare* was definitely the only one to show any sign of combat, although there could be little pride in the wounds. During her absence a prize had certainly been taken, but was lost almost as quickly, along with a fair proportion of her crew.

"*Athena* is signalling," Dilson reported, his glass already raised. "She's repeating from the Commodore; we are to close with him without delay."

"Acknowledge," King grunted. There was little else to do; *Hare* was already making good speed as she had done for the last few days. Banks would be keen to know how they lost contact with the convoy and what had caused their delay in joining up, although King had a deal more to tell him than that.

Part Two

1.

The great cabin in *Relentless* seemed unusually orderly after the chaos of King's own battered quarters. Even the ship herself, being built with timbers originally intended to support the bulk of a battleship, made him feel even more of a nonentity when he remembered his own command's frail and leaking hull. But Banks was as genial as ever and greeted him with the well remembered smile as he indicated a particularly comfortable chair that benefited from the last of the afternoon's light from the stern gallery.

"You cannot blame yourself," Sir Richard told him firmly when King had finished his sorry tale. "A large schooner will always require a sizeable prize crew and there were a great many prisoners to consider as well."

That was a major point; without the Frenchmen, fewer seamen and none of the marines would have been needed. But now *Hare* had lost more than fifteen hands and all her marines, together with the junior officers.

"I think perhaps I should have abandoned the prize," King admitted finally. "Cast her adrift with cannon over the side and all lines cut, then let her people make what they could of her."

"Maybe so," Banks allowed. "Although such an action would not have looked so well in your report."

"I should still have my men," King pointed out. "Adams was amongst them, and young Summers."

"Hindsight is a wonderful thing," Banks told him briskly, "though rarely of any true value. You can cope without marines for now. I shall send a draft of seamen from *Relentless*, and signal for Granger and Bruce to do likewise, though I fear we are all relatively light in that department."

"Thank you, sir," King replied. He could not expect his fellow commanders to provide him with trained hands, but even landsmen would be welcomed. "What of the Indiamen?" he asked. "Might we press a few from there?"

Banks shook his head. "I fear not," he said. "They are still officially outward bound, though there are other considerations that make such a move unwise."

"When we reach St Helena, perhaps?" King suggested.

"Not even then, Tom," Banks told him in a softer tone, "as we shall not be calling."

"Not calling at St Helena?" It seemed a strange move, especially considering there were no other friendly ports for thousands of miles.

"Have you not noted our position?" Banks was grinning now.

Since the loss of the prize, King felt every moment had been spent dealing with the immediate problems of a leaking hull and the lack of suitable hands, so was momentarily at a loss. Then realisation dawned: they had passed the tenth parallel south. Sir Richard's sealed orders must have been opened and he might be prepared to share a little of their contents.

"So, do I gather we have another destination?" he asked, eyeing his former captain quizzically.

Hearing they were not bound for St Helena had changed things dramatically, for the island was not just a provider of water. Despite Anderson's attention, *Hare*'s hull was continuing to leak and, although Jamestown had little in the way of dockyard facilities, King had been depending on what assistance it could offer.

"We have indeed," Banks confirmed. "I cannot say more for now, but the convoy will continue on the current heading for the time being." He paused and raised an eyebrow. "And I mean the convoy: the Indiamen are remaining with us throughout."

"Are they indeed?" King now felt nothing could surprise him further.

"It would be wrong of me to say more as the other captains are yet to be informed."

"Of course, sir," King agreed. "Though I presume we shall water at some point?"

"*Hare* should have been provisioned for three months," Banks replied.

"Indeed she was, but the merchants?"

"They were also provided for," Sir Richard now gave a slight snort. "It seems their Commodore was given greater insight into our mission than myself. Understandable in the circumstances, though I cannot help but feel a mite aggrieved."

But King's mind was exploring the more important ramifications; so the Indiamen were not just a group of merchants to be protected, they actually had some bearing on the squadron's ultimate goal. A fleet of such a size could be carrying anything from trading goods to armed men, while their southerly course opened up much of the world as a final destination. They might round the Cape and head east for India, China or New Holland, or turn west for South America and the Pacific. Then cold reason returned as he remembered that any distant station would be denied him; *Hare* was simply not seaworthy enough for a lengthy trip. Even with fresh men and favourable weather, she would founder within a few thousand miles and, once more, he began to resign himself to leaving Banks and his force behind.

"I shall certainly tell more in time," Sir Richard confirmed, "but can promise you this for now; where we are bound is not so very distant. Once there, we shall find additional crew for your command, as well as shipyard facilities to see her sound. And I definitely have no intention of leaving you behind."

* * *

The former prize crew had been treated well enough by the French. The one slightly wounded marine was taken straight to the surgeon while the officers were removed, presumably to speak with their French counterparts in the luxury of quarters set apart for those of higher rank. Meanwhile the rest, the petty officers, seamen and marines had been herded below and placed in an unlit storeroom.

"Strike a light someone," Sergeant Bates ordered once the door had been closed and soundly bolted.

There was a brief rustling from the throng of men, then a small bright flame flared up, illuminating Parker's face and the area about him.

"Not much in the way of tinder," the topman muttered.

"And nothing to light as far as I can see," another added.

"Never mind, it will serve to see us settled," Greenwood assured them.

"Can't see that takin' long," Oats, a marine private, commented. "Ain't nothing to sit on."

"Place is empty, as far as I can see," a seaman agreed. "Belike the Frogs are short on provisions."

"More likely they've cleared it for the likes of us," Sergeant Bates stated with more authority.

"Well if that's what the French call clearing, I don't think much of it," Oats grumbled. "Hasn't seen a swab in ages and the stink is rich enough to peel paint."

"Every orlop smells," Greenwood told him levelly.

"*Hare*'s never did," someone at the back countered.

"That's 'cause she were leaking so bad she never got the chance," Greenwood insisted, turning in the general direction of his unseen critic. "The amount we must have been pumping out each day don't bear thinkin' about."

"I wonder if they got away," Parker pondered as he blew gently on his flame.

"Last I saw she were making good speed," Russell remarked. "As long as she don't take any shot, I reckon they'll make it."

There was general agreement from the crowd, something that pleased Russell. A few weeks ago he would never have chanced such a remark, but had learned a great deal since and it seemed the others were ready to accept this.

"We wouldn't have been caught if it weren't for the rudder," Goodridge, the elderly quartermaster declared. "As it was, there weren't nothin' I could do."

"No one's blaming you," Greenwood assured him. "It were just bad luck, that's all."

"So what happens now?" someone in the darkness asked.

"We sit tight," Henderson, the boatswain's mate, replied.

"Don't see we has any choice," another anonymous voice remarked.

"The light won't last much longer," Parker told them as he began passing the hot tin from hand to hand. "We needs a bit of tow or something to keep it going."

"Ain't nothin' here – 'cept rat's droppin's."

"May as well blow it out," Greenwood directed. "We might need it later."

Parker paused for a moment in case any of the petty officers had a better suggestion, then blew firmly on the light. The flame flared briefly before dying, and then all were left in darkness.

* * *

Adams supposed the reversal of circumstances was not as bad as it might have been. The final taking of his command had been well handled, with three boats arriving from the leading frigate. Between them, they must have carried more than seventy armed men, although he had no thought of opposition and had already stuck his colours. Then there had been a brief interview with a French officer; Adams had not spoken the language for some while and, with the shock of having been captured, the words simply would not come. But the young man had known English tolerably well and there was little confusion. Callahan and his wife appeared on deck and explained themselves then soon all were being taken back to the frigate.

As the cutter pulled alongside, Adams remembered looking back at *Hare*. The brig was in plain sight and still heading stoically for the horizon with two Frenchmen in pursuit. His eyes stayed on his former home for several seconds; King would be aboard and probably watching him. It was quite possible – likely even – that the two would never meet again. Adams felt a mild pang of regret, but there was little room for more. Then, after some urging from behind, he heaved himself up the warship's tumblehome and squeezed through the narrow entry port.

Once on the frigate's deck, all was very orderly, even if Adams seemed to be viewing everything through a faint mist. There were further armed and uniformed men waiting for them – French marines, Adams supposed – along with many more officers, one of which appeared to be the ship's captain. Then he, Summers and Bates, the marine sergeant, had been singled out, with Bates soon being sent to rejoin the others as it was realised his rank had been wrongly assessed. Handshakes were exchanged along with names that meant nothing to him and were immediately forgotten; it was only later that he realised his sword must also have been removed. Soon he was being guided along the quarterdeck and then found himself entering the officers' quarters, which were larger than any he had encountered for some while. Chairs were found for him and Summers, the captain reappeared and took a seat behind a desk, then another entered and all stood once more. This was an older man but even more splendidly decorated and introduced as a

Contre-Amiral by the young man who had accepted Adams' surrender. There were further handshakes before all returned to their seats and the interrogation began.

And it was at that point when, for some reason that he was never to understand, Adams found his knowledge of French returning. He even felt a degree of pride when a question phrased in broken English was answered more fluently in his captor's language. But the satisfaction did not last long and soon was replaced by another sensation: the utter desperation of defeat.

"So, you originality came from a warship?" The captain himself had taken up questioning when it was realised Adams understood the language.

"*Hare*," Adams agreed, ignoring the slight intake of breath from Summers. "She is of four hundred tons and carries sixteen guns." He knew Summers was regarding him curiously but there seemed little point in keeping such facts secret; the French would have seen the brig and guessed her strength. If they did not discover her identity from him, they would doubtless do so from his former prisoners.

"And where is she bound?"

That was another matter, and this time Adams shook his head. "I cannot tell you," he said. Then, before the Frenchman could ask more, added, "I cannot tell you because I do not know myself; we were sailing under sealed orders. Not even our captain is aware of our final destination."

The Frenchman considered him thoughtfully. "It is a small ship to send on an independent commission," he said. "Surely there will be others she is in company with?"

Adams went to explain but something made him stop and the older man nodded in apparent understanding.

"Very well, though I shall doubtless learn more in time," he replied mildly.

"And I have less reluctance in telling of our own plans." This time it was the *Amiral* who spoke, and did so with a far stronger accent forcing Adams to concentrate harder.

"My ships have been at sea some while and have taken a number of your country's vessels." The last part of his statement was made with a glance towards the captain who nodded in confirmation.

"So far we have captured five, not counting your own. Three merchants that are now on their way to French ports, and two small Royal Navy warships which were destroyed –they were poorly built and required extensive repair," the Frenchman explained curtly. "Their officers and men were sent back to France with our other captures."

Adams found that easy to understand; his recent experience confirmed that taking a warship as a prize could easily turn out to be a two-edged sword.

"But you will not be travelling back to France," the *Amiral* continued. "We now require water and other supplies so I will be despatching each of my force in turn to replenish at Cape Town. This ship will be first; Captain Brunelle shall be pleased to see you and your men safely to the port, and there pass you to the Batavian authorities in control."

Adams found himself nodding politely. So, he was to be held by the Dutch, or at least the force that currently occupied the low countries; he supposed it would make a change from being a prisoner of the French.

At that moment a hesitant knocking interrupted the proceedings; a young *aspirant* entered and approached the *Amiral*. The lad was flushed and nervous but clearly had an important message which he passed on in a low tone that Adams was unable to overhear.

"I understand you were carrying passengers," the *Amiral* told him when the boy had been dismissed.

"I was," Adams confirmed. "Mr and Mrs Callahan," he continued. "An American couple who were aboard the schooner when she was taken."

"It seems they are also wishing to visit Cape Town," the *Amiral* added with a wry smile. "And Monsieur Callahan would appear to be an important man who has great plans for the destruction of your country. So for us it is a fortunate day indeed."

* * *

It was not long before a measure of routine became established. On pledging to cause no difficulties, Adam and Summers were given a small berth to themselves. It was on the orlop deck and next to the warrant officers' mess, where the pair were also allowed to take their meals. At first their French contemporaries treated them with caution but, with the help of the lads' knowledge of their language, they were soon accepted and the first shoots of friendship began to sprout.

But for others, the lower deck men and more junior officers, things were not so civilised. The store room that had first housed them became their permanent home and, though benches, necessary buckets and a selection of worn hammocks were provided, they were hardly any more comfortable.

"With all this talk of revolution and equality, you'd think we'd be treated a bit more fairly," Oats grumbled over his portion of pickles, hard cheese and ship's biscuit. "We've had the same scran now four days in a row; you can bet Adams is eatin' better."

"I hope he is," Greenwood told him.

"Yes, but why ain't we been treated the same?" the marine persisted.

"How do you know we ain't?" Parker asked. "Just because he and Mr Summers aren't with us don't mean they're living the high life."

"Oh, you thinks they're in the berth next door do ya?" Oats snorted. "Na, officers are always treated better, it's the way of the world."

"But they're not really officers," Long, another marine, added.

"Mr Adams 'as passed his board," Sennett reminded them.

"Aye an' don't we know of it?" Oats replied. "But he ain't a lieutenant – not yet anyways. He and that boy are still midshipmen, which don't make them much different to you, Sarge," he added, glancing at Bates.

"Oh, it does," Greenwood told him firmly. "They might be juniors, like me an' Mr Henderson here, but they're still of the quarterdeck."

"And that makes a difference does it?" Long demanded.

"It means they're treated like gentlemen, even by the French."

"I've heard it all before – 'Aft lies the honour, but forward the better man'. Ain't that the case?" Oats grumbled.

"You've got that wrong," Sergeant Bates told him firmly. "An' if you go on spoutin' that sort of Frenchman's talk, won't stay a Royal much longer."

"But that's just it!" the marine wailed despondently. "The Frogs don't believe it any more than the English. Otherwise we'd be sleepin' in the captain's cabin and dining off goose liver and snails."

"You got it," Greenwood told him. "The world's a topsy-turvy place where nothin' can be depended upon 'cept the poor gets mistreated. So what do you want to do about it; start a revolution?"

Oats went to speak, but knew when he was beaten.

"And you won't find me eatin' no snails," Bates added.

* * *

The ship that held them was a heavy frigate: a powerful beast that also handled well. But though Summers was experienced enough to appreciate her design, there were various less attractive aspects.

For a start, discipline aboard the Frenchman was very different to that of a Royal Navy vessel. On the lower deck there were two distinct groups; the regular hands who carried out most work aloft as well as anything that required a degree of seamanship elsewhere, and younger men, some no more than boys and all far less experienced. Many bore the vacant and mildly frightened look of conscripts and were barely tolerated by the older men who made little effort to pass on their skills. As a relatively new addition to the Royal Navy himself, Summers could equate with the youngsters and readily accepted that most of what he knew had been learned from those more experienced who were willing to share.

And the ship was also poorly cared for; her crew handled her competently enough and there was little to criticise in the officers, the basic rigging was properly maintained as was each individual piece of equipment, including the massive cannon that made up her main armament. But general cleanliness was lacking, with no sign of silver sand or holystones for the decks. Brass was tarnished, there was little evidence of blacking and Summers could only be mildly appalled at the regular hands' messing arrangements.

Some of this he had tried to discuss with Adams, although his friend was strangely indifferent. Summers had no idea why but, whatever the reason, the old rapport that had been a feature of the life they had shared in *Hare*'s cockpit was definitely missing.

He had even been unable to evoke any sympathy for their own lower deck men. They were being held in a former storeroom on the orlop and the first three days had been spent without any being given the chance to exercise or take fresh air. It was only after he made a personal representation to one of the senior French officers that anyone saw the need to make changes. As it was, each were only allowed an hour on deck every day – a small victory maybe, but one Summers had won on his own; Adams could not have been less interested.

He supposed that much might change when they reached Cape Town. Both men were accustomed to being held captive and knew it to be a different prospect on land than at sea. But even if Adams came round and began to behave more like the friend and confidant he remembered, Summers sensed something of their former relationship would never return.

* * *

Adams was also aware of the souring of matters with Summers but, as with so much of his present life, cared little. Since losing command of the schooner a cloud of apathy had descended to the point where little seemed able to affect him. It was as if all that happened did so to another person; his mind was numb, sounds were barely heard, faces remained indistinct and the cycle of daily living continued without his actively willing it.

As with any lengthy journey without sight of land or change in weather, each day began to merge into the one before. Soon time ceased to have meaning and monotony set in; something that was positively welcomed by Adams, who was only too pleased to notice details of both his capture and the duties of a King's officer were starting to fade. Consequently Summers' quirky conversation or foolish suggestions were simple to ignore and he found himself seeking what solitude there was in a ship that crammed four hundred souls into a hull little more than a hundred and fifty feet long.

But at least he had been accepted by the French officers and soon was permitted to spend most evenings on the quarterdeck. There many of the darker hours passed with him staring out over the taffrail although the beauty of the ship's short, translucent wake went unnoticed. The officers grouped further forward were inclined to give him space. They could guess at a defeated enemy's need for isolation although Adams' thoughts were far from morbid and he had few concerns for his immediate future.

He had quickly decided that the recent defeat would effectively write off any chance of his returning to the Navy and trying for a commissioned post, although that did not mean there was nothing to look forward to. From what Adams knew of his destination, Cape Town had been under Dutch control since being handed back by the British in the recent peace. That might mean anything, as Holland had been overrun by the French many years before and the Batavian Republic, now known as a Commonwealth and controlled by Napoleon, had a very different constitution to the old regime. Nevertheless, he sensed his impending imprisonment would differ to that encountered while being held captive in France.

For it was almost customary in foreign bases to allow captured officers some freedom; not on the same lines as that of Verdun, perhaps, though possibly superior and certainly a lot more transparent. He had heard many tales of those captured in distant lands who came to call the country home and, with his service career apparently over, the idea was not totally abhorrent.

It was still summer south of the equator and the long hot days in which nothing was demanded of him allowed his mind to wander, with space for the strangest thoughts to present themselves and be seriously considered. Perhaps, after a spell in captivity, he might be allowed to start up in business; after all, the Cape was a major port on the Eastern trading route. He already knew a certain amount of French; Dutch could be as easily acquired and in time there might be a position for him with the VOC, or rather whatever had risen up in its place. And it would not be too wild a stretch of the imagination to see himself growing old in a pleasant climate many miles away from the war and past failures, with a modest house, perhaps some land and, the most ludicrous thought of all, a wife to love and care for him.

In reality this last aspect had been very much on Adams' mind as he considered his prospects and, though he would never have admitted it to himself, was one of the main reasons for taking the air in the early evenings. And so, on the fourth day and just before the sun began its downwards plunge, it was no surprise and something of a relief to hear the faint rustle of material and, looking round, see Anne Callahan standing near to him.

Each acknowledged the other's presence with little more than a polite nod, but in no time the gentle discourse that had become customary aboard the schooner resumed, seemingly unchanged, even if the circumstances were so very different. And as the dark night surrendered to a full and brilliant moon, it was entirely natural that their conversation should deepen further.

2.

Aboard *Hare*, King was now feeling far more optimistic. Anderson had made no further progress with their leaking hull and the problem was steadily growing worse, with pumping now required almost continually. But they had found the convoy again; should there be a major problem, if one of the pumps were to fail, or the leaks become truly unmanageable, there were three large warships packed with skilled men and an assortment of replacement parts close at hand. He could also relax in the security the accompanying frigates offered. There might be five powerful Frenchmen in the vicinity – a force that outnumbered theirs considerably – but still he remained unconcerned. The French may hold the upper hand on paper but, in common with many British sea officers, King remained certain of victory at almost any odds. It was a confidence that ventured dangerously towards arrogance, yet would still be a major asset if it came to actually mixing with an enemy.

Another contributory factor to his change of mood was the entire British escort force was under the direct command of his former captain, someone who came as close to a father to him as was possible. The pair had been through much together and that included defeat as well as victory, but the fact that both had survived and seemingly prospered was enough to convince King he might relax a little. Banks had assured him their final destination was close enough for his leaking hull to make without difficulty, especially if the weather remained so agreeably placid, and by not calling at St Helena he would also avoid any chance of an awkward reunion with Julia Booker: the girl he had left behind on the small island.

And finally there was the additional information Banks had let slip; not the full extent of his sealed orders perhaps, but probably more than had been shared with Bruce or Granger, who captained the other escorts. Now King was not only reasonably certain of remaining with the squadron, the rest of the commission would appear to be eventful indeed, and it would be strange if he did not return with a decent amount of prize money with which to dazzle Aimée.

Strangely this last point was the only one that contained any measure of doubt for King. Due to the convoy's brisk progress there had been no opportunity to receive or send mail and his last memory of her was their graceless parting at *Relentless*' entry port. If he were honest, the prospect of returning with pockets brimming with gold was more the product of sailors' dreams; what he truly wished to bring back was something considerably more valuable than riches, and far harder to obtain.

* * *

"You must not judge my husband too harshly," the girl told him on the third night they met. Adams turned to her. Dusk was falling quickly: soon it would be dark and he was suddenly unwilling to waste the precious twilight in talking of another man.

But that was sheer nonsense, for a start the fellow in question was her husband. Strange thoughts might be fermenting inside Adams' own head, but Anne had yet to express any interest in him, and neither did he have any right to expect her to.

"I do not judge him at all," he replied, mustering every ounce of dispassion. "He has chosen his country – you both have," he added quickly, remembering. "And as America has no part in this war, you are free to side as you wish."

"But do you not know of his plans?" she asked.

"Not in any great detail. Mention was made in the interview with the *Contre-Amiral*, but no more." He paused. "I had considered they centred about Cape Town, so were truly not of my immediate concern."

She looked down and began to fiddle aimlessly with the buttons of her jacket.

"He only assumed American nationality three years ago," she admitted. "Until then he was Irish and inordinately proud of the fact."

"That comes as no surprise," Adams laughed. "Indeed, most would have guessed as much. And I assume he fought in the troubles?" he added.

"No, he did not," she replied. "David was living in America at the time and tried to return home but it were not possible. Though his family certainly did and you may as well know, my husband's cousin was Father John Murphy."

The name sounded familiar, although Adams could not place it. "A papist?" he asked.

"A Catholic Priest," she corrected. "And one of the leaders in the uprising."

"'Ninety-eight?"

She nodded. "Father Murphy originally urged his followers to pledge allegiance to the crown, but circumstances turned against him."

Adams was starting to recall now and the woman gave more details as he did.

"He took command of a small army of rebels and was initially successful, but there were many more defeats and finally he was captured."

"I see," Adams commented softly.

"Forgive me, but I don't believe you do," she insisted. "The English tortured him as they did so many who opposed them. Then, when he would give no information, he was killed in the most brutal manner imaginable. They set his head on a pike to face a Catholic church and burnt his body in a barrel of tar so the worshippers could scent his funeral pyre."

"War can be vile," Adams murmured, "and civil war undoubtedly so. Though I understand the rebels were no kinder to the British."

"Some might say they had more reason."

"But your husband was not involved," Adams reminded her.

"I said he did not fight," she pointed out. "When the uprising was put down so decisively David remained in America. At the time he had just started the trading company and threw all his energies into that. It was before we knew each other well, but I think he had some idea of forgetting the troubles in his homeland. Then came the news of his cousin's death. That was when he started to drink more than he should: I think he has been torturing himself ever since."

"So what does he propose to do now?" Adams asked and the woman shrugged.

"His business is successful and we are well provided for," she replied. "More than that, he has contacts and can now call upon a fair amount of shipping."

"He owns ships?"

"No, but there are many who do that are obliged to him in some way. And he will not be afraid to call in past favours."

Knowing what he did about the man, Adams was not surprised at that. "For what purpose?" he asked.

"That is where matters are not so clear," she admitted. "I know he has plans but, beyond the general outline, not in any great detail."

Adams began to consider this and, as he did, was conscious of interest stirring in his brain. It was a sensation that had been absent for far too long. "But you know what he intends?" he persisted.

"Oh yes," she replied, as if it were the easiest thing in the world. "He wishes to start another uprising in Ireland."

* * *

"When we gets back to England, we're goin' on the biggest spree ever," Swain announced with satisfaction.

"You're talking a long way off," Jackson, the gun captain, warned.

"Maybe so," the holder agreed. "But it can pay to plan these things."

"Aye," Sayer nodded eagerly. "Nothing wrong with a touch of wool gathering. What we going to do then, Swainie?"

The mess felt uncommonly empty with Greenwood and so many of the others gone, while knowing their mates were in the hands of the French made those that remained especially uneasy.

"Well, let's assume it's Portsmouth," Swain began.

"Aye, Pompey," Jackson concurred. "My home port."

"And mine," Seldin agreed. "None finer."

"Start at the Kepple's Head."

"The Kepple?" Jackson exclaimed. "Bit warm for us, ain't it?"

"We've been particularly lucky with prize money," Swain assured them dreamily. "Sink a few there, then on to Mrs Flanagan's."

"Pushing school, is it?" Sayer asked, but the other men shook their heads.

"Best chop house on the south coast," Jackson assured him. "Don't know what she puts in her gravy, but they're queueing in the street some nights."

"What's a pushing school then?" This came from Georgie, the lad.

"Best you don't know," Jackson grunted.

"It's a brothel," Swain told him before adding, "Lad's got to know sometime."

"No reason to tell him sooner than he needs," Jackson insisted.

"Anyway, we're eating at Flanagan's..." Swain prompted.

"That's right," Swain agreed. "So where do you want to go next?"

"Cock fight," Seldin proposed. "You get the squarest pits in Pompey."

"Or a Penny Gaff," another suggested.

"I still like the sound of an academy," Sayer sighed. "Not had a decent press since I came aboard."

"It's a lot longer for some of us," Seldin agreed. "And with Parker as a mess mate, we missed out last leave."

"Aye," Jackson agreed. "Folk like him ain't the most popular at such places."

"So why don't he go to a Molly House?" Sayer asked and Jackson shrugged.

"Never seems to want to," he said. "Don't go much for drink neither."

"Has too much fun messing with other people's pleasures," Swain snorted.

"Na, Parker's not like that," Seldin insisted.

"But just because he don't want to, don't mean we can't," Sayer stated determinedly. "I say we get corned and make for the brothel!"

"What's a brothel?" Georgie asked and Swain's eyes flickered towards Jackson for a moment.

"It's where they sells soup," he said.

* * *

"An uprising in Ireland? But what of the Act of Union?" Adams felt the need to protest, even when such a foolish ambition had been mooted.

"It is because of that he wishes to rebel," the woman replied adding what might have been a laugh. "And claims he knows of others with like minds, while England has withdrawn much of the army that was stationed there. David believes all that is needed are funds and a small band of disciplined men; once both are in place there will be little to stop them. He has money and access to shipping, and we are currently travelling to the Cape to investigate the troops."

"He intends using Dutch?" Adams asked.

"No, but there are native soldiers to be had in the colony. They will be mercenaries of course, but supposedly well trained and can be relied upon."

Adams was silent for a moment. What she said was logical but only to a point. Britain had certainly withdrawn men from Dublin, but there remained a considerable number garrisoned in the country, with further to hand if required. Whatever Callahan's dreams, it would need more than a few hundred armed men to make any sort of impression and they would have to be highly disciplined. And even if such a force were found, after the recent and crushing defeat, he doubted the civil population could be stirred into repeating the process.

"So, that is the importance of your journey," he mused. "I had thought it on account of your brother."

"Oh Wieb is there," she confirmed, "as are his wife and family. My husband hopes he will help him raise the army though I doubt such a thing will be of interest. From his letters I would judge Wieb to be enamoured with the country."

"How long has he lived there?" Adams asked.

"Since the British gave up the colony, which is a short time indeed. But I know my brother well, and it does sound such a wonderful place. Oh, John," she continued, unconsciously taking his hand. "It is so far away from Europe with all its troubles. A new land, where all can begin again: it sounds perfect!"

The touch of skin together with her use of his Christian name sent a physical thrill through Adams' body and he had to take a grip on himself before continuing.

"So will you allow your husband to stir up more trouble?" he asked, his voice unnaturally harsh. It was now late into the evening but the moon had risen to show her features perfectly and, once more, Adams was struck by her delicate beauty.

"You know the kind of man he is," she shrugged, "and in truth, I wish it were not to be. But he will hardly listen to me, or anyone else for that matter. I am simply his wife: someone he regards as good enough to care for him and nothing more."

"But are you in favour?" he asked. "Of his plans, I am meaning."

"Lord, no! I credit myself with some sense and think him a fool to even consider the prospect. From what I know of Ireland, it would need a vast army to make any change to the country," she continued. "And a force of that nature would surely require shipping way beyond anything even David can summon. Besides, when all is said and done, if a rebellion were so easy to start, why have not the French attempted it already?"

"They have," Adams replied. "On a number of occasions, and each ended in disaster."

Again the smile. "As I suspect this will also," she sighed. "Tell me, John, why does it need to be so very difficult to find happiness?"

3.

"Well there it is, lads," Greenwood announced. "Cape Colony: our new home. So feast your eyes upon it!"

The view from the frigate's waist was not great and no prisoner was allowed upon the gangways during their brief exercise period, but enough could be seen through the open ports.

"It's a bloody island!" Oats exclaimed in disgust.

"Beyond that," Greenwood told him sharply. "You see the mountain?"

The seaman pointed out to a range of grey hills capped by several massive peaks, one of which rose higher than the clouds that surrounded it. Despite its height, the edifice was considerably wider than it was tall, and looked more like some mystical fortress.

"That's a mountain?" Sennett asked in disbelief. "I always imagined them having a sharp bit on top."

"Most do," Greenwood agreed, "but not this one. She's bigger than many though."

"You been here afore then, Greenie?" Sergeant Bates enquired.

"Aye, in 'ninety-seven," the seaman replied. "We held the place then – took it from the Dutch a couple of years earlier."

"So how come it ain't ours now?" Oats whined. "Frogs take it off us, did they?"

Greenwood shook his head. "We had to give it back in the Peace."

"So what did we get in return?" Oats persisted.

"Not a lot," Greenwood answered. "Couple of islands in the Caribbean and one further east they calls Ceylon."

"Sounds like a regular sailor's bargain to me," Oats grumbled and Greenwood didn't feel inclined to argue.

"A busy enough port, though," Russell remarked, his thoughts more firmly centred on the approaching land.

"Oh it is," Greenwood agreed. "Major stopping point for the Eastern trade; probably means as much to John Company as Malta does the RN. And we weren't so dumb as to give that up," he added with a significant look at Oats.

"There's traders a plenty there," Sennett pointed out as the frigate eased steadily in with the breeze and the full extent of the waterfront was slowly revealed. There was no regular harbour as such, but a forest of masts could be seen at a nearby anchorage with a number of low lying buildings and what might have been a shipyard to the south. But all signs of civilisation seemed humble when judged against the natural phenomenon that towered above. And the huge mass of rock was only part of a ragged backdrop that was equally imposing. There were peaks to either side of the monster and each would have looked large in any other setting, although all seemed dwarfed by the massive, flat-topped form that claimed centre stage. From the main deck of a frigate it was impossible to tell how far off the range lay but, even if close to, it must be vast indeed. And beneath, sheltering in a separate mooring appropriate to their station, was a small collection of warships.

"I see the Navy's here," Bates announced flatly as he noted these.

"Aye, well in evidence," Greenwood agreed. "Must be the escort for them merchants; it's the time of year for such a thing."

"If that lot sets sail and meets up with *Hare* or our old squadron, there'll be hell to pay," Sennett commented flatly.

"What with them about, an' the French what took us, I'd say we did well to get captured," Oats agreed, giving a wry look. "At least we'll live to see out the war."

"Who's saying they're French?" Greenwood asked and, sure enough the red, white and blue of Batavian ensigns could be seen flying from several of the anchored shipping, as well as a few of the larger shore emplacements.

"Dutchmen," Bates noted scornfully adding a sniff. "Never know where you is with them square-heads. One minute they're trading partners and marrying your sister, the next we're having to take their fleet to pieces at Camperdown."

"Well they're firmly under Boney's thumb now," Oats grunted. "An' have been for a while. See a Dutchman's flag and you may as well be lookin' at a tricolour – makes no difference."

"And we're about to get a closer look soon," Bates added as he nodded towards one of the warships currently recovering her anchor. The men watched in silence as she squared away; it was another frigate, though smaller than the Frenchman that held them. She was more graceful, however, and there was no hint of clumsiness in her handling. Soon she had caught the breeze and was standing out to sea.

"Must be a welcoming committee," Bates commented dryly.

"No, she'll steer to pass us," Greenwood predicted. "Heading for False Bay more'n likely. That's a few miles to the south and far larger, though not so well protected."

"Bit of a turnaround," Bates snorted. "All this enemy shipping splashin' about as if they owned the place and not a British flag in sight to tell them otherwise; hardly what we're used to."

"Maybe not," Greenwood agreed. "But then we're a long way from home."

* * *

"Well we seem to be making progress," Callahan muttered as he stood with his wife on the quarterdeck. "Ask the Captain how long until we can go ashore."

"But I do not like to bother him..." Anne began, before noticing the look of sudden anger on her husband's face and hurrying away without another word.

"We should take up our mooring within the hour," she announced, returning. "The captain expects to meet with the port authorities immediately afterwards. He is happy for you to accompany him if you wish."

"Most kind, I am sure," Callahan grunted and he withdrew his watch. "Our luggage is packed, I assume?"

"Very nearly," the woman assured him. "I just have your shirts to attend to."

"Nearly?" the man questioned. "My dear, I have not spent the last few years of my life planning this operation to have it delayed in any way. Kindly cease your prevarications and be sure we are ready to leave as soon as the captain sees fit."

* * *

Summers and Adams could see the approaching frigate equally clearly. They were also in the waist but further aft of the other British prisoners and the two lads were getting on rather better.

In the last week or so Adams had resolved much and was finally able to cast off some of the self-indulgent melancholy that had haunted him since the loss of the prize. And though he remained convinced his career as a Royal Navy officer had ended, he was now even more sure it need not be the finish of all ambition – or life in general if it came to it. There were still many ways in which he might progress, even if one of the reasons for this was hardly positive. For, although she had done nothing to actively encourage it, he was now quite certain that, whatever his future turned out to be, it would be shared with Anne Callahan.

During the latter part of the journey their regular rendezvous on the quarterdeck had become the highlight of his day; a tranquil time when the pair could talk openly and in increasing confidence about a variety of subjects. As the voyage wore on, these became intimate to the point that he now felt he knew the woman as well as any, and undoubtedly better than the arrogant pig who had taken her for his wife.

Actually, his education had also included her husband or, more specifically, his plans for the invasion of Ireland. Callahan had not trusted his wife with the finer details but what little she did know had been freely passed on to Adams, who was both disturbed and amazed by what he heard.

Of course, the scheme had no chance of success. Too much depended upon a dozen imponderables and the failure of any single one would see the whole thing collapse in dismal failure. First, men had to be recruited; Callahan's initial estimate had been for two thousand fully trained troops although the number and their level of expertise varied whenever they were mentioned to his wife. But even a small army must be recruited and probably from several locations, yet all must arrive at the same place and time to have any chance of success.

Victuals and equipment must also be arranged, and there would be a need for an equally large number of horses, creatures that were difficult and expensive to transport by ship and required a deal of care that would entail recruiting even more manpower.

And even assuming all that could be arranged, along with the vast amount of finance required, transport wagons, field shelters and medical facilities, there would come the problem of attracting support from the civil population. Adams was no expert on Irish politics, but doubted if much could be expected of a country still reeling from an unsuccessful rebellion less than ten years before. There may be small groups of dissidents ready to rise to the cause but, despite having strong family connections, Callahan had not attempted to contact these, and neither was he willing to share the planning with anyone who had a better grasp on military strategy. Anne was sure his intention was simply to march at the head of an all conquering army and single-handedly rid his home of British oppression.

Which was a fool's dream and one that could only end in disaster; even Adams, a passed midshipman with little knowledge of land-based campaigns, could see that. But discovering more of Callahan's plans and discussing them in detail with his wife during their twilight conversations had brought one positive side effect; the young man's previously dormant mind was now very much awake.

Almost overnight he had begun to take more interest in events aboard the frigate as well as life in general. There was no wavering in his intentions; Summers remained unable to convince him he was not totally finished as a Navy officer, but at least something of their former friendship had been restored. And while one relationship was rebuilt a second, and very different one, also flourished. Adams now knew he loved Anne Callahan beyond measure, and the fact of his love, though it must remain secret even from her, had made him happier than he could ever remember.

Even knowing his affections might be unrequited made little difference; such trivialities could be addressed in time, as could the fact that, as soon as their current ship dropped anchor, he was likely never to clap eyes on the woman again. For despite all the evidence to the contrary, he remained inwardly certain they shared something far greater than a few whispered confidences and they would never be parted.

"She's a pretty little thing, for sure." Summers' casual remark caught Adams by surprise and he turned to glare at his friend.

"What did you say?" he demanded.

"The frigate," the lad replied innocently. "Well set up and sailing nicely."

"I-I suppose she is," Adams agreed, finally allowing his eyes to rest upon the oncoming warship. She was close-hauled and her sun-kissed canvas contrasted beautifully with the harsh backdrop of dark, distant mountains.

"French would you say?" Summers mused, but Adams shook his head.

"Too heavy in the beam," he answered absent-mindedly. "Dutch more like, though she looks to have a sizeable draft, which is rare. To be honest, I'd reckon her more likely British."

"British?" Summers questioned in barely a whisper.

"Aye, but probably a capture," Adams added more firmly. "At least they haven't covered her in spars, like some continental navies."

The pair continued to gaze at the ship; the Batavian ensign was quite prominent yet both could ignore this and appreciate instead the grace and purpose of her lines and that she was being singularly well handled. And then something else in Adams' mind began to stir; something that told him the frigate might not be all she appeared and soon all thoughts of Anne Callahan and their future together were totally forgotten.

* * *

"So we are heading for the Cape?" Croft mused, while Brehaut whistled softly through his teeth. They were in King's quarters aboard *Hare*; the place was still showing signs of the recent battle and not all the furniture had been restored, but neither fact was on the minds of those present.

"Cape Colony," King confirmed. He had only just returned from a similar meeting with Banks and the other captains and was still digesting the information himself. But now he knew their final destination it was essential his fellow officers were equally aware. "Commodore Popham set off last August to take the station back," he continued. "Though understandibly nothing was made of the fact at the time."

"Must have been a considerable fleet," Brehaut supposed. "And strange that none got wind of their leaving."

"They sailed from various ports and assembled at sea," King explained. "But the force was considerable and contained enough troops to carry the place."

"And did they?" Croft asked. King smiled; it was one of the first questions asked at the earlier meeting and he could only give the same answer as Banks.

"That is what we are to discover," he replied. "The escort was relatively light; three sixty-fours, a couple of frigates and some small stuff. Nothing has been heard from them since."

"Might they have known more at St Helena?" Brehaut suggested cautiously.

"They might," King conceded, "though we could not spare the

time to find out. And it would have made little difference: Commodore Popham's squadron was not due to call there on the way and, as the mission was housed in the deepest secrecy, most on the island probably remain unaware it was ever mooted even now."

"A force that size yet they did not call at St Helena?" Brehaut marvelled.

"That was the intention," King confirmed. "To have done so may have given the Dutch prior warning. As it was, they were expected to water at Salvador, then cross the Southern Atlantic and catch them unawares."

"That would be a hefty feat of navigation," Brehaut pulled at his chin in doubt.

"Well, let us hope they were successful," King answered softly.

"So what is our part in this?" Croft this time.

"We are to assess the situation and provide reinforcements where needed." King leaned back in his chair and considered his two officers. One he had known for many years, the other was a relatively new acquaintance, but neither were fools. And he realised then that it had become all too easy to regard them as confidants and allow far more licence than had been his custom in the past. On finally hearing the details of their mission from Sir Richard he had also been mildly disconcerted, and it was reassuring to note the same emotion on both their faces. "Since Commodore Popham left there have been reports of various French squadrons operating in the area; something we have been able to confirm for ourselves," he added with a touch of irony. "And there are more beyond the Cape; *Amiral* Linois is understood to be operating off the *Île-de-France* and has at least one eighty-gun ship in his command."

"And you think he might have run in with Popham's squadron?" Croft asked.

"It is a possibility; as I said, the escort was not large and there would have been a number of unarmed transports to protect."

"So are we to seek him out?" Brehaut this time.

"No," King replied firmly. "Our first and main consideration is to make for the Cape. If Commodore Popham has been successful in recapturing the colony, we must reinforce his troops while defending against counter-attack from the sea. Once the place is safely back under British rule the loss of supplies and repair facilities will confound an enemy squadron as effectively as if we had defeated them in combat."

"And if not," Brehaut again, "if Popham's force has been unsuccessful, or a French squadron has already met with them..."

"Then we must attempt to locate those of our ships that remain." King's tone, though positive, hid a myriad of doubts. "We might still mount a joint assault on the base using those reinforcements we are carrying, or try to establish a stronghold somewhere else but, either way, I think we may all now appreciate the need for haste."

"Linois is a tough character," Croft mused. "Gave Admiral Saumarez a run for his money at Algeciras."

"And he has not been idle whilst in Indian waters," King agreed. "We understand his squadron has taken a considerable number of our vessels while the fear of running in with him has dissuaded many more from sailing."

"Though he is not without fault," Brehaut added more optimistically. "Why I understand he was seen off by a fleet of Indiamen disguised as men-of-war in the past."

"Well, it will do little good to surmise further," King said, sitting forward in his seat. "Let us hope Commodore Popham has been successful, while being prepared for other measures if he has not." He paused as another thought occurred. "Though we have more reason than most to want the British flag flying over the Cape, for we are in dire need of a dockyard."

* * *

"She's *Narcissus*!" Adams whispered urgently whilst tapping Summers on his shoulder.

"What do mean?" the lad asked.

"*Narcissus*!" Adams repeated, his face now reddening with excitement. "Donnelly had her when we were blockading Toulon in *Prometheus*."

"You mean she's British?" Summers gasped.

"She were then," Adams confirmed only slightly louder.

Both turned their attention back to the warship that was

steadily closing on them. Though still apparently heading for the deep Atlantic, she would be passing them far closer than was normal.

"If so, what's their game?" Summers pondered softly.

"She may have been captured," Adams supposed as the doubts began. "But I'd recognise that prow anywhere – saw it often enough when we were on station."

As one, the pair looked over to the dockyard that was becoming more distinct with every moment. Nothing appeared untoward; the Batavian flags remained in evidence and there was no sign of military activity on the foreshore. To all intents, the French frigate was approaching a friendly port and would soon be dropping anchor.

"Are you certain?" Summers asked in a slightly louder tone.

"As I can be," Adams replied.

A party of Frenchmen pushed past them carrying small packages and heading for the foremast.

"They'll be preparing to send today's private signal," the younger man guessed, glancing in their direction. "Hoisting it for'ard to make sure it's seen."

Adams watched them go in silence although his mind was continuing to work. What he had said about being certain of *Narcissus*' identity was quite correct; he knew her as well as any vessel he had served alongside and was positive she now lay off the larboard bow and soon would be passing close by their beam. But quite what that meant when the Cape was still in the hands of the Dutch he could not comprehend. And there was something else, something that vaguely troubled him. The signals party that even now was attaching a series of canvas bundles to one of the fore halyards; they also had a bearing on matters although what exactly remained a mystery. And then it came to him.

"Come, Michael – we must move!" he cried urgently.

Summers' glance contained both alarm and concern; his friend had been behaving strangely for some time and now seemed to be including him in his madness.

"Move? But where?" he asked, but Adams had already grabbed his arm and was dragging him forward.

* * *

“Frigate's cutting it fine...” Greenwood commented as he peered forward through the open port.

“Aye,” Oats agreed, following his gaze. “What's that about then?”

“P'raps they means to speak with us?” Sennett suggested.

Rather than take advantage of the wide bay, the approaching warship continued to bear down on them in a manner that was, at the very least, foolhardy. And she seemed to be sailing with a minimal crew; hardly a man was visible on her main deck or forecastle while the quarterdeck only held a scattering of figures. Then, the final part of the puzzle; those that could be seen were stoically ignoring the waves and shouts rising up from the shore-starved crew in the French ship.

“Blowed if I knows,” Greenwood confessed, although he did have an idea that had already started to form. But it was such a foolish one that, however perfect it might seem, he instantly discounted it.

The two men detailed to guard them had also noticed the frigate's unusual behaviour. They, along with others close by, were obviously discussing it in thick guttural comments and Greenwood could also see Adams and the other young British officer pressing through the throng and creating all kinds of annoyance as they barged their way towards them.

“What's about, sir?” he asked, as they passed close by, but neither so much as glanced in his direction.

“Rum times,” Sergeant Bates muttered as all eyes returned to the frigate. She was now almost level with them and clearly preparing to turn.

“Less than a cable off now,” Sennett snorted. “An' looks to be wanting to round our stern.”

“That's damned queer sailing,” Oats murmured.

“Queer sailing? – I calls it something else,” Bates grunted. “What odds that we lose our gingerbread?”

“Aye,” Sennett agreed hesitantly. “If it weren't for them ensigns I'd say she were lookin' to rake us...”

And then, in what appeared to be one swift movement, the oncoming frigate's ports opened and her guns were run out, while the yards were brought round by men who magically appeared from the shelter of the bulwarks and the ship was thrown into a tight turn. Her hull dipped deeply and a cloud of spray rose up before the Batavian flags were finally whipped away only to be instantly replaced by British ensigns.

* * *

"What the devils going on?" Callahan demanded as he glowered about the quarterdeck. His wife's insistence on seeing to their luggage had left him without the means to communicate with the French crew, and now all hell seemed to be breaking loose.

"Damn it, man, can't you see they are British flags?" he bellowed at the captain, who gave him little more than a glance, although another officer shrugged in resignation. "You don't mean to let them take us, do you?" Callahan demanded.

There was no answer to his question and the American turned back as the oncoming warship cast a shadow over the quarterdeck. Then it was close alongside with men aboard her poised ready to clamber over their stern. A sudden thump sent a shudder throughout the French ship and there was the squeal of wood grinding against wood before the British were upon them, swinging themselves over the bulwarks like so many trained monkeys.

"Do you mean to offer no resistance?" Callahan all but screamed, although no one paid him any attention. Strange men were on the deck and advancing toward them; Callahan glanced at the captain who seemed determined to give up without protest. For a moment blind fury took hold; this was the end of his dream, of the work he had put into freeing his homeland from foreign rule. His plans were to be scuppered by timid Frenchmen in a land many miles from home. Well it would not do and, in a flash of anger, Callahan pulled out a small pocket pistol from his jacket and took aim.

* * *

"Get the code book!" Adams bellowed as the pair reached the break of the forecastle. Summers, who was slightly ahead and had now grasped what was about, dutifully snatched the leather-bound file from the hands of a bewildered signalman and headed back towards his friend. The French signals officer cried out in alarm and tried to grab it back, but Summers was too quick and tossed the thing to Adams.

The older lad caught it in a flutter of pages, but there were several French seamen close by and he looked around in desperation.

"Greenwood!"

The topman looked up at the call of his name and almost had to dodge the book that came spinning in his direction. But the thing was recovered easily enough and Greenwood tucked it firmly under his arm as he barged the guard that showed signs of wanting it back. The shrill scream of a whistle cut through their shouting; a single gun shot rang out and there was a cry from closer by as the second guard drew his sword. A quick glance was enough to show that the oncoming frigate was now firmly across the Frenchmen's stern and ready to deliver a devastating broadside.

"Secure yourselves!" Greenwood bellowed in alarm, while grabbing at Russell with his free hand and dragging him to the deck. For several seconds everyone waited but, rather than the crash of cannon fire, there came the almost gentle popping of small arms. Then the whistle sounded again and was followed by an angry voice bellowing in French. From his position on the deck, Greenwood tried to look round but he could see little and all he was really conscious of was the pain in his chest caused by concealing a remarkably hard little book.

4.

It was noon and they had been climbing for much of the morning yet still had a good deal further to go. Adams glanced up at the mass of sandstone that towered above them. Despite being in the midst of summer, a layer of cloud hung just above their heads that all but concealed the top of the mountain.

"What say we rest here and consider the view?" he asked.

Summers, some way behind and just as flushed, grunted in agreement before flopping down on a patch of short, tufted grass; one of many that maintained a perilous hold on the rock. Adams followed and for a moment neither spoke. Then, as strength returned, both hauled themselves up to their elbows and, still in silence, stared down at the town that lay beneath.

It was a small place and, from their viewpoint at least, appeared orderly and neat; long, straight streets that crossed at right angles to reveal the meticulous minds of their Dutch planners while the smart stone buildings with tiled roofs and square windows were the epitome of stability and order. From that distance there was no suggestion of the violence, confusion and occasional squalor that the pair had encountered over the last three days. But then the British had not been in control for long; it was only a month back that the expeditionary force had first laid sight on Table Bay and set about capturing Cape Town itself. Adams and Summers had heard the story a dozen times from as many sources and, if they were entirely honest, the exact details meant little; both having just been through enough dramas in their own lives to be totally uninterested in other people's.

The confusion would be temporary however as the British were well on the way to re-establishing order. Not all the inhabitants turned out to be Dutch, there being many other nationalities in the colony including a good many Huguenot French. Most cared little about their overall masters and were content to allow the British to resume rule if it meant their own lives could continue uninterrupted. And the capture of the ship that had held them both prisoner had been handled competently enough. With the sudden revelation that he was deep inside enemy waters, aided in no small way by Captain Donnelly's astute positioning of *Narcissus* across the stern of his ship, Captain Brunelle soon realised the futility of his position and his entire crew capitulated with little protest other than a few sour expressions. The frigate was brought to her mooring under the command of an immaculate Royal Navy lieutenant and a prize crew of grinning Jacks.

And then it had fallen upon Adams to do the explaining. Apart from his two examination boards and whoever commanded his particular ship, he had had little experience of dealing with senior officers, yet found himself positively bombarded with questions from any amount of gold braid. And not just the Navy; there were Army officers a plenty who would know more of his story while the make up and purpose of his original squadron was of interest to all. Most were convinced that Commodore Banks' final mission must be connected with the colony; something Adams was patently unable to confirm, but he was more capable when it came to providing information about Callahan.

The American had been the only casualty during the frigate's capture, a fact that still seemed remarkable and on so many levels. Callahan had been on a crowded quarterdeck when the British frigate came upon them, yet he alone offered any real resistance. Rather than bowing to the inevitable, the man had aimed a pistol at the first to board; the shot had gone wide but still provoked his own death, which had been instantaneous. Anne was understandably upset at the sudden killing of her husband, although privately Adams found it hard to feel anything other than relief, an emotion mingled with more than a little hope.

So he had answered the questions as they were posed, being careful to add nothing to implicate Anne who, with her husband dead and his plans apparently at an end, was allowed to go free. Soon she would be returning to Holland probably along with her brother and the rest of the defeated Dutch army although Adams was intending to see her before then. But he was in no rush; first a spell of peace was needed, a rest from the intensive questioning as well as those weeks of tension that had gone before.

Which was why he suggested the day out to explore the mountain and now felt glad he had, and that his old friend was still willing to accompany him.

"Seems a peaceful place from up here," Summers remarked as they continued to look down at the town below. Adams nodded in agreement; it was certainly good to be away from streets that echoed to the sounds of marching men, screaming children and the bellowing of wild-eyed officers. As part of the terms of surrender, their former enemies had been given relative freedom, along with the promise of return to Europe at Britain's expense, but that did not mean there was no friction between the two forces. Despite Governor Janssens' assurances, some of the Dutch or, more commonly, their French administrators, were still proving troublesome. Even in Adams' short stay there had been confrontations that ranged from slight scuffles to one outright pitched battle and, even though they concerned a minority of the former rulers, it was generally agreed that the sooner the old guard were gone the better.

And he supposed Sir David Baird, the new Governor, would have other problems; apart from those enemy merchant ships captured when the British took possession, there were a good many neutral traders, either in the various bays or attempting to gain entry, who wished to continue commerce with independent dealers in the town itself. These hailed from an assortment of impartial countries and no administrator could afford to offend any if they wished to protect future trade.

Governor Baird also had to see the civilian population were fed; after the British landed, warehouses had been closed either through fear of looting or with an eye to potential profits when resources ran short. There was little possibility that any would starve, but the situation must be eased as quickly as possible, and with the least offence to either party.

Then there were matters naval; Commodore Popham's original escort force had included three line-of-battleships and, even though these were antiquated sixty-fours, they could still put up a reasonable fight. But more would be needed if they were to properly defend the base, something that must surely be a priority.

The whole point in recapturing Cape Town had been to see it resume its place as a vital British outpost so it was important the station remained under the union flag. Troops from eight foot regiments along with a detachment of artillery had been used to retake it and men had certainly died, both while being tendered ashore and in what was now being referred to as the Battle of Blaauwberg. Adams was no expert on matters military but guessed enough remained for a healthy standing garrison, although how Bonaparte would react to learning one of his most valuable bases had been taken was another matter. More men might be brought from St Helena, but that was several weeks' sail away, and only a fool would weaken one stronghold in defence of another.

But these were someone else's problems and Adams was glad of the fact. After his brief sojourn into the world of higher responsibility, he had no wish for more and was content to lie back, breathe in clean fresh air and enjoy the fine weather.

"What say we eat?" Summers asked, casting a sidelong glance at his friend.

"I say we do," Adams agreed as he reached for the small

canvas bag that held their food.

It was beef, recently roasted and with equally fresh bread that was warm from the sun and smelt delicious. The two ate in silence and only when everything had been consumed and both were silently regretting not bringing more water to drink did Summers make the sighting.

"Topmasts," he said, pointing far out over the blue Atlantic.

Adams slowly opened his eyes to follow his gaze, then sat more upright as the significance registered; Summers was right, there was a positive fleet on the very edge of the horizon.

"A way off, but quite a force," he muttered as recent thoughts came back to worry him. "Do you think them British?"

"One can only hope," Summers replied. "News of the Cape's capture could hardly have spread far, so we cannot expect the French to have reacted quite so quickly."

Adams looked again, then found himself suppressing a yawn. The fleet, though large, was still a good way off, while the two of them were suitably hidden on a deep and anonymous mountain range many miles from the town. And with no ship to serve, or position to maintain, little would be required of them; a state of affairs that suited him perfectly. "You may well be right," he finally agreed, resting back once more and closing his eyes against the hot sun. "In fact I am sure of it."

* * *

Actually, Summers was spot on; before the pair had finished their day's excursion, the first of the ships had entered Table Bay. She was *Relentless*; the frigate's broad beam was especially noticeable as she rounded Green Point and, with the wind agreeably on her quarter, dropped anchor. *Hare* followed close behind for, such was the state of her hull and despite both pumps being manned continually, the brig had begun to settle.

King, standing on the quarterdeck as Banks exchanged signals with the shore, had seldom felt a deeper feeling of relief. The Indiamen were diverting to the merchant's anchorage and would probably begin disembarking their troops the following morning, and there was bound to be much coming and going before *Hare* was finally taken in hand. But the last few weeks of riding a steadily increasing swell had been a constant strain and he was now almost giddy with fatigue.

"Good to see solid ground once more."

It was Croft, the first lieutenant, although he was not addressing King, but Brehaut the sailing master.

"Aye," the Jerseyman agreed. "Good indeed."

* * *

"Have you met Sir Home before?" Faulks, the HEIC Commodore enquired, placing a comradely arm about Sir Richard's shoulder.

"I have not," Banks admitted as the two walked down the shabby corridor. "But have heard of him for sure."

"And will doubtless have utilised his telegraph book," the Company officer assumed. "I understand you men-of-war types swear by the thing."

"It has proved useful," Banks agreed more cautiously. "Though some messages are still sent in the former code."

"Indeed so?" Faulks reacted in mock horror. "Though Popham's was used at Trafalgar, were it not? 'England expects that every man shall do his duty' – was there ever a finer rallying cry?"

Sir Ralph Faulks was a Company officer of note and one with many connections in parliament, as well as commerce. But that hardly made Banks like him more – the reverse, if anything – and certainly did not grant the right to clasp him by the shoulder as if they were close acquaintances.

"Though even that had to be modified to comply with the code," Banks told him firmly. To his mind the signal had done little more than amuse the fleet, which had been Nelson's intention. The one that followed, 'engage the enemy more closely' came from the previous signal book and only required two flags and a single lift to convey a far more potent message.

"In truth, I am surprised two codes need be used," the larger man told him. "Rather typical of my lords of the Admiralty, would you not say?"

"How so, sir?" Banks enquired, his hackles rising slightly.

"Why, none will accept change!" Faulks declared in a bellow. "It is the same with all government departments and what separates them from honest traders. I tell you, sir, they would behave differently were the cold chill of impending debt playing about their shoulders!"

"Though they usually act when the time is ripe," Banks replied more levelly. He was aware of defects in the chain of command and had frequently discussed them in detail with officers of his own service, but when a man from private enterprise sought to criticise he was the first to jump to the Admiralty's defence. "More mistakes are made through haste than caution."

"Possibly," Faulks allowed. "Though at times it seems an idea might be rejected wholly because it came from Sir Home."

"Indeed?" Now Banks was genuinely interested. "Why so?"

Faulks paused for a moment and looked Sir Richard in the face. "I do know the man – know him quite well, actually," he confided in what was, for him, a soft tone. "And he is rather like yourself, if I may," Faulks added. "Not the kind that makes acquaintances easily."

Banks actually took a step backwards; it was an odd assertion for one senior officer to make to another and for a moment he was lost for words.

"Oh yes, I have worked alongside Commodore Popham on several occasions," Faulks continued, oblivious to any offence. They began to walk once more and the Company officer returned to speaking in his customary brash timbre. "And can verify for his competence – indeed, he has a brilliant mind... a brilliant mind," he repeated, the genial hand firmly back in place. "But not everyone can cope with such energy. The man has an enthusiasm rarely encountered, and such things are liable to offend those less talented."

Banks glanced at the fellow sharply, but Faulks' eyes were set ahead and he was now comfortably into his flow.

"Lord St Vincent does not have a kindly word to say for him," he continued. "And my Lord Howe likewise, though they do not know him as I, so truly should not be permitted to judge."

From what Banks knew, Lord St Vincent had openly accused Popham of corruption, a charge that had come about after his personal cargo was seized by the Royal Navy. It was one of several such stories currently circulating and many concerned the vast sums made through Popham's association with the East India Company; something that probably explained his friendship with

Faulks.

"Comes from a large family, some say fifteen siblings, others more, but there are as many half-brothers or sisters," the Commodore rumbled on. "Father was Britain's consul in Tetuan, don't you know?"

Banks didn't.

"And he were present aboard a frigate at St Vincent," Faulks added.

"As was I," Banks interrupted firmly.

"Ah, but this was the earlier battle," Faulks countered airily, as if dismissing Jervis' action as a mere skirmish. "And I understand Sir David Blair is a sound chap," Faulks continued. "Don't know the cove as well, of course, but he seems as solid as they come. I'd say that with him as Governor, and Sir Home our Commander-in-Chief, we are in excellent hands. Frankly, Sir Richard, nothing but good can come from it."

* * *

"Don't know about repair," Brown stated gloomily as he gazed out from the hard. "I'd say the old girl were ready for the knackers."

"It don't look good," Greenwood agreed.

Hare had originally been secured to a jetty but after the following tide had all but swamped her, now lay beached at an ignominious angle nearby.

"They say there's a dry dock of sorts hereabouts," Parker added more brightly. "Might only be a spot of trouble; she could be tight as a tick in a couple of months."

"Don't see it myself," Brown countered. "Way she were sitting, we're talking a total rebuild. Could take years, and who's going to waste a dock on a nothing brig-sloop, not when there are battle-waggons and Company liners what might be needin' it."

"So what would have happened to the men?" Russell asked. After their release from the French frigate, the former prize crew had been found accommodation in a military barracks. The place was comfortable enough but he had been looking forward to regaining his berth aboard *Hare*.

"Can't say," Greenwood shrugged. "If the barky really is crank, they're likely to have been turned over – as we probably will."

"Turned over?" Russell asked doubtfully.

"Moved to another ship," Parker explained.

"Does that mean we'll be split?"

"Not necessarily," Greenwood replied. "Might keep us together, though it ain't assured."

Russell stared morbidly at his former home. He might only have been aboard a matter of months with much of the time spent getting used to his new life. But now that he had, the prospect of a permanent move to another ship, with a different set of men and fresh routines, was strangely abhorrent.

"So there's a chance we'll stay as one crew?" he asked at last, and Greenwood regarded him with interest.

"Matters, does it?"

Russell nodded.

"Well, who'd have thought?" Parker pondered.

* * *

"You captured an enemy's signals book?" King remarked, the surprise evident on his face. Adams silently agreed.

"We figured such a thing would be useful, sir," Summers piped up from his side of the table.

"Forgive me, gentlemen, but they are not uncommon," King was speaking with obvious care as he looked from one to the other. "Why there are already several examples in British hands and few secrets to be found within."

"So we have discovered," Adams agreed.

"It is the daily codes that we are more in want of," King continued, adding, "though the signalling system itself may have changed," in an effort to appease.

They were sitting in the parlour of Johnston's, one of three large boarding houses in Cape Town's Keizersgracht. Despite the apparent choice, each differed little from its neighbour: solid houses, soundly built of whitewashed stone with three full stories and large squared windows that let in both light and air. The owners, a middle-aged couple whose original roots may have come from any of a dozen continental countries, were as happy to take English coin as Dutch or French. The food was reasonable as well and the four daughters kept it spotlessly clean. Adams and Summers had been sharing a room there since being freed and King, with the rest of *Hare*'s former officers, soon joined them.

"No, the system is the same," Adams confirmed sadly. "Nothing has changed and I should have made for the code book," he continued sadly, meeting King's eyes. "Though it were on the quarterdeck and was ditched with the other confidential papers."

"It is of no matter," King hurriedly assured the pair. "And your action shows remarkable spirit."

"That's not what Lieutenant Murray said," Adams sighed.

"Murray?" King questioned.

"Fellow what led the boarding party from *Narcissus,*" Summers explained.

"Told us we'd wasted our time and might have got killed," Adams added.

"Well it is no matter, and I am sure he will mention your action in any report, as I surely intend to," King continued. "For I still say it shows spunk."

Adams nodded silently once more and King sensed he was troubled.

"You have nothing to condemn yourself for in losing the prize," he added softly. "There is no shame in surrendering to such a force, as I myself can testify."

"I were out of station," Adams maintained. "With the same wind, both of us could have escaped."

"But we were in the midst of the doldrums," King reminded him. "Such latitudes are famously fickle; you cannot be held responsible for the weather."

"You don't understand, sir, I were distracted," Adams replied and the words had an element of final confession about them.

"Distracted?" King asked. "In what way?"

"One of the passengers," Summers interjected when no reply was forthcoming. "Tasty little mot with nice eyes," the boy added. "Especially the left one."

Adams glared at his friend but Summers was enjoying himself and paid no attention.

"John and her used to talk on the quarterdeck most evenings. Though there was nothing in it," he added quickly, sensing he may have gone too far.

King's mind went to Callahan's modest wife. He had been concerned about the woman, but only on account of the possible connection to Juliana; he could never have thought her capable of sabotage. "And did she encourage you to lose contact with *Hare*?" he asked seriously.

"No, no, of course not," Adams answered quickly. "She would never have done such a thing – I should not have let her. The fault were mine, I lost sight of what was about."

"And had been standing watch double tides for several days," King reminded him. "Being in command would also have been new to you, while there were prisoners to consider as well as passengers..."

As he spoke the words, King realised quite how much he had placed on the young man's shoulders and felt a pang of guilt. Perhaps Croft would have been a better choice after all? But then no officer progresses without a degree of stretching; it was simply a shame that, in Adams' case, he had been forced too far.

The man had his head down now and was staring at his hands. King glanced across at Summers who gave a barely perceivable shake of the head.

"Nothing will count against you for what happened," King spoke slowly and clearly, even if Adams did not appear to hear. "You will find a posting as lieutenant and continue your career and be all the better for the experience."

"You think so, sir?" he asked, looking up.

"I am sure of it," King told him firmly.

* * *

"Gentlemen, please be seated." The tall man who had been introduced as Sir David Baird was dressed in the uniform of a Lieutenant-General. He smiled easily as he stood to greet them, and waved to chairs on the opposite side of a large oak desk. It was a big room with a high ceiling although the carpet was scuffed and the windows that looked out over Table Bay decidedly grubby.

"You will have to excuse the state of these quarters," the man continued in a deep, pleasant tone that had the hint of a Scottish accent. "We have only been in place a matter of weeks and there has been much to do. My offices are elsewhere, as are Sir Home's," he added, "who will no doubt join us shortly."

At that moment the door behind them flew open and a slighter figure in Naval uniform propelled itself into the room.

"Ah, Sir Richard, Sir Ralph, my apologies," Commodore Popham announced while crossing the floor in several quick strides. "I have been with General Janssens, the former Governor, and he is not a man to rush."

"Our visitors have only just this moment arrived," Baird explained as the Commodore took a chair next to him and immediately began to fiddle with the arm rest.

"Well, doubtless you have heard our news to date," Popham remarked, abandoning the furniture and fixing his entire attention on Banks and Faulks. "We took the place from the Dutch without a great deal of trouble, though recapturing a port is never the simplest of procedures."

"In truth, there is still much to be done," Baird agreed more moderately. "And the convoy home is currently in preparation, it should be departing within the month."

"That will be transferring captured troops back to Europe," Popham interjected. "Together with their commanders and any civilians who have no wish to remain."

"Are they all Dutch?" Banks asked.

"In the main, yes," Baird confirmed. "Though some officials are French."

"And a few of the rank and file are local; most of whom have agreed to serve His Majesty," Popham added with a glance at Baird, and Banks was strangely reminded of past conversations he had held with long-married couples.

"But first you must tell of your own exploits," Baird suggested. "Though we have heard much from Mr Adams, of course."

"Then there is little that either of us might add," Banks responded quickly as he sensed Faulks might have a monologue planned. "My ships are at your disposal, of course."

"As are my men," Faulks agreed. "There are slightly over five thousand Company troops disembarking as we speak and I also have a deal of administration officers who will do what they can to take pressure from you both."

"Which will be welcome," Baird assured him with a polite nod.

"With luck we should have the post running efficiently for the rest of the season, then can begin the next on a surer footing," Faulks added and was about to elaborate when Popham cut across him.

"Remind me of your exact force, Sir Richard," he demanded, oblivious of any offence caused to the Company officer.

Banks drew breath. "I have *Relentless*; she is a nominal thirty-eight, though a razee, as I am sure you are aware. There are two further fifth rates and a brig-sloop; the latter requires immediate dockyard attention."

"Dockyard attention? Ha!" Popham fairly exploded. "That is something we cannot provide I fear."

"*Raisonable* has need of what provisions there are," Baird explained more gently. "And we have several Indiamen with prior claim."

"But your ships are a useful addition, none the less," Popham conceded quickly, "though I had hoped for more; a couple of seventy-fours at least or perhaps a three-decker..." he added, his mind seemingly drifting to another place.

Banks made no reply; it was not for him to justify his masters' decisions although frigates would surely be of more use where long-distance policing against pirates and privateers would be a major consideration.

"We have to guard against the French taking the station back," Baird explained.

"And not just that," Popham added. "Now that we are in place, there may be other conquests to be made."

Banks tried to show no surprise. All he had heard of Popham was certainly proving correct: the man was a positive firebrand. But as to extending his domain, he could see little prospect of that – unless the Commodore nurtured plans on taking the *Île-de-France* or somewhere even further afield.

"But for the time being we are well enough served," Baird assured them hastily. "For we have also been provided with an excellent French vessel that is ready to take into the service."

"Indeed, she all but fell into our lap!" Popham exclaimed with delight. "Kind of the French to deliver such a present."

"She appears a fine ship," Baird agreed.

"Which will need a crew, though that will not be so much of a problem. With Sir Ralph's additional troops now on station I shall approach my Marine Brigade," Popham continued. "They are the seamen and marines I led during our action on land," he added for his visitors' benefit. "A few will never become land animals and would be better placed at sea – I always believe a man is most useful where he feels comfortable, don't you agree Sir Richard?"

Banks went to reply but it seemed none was necessary, for Popham was talking again.

"Yes, get them back on the briny, they will be less trouble there – for me at least," he added with a sudden grin. "And such a fine frigate shall make a desirable berth indeed. Now who can we find to command her?"

5.

The news that *Hare* was to be condemned hit King far harder than he anticipated and, though not exactly taken to his bed, he had been unusually listless ever since. Of course, it should not have been a great surprise; an immediate start could never have been guaranteed and he had already resigned himself to wasting a good few months on the beach, as well as possibly losing some of his key men, while the hull was rebuilt. But even before the brig's holds were emptied it became apparent she would need more than a simple re-caulk. The lower frames and strakes were rotten to the extent that how *Hare* could have been presented as seaworthy when he took her over was a mystery.

All the brig's officers had taken up residence in Johnston's, the boarding house discovered by Adams and Summers. Together they had effectively turned much of the place into a combination of great cabin, gunroom and cockpit, with King's own quarters appropriately occupying three rooms on the top story. It was comfortable enough, and something of the former hierarchy of *Hare* had been preserved although he knew it would not be long before alternative employment were found for Croft, Brehaut and Manning, with Adams and the more junior men probably leaving even sooner.

But he would not be so fortunate. The opportunities for a Commander were far more limited; most warships were too large for one of King's rank to legally captain while he was equally too senior to take up a lieutenant's post. The answer would probably turn out to be a permanent shore berth, and that was not a prospect he welcomed.

The months spent on Sir Alexander Ball's staff had been enough to show how totally unsuited he was to desk work and, since then, King had been promoted, then gone on to command two minor warships. To return from such a position and face a future filled with files, agendas and innumerable meetings seemed bleak indeed. He would be entitled to full pay, so Aimée could continue to draw her allowance, but without a command any chance of earning prize money must go by the board. He supposed he might opt to return home; a berth would be available in the convoy due to return the Dutch military to Europe; he might be back with Aimée in time for the start of summer. But although prospects for employment were ostensibly better there, the competition for posts would also be high, and a man who had allowed one command to be taken from him while the next rotted away beneath his feet would not be valued greatly.

However, that was for the distant future. Nothing would happen for several days and he was more than content to spend the time lounging in the unusual comfort of a fine arm chair, his stocking feet stretched out upon a carpeted floor in a house that, for the time being at least, still housed so many close friends.

"There is a visitor to see you, sir."

So intent on his idleness had he been that King totally missed hearing McNamara enter and the servant's soft voice actually made him jump.

"A visitor?" he asked vaguely

"Commodore Banks, sir. He is waiting below. Would you have me show him up?"

"No, I shall come down," King struggled to his feet. He had truly meant to call on Sir Richard; the brief interview after *Hare* was condemned hardly being sufficient to sort out all the implications. Then, as he allowed his servant to help him on with his boots, another thought occurred.

Banks was a man of action and hardly in the habit of making house calls. He may be bringing important news, in which case King was especially intrigued. He knew him well enough to guess he would equally welcome fresh air; a decent stroll along Gentleman's Walk would do them both good and was the closest he was likely to come to pacing a quarterdeck for some time. And even if this turned out to be nothing more than a social visit, it would be a chance to get free from the uncomfortable little chair and the claustrophobia of a crowded house.

* * *

"Should you be here?" the woman asked and Adams shrugged.

"No one stopped me," he said, sensing slight hostility. "And I wanted to see you again before you left."

Anne looked at him for a moment, then up and down the empty corridor before opening the door wider. "You'd better come in," she said at last.

It was a plain little room set amid the boarding house's copious attic: two floors and a decent walk away from Adams' own quarters. And it was furnished far more sparsely, with no rugs or carpet. Anne indicated the only chair and the lad took a step towards it but did not sit.

"You are well, I trust?" he asked, looking into her eyes and finding them slightly reddened.

"My husband is dead," she replied coldly, "and I am miles from home – how should I feel?"

"But your brother?" he asked.

"My brother is dead also; at least that is how it appears." She had turned away and was considering herself in a small mirror over the washstand. "And if so, it would be at the hands of the English when they invaded this place."

Adams closed his eyes for a moment. "Anne, I am so sorry," he said, "though I had nothing to do with it."

"No, I do realise that," she agreed, returning after the briefest adjustment to her hair. "And you must forgive me, I am not quite myself at present." For a moment she put a hand out to him; he went to take it, but the thing was gone and she had stepped back before he could. "It is nothing to do with you – nothing to do with either of us, though a mess we are all caught up in." The woman's voice had lost its previous intensity and was now little more than a murmur while her expression was visibly dissolving even as he watched. "Oh, John why did it have to be this way?"

Then she was in his arms and the tears began.

"I'm sorry, Anne, truly," he mumbled, awkwardly patting at her shoulder. With much of his adult life being spent at sea and in the company of men, this was as intimate as Adams had been with one of the opposite sex and he was feeling his lack of experience.

"It's not my husband," she assured him through gasps. "Or even Wieb really – I just don't know what to do. I feel so alone."

"You are not alone," he told her softly. "I shall take care of you."

She leant back and considered him for a moment. "But you do not know me; not truly," she protested.

"What I know I like," he answered with the simplicity of youth, "and think we were meant to be together."

She smiled faintly and shook her head. "How can that be? You are an Englishman; we are enemies."

Adams led her across to the bed and, after an awkward pause, they sat down beside one another.

"My captain is English," he said, her hand still resting in his, "yet his wife Dutch – nothing is impossible."

"But the plan David had for invading Ireland..." she began.

"Has any more been said of that?" he asked.

She shook her head though the tears were still close by.

"Then you must not, nor will I," he said. "With your husband's death the whole matter may be forgotten and you can return to Holland with others of your country – if that is what you wish, of course."

"I see little choice," she sighed. "Though it is not my country and hasn't been for many years. And I do not mean because I am now an American," she added before he could interrupt. "That was to please David, and so we could be married. Holland is my home and always will be but it is not as I remember, not since the French came."

"Then why not England?" Adams asked, and her eyes opened wider.

"England?"

"As I have said, Commander King's wife is Dutch, and lives in London. There is no reason why you should not do the same."

"But you do not understand, the English killed my husband and probably my brother – if it were not for you I would hate them more than any other nation."

"Then stay here," Adams suggested. "We might both – with no ship I have every reason to resign and find work as well as a place for us to live. There is the East India Company; they are setting up their base once more so must have employment for someone of my experience. I could look after you and we might be happy."

"It is a consideration, I suppose," she allowed at last. "But I cannot ask you to change your life, not for someone you have only just met."

"It is something I am willing to do," he assured her.

"I have no money," she finally confessed. "David was so strict with such things and always paid for everything. All I could find were a few coins and they are spent. Oh, he has other funds but was intending to raise them from a bank in Cape Town. And I suppose I might discover which in time..."

"I do not have much," Adams admitted, "but you may have it all. And I can raise more, I am sure of it," he added encouragingly.

"I do not like to ask," she declared. "Though even a few pounds would mean so much..."

"Of course," Adams assured her. "I will come back this very afternoon."

"Then I shall wait for you," she said, smiling also.

* * *

"A frigate?" King gasped in disbelief as he and Sir Richard strode away from the boarding house.

"Indeed," Banks confirmed with a grin. "The Frenchie that were taken afore we arrived."

King nodded; he knew the ship well. She had held Adams and the rest of the prize crew prisoner and since been much admired by every sea officer on the station.

"But I am not made post," he protested. They paused as a

small carriage passed by, then both hurried across the street.

"It would be a temporary position to begin with; as Commander-in-Chief, Sir Home is privileged to make such appointments," Banks explained when they reached the other side. "Why I understand he has already given another commander charge of a fifty-gun fourth rate and made a lieutenant captain of a brig similar to *Hare*."

"But can he truly do such a thing?"

"Tom, do you not remember your own commission as lieutenant?" Banks asked, the grin still firmly in place.

"Why yes, it were down to Sir John Jervis," King agreed.

"When he was C-in-C Mediterranean; the Admiralty confirmed it immediately afterwards as I recall, as is usually the case. And I might also add that Sir Home's own promotion to commander, and then subsequently post captain was entirely at the bequest of the Duke of York in very much the same manner."

King nodded meekly as the full realisation dawned on him.

"She is a fine ship," he muttered eventually.

"I should say," Banks agreed. "Not as stable or strong as *Relentless*, but a worthy fifth rate none the less. Long eighteens as a main battery – or at least the French equivalent, and I understand she left the shipyard no more than a year back. We're retaining her name as there is nothing like it in the fleet."

"Which is?"

"*Mistral*."

"Appropriate," King mused before adding, "I shall need officers," as the thoughts began.

"You may take all available from *Hare*," Banks reminded him. "Adams can use his commission as lieutenant and the other juniors will surely follow, though more shall be needed for such a vessel."

"And men?" King asked, still hardly daring to believe.

"Sir Home is willing to allow any from the Marine Battalion ashore to volunteer."

"I don't know what to say..." King finally confessed.

"Then say nothing," Banks instructed. "There are still several hours of light left, and I would welcome the distraction. What say we go and inspect your new command?"

* * *

"How much?" Summers asked.

"Ten guineas," Adams told him and the lad shook his head.

"I don't have anything like that sort of chink," he admitted.

"Well, what can you summon?"

"Perhaps one, if I count everything."

Adams sighed; that would not do at all. Ten guineas was actually quite an arbitrary figure: one he had summoned up as being suitable for the needs of a mature woman who would be waiting for him while he, her partner, earned more. But he could barely raise four himself and had been depending on Summers for the lion's share. That is until his so-called friend let him down.

"What do you want it for?" Summers asked.

"It's not for me," Adams snapped.

"And I suppose that Callahan mot has nothing to do with it?"

Adams' face reddened suddenly and Summers thought he might have over-stepped the mark, but the older lad soon recovered.

"What if it is?" he demanded.

Summers shrugged. "I'm simply surprised, that's all. Her husband made himself out to be warm enough; she can surely get an advance from his bankers."

For a moment Summers' reasoning broke through and Adams was in irons, then a fresh wind caught him.

"Look, if you don't have any rhino, can you not borrow?"

"I suppose I might approach the purser," Summers replied doubtfully. "Though old man Foil charges ten in the hundred."

"Do that," Adams instructed. "And I shall also: we can visit him together – do you know where he is berthed?"

"This very building, as I understand," Summers answered. "But wait – there surely cannot be the need for haste?"

"Oh there is need all right," Adams assured him as he turned for the door. "As you yourself will know one day, when you are in my position."

* * *

For many years Croft had purposefully lived without ambition; that he had managed to secure his post aboard *Hare* was fortunate enough and he had stoically stuck by the old girl through several gruelling years and three increasingly younger commanders. Throughout that time both he, and the brig, had grown more weary and it had been a private assumption that, when the time came for her final paying off, he would also retire. But such a thing was hardly feasible on a South Atlantic station many miles from England. Besides, it seemed others held greater confidence in him than he did himself for, by some unexplained miracle, he had been appointed first lieutenant of a prime frigate.

It was a position that carried far more strain and responsibility than his last posting and even that had been dragging him down of late. But as soon as he stood on the new ship's quarterdeck and took in her size; the height of the spars that towered above and gauged the weight of the hull beneath his boots, he was filled with a new and welcome energy.

Quite where this had come from Croft had no idea; he could only suppose it was one thing to have charge of a worn out brig-sloop with a leaking hull and no other lieutenant to share the pressure, and quite another to manage an all but brand new warship with able officers aplenty to support him.

And what a fine craft she was – Toulon built from Adriatic oak, and with surprisingly good masts that would serve for many years. There were areas that betrayed her French origin: she lacked adequate supplies, stores of both canvas and cordage were pathetically low and there were no replacement spars of any variety. But much would be available from the Company yard; he would simply have to indent for them, as he would turpentine, tar, pitch and other consumables they were likely to need. He did have round shot for the cannon, as well as canister and bar, though very little powder, and he would have to discover if the slightly oversized French pieces would take standard cylinder or prefer something less volatile.

The more he became involved, the greater his responsibilities for commissioning such a warship appeared; there would be far more complex station and watch bills to write up, not to mention the less official organisation required when so many men are managed. But he already had the core of an experienced crew from *Hare*'s people, the rest were to be provided by Commodore Popham and they would not only be trained hands but men who had volunteered for the posting. A seemingly sufficient number of junior officers had also been promised so, after only a short period of working up, they should have a good, tight complement. And, though the task that lay before him still seemed enormous, he was surprised to discover himself relatively undaunted.

Since being appointed to the ship, Croft had barely been ashore, the rest of the time having been spent inspecting every inch until he knew her better than any and, though they had yet to take her to sea, already had a fair idea how she might handle. With principle dimensions greater than most British vessels of her class and an elegant hull that was far more graceful, she would be both stable and fast. Whether her slightly lighter timbers would stand up to as much punishment, both in battle and from prolonged exposure at sea, was another matter although, as far as Croft knew, there were no plans for using her for blockading duties. Instead, they were on a South Atlantic station where speed and firepower were at a premium, and Croft felt she could not have been better placed.

And the strange thing was that, though he had barely slept since being told of this new challenge, and despite all his waking hours having been fully used ever since, Croft did not feel in any way tired. The reverse in fact: he now found himself drawing on previously unknown reserves of energy while his general temper, which he privately acknowledged had become fraught and brittle whilst maintaining *Hare*, was now far more sanguine. Though physically exhausted at the end of each day, he slept better and generally felt more relaxed than he had been in ages. His appetite was also improved and he could deal with awkward situations or seemingly impossible people far more easily. But the main change was one that did not spring immediately to mind, and only occurred to him now, in a moment of rare reflection. The position of first lieutenant was a difficult one, and carried more responsibility for the actual fabric and working of a ship than even the captain. Yet he felt he was up to it: more than that, it was as if he were born to the task. And not for some time had he even entertained the thought that he might be too old.

6.

Hare was the only warship Russell had served aboard so he naturally assumed her cramped quarters and the permanent odour of rot to be standard for the breed. His time as a prisoner in *Mistral*'s stuffy forward store room had hardly altered this opinion so, when he finally stepped on the frigate's berth deck as both a free man and part of her crew, his surroundings came as a pleasant surprise.

"This is far more the thing," he remarked, gazing in wonder at the empty space that smelled of nothing worse than pitch and mildly stale humanity.

"Frigates are known to be a deal more airy," Greenwood agreed while the rest of his mess examined their new quarters. "And the old *Hare* was about as tight as you can get."

"Mind, she's not been long afloat," Jackson added as he fingered the spirketing doubtfully. He, along with some of the older hands, were not so impressed and found no difficulty in saying so. "A year at the most – not even the French could mess up a ship in that time."

"I hears the Frogs have some nasty habits," Swain agreed. "Like burying their dead in the ballast."

"Is that right?" Russell asked doubtfully.

Greenwood treated Swain to a stern look. "Might have done so in the past," he allowed. "Though I've never come across it m'self."

"When you works below, such things is important," the holder assured them.

"Well this one's not been at sea that long," Greenwood maintained. "Few gallons of vinegar and a dab of elbow grease and you won't find a better berth south of the line." He had heard there was usually a degree of resistance when a fresh crew took over a captured enemy ship and the last thing Greenwood wanted was his mess getting off on the wrong foot. But Russell had no argument; whatever her origin, to his eyes the frigate was a distinct improvement to the dingy little brig-sloop they had left behind.

"Might seem large enough now, but there'll be more'n two hundred down here, if they gets all they want," Jackson persisted as he stared down the length of empty deck.

"And still she won't feel full," Greenwood added.

"Deckhead's almost a foot higher," Parker pointed out more positively as he examined the hammock cleats on one of the oak beams.

"Then there'll be draughts," Swain countered. "Known it before in frigates; far too open. Give me a thumper every time – they has the best messes. Nothing like a pair of decent sized cannon at either side to make for a warm caulk."

"If you want a two-decker there are three on the other side of the anchorage," Parker replied. "Though they're nought but tiddlers – sixty-fours – hardly large enough to stand in the line while a frigate like this can give royals and t'gallants and still leave them in her wake."

"Besides, if there are draughts they'll rig screens," Greenwood told Swain firmly. "Ask me we got ourselves a sound ship and, after what happened to the old *Hare,* should be grateful – it's a long way back to England and this one feels like she might make it."

"Aye, I suppose she's sound enough," Jackson agreed reluctantly. "For a Frog build."

"French build good ships otherwise we wouldn't be copying them so," Greenwood maintained. "There are plenty of decent barkies in the fleet what started out in French yards."

There was a pause while all digested this.

"I suppose the scran might be better," Swain speculated. "Did you see the size of the galley?"

"Frogs carry more men," Jackson grunted. "An' they do so like their grub."

"So when we going to get underway?" Swain demanded.

"When the rest joins us," Greenwood replied. "Buzz is there's a draft coming over from a marine battalion."

"Jollies?" Brown asked in mock horror and Greenwood shook his head.

"They're Jacks like us what's been drafted ashore and now want for a new home."

"So when they going to get here?" Jackson again.

"Soon," Greenwood's answer carried more than a hint of annoyance.

"An' what they going to be like?" Swain this time.

"Well, we don't know that do we?" Greenwood snapped as exasperation finally set in. "We'll just have to wait and find out."

* * *

Mistral's great cabin was also a spacious area and made the more so by its lack of furniture; King had been in command of the ship for barely two weeks and there had been so much to do that little attention could be spared for fitting out his own quarters. But his old mahogany table had been recovered from *Hare*, as well as the chairs used for dining. All of these were currently in use as King had called a meeting for his more senior officers and, as he surveyed the two rows of faces, he was mildly gratified by their number.

In addition to Croft, Brehaut, Manning and Adams – the latter having finally been fully commissioned as a lieutenant – there were two additional men in the form of Murray, the new second officer, and Hopkins who was to lead their marines. King considered the newcomers as they sat amidst the more familiar faces. Murray was older and doubtless more experienced than Adams, though King still wondered if he were still a little young for such responsibility. He had come across from *Narcissus,* where he was fourth lieutenant, so personal advancement gave sufficient reason for the transfer even if it was slightly disconcerting to note the willingness with which Donnelly had let him go. Despite the name, Murray came from Sussex and carried with him an accent and manner that suggested the aristocracy. But there had been something about the man that worried King and, when he pressed him in private, he had reluctantly admitted his father to have been a blacksmith. To King's mind there was no disgrace in that; it might even be considered an attribute, although trying to disguise the fact was definitely not.

Hopkins was more easily classified, however; King had met a dozen like him in the past and was inclined to treat all of the type with caution, for there was little of the salt in the man. He might as easily have been a guards officer and, like Murray, appeared far too confident for his position. The trait was hardly eased and may even have been caused by his lack of stature. Should he take the trouble to check, King was sure Hopkins met the regulation height for marine officers but that hardly compensated for his slight frame which made him look almost frail when seen in company with some of the brutes he commanded. But a lack of physique did not bother King unduly; Hopkins still behaved as if he were God's gift and only tolerating a position aboard *Mistral* until something better came along.

Being that they had joined together, King supposed it natural that the two new men should have struck up a friendship, although their mealtime conversation, frequently interspersed with resounding guffaws, was powerful enough to infiltrate King's own quarters on the deck above and make him glad he did not have to share the gunroom.

With Croft very much on the old side and young Adams still finding his feet, these were not the tight set he could have wished for as his senior men. But he had worked with worse and, with the reassuring presence of Brehaut and Manning, King still felt much could be made of them.

"I realise every one of us have many tasks in hand and assure you this will not take long," King began. "Though I felt it best if we all met officially and discussed the ship's future."

There was a general nodding of heads and perhaps it was nerves that made Hopkins give a toothy grin, but King overlooked that.

"First I have to inform you that we are to be leaving for St Helena the day after tomorrow."

That evoked far more reaction; Croft, Brehaut and Manning exchanged glances, while Hopkins reddened slightly and Murray began to blow through his lips as if he were in the act of deflating. Only Adams remained totally composed; something that surprised King and was a point in the lad's favour.

"Accordingly, there will be no working up, as such," he continued. "On leaving Table Bay we will head straight for Jamestown carrying despatches for the Governor there, so I have no wish to turn back or delay in any way." King knew not taking the customary month or so of short trips to allow the new ship to settle was a risk; much could happen during the first few days at sea and to commit to a long journey immediately was almost asking for trouble. But with other frigates on the station, the competition for independent jaunts was strong and he considered it fortunate that *Mistral* had been given this opportunity. Besides, he assured himself, if the hands were thrown into active service, they may settle all the quicker. "Is that of concern to anyone? Mr Croft?"

It was fitting that the executive officer should be consulted first, if perhaps a little unfair, although King was pleased to note him more than ready to respond.

"I can foresee no problems, sir," the older man replied confidently. "We are still awaiting some purser's and gunner's stores and I should like to refresh all our water, though, in every other respect, *Mistral* is ready to sail."

"Gunner's stores?" King questioned.

"Refinements for the French cannon," Croft explained. "Nothing that we cannot do without."

"Very good," King allowed. "And our complement?"

"The last of the people were received this morning; if anything we are slightly over subscribed," Croft answered with a rare smile. "It would seem that service in *Mistral* is a popular option with the Commodore's land forces."

"Probably glad to be away from the old man," Murray interjected with a smirk that was mirrored by Hopkins, and King directed a cold look in their direction.

"Whether that is the case or not I cannot tell," Croft continued, "though we have a proportion of able to ordinary, and indeed ordinary to landsmen, that is quite unheard of. Some are native troops that were originally recruited locally, though most have seen extensive service in a man-of-war before joining the Commodore's Marine Battalion."

"And petty officers?"

"Sufficient," Croft was less positive. "There are no gunner's mates, though I have singled out three quarter gunners that may be suitable and the cook is not experienced. He is well supported, however, and I do not think there will be a problem on that front."

"Mr Manning, can you comment on their general fitness?"

"The new men are generally healthy, sir," the surgeon replied. "A few were rejected due to abdominal strain and there was one whom I suspected of harbouring the flux, but the majority are sound."

"That is good news indeed," King, who had already been

aware of each point, nodded. “And Mr Brehaut, are you satisfied?”

“I am, sir,” the sailing master agreed. “I have reliable masters mates and Summers is proving a very able midshipman as will Dilson in time I am sure. Cole is also improving and may be considered as midshipman before long; he definitely has the mind for navigation, though there is yet more space in the starboard cockpit.”

Brehaut's last point was not to be surprised at considering their station; had they been nearer England, King might have filled both midshipmen's berths with the sons of fellow officers or minor dignitaries and made a fair amount for himself into the bargain.

“May we promote from within?” he asked.

“There are a number of hands who have shown aptitude and might be considered as volunteers,” Brehaut replied thoughtfully.

“Then I would be glad to hear of them,” King declared, adding, “Speak to me at some point, if you please,” before turning to the new second lieutenant.

“Mr Murray, you are settling in, I trust?”

“Never better,” the young man assured him with perhaps too much bonhomie. “She's a fine ship and will serve us well, I think.”

“I am very glad to hear it,” King confirmed. “And Mr Hopkins, how are your men?”

“They are in reasonable shape,” Hopkins announced, “though would benefit from a deal of exercise.” King nodded in apparent satisfaction although he still retained serious doubts about the new officer. Perhaps it was his pale skin that was surely a sign of time spent indoors, or maybe the fair hair that was faintly tinged with red, but Hopkins did not come across as what the men would regard as a hearty.

“And Mr Adams?” King said, turning with relief to the last face. “I am sure you have already been welcomed into the gunroom, but I wanted to say how glad I am your commission is finally confirmed.” King beamed at the lad with genuine pleasure.

“Thank you, sir,” Adams replied, although there might have been a trace of doubt in his voice.

“Are you settled in your duties?” King enquired.

“Oh yes, sir,” Adams confirmed with rather more certainty. For a moment King considered him; he could not be sure, but there was something about the young man that seemed different. It was as if he were keeping a secret, or had something else on his mind. Or he could simply be adapting to a very different life amongst commissioned officers. Stepping from the cockpit to the illustrious world further aft was a major change, and the lad should be allowed a little leniency. Although not too much, King decided privately. For there was an aspect in that look of preoccupation that he did not like at all.

"Then there is nothing left to say," King concluded, turning to the group in general. "All look to your various departments and prepare to be underway at first light Tuesday morning. Are there any questions?" His glance took in every face in less than a second, but was sufficient to tell him all appeared ready. Though whether they truly were was yet to be seen.

* * *

"Look alive there!" Harridge, the boatswain, bellowed. The new men had been aboard for more than a day and all had claimed to be proper Jacks, yet there were some that seemed as bewildered as any landsmen. "We stows our hammocks like so," he continued, snatching the thing from the bemused man's hand and thrusting it into the netting correctly. "That way they forms a decent wall and one you'll be grateful for when the shot starts a flyin'." He turned away in disgust and met the eyes of Adams, the newly appointed lieutenant.

"New intake giving you a hard time are they, Pipes?" Adams enquired.

"Oh you wouldn't believe it, Mr Adams – sir," Harridge hastily corrected himself as he remembered the young man's new rank. "Most is all right but some are the biggest bunch of lubbers I've ever had to deal with. An' I seen a few."

Adams grimaced in sympathy; he supposed that if some exaggerated their experience to gain a higher rating it wasn't to be surprised at, such a thing was common amongst new recruits. The majority looked sound though and they were fortunate to be allowed so many. "They'll settle," he assured the boatswain. "It's always the same with new men."

“Not all new men,” the voice came from behind and interrupted Harridge's chuckle. Both turned to see Murray, the freshly appointed second lieutenant, standing stiffly behind them. As always, he was dressed in a crisp tunic with britches and stockings whereas Adams, who had more excuse than most to be wearing fresh cloth, wore an old blue round jacket and seaman's trousers.

“We were not meaning yourself, sir,” Adams hurriedly assured him.

“I should think not,” Murray agreed as he stepped forward. “New hands being put through their paces are they?”

“We've just piped 'up hammocks',” Adams explained diffidently. “Though there are exercises set for the rest of the forenoon watch. Topmen aloft and drill for fo'c's'le and quarterdeck servers. Then a general drill for the main battery this afternoon.”

“Indeed, I shall be supervising the gunners myself,” Murray assured him as his eyes pointedly swept down Adams' shabby attire. Sensing possible trouble Harridge had already melted away and the pair were as alone as was possible on a crowded deck. “And I gather you will be assisting me?”

“Yes, sir,” Adams agreed.

“Well try and spruce yourself up before then,” Murray advised. “Doesn't do to dress like a warrant officer, not when there are new hands about.”

“I have just the one tunic, sir,” Adams replied guardedly. “My commission was only recently confirmed.”

“And do they not have any ashore?” Murray enquired with an ironic lift of one eyebrow.

“Probably, sir, though I have been committed on board and not had chance to enquire.” Adams had already marked out the new man as something of a stickler; his insistence on being addressed formally even when below deck and off duty, was one indication, as was his own dress, which was invariably immaculate. And he was clearly not without means; to maintain such standards would entail several changes a day. Whoever had been allotted to attend him as steward had certainly drawn the short straw.

“And try not to be too familiar with the petty officers,” the new man continued in a slightly softer tone. “Addressing the bosun as Pipes is a lower deck trick. You are commissioned now and of the quarterdeck; it would be better if you behaved like it.”

* * *

But though some habits remained unbroken, and even with Adams unable to source a second tunic, *Mistral* sailed with the tide on the following Tuesday morning. Standing on the quarterdeck as the wind caught each successive sail, while breathing in the warm salt air and feeling the deck come to life beneath his feet, King discovered he was more than satisfied. To all intents he had been made post and, more immediately, had a fine frigate to command. Things would have to go very wrong indeed for the Admiralty not to approve either promotion or appointment and, considering their remote location, even that eventuality must be several months away. So for now and the foreseeable future he was free to improve what he knew to be a fine ship while looking forward to the day when formal confirmation was received.

And then he would have truly arrived. Once officially on the captains' list, King need only survive and remain in service long enough to hoist his flag, something he was still young enough to regard as a distinct possibility. More than that, his wages would rise significantly as must the chance of earning prize money. Considering her class and the rich pickings from India and the East that regularly passed by the Cape, the likelihood of him making a substantial pile had definitely increased and, with no Admiral on station, would not be depleted by an extra share elsewhere.

This first independent commission was not likely to be the last either. He could look forward to several such solo missions away from any overbearing flag officers; time when he was the ultimate authority and in total charge of the ship and where she might carry them. Admittedly the current mission was little more than an outing: a mere run to and from St Helena. If all went well they could be back at the Cape within a month. But he would be in sole command throughout and, once the despatches were delivered, free to take a little longer in returning, especially if the prospect of a prize, or some other action, came his way.

St Helena might hold some memories that were probably best

left undisturbed but old friends could be found there as well. Fraiser, the elderly Scottish sailing master from *Scylla*, had chosen to retire to the island and may yet be alive, and there were others who would doubtless remember the young and foolish lieutenant that had once been Tom King. It would be good to return as a more mature senior officer; one who, though wounded, had evidently progressed and now held command of his own ship. And what a ship she was; King glanced up at the pyramids of unusually white canvas that towered above him as they powered the ship through the rich, blue ocean. Yes, *Mistral* was a frigate anyone would be proud to command. And then, as if connected, his thoughts turned to Julia Booker.

Unless her father had died or moved away, she was likely to be on the island still and must surely hear of his return. Being that St Helena would become a regular calling point for *Mistral*, it would seem foolish to avoid a meeting, but equally he wondered if he truly wished to seek her out. King thought not: too much had happened since they were together and he could see little point in reviving ancient history. But of one thing he was sure; even if they did not actually meet, no ship calls on the small community without all ashore becoming aware, and he was secretly glad she would hear of him, along with all he had achieved. What they had shared might be many years in the past but she would not have forgotten. And though he could not explain it even to himself, it was particularly important that she knew exactly how much he had changed in the meantime.

7.

After six days at sea, when Cape Town was little more than a memory and the promise of St Helena still lay some way in the future, they began to see progress. Adams' guess had proved correct: not all the new draft were as experienced as they claimed. But with patience, and after several alterations to the watch bill, order was slowly becoming established.

Croft glanced surreptitiously forward to the break of the quarterdeck where a party of new hands were coming to the end of that morning's holystoning. The strakes were still damp but a thin haze showed how the morning's sun was finishing their work. And though they might not have achieved quite the brilliance some first lieutenant's would demand, it was a fair effort and he was quietly satisfied.

As he was in other areas. After a few initial mishaps the cook's department was becoming more efficient with food no longer being served cold, late or raw. And the deficit in shirts discovered when the slop clothing was unpacked had been made up; members of the sailmaker's team, aided by a few volunteers, had taken extra sewing duties and now there was a surplus. But to Croft the most important improvement was a personal one and far more private.

The new found energy that had appeared after his appointment was not failing him. With nearly three hundred men to look after there was definitely more to do, and the responsibility for a fair sized warship lay very firmly on his shoulders. But he seemed to be keeping up reasonably well; perhaps it was a little harder to raise himself after sleep, but even that was improving. And at least he now had a core of assistants to call upon.

At most times of the day the gunroom contained at least one other trained and responsible man willing to assist with small matters or simply give an opinion. Some were better than others; Croft still had reservations about Hopkins, the fair-haired marine officer, finding him unusually arrogant for one of his station, and Murray, their new second lieutenant, was possibly more so. But if only by their presence, both contributed to the general atmosphere of what in larger ships would be known as the wardroom. Adams, the youngest and most recently promoted, was also adjusting to life as a commissioned man extremely well. At meal times there were always enough to make discussion lively and the new influx of junior and petty officers that managed the lower deck had done much to take the drudgery out of the more mundane duties.

And they had been lucky with the midshipmen; on leaving *Hare* and after Adams' promotion, the only "young gentlemen" aboard had been Summers, Dilson and Cole with the latter two officially being rated volunteers. No further suitable candidates had come with the new draft but it had been no hardship to promote them both, giving Summers some contemporaries. Then, after a deal of discussion, four more were selected from *Hare*'s regular hands and informed they were to be volunteers. All would need time to work up to the new role of course and some might not make it, although one, a member of Greenwood's mess, was already showing real ability. Sennett had been pressed into *Hare* shortly after Croft was appointed to her and had apparently taken to the life to the extent that he was now a useful hand. But unusually for a lower deck man, he knew both his letters and numbers and was already showing a fair aptitude for navigation. With luck and a following wind, Croft felt he might one day walk the quarterdeck as a lieutenant.

The hands themselves were also settling. Trouble could always be expected when a new draft was introduced especially, as in this case, when they were an established unit already acquainted with one another. The recent intake also outnumbered *Hare*'s former hands and, as the ship was new to both groups, there had been a few confrontations between the two. The situation was made worse by the inclusion of foreigners in the fresh hands; when he had been told there were native men amongst the draft, Croft had expected something on the lines of freed slaves, as the Dutch were known to be enthusiastic keepers. But though there were some black faces he also noticed a scattering of other locals who were of a very different ilk.

Croft had yet to learn much of their backgrounds but it was obvious that none knew a great deal about ships or the sea and, unlike the former slaves, they showed little inclination to learn while seeming to radiate an atmosphere of belligerence and discontent that was noticed by all. They were, however, strong, so could be used for any work where muscle was the main requirement and a poor attitude might more easily be dealt with. As a consequence, most had been drafted into the afterguard or sent below to join the holders. With careful watching and the judicious application of a rope's end, there had yet to be any significant breaches of discipline, but Croft was not so foolish as to think such a situation could continue. Before long one would step out of line to the extent that a more official punishment was called for, and when that happened it might cause trouble from the rest. That time was yet to come, however, and he now felt more able to cope when it did.

And at least they had a force of men trained for just such an emergency. At first the rumour was they were to receive regular soldiers in place of a Royal Marine contingent; something that Croft would have objected to most strongly. However disciplined land troops might be, they could never emulate true marines. The highly discipled force of sea soldiers might provide regular fodder for japes amongst the seamen, but they also carried out a difficult task in maintaining order whilst living in conditions that were hardly conducive to military life. The forty or so men that made up *Mistral*'s contingent would be a negligible force in most land actions, but aboard ship they represented a major asset, and one that could be relied upon to settle disputes amongst the crew as much as mounting more conventional assaults against an enemy.

But that brought his mind back to the one potentially weak link in the chain; Sergeant Bates had followed them from *Hare*, and the new corporal seemed just as solid, although Lieutenant Hopkins was their overall leader. Try as he might, Croft could place no confidence in the new man who, being ill mannered, proud and often downright lazy, seemed the very antithesis of those he was detailed to command. Such qualities may not have been so important in other officers – an arrogant sailing master might still carry out his duties well enough, as would a self-important surgeon or a haughty cook. But a marine lieutenant had to be both morally and physically strong if he were to attract the respect of those he led and, though Croft had yet to see Hopkins in action, he could not imagine him having such qualities. Much of the everyday organisation was done by Bates and the other NCO, of course, and Croft remained hopeful that Hopkins would either modify his attitude or make way for a better man. Only the former could happen in the next few days, however, and that was when Croft was privately expecting any trouble to erupt.

"Fine morning, sir," a voice informed him and Croft glanced round to see Murray, the second lieutenant, standing behind.

"Indeed," Croft agreed a little crisply. The watch would be ending in fifteen minutes and Murray was his replacement. As usual, he was punctual and dressed immaculately; two things that Croft could hardly complain about, although he did so dislike being crept up upon, and the young lieutenant's pathological hauteur never failed to annoy.

"Yes, it will be another splendid day," the junior man continued airily, while ostentatiously taking in the beauty of his surroundings before reaching for the traverse board. "Can't beat the southern latitudes for such weather, and it is a comforting thought that those in England are still in winter."

Croft said nothing; he supposed there was no harm in such familiarity and Murray was doing his duty in checking the ship's current position as well as all that had occurred over the last four hours. But it was still a relief when another figure appeared at the aft companionway and Brehaut, the sailing master, joined them.

"We seem to be making good progress, master," Croft announced.

"Aye, we shall raise the island in under a week if this continues," the Jerseyman agreed. "Though I sense a change in the weather afore then."

"A change?" Murray asked, shifting his attention to the pair. "I hope you do not mean ill weather."

"Possibly a storm," Brehaut replied easily, "though not a bad one. However, I don't expect to keep this wind for much longer."

"And on what do you base your supposition, Mr Brehaut?"

The sailing master considered the new man for a moment. His attitude was hard to like although equally difficult to define.

"Nothing scientific," he answered with a generous smile. "Call it an inkling if you will."

Murray closed his eyes briefly. "Then perhaps you should keep your inklings to yourself?" he suggested. "As sailing master I should have thought you would concern yourself with fact rather than fantasy."

Croft and Brehaut briefly exchanged glances. There was nothing exactly wrong with what the new man had said; as a commissioned officer he was undoubtedly superior to Brehaut in rank so could address him very much as he pleased. But though hard to object to officially, it had not been a polite comment and Murray would obviously have to be handled carefully.

"So I assume you do not sense a change in the weather, Mr Murray?" Croft asked coldly.

"I should not attempt to, sir," Murray replied with a supercilious look. "Such things are quite beyond me. Though I understand some animals are famed for their ability to predict rain."

* * *

There was no storm; something that Murray was careful to make mention of on at least two occasions. But the weather did indeed alter and the west-north-westerly that had been blowing steadily for the past week or so died, only to be replaced by a far stronger breeze from the south. That afternoon it became necessary to take in the topgallants and add a reef to the topsails, yet with the wind now more comfortably on her quarter, *Mistral* continued to cut through the crested waves with all the grace and elan of the thoroughbred she was.

"Fine sailin'," Greenwood muttered contently. It was a rare rest period in the regular exercises that had been called for since the ship was commissioned. No department had been spared, with even the holders set to endlessly rearranging stores to alter the ship's trim and, as the seamen rested on the forecastle, all were glad of the break. "This sou'-easterly will carry us all the way to the island and then some, if we has the wish."

"But won't we be heading back for the Cape after?" Russell asked in doubt. Of them all, the drills had pressed him the hardest, yet inwardly he knew himself to have learned a good deal.

"Maybe so, an' then, maybe not," Greenwood shrugged.

"Don't you care where you're bound?"

"St Helena," Parker told Russell firmly. "We're bound for St Helena: they told us that as soon as we left the Cape."

"Yes, but after that?" Russell insisted.

"Captain don't make a habit of referring to me, not when he makes his plans," Greenwood replied evenly. There was a pause as a high flurry of white water came further aft than was usual and scattered itself over the small group in a mist of fine spray. "But we got good weather to travel," the seaman added, glancing at the droplets on his bare arm with apparent satisfaction. "And a sound ship, so anywheres is right with me."

"And me," Parker agreed readily.

Russell considered them both, noticing especially their look of total fulfilment, and then realised that he was content also.

* * *

There was just the two of them in the gunroom, the rest of the officers being on deck or busy elsewhere and, though an invited guest, Summers still felt very out of place. Adams seemed to be aware of this yet strangely made no attempt to put him at ease.

On one occasion he summoned the steward to order fresh tea, even though there was a perfectly good pot not yet cold, and insisted that the remains of the last meal's duff was served to his young guest. He had also risen from his chair twice and begun pacing about the place as if to properly demonstrate the amount of space available in his new quarters. And Summers noticed another way in which his friend had changed: he was always the senior man. When Summers had joined as a raw volunteer, Adams was already a midshipman, while the simple act of being older gave a measure of seniority. But now, rather than a handful of years, he behaved as if many decades separated the two and the white facings to his lapels were actually a pair of epaulettes.

It might have been due to his promotion, Summers mused as he sipped tea ostentatiously sweetened with too much sugar, or perhaps his association with Anne Callahan, but the change was definitely for the worse. And, as his friend launched himself into yet another lecture, he became increasingly convinced that the woman was at the heart of it.

"Yes, you should get a girl, Michael," Adams told him, as if in confirmation. "There ain't nothing like it."

"Is that what she is?" Summers enquired artlessly and Adams broke out of his trance to consider him.

"What do you mean?"

"Well, she is hardly young," the lad continued, digging deeper. "And must have been married to old man Callahan for ages."

"A couple of years at most," Adams replied crisply. "And she were nought but a child when they wed."

Summers acknowledged this with a nod; it really meant nothing to him although Adams, it seemed, wished to thrash out the matter.

"Besides, it was not a real marriage, not in the normal way."

"Not proper – you mean, not church?" Summers enquired.

"No," Adams stated firmly, "I mean the way they lived. They were not... together. Not much anyways."

"Told you that, did she?" Summers asked, sipping at his tea once more.

"Didn't have to," Adams assured him. "I can tell; when you know someone properly, you don't have to ask."

"Is that so?" Summers eyed him thoughtfully and Adams had the grace to blush.

"I mean, some things need not be said," he flustered.

"That's convenient," Summers told him. "Can I have some more of that duff?"

* * *

"I've had a complaint from the marine officer," Harridge told Greenwood's mess just as they were finishing their midday meal. "Says some of your lot been disrespectful," he added, now looking directly at Greenwood.

"I'm sorry to hear that, Pipes," Greenwood answered easily from his place at the mess table. The men were tired from the morning's exercises and, with a full afternoon ahead, would be in no mood for trouble. But then the boatswain was a reasonable sort and entitled to a degree of respect. "He ain't said nothin' to us, and a cull like that's not the kind to keep his trap shut."

"Weren't directly said to 'im," Harridge allowed. "Though he thinks he were being referred to. Empty bottle, does that sound about right?"

The boatswain's remark brought a smattering of muted laughter from the mess.

"Belay that!" Harridge ordered, suddenly gruff. "You might think it amusin' but he clearly don't and that kind ain't the type you want to annoy. So come on, which of you bastards called the lubber an empty bottle?"

* * *

And so the voyage continued. They did not make the fast passage Brehaut had hoped for but, by the time the grey dot that was St Helena finally came into view and grew into the stark silhouette that made the island so distinctive, it was clear that the regular drills had brought about a noticeable improvement in both ship and crew. And as *Mistral* drew closer to the well remembered anchorage at Chapel Bay, King's thoughts finally began to extend beyond the confines of his new command.

He hadn't actually been expecting many changes in such a remote outpost yet it was still mildly disappointing to note Jamestown was apparently unaltered. He stood on the quarterdeck with glass in hand, although there was no need for any artificial aids – he could see all he wished clearly enough. The brown-grey cliffs that ringed the bay were just as imposing and dipped only long enough to allow a glimpse of the small group of buildings that made up all the island offered in the way of a decent sized town. And beyond that, more hills, but this time totally concealing the rich and fertile hinterland that he could so easily remember crossing. Closer to, there were a dozen or so heavy Indiamen sleeping at anchor, which was novel; his last visit had been between seasons and the roadstead was almost empty, but all else seemed very much the same with no obvious changes.

He understood a Company man named Patton to be the present Governor – King had neither met nor heard of him; in his time the post had been filled in an acting capacity by Francis Robson, an HEIC colonel. And others would have come and gone since he last visited the station. His mind briefly played upon Julia Booker, the girl he had left behind or – as he quickly acknowledged – had refused to come with him. Once more he decided if her father were still on the island it was a fair bet she would be also and yet again wondered about seeking her out before deciding against it. But now that he stood on the very threshold of the place, his reasons had altered slightly, and he wondered if all the changes that he was so proud of in himself would be fully appreciated.

There was the empty left sleeve to start with, he had since won an epaulette for the same shoulder that was now being worn on the right and announced him as a junior post captain, though that could be classified as mere ornamentation. The loss of a limb was far more fundamental and, possibly for the first time, he almost felt ashamed of the wound. He had also altered as a person and probably just as much; there was less of that devil-may-care about him, an attribute that Julia would have known and perhaps loved. Now he was more circumspect and, he hoped, mature, which was fitting for a gentleman of his rank. Mistakes he may have made in the past would not be repeated now; he could hardly imagine expecting a respectable young woman to accompany him back to England, not when he had a perfectly legal wife waiting for him there. Admittedly he might have asked something similar of Aimée, and less than a year ago, but that was only after his relationship with his wife had deteriorated further. No, he would not seek her out but, if luck should see King running in with Julia Booker, she would definitely find him to be an altered man – and a better one as a consequence.

"Been here afore have you, Master?" he asked genially of Brehaut who was preparing to take bearings as the ship made ready to anchor.

"Many years ago, sir," the sailing master replied, briefly taking his eye from the compass as he remembered. "Though I can't admit to remembering much about it. We'd been at sea for more than six weeks without sight of land an' I were so glad to finally strike soundings that much of my time was spent in a pot house." He grinned at the memory. "Mind, I were little more than a lad in those days," he added more seriously. "You wouldn't catch me doing the same now."

King nodded politely. He supposed that very much the same could have been said about him.

8.

But whatever his first impressions had been, when he reached the shore things were not exactly as King remembered. For a start, the place was far more crowded; some of the throng would be from the visiting East India Company ships but the rest gave an impression of being residents and there were a lot more military than on his last visit. During the short trip to the Castle he lost count of the times he had to give or receive salutes and, despite no other warship being at anchor, a good proportion wore Royal Navy uniforms. Even Jamestown itself felt larger, with a greater number of businesses that now filled both sides of the main street, although the place had lost none of its inherent friendliness and the savage, bare hills that towered to either side were every bit as imposing. But still he felt much of the former magic of the town was somehow missing and, as he finally made his way back down the steps of the decidedly unfortified government building, King could not ignore an inner feeling of regret.

But he was in no mood to delay; having spent the best part of three hours in various meetings the lure of his ship was strong. His first interview had been with the senior naval officer; a rotund and decidedly land-bound post captain who viewed King's single epaulette with obvious disdain. And matters did not improve when he confirmed Cape Town was indeed back in the hands of the British and had been retaken without reference to anyone on the island. The same resentment was apparent when speaking with the Governor a little later. He was an equally antiquated Company officer who spoke in a broad Scott's accent and apparently regarded his domain's lack of inclusion in Commodore Popham's plans as a mark of mistrust. King had been quick to sooth hurt feelings, though this was only by yet another account of Strachan's action; something which had only been briefly alluded to in official reports.

And now, with the sun well past its apex and a throat uncommonly dry from talking, he began threading his way through the crowded streets once more. His gig had been left at the jetty; the crew would be getting restless and Summers, the midshipman in charge, might be having problems keeping them in check. But the quay was not far off and *Mistral* lay at anchor only a short distance out in the bay. In under fifteen minutes he should be free of this crowd and it was just as he was starting to relish the thought that it happened.

He told himself later an able-bodied man would not have disgraced himself so; certainly if he had been capable of throwing both arms out the fall might have been less undignified. As it was, as soon as his heel slipped on the small, irregularly shaped cobblestones of Castle Terrace, King knew he was heading for a spectacular tumble.

He lay for a moment on the hard ground which was now revealed to be slightly damp while the crowd passed him by with little more than amused comments. Then slowly, ever so slowly, began to ease himself upright.

"Take a spill, did we, sir?" a uniformed figure enquired as he alone stopped to help. King glanced at the green tunic which he did not recognise, although the man was probably a private. Usually the pair would have exchanged little more than silent salutes but now, united by his accident, all difference in rank was temporarily suspended.

"Here, take a seat on the wall," the Samaritan suggested as he collected King's cocked hat before leading him gently by the arm to the refuge. King obediently followed; promotion and injury had long since put paid to any need for physical exertion in the course of his duties and the simple incident had left him both stunned and mildly disorientated.

"Set y'self down and take a breather," his helper advised, laying the hat down next to him. "You'll feel better in no time."

King muttered his thanks and the solider gave a generous grin before moving off into the throng. He collected the hat and examined it; there was no damage other than a scuff to the rim. Apart from that he had a slight tear in his britches and quite a bit of Jamestown dirt had spread itself about his person. He brushed off what he could then remembered more important matters. The slim envelope addressed to Sir David Baird, presumably a hastily written personal note from the Governor, was still inside his breast pocket and he could also feel the reassuring bulge of his purse. Other than the letter, there were no despatches to carry back to the Cape and the only thing that actually kept him on the island was the need for water. This had been arranged for first light the following morning; *Mistral* could square away as soon as her casks were filled and, by the same time tomorrow, St Helena would become a memory once more.

That time could not come fast enough for him, he decided; he had already seen more than enough of a place he once loved and now wished only to be gone. But it was then that a face in the crowd passing by caught his attention, and suddenly he found himself looking straight into the all too familiar eyes of Julia Booker.

* * *

"Will we be getting leave, sir?" Adams enquired, and the first lieutenant eyed him quizzically.

"Is there something ashore you require?" Croft asked sharply, remembering a similar conversation with the same young man.

Adams shook his head. "No sir," he replied. "I have everything I need aboard ship – or waiting for me at the Cape."

"I am glad to hear it," Croft told him, purposefully ignoring what might have been a particularly smug expression. Snores from a sleeping officer could be heard through the thin deal door of his cabin but, apart from that, the two were alone in the gunroom. Croft had been waiting for a chance to check on the young man's progress and this was too good an opportunity to pass by.

"So what is at the Cape?" he asked, indicating the chair opposite. "Might it be a young lady?"

"Indeed, sir," Adams admitted as he seated himself and the look of both pride and satisfaction was not lost on the older man.

"I am glad to hear of that also," the first lieutenant confirmed. "Though would caution you to be careful; sailors do not make the best of husbands."

"No, sir," Adams replied seriously. It was good to be speaking with Mr Croft in such a manner; almost as if they were on a similar level.

"And what of your new rank and position?" the older man enquired. "I trust you are settling well?"

"Oh yes, sir," Adams grinned. "And I like it fine."

"No problems with the men?"

"None, sir," Adams was reassuringly positive. "There seems little difference; they have accepted my promotion well."

Croft nodded; Adams had acquired the skill of commanding respect when a senior midshipman so, whatever the mystery female had done to his heart, his mind was apparently unaffected.

"And your fellow officers?" he persisted in a slightly softer tone.

"I'm getting on well enough, thank you, sir."

"There is no need to call me sir below deck, John," Croft reminded him gently. "We are considered at our leisure."

Adams paused; that was how he had always read matters although Murray, the second lieutenant, insisted on the honorific.

"I think I'd prefer to, sir," Adams replied awkwardly.

"That is your choice," Croft told him easily although there might have been regret in his tone, "but I repeat, there is no need."

Adams now felt totally unable to reply. He had always held the executive officer in high regard although, since attaining the status of lieutenant himself and learning more of the man and his duties, was now almost in awe. The transition from organising a worn out brig-sloop to a crack fifth rate frigate with more than double the crew had hardly phased him; something that was truly remarkable in the younger man's eyes. And as well as appreciating his talents, he had also come to like the person himself, whereas three weeks of close association with Murray had only increased his loathing for the fellow. There was no way of conveying this without risking a serious breach of discipline but of one thing Adams was certain: if he had to continue addressing the second lieutenant formally, he had no intention of treating Mr Croft with any less respect.

* * *

"Tom, it *is* you," she announced, drawing closer and lowering her small bag to the ground. "But you look so different!"

King rose quickly; meeting with Julia again had certainly been on his mind, but now she was there, large as life and directly before him, he had no idea what to say.

"But your arm," she added, indicating his empty sleeve and he remembered how direct she could be at times. "You have been wounded?"

"Indeed," King confirmed hesitantly, "though all is well now. And I have been made post – I am a captain," he added foolishly.

"That is good to hear, Tom," she replied, barely suppressing a smile. "Is your ship at the anchorage?"

"She is – a frigate – and a fine one. Might I show you?" King suggested but Julia shook her head.

"I have to be gone, Tom. The market closes at two and I am late already. But will you be on the island for long?"

"Oh I must leave tomorrow," King explained. "On the morning tide."

Of all the foolish things to say; *Mistral* was anchored in more than fifteen fathoms, and the sea bed dipped steeply beyond;

besides there was the small matter of ten tons of water to take on first. In the space of a minute he had revealed himself to be boastful, self-important, a fool and a lubber.

"But it is so good to meet once more," she said, and her smile seemed genuine.

"I have not asked," King muttered, finally coming to his senses. "What of you?"

"I am well and a married woman now," she blushed faintly and added a glance towards her left hand. "Joseph and I have a young boy, he is almost three and a handful – I truly must go to the market and return to them both."

"I give you joy of your family," King stated formally, although his voice cracked as he did. "And what of Adam Fraiser?"

"Ah, I fear he passed last winter," she answered more sadly.

King closed his eyes for a moment. "He was a fine sailing master," he said softly.

"He was a fine man, Tom," she corrected with a hint of rebuke and nothing was said for some seconds. Then Julia broke the spell.

"I do really have to go," she bent to collect her bag. "Though it is good to see you." For a moment she hesitated. "There is no chance that you might dine with us this eve? We have a small house that looks over the bay and young Jamie is especially fond of sailors."

Their eyes met again but King shook his head. "There are matters I must attend to," he explained with a degree of gravity he did not feel.

"Than I shall leave you to them," Julia nodded and cautiously held out her hand. King took it in his and they were united for a moment before she turned into the crowd and seemed about to disappear as totally as the soldier had. But at the last moment she paused and glanced back.

"And Tom," she said as the smile returned. "There may be a difference in appearance, but you are definitely the same person; truly you have not changed one bit."

9.

Five days later, when St Helena was several hundred miles over the horizon and the incessant exercises had resumed, *Mistral* was ordered to clear for action. The call came half way through the morning watch and this time was not a drill; a sighting had been made by the main masthead several hours before and by the time King finally ordered them to prepare for battle, the topsails of several approaching ships were in plain sight of all on deck. Russell actually paused to look at them as he emerged from below before a shout from Henderson, the boatswain's mate, sent him scurrying for his proper station at the forward battery.

"Reckon they're French, Greenie?" he asked his mess captain as the pair began to free one of the trussed up monsters they served.

"Belike," Greenwood muttered in reply. He had just returned from aloft where he and Parker had fitted chains to reinforce the fore lower yard slings and so been able to study the ships more carefully. "Or Spanish, or Dutch – it makes no difference. Though I'll tell you one thing," the topman paused. "They ain't British. And here's another: neither are they warships."

Others were of the same opinion and the news spread quickly. Soon the entire upper deck was abuzz; an enemy merchant fleet was in sight – five ships, possibly more – and all certain to be loaded with riches. No other British flag was in sight so, though they would be lucky if *Mistral* took more than one, it would become their sole property. In the next few hours every man Jack of them was liable to become extremely rich and all were instantly transformed.

It was as if the past few weeks of trying to mould them into a workable crew had been time wasted, for more progress was made in a single hour and morale had never been higher. Now they stood as one body: a group united by a common goal and with all petty conflicts and disputes forgotten. Across the water lay riches beyond measure; all it would take was a degree of co-operation and their lives would be changed forever.

* * *

“You're sure they're Dutch Indiamen?” King asked when the leading ships could be seen in more detail from the deck.

“Sure as eggs is eggs, sir,” Brehaut replied, the excitement having infected even the Jerseyman's sober countenance.

“Not the prisoners returning home?”

“They were due to leave Cape Town just after us, and we've been gone several weeks,” Croft answered this time and was just as positive.

“Nothing could have delayed them so long,” the sailing master agreed.

“Besides, you only have to look at their beams, sir,” Croft added. “There is no doubt of it.”

King nodded; he had made the same assessment, as had the masthead lookout several minutes before, but still they could not afford to take chances. Since they left St Helena, nothing of interest had been sighted and he had almost resigned himself to an uneventful trip back to the Cape. But now, suddenly, all that had changed and it seemed *Mistral* was to be tested in action for the first time.

To all appearances the heavy hulls currently rolling towards them belonged to homebound merchants, Indiamen similar to those of the HEIC but serving a very different country: one that was at war with England and so fair game. They would be loaded to capacity with anything from tea to spices, silks to precious jewels, with each potentially worth several hundred thousand for their cargo alone. But at such a distance they were almost indistinguishable from men-of-war and, if he were going to risk his precious frigate, King would prefer to be certain.

“Deck there, I've another!” the masthead roared out and all instinctively looked to the cluster of masts on the southern horizon that was growing more distinct with every passing minute.

“What do you see there?” Murray called up impatiently; he had been officer of the watch and was yet to take up his action station on the main deck.

“Looks like an escort, though not a large one. She's standing towards us an' forereaching on the merchants; she'll be up with them in no time.”

“Standing towards us?” Murray muttered in doubt. “But we must be in sight. And why have the merchants not divided?”

King thought he knew, but needed confirmation. Catching Croft's eye, he led the first lieutenant to a quieter area of deck where they could speak more privately.

"What think you?" he asked.

"I'd say there are others on their tail," the older man answered with reassuring certainty. "A group of VOC Indiamen positioned so would be coming back from the East. They may have tried for the Cape and found it to be in our hands. If a scratch fleet of our own forces were roused and upped anchor to give chase it would explain why the sight of a single frigate has not deterred them. And why they're still heading straight for us."

Yes, it did make sense and once more King was pleased to have his suspicions confirmed. Even if just two British frigates had set off in pursuit, *Mistral*, on her own, would still be the softer option.

"And there's smoke!" The lookout again.

Once more, all turned to peer past the forecourse and this time were rewarded by a faint haze rising from beyond the oncoming ships.

"Gunfire," Croft announced with the air of one proved correct.

"Add t'gallants if you please," King commanded and Brehaut bellowed out the orders that would see the extra canvas set. Until that moment King was in no rush to raise the Cape and *Mistral* had been cruising under topsails and forecourse in the hope of just such an encounter. But now, with an enemy in sight, he must pick up speed and do all he could to block their escape. "And take her two points to larboard."

"Starboard the helm: two points to larboard!" Brehaut dutifully roared out as the fresh sails started to fill.

Mistral was taking up position directly in the merchants' path. She might not stop them all, and there was the additional factor of the armed escort whose upper sails were now becoming visible from the deck. But if they could knock away a few spars and slow the Indiamen down, some should be taken, especially if a considerable force were truly in pursuit.

Such a stance was not without its dangers, however. Even ignoring the escort, which could be anything from a sloop to a frigate as large as *Mistral*, the merchants themselves would be armed. Each may not have the firepower of a warship but even a seven hundred ton trader could mount a broadside of several twenty-four pounders and there were five of them. It was heavy metal that would do a fifth rate no good at all, especially if he were foolish enough to draw in close. But then such a prize was worth a few risks. Ever since leaving St Helena, King had been in the mood for a gamble; now one had come his way the odds did not unsettle him at all. In fact, he welcomed them, and the higher the better.

* * *

Croft's meticulously planned station bill had placed Adams in command of *Mistral*'s two forward batteries; twenty of her main cannon fell under his direct control as well as the two forecastle mounted chasers, while Murray had charge of the aft long guns as well as all quarterdeck carronades. Both lieutenants were well supported with Cole acting as deputy to the second lieutenant while Croft, recognising Adams' friendship with Summers, had placed the two together further forward. The theory behind this was, if either lieutenant were to be incapacitated, the other could assume overall control of the ship's weaponry – although Adams would have preferred another arrangement.

For in each successive great gun exercise, the friction between the two men had grown. In Murray's eyes, nothing Adams did was correct – his crews were sloppy, their timing erratic and, whenever live firing was allowed, he found fault with their marksmanship. Not that the second lieutenant's men were any better; both sets of servers were working with unfamiliar French guns that were of a slightly larger calibre than equivalent British weapons and fired by a different mechanism. And there were no flexible rammers, the double-headed tool that made serving any cannon so much faster. Williams, the gunner, had indented for them and they would doubtless be provided in time, although *Mistral* had sailed before that could happen. Instead, they had to wrestle with the archaic French implements that required more space, time and practice to handle.

But there was no one to cajole Murray or his men; they were allowed to make mistakes and find their feet, whereas Adams' servers worked under the added strain of having two officers supervising their work, with one being far less constructive in his criticism. So now that *Mistral*'s cannon looked like being used in anger, Adams was more anxious than he might have been. This was also his first action as a commissioned officer, while the last time he had faced an enemy it ended in defeat and capture.

Summers, to his right, seemed no more relaxed. Twice he had admonished servers for not rigging their train tackle correctly and each time looked across to Murray to make sure the lieutenant had not noticed. It was hardly the right attitude to carry into battle and, unless something dramatic happened, Adams could see no way in which the situation would improve.

* * *

"Square-heads is holding their course," Greenwood murmured as he peered through the gun port. His augmented mess was responsible for two cannon; numbers five and six of the forward battery. But the new additions had arrived at their station first and been mainly allocated to the starboard piece, leaving the core crew of the larboard weapon to men who had served together for some while. Most would have preferred the starboard gun, as they had drilled on it for longer, although their current piece was perfectly serviceable and they were in a better position for considering the oncoming enemy.

"They're large," Russell said with a hint of concern.

"They're Indiamen," Greenwood countered. "Don't be put off by the size."

"Don't they have guns?" Sayer asked.

"Might have," Parker replied.

"We've more," Greenwood assured them.

"Aye, but Frog built," Swain added with disdain.

"You don't want to worry over that," Parker chuckled. "These buggers can still cause a stir."

"They're nothing more than continental rubbish," the holder declared, giving a derisory slap to the two tons of cold iron that lay between them.

"Maybe, but they're all we got to work with," Greenwood replied. "So best get used to it."

The cannon concerned was one of twenty-eight that lined the

frigate's main deck. Mounted on a conventional carriage, it was also considerably larger than the carronades they were more used to aboard *Hare*, although the weapon actually threw a lighter shot. But it could do so with far greater accuracy over a longer distance and should also prove more reliable in battle for carronades had a habit of exploding if allowed to become too hot – an attribute that hardly endeared them to their crews.

Yet the two French monsters they cared for were equally unpopular. The beasts might be superior weapons but they had still to reveal their souls to the trespassers and, like the ship, the English had yet to love them.

"So how much do you think we'll get?" Jackson, the gun captain, spoke from the back of the group and there was a pause. Such a question deserved an answer from their most experienced member, although Greenwood, it seemed, was showing reluctance.

"Can't say," he muttered at last. "So much depends on how many we take and what they're carrying."

"Knowing our luck they'll be in ballast," Sayer grumbled.

"No ship rounds the Cape in ballast," Greenwood stated more firmly. "Even if we catches one, and has to share between a couple of other ships, we won't go short."

"Hundreds?" Jackson asked. "Thousands?"

"Not thousands," Greenwood replied. "Not for the likes of us, unless we gets them all and there's no one else to share with. But a pile; maybe as much as a hundred a piece plus a little extra for the hull."

Now the silence was more meditative than expectant. Such a sum was true riches when a sound cottage could be bought for sixty guineas and a thriving business not much more. In the next few hours all aboard *Mistral* were at risk of becoming dangerously rich and it was a concept that deserved serious consideration.

Swain broke into their thoughts with another pat to the cannon's barrel, and this time the action carried a deal more affection.

"What's that about then?" Greenwood asked, and Swain grinned.

"Looks like we're going to be relying on chummy here for the rest of the afternoon," he replied. "So we may as well get along."

* * *

By two o'clock the situation had developed further; the ship remained at action stations with no mid-day food or grog being served and neither had the men been stood down. But for once no one was thinking of their bellies or comfort; the Indiamen's hulls were now in plain view and had closed to the extent that King ordered *Mistral* to block their path. Currently she lay hove to, broadside on and almost stationary in the gentle swell. The escort, a sleek little corvette not unlike *Kestrel*, King's first true command, had also revealed itself, and now stood to windward of the column of traders it protected. Beyond, three ships were in pursuit; a liner and two frigates, although none appeared to be from Banks' squadron and neither were they close enough to exchange signals with *Mistral*.

King turned away from the sight and met the eyes of Croft and Brehaut; the two officers he had come to rely upon far more than he had ever expected.

"When we turned I had thought them to split," he confessed.

"It was a fair assumption, sir," Croft assured him.

"And would have made matters a deal easier," Brehaut added.

King was not so sure of the last point; five merchants heading in disparate directions would have been harder to catch, but he let the matter pass. As it was, the Indiamen had stayed as one body and roughly in line ahead, with the saucy little corvette abreast of the leader.

"Well, they are closing fast," he continued. Then, after a pause, "Bring her to the wind once more and set the royals."

A plan was steadily forming; adding additional canvas might be a mistake, and would certainly make *Mistral*'s own masts more vulnerable, while the extra pace might actually work against them by not allowing their gunners time to reload. But speed was one of a frigate's major attributes and, if managed properly, could be used as a weapon in itself.

Brehaut detached himself from the group and saw the ship brought back to the wind while King turned away from Croft to discourage further conversation; he needed a moment or so longer to think everything through.

The wind was coming steady and strong from the north west;

ideal for the hit and run tactics he had in mind, especially as the merchants were continuing to beat into it in an irregularly spaced column. On the face of it, he might launch a frontal assault, tackle each ship in order and try to slow at least some of them down, but that plan had obvious flaws.

First, he could not give *Mistral* her head – the merchants must be making three, possibly four, knots; even if he hauled his wind they would close far too quickly to see the job done and, were any allowed to pass without being disabled, they must be considered lost. Having a warship to windward was another disadvantage; the corvette could be counted on to close and engage at precisely the wrong moment, giving yet more chance of a trader escaping. No, there had to be a better way.

With such a breeze and the added sail, he knew *Mistral* would be blisteringly fast: if he could break their column and pass between each in turn, while shooting away as much of their tophamper as possible, several, if not all, might be slowed sufficiently to make their capture a certainty. The corvette remained a problem; she would be less predictable in her movements and could only be tackled as luck dictated. But what he intended would at least use *Mistral*'s speed to its true advantage. It would still be better done in one pass, of course, and if he failed, if his raw crew were unable to coordinate sufficiently and no great damage were caused, all King would have achieved would be to join up with the pursuing ships.

"Starboard the helm; take her three points to larboard," he murmured, giving the order that would both bring *Mistral* on an oblique towards the enemy squadron and the wind more on her quarter. "And pass the word for Mr Murray and Mr Adams so I might brief them."

He watched as the messenger scurried away, then looked up at the sails that were being set competently enough. The ship heeled only slightly as the yards came round but quickly gained pace. The first Indiaman was now less than three miles off their starboard bow; they would be in range in no time. King gave a surreptitious glance about the quarterdeck; the servers were standing prepared at their carronades and there were the afterguard, all apparently alert and anxious for what was about to take place. But just how ready they truly were had yet to be proved.

* * *

"It will be the starboard battery first," Murray announced importantly as he returned to the main deck. "But both will be in use, so divide your teams accordingly."

Summers touched his hat in acknowledgement and looked towards Adams as his friend joined him. *Mistral* was continuing to bear down on the merchants yet at such an angle that, if she remained so, the Indiamen would escape entirely. He was certain that was not what the captain intended, but then so much had altered of late he really could not be sure.

"We are about to turn and will then head to break the line of merchants," Adams informed him. "That is when the fun will really start."

"Why did we not turn to windward?" he asked softly. "That way we would have made our run with the breeze on our quarter rather than close-hauled."

Adams glanced across to the Indiamen. "The escort," he replied. "She's a French warship and a twenty-gunner, so will be something of a nuisance."

"Though surely no match for us?" Summers asked anxiously and his friend considered him for a moment.

"She's as powerful as the old *Kestrel* and doubtless every bit as fast," he said. "And might still cause damage."

"So what is intended?" Summers persisted.

"We are to pass between the two leading merchants," Adams replied. "Discharge our guns to both sides, then turn about and attempt to do the same with numbers three and four."

"And the escort?"

Adams gave a grim smile. "We will deal with the escort as we can; it is hard to plan for a quarry so manoeuvrable."

Summers swallowed. "It is somewhat vague," he said.

"There is no doubting that," Adams agreed. "We are dealing with six enemy ships, any of whom may break off on their own. Much will have to be improvised as we go and a good deal more is dependent on how our people work together." He gave a cursory glance at the men standing ready at their stations, then a movement from the quarterdeck caught his attention. "But hold fast," he said. "It appears we are about to start the first turn."

* * *

Mistral came round sweetly; soon her bowlines had drawn tight and she was powering along as close to the wind as the quartermaster could hold her. The enemy were making considerable way, so it was impossible to aim directly for the gap that was King's goal; all he could do was estimate. But it would be tight – too tight possibly – and as he watched he wondered if the turn had been postponed unnecessarily; certainly he could have wished for another half a cable to starboard. And what exactly had become of the corvette he could not tell for her masts and sails were now shielded by those of the leading Indiaman. But *Mistral* was making a good pace and closing fast; all would be revealed soon enough.

"We shall be able to open up with our bow chasers in no time," the first lieutenant remarked.

"As will the merchants with their broadsides," Brehaut agreed less enthusiastically.

King gave no reply. Normally he disliked unsolicited observations from his senior officers although supposed he was partly to blame for consulting them more regularly of late.

"I assume our weapons are ready and the men told off?" he asked sharply, and it was an unnecessary request; all knew every piece had been drawn and reloaded with bar shot some while before and Murray and Adams were well aware of what needed to be done.

"Ready sir," Croft confirmed crisply.

King gave a brief nod in acknowledgement; his question obviously had the desired effect and a silence descended on the small group. But there was no time for hurt feelings, his eyes were fixed on the leading merchant. She was taking the wind just forward of her beam, causing the tanned canvas to fill with a graceful curve that, when highlighted by the afternoon sun, turned her into a thing of beauty. Yet all King registered was the row of cannon that had been hauled out to meet him; that and the space between her and the next ship – a space that he needed to shortly fill.

As Brehaut had stated, they were close to the arc of the Indiaman's guns and *Mistral* would be taking any shot on her fragile bows. Yet again he assured himself that the standard of merchant gunnery was not high, while their weapons, though heavy, were often antiquated. But whether they could be laid accurately or not, it would only take a significant hit to *Mistral*'s prow and his careful plans would be turned into chaos. Were a mast taken down, or even a vital spar – the jib boom or one of the lower yards – they would be as good as dead in the water. And unless he were able to manoeuvre, *Mistral* must then be at the mercy of the merchant's cannon, which could pummel her with shot to their hearts content.

But it was relatively easy to dismiss such negative thoughts, especially as there were other matters to consider. They could indeed open up with their bow-mounted chasers; one merchant was comfortably in range of the two light guns and a lucky hit might make matters easier. However, he felt reluctant to do so as the almost gentle pop of the long guns would be a rather feeble opening to his part of the action. Besides, there was the prospect of the corvette, still lurking somewhere behind the leading ship.

She had probably been the cause of the smoke sighted by the masthead, so must be fast enough to escape the oncoming frigates, while her captain was clearly not afraid to take on a superior force. If *Mistral* were to burst through the merchants' line after despatching both broadsides, only to meet a barrage of twelve-pound shot from what was effectively a minor frigate, it would hardly be pleasant.

"They're leaving it late," Brehaut remarked quietly and King had to agree. That might mean anything from the merchants' cannon being quakers – false barrels set in place to frighten off pirates – to the gunnery being under the charge of an unusually cool head; someone who wanted the very best from his weapons. But *Mistral* was committed now; to turn away must only make her more vulnerable and it would not be long before she was in the perfect position to release her own broadsides.

And it was just as King was thinking so that the leading Indiaman finally opened fire, and did so with commendable efficiency. The line of seven discharges flowed in an even wave that would have done credit to any warship. For a few desperate seconds King wondered if they might have met with a truly experienced opponent and were about to receive a drubbing, but the fountains of spray that eventually erupted were poorly grouped and fell well short.

That was the first obstacle tackled; merchant servers could not be expected to reload in less than five minutes and in that time *Mistral* should have been through the precious gap that was growing closer with every second. His eyes switched to the next ship. She was further back; they would only just be entering her arc of fire. Then, even as he watched, the first tongues of flame burst out from her broadside.

They were less regular, although three shots fell close with one actually passing through *Mistral*'s rigging. No damage was done, however, and King breathed a heavy sigh; all that remained now was to see their own shot was more effective. That and deal with the hidden escort.

* * *

"Ready lads," Greenwood warned as the second merchant's broadside was released. Standing nearby with the hated fixed rammer in his hand, Russell watched as the shot flew towards him. They were on the larboard side, so this was the first time he actually felt in danger from the heavy weapons, yet still he stayed remarkably detached. For this was not his first time in action and he now judged himself truly hardened.

"There we go," Jackson, the gun's captain, remarked as the last fountain subsided. "Nothing but wind and smoke, like most merchant artillery. Now close up; we'll show them what proper gunners can do."

* * *

King had been right: it would be close. Although, now they were almost upon the ragged line of Indiamen, he was finally able to aim directly for the oncoming gap. But, in the last few minutes before they broke through, the tension aboard *Mistral* had grown to the stage when it was hard to concentrate on anything other than the towering masts steadily growing closer.

"What of that corvette?" King bellowed to the masthead.

"No change, sir, though I can't see her too clearly," the

lookout replied. "Indiamen are near enough on a close reach, so their sails is masking. But she's gone about for sure and is heading back to meet us."

King made no reply. If he were the escort's captain he would have done exactly the same; the leading merchant would provide shelter as well as acting as a depository for *Mistral*'s opening barrage. He supposed he might save his starboard broadside to use on the corvette, but that would mean the first Indiaman would probably escape and he was suddenly very anxious that this must not happen. But as soon as he was clear of her he must face the escort which would surely be attempting to cross his bows. His gunners would have to work fast if they were to be ready to meet fire with fire and, having a relatively raw crew, that was asking a lot. But his primary mission was to stop that merchant and he must do so, even if it meant taking damage as a result.

Forward, Adams was signalling his starboard guns could now bear on the leading trader. King glanced down; Murray had yet to follow suit, but it could only be a matter of seconds. There came a popping of muskets from the Indiaman's stern, although *Mistral* was comfortably out of accurate range of such fire. Then the second lieutenant raised his sword and, at a shout from King, the entire starboard battery was released.

The smoke immediately blew clear and King could tell their shots had been well laid. Damage was caused to the main shrouds and most sails were pockmarked with holes. Then the enemy's mizzen began to totter before falling to leeward and dragging the main topmast with it. For a moment the Indiaman continued on her course before the wind, acting more on the foremast and jib, began to turn the entire hull like a gigantic weather vane. Soon what canvas remained was flapping impudently as the vessel began to wallow in the swell.

"Well, she won't be going far for a while," Brehaut announced with evident satisfaction.

"It was good shooting," Croft agreed.

"And now we shall have to do the same again," Brehaut added, as he turned to consider the second in line that was approaching on their larboard bow. If anything she was moving faster and would be ripe for a broadside within seconds, although King's mind was elsewhere.

The corvette had indeed been sheltering behind the first Indiaman and, now they were passing the merchant's rolling hull, lay in clear sight. The small warship had turned completely and must have hauled her wind. Now she was underway once more and soon would be heading to cross their bows. She was a good distance off though; there may well be time for what he had in mind, although that was by no means certain.

King pursed his lips. There was little alternative; the only thing he could realistically do was stick to the original plan and trust as much to luck as his inexperienced crew. He glanced about; the starboard carronades were being loaded with reasonable efficiency and those further forward were making good progress with their carriage pieces. If they could work quickly enough, they might be able to deal with the escort without taking too much damage in return. If not – well he would simply have to face that prospect if it came about.

10.

The roar of the starboard battery's broadside had been literally deafening and even now, with the prospect of firing their own cannon on the second enemy closing to larboard, all Russell could think about was the dull throbbing in his head. It was partly his own fault; he knew the importance of wrapping a neckerchief tightly about his ears and had been a fool to forget.

For as well as learning much of seamanship in general, he was now a reasonably experienced server; there had been more than a few drills with *Hare*'s carronades and, despite the shorter period, almost as many using *Mistral*'s mighty long guns. When at sea it was customary to finish off the exercise with target practice from each individual cannon, but to hear all the starboard monsters speak as one had been a novel experience, and doing so without protection made it stunning as well. Beside him, Jackson, the gun captain, was saying something and he rubbed at his ears in an attempt to make it out.

"I said, look to the recoil!" Jackson's words got through on the third attempt; Russell nodded dumbly and stepped away from the long gun's cascabel. The heavy iron barrel was mounted on a wheeled carriage that allowed the entire weapon to move further than the lighter carronades he was more used to. But there was less chance of the gun actually leaving the deck on firing, and none of the "barrel bounce" so common with the shorter weapons. Russell fingered the hard shaft of his rammer as he considered the piece; it was almost elegant when compared with the stubby carronades and looked far more businesslike. The starboard guns had made short work of the first Indiaman's tophamper; he just hoped the larboard battery would be as successful.

Meanwhile, Jackson had forgotten all about Russell; he had had more important things to do than worry about wayward servers and was concentrating all his attention on lining up the forthcoming target in the cannon's crude sights. The quoin had been removed to allow for maximum elevation and the entire piece was slewed to face as far forward as possible. But still the Indiaman remained a little beyond his reach, even if the time when it might be successfully hit could now be measured in seconds rather than minutes. Behind him Adams and Murray, the two lieutenants who commanded the deck, were disagreeing over some matter but Jackson had no mind for them either. It was down to him to see the weapon properly laid, then despatched with the least possible fuss and, as a responsibility, it figured highly in Jackson's life. Having already failed as a barber on land then risen no higher than ordinary seaman at sea, the ability to lay a gun accurately was about his only skill. But it was one he remained inordinately proud of and anything remotely connected with gunnery was taken with the utmost seriousness.

The firing line was gripped firmly in his hand. If the gunlock failed, there was slow match burning in a bucket nearby and, however heated the argument behind him, the despatch of their broadside was bound to take precedence with both officers. For it certainly would with Jackson.

* * *

"Do you not see the enemy?" the second lieutenant demanded, pointing at the corvette still creeping towards their starboard bow. "Order your men to load with round shot – and target the hull!"

Adams shook his head defiantly. "We were told bar," he

maintained, glancing back to the quarterdeck, "and have received no subsequent instruction."

"Bar against the merchants," Murray hissed, his eyes shining bright from within a flushed face. "But what comes up to starboard is a warship. I am your superior officer, and I say round!"

"Then your order has come too late," Adams replied firmly. "My men are ahead of yours and already loading their shot."

So saying he turned away to meet the look of an anxious Summers. But Adams had no doubts: if anyone on the quarterdeck had wished for a change they would have been told and he was damned if he were going to waste time by asking for confirmation himself. Besides, the second lieutenant's domineering manner had gone on long enough, though it was strange that the fervour of action had been needed to spur him to rebellion. "Are the starboard cannon ready, Mr Summers?"

"Some are coming up to priming now, sir," the midshipman replied. Then, greatly daring, "And all are loaded with bar."

"That is as it should be," Adams confirmed. "And be sure we aim at the corvette's spars."

The comment was not lost on Murray; Adams' men were indeed faster than his own and further argument would only make that more obvious. "You shall hear more of this," he promised. "I shall be taking the matter up with the captain!"

"You are welcome to do so, Mr Murray," Adams answered without looking back, although he did add a wink for Summers' benefit.

* * *

At the larboard battery, the second Indiaman was in range and making a fine target. For a moment Jackson wallowed in the sight of the stumpy foremast, so invitingly festooned with billowing canvas that it almost hurt. Flashes of small arms fire sparked from her forecastle; the enemy was taking pot shots at them and they were welcome to – *Mistral* was about to reply with proper artillery.

He measured the distance to the foremast with his eye, then considered how quickly the spar was moving across his sights. There was nothing mathematical in his calculations, it was a simple and natural skill; one he had perfected over several years of practice. A lot would depend on when the broadside was ordered, but he could also estimate that, along with the all other computations that were running, unbidden, through his mind.

"Larboard battery be ready!" Adams' voice rang out, just as Jackson sprang up and raised his arm. And then, from further aft came the order to fire.

The line moved in Jackson's hand without him consciously willing it, and there was an agreeably bright spark from the lock. Then the weapon itself exploded with a sound too vast for simple men's ears which was instantly echoed by the pieces to either side. Jackson stood back as the tackle men moved in to control the smoking beast. He checked the rest of his servers; no one had been hit by the recoil and all were about their business correctly. There was Russell wrestling with the unwieldy French rammer, Greenwood and Brown attending to their duties with shot, powder and wad while the lad, Georgie, arrived with a fresh cartridge for the salt box. As the weapon's captain, Jackson had nothing to physically do until the cannon was presented to him with charge and shot in place and then it would be a simple matter of pricking and priming before the business of laying the gun could begin once more.

But now he had a moment to consider the enemy that still towered above them. *Mistral* had covered a considerable distance in a short time and, when loaded, the cannon would need to be slewed considerably aft. There was no need for haste, however; whether it had been his own eye and gun that caused the damage, or a combination of several, would never be known, but the trader had already been soundly struck.

Not only was her fore topmast in tatters, the jib boom, martingale stay and dolphin striker had completely disappeared, while the amount of canvas that flapped uncontrollably from the main showed that a good deal of cordage had also parted. The stricken merchant was turning as well, although in the opposite direction to her leader, with the bows now facing defiantly into the wind. From behind he could hear shouts from men still loading the starboard battery; they should be opening fire again soon and doubtless *Mistral* must then start to turn. But whatever the outcome of the action, that first broadside had been a proper pearler and Jackson was more than satisfied.

* * *

The starboard servers were making reasonable progress, but only just. Some, the older hands from *Hare* who had been retained as a team, were performing well together although a few of the new men were not so experienced. King had noticed several knock into each other as they worked and a bar shot dropped by one of Adams' servers had flattened the man's foot and sent the entire team into disarray. But he should not be surprised; a lot had been asked from relatively raw gun crews. The recent drills had done much but were still not sufficient to turn groups of men into proper working units.

And he was certainly pressing them hard. The enemy corvette was creeping up on their bow; really *Mistral* should turn now to both meet it, and be in a position to take on the rest of the merchants. Expecting those less experienced amongst the waisters and afterguard to attempt such a manoeuvre while the guns were still being served might well be a step too far, but delaying must surely make the capture of the other Indiamen less likely, to say nothing of the sound raking they could expect from the corvette.

He watched as *Mistral*'s two bow chasers were despatched at the small warship. The shots may well have struck home; it was difficult to see as the smoke rolled back over the ship although, once it had cleared, no damage could be detected. And the French captain was undoubtedly playing a cool game, he might easily release his broadside now but was waiting for *Mistral* to creep just that little bit closer, when the angle and range would be ideal.

Noticing that, King knew he had no alternative. They had to turn and turn now, whatever the state of his starboard broadside.

"Take her about, if you please, Mr Brehaut," King gave the order formally, and the sailing master responded in kind with a polite touch of his hat, although all on the quarterdeck understood exactly what was being asked.

As soon as the enemy guessed King's intentions, they would open fire themselves, even if it meant missing the optimum position, and the warship's broadside could be expected just as half his crew were in the midst of a complex manoeuvre while the rest struggled to serve their guns. But there was no option; to remain on their previous heading would only make the raking more devastating and King was as keen as any to take all the remaining merchants.

The ship baulked slightly as the helmsman took her round, but the eyes of the small command group were fixed on the corvette now less than five hundred yards off their starboard bow. The Frenchman might only be carrying twelve-pounders, but that was still heavy metal to receive at such a range, and it would only take a couple of lucky hits to disable *Mistral*.

And then, with a ripple of fire that flowed steadily down her sleek hull, the corvette spoke.

* * *

The broadside arrived just as *Mistral* was presenting her own beam to the Frenchman, but her guns were not ready and, when the enemy shot began to fly amongst them, it caused true consternation. There was physical damage as well: the British frigate's main topmast was struck. Only a glancing blow and the spar remained firm, but would doubtlessly be weakened, and she lost her fore topsail yard as well as the topgallant mast above. Other shots punctured canvas or took away line and tackle and several were wounded by falling blocks. But, as the dust began to settle, *Mistral* remained under control and, apart from an imbalance forward, still able to manoeuvrer.

King stepped forward to the break of the quarterdeck and considered the starboard battery. Some of the servers had finished their work and several gun captains had their hands raised to signal their weapons ready. Murray was there and apparently on top of matters, although the fool was waiting for a full broadside to be prepared and there was simply not the time.

He drew breath and bellowed out across the waist. "Mr Murray – fire as you will!" The young man spun round as if in surprise, then touched his hat, and shouted to his men. The order was repeated by the junior officers and there was an agreeable pause as the guns were sighted afresh. Then the starboard battery began to speak once more.

There was no devastating crash of a simultaneous broadside, nor the measured pace of controlled ripple fire, instead, *Mistral* gave forth with a clatter of reports that sounded like the barking of a particularly mad dog and ended, many seconds later, with the despatch of two quarterdeck carronades close to where King stood.

The spasmodic fire might not have been impressive but, as the shots began to tell, King was more than pleased with the result. Several of the frigate's aft long guns appeared to have targetted the hull, which was a waste, as far as he was concerned. Small though she might be, it would take a lot to actually sink the corvette, and not enough men would be injured by such fire to affect the combat significantly. But Adams' guns had been more purposefully aimed and, once more, did damage aloft. Even as he watched, the corvette's main topmast fell; the jib boom followed and in no time what had been a proud warship was little more than a tattered wreck. It was all he could have hoped for and, turning back to the command group by the binnacle, King found he was grinning like a child.

It was a joy shared: both Croft and Brehaut were equally pleased, or perhaps it was relief than made them appear so. Whatever the case, at least the escort could now be discounted and all *Mistral*'s might used against the three remaining merchants.

But even as King switched his gaze to the remaining ships it seemed further action might not be necessary. Two of the Indiamen had veered away to avoid their wounded colleagues and had done so in such haste as to throw their sails into a confusion of flapping canvas, while the last, and sternmost, was luffing up and apparently surrendering. And the cause was equally plain; while he had been concentrating solely on other matters, the pursuing British had closed up and would soon be bringing their own great guns to bear. One, the leading frigate that might well be Donnelly's *Narcissus,* was showing a line of bunting from her fore topsail yard. King glanced back for the signal midshipman but Dilson, who had adopted the position permanently on being promoted, was already rustling through his code book.

A series of crashes came from the larboard battery; some of the servers to that side must have made better practice than their colleagues and were able to bring their pieces to bear on the corvette. King turned away from the sight and knew he should count himself lucky; they had taken damage, but all could be repaired, *Mistral* might not carry spare spars but such things should be found in Cape Town and they could easily make that under a jury rig. The day should also see them bagging five juicy merchants as well as a small warship. Even with three others in sight, his share would be more than substantial; certainly enough to set himself up for a pleasant life at home with Aimée.

And then it struck him that home was probably where he should be. It was a strange thought to occur at such a time, but he had heard others describe odd emotions after battle and supposed he must be experiencing something similar.

It was not that *Mistral* had fared badly; the crew were still settling down and could be expected to do better next time, and there was a good deal more he had yet to discover in his new command. But those moments spent wondering if they could silence the corvette seemed to have sapped something vital from within; he felt exhausted and not a little dispirited. The hands had taken to cheering, something King could readily understand though not condone. Normally such an outburst would be contained by his lieutenants, but through the gaps in the hands' yells he could also hear Adams and Murray. The pair were further forward in the waist and apparently in the midst of a heated argument.

Croft began to bellow for silence and, when it finally descended, strode forward to the break of the quarterdeck to attend to matters forward.

"Corvette has struck, sir," Brehaut reported more solemnly. "As has the first Indiaman."

"Very well," King replied automatically.

"*Narcissus* is signalling for us to engage the second merchant," Dilson looked up from his signal book. "Though I believe she is surrendering also."

"Acknowledge," King ordered. "And ready the cutters. We shall need marines to secure prisoners, so notify Lieutenant Hopkins." There would also be prize crews to organise, repair parties that must be selected then sent to the damaged ships and a whole raft of sorting, while they would have to see their own rig was put to order as soon as possible. With several hours of daylight to come there should be plenty of time, although it still seemed a massive task and King could not shake the sudden feeling of apathy that threatened to take him over.

He took a turn along the deck to clear his mind. He had gone through much in the past few years; the loss of *Kestrel*, then capture and escape, followed by the scrapping of *Hare*. But he had also archived a great deal: so many ambitions – post rank, command of a prime frigate and now, with the capture of an India convoy, there was finally the prospect of a comfortable living for the rest of his days. So why did he find himself wondering if it had all been worth it?

He didn't have the answer, although one fact was beyond question: for the first time in his life King was starting to question whether he had the energy, spirit or inclination to remain in the Royal Navy.

Part Three

1.

On the few occasions that Banks had met and spoken with Commodore Sir Home Riggs Popham, he had always considered him pleasant and gentlemanly enough, if undeniably excitable. His movements were quick and jerky; he seemed to think faster than he could talk, constantly changing the course of conversation or challenging seemingly indisputable points, and all the time there was the impression that he might break into hysterical laughter at any moment. But on that particular day, and in the clean, orderly yet somewhat bare surroundings of his office, the man was excelling himself.

"The two we have examined to date are well loaded," he enthused, his eyes sparking with life. "Mainly silks and spices of course, but worth a fair deal, and we have great hope for the others."

Banks sat stone-faced and said nothing. He had left Portsmouth under Admiralty Letter, which meant no share of any prizes they took would be going to an Admiral. Though Commander-in-Chief, Popham remained a fellow Commodore so surely had no claim. Such things were for others to decide, however, and he had no intention of raising an objection now; especially as the man opposite would not be easy to argue with.

"And the corvette will repair well; she shall make a tidy command for an aspiring officer." The thought seemed to strike a chord with Popham and his eyes flashed. "Tell me, Sir Richard, how are repairs progressing with Mr King's frigate?"

"Well, I believe," Banks replied. "Damage to the tophamper is currently being addressed, they are only awaiting a t'gallant mast that must be cut down to fit."

"Splendid, splendid. And the vessel, she pleases him?"

"So I understand. He undoubtedly gets the best from her."

"Fellow did well – damned well," Popham declared. "I would that there were more like him. Still, we must make do with what we have, what? I assume he will be back at sea forthwith?"

Banks blinked; he had just explained *Mistral*'s need for a topgallant mast. One had been located and the work on it would not take more than a day or so, with slightly less to see the spar in place, but Popham seemed happy to disregard such technicalities.

"As soon as his ship is ready, yes," he finally confirmed.

"Good, then I might impart more news," Popham announced suddenly as another thought occurred. "An American brig called here recently; the *Elizabeth* – you will see her anchored under the fort." Now Popham's eyes grew distant. "My wife's name, don't you know?" he added and Banks shook his head a little awkwardly.

"I am a lucky man indeed," Popham continued unaware. "With a wife who compensates for all that is frail in friends and malignant in enemies."

There was a pause, which Banks gathered to be unusual in conversations with the Commodore. "You were speaking of a brig, sir?" he prompted.

"Indeed, Captain Waine, the American – fine fellow, you must meet him," Popham continued, his usual mode of speech returning. "He has offered me his vessel and full support; says he will accompany any force I raise personally, so there's no doubting either his information, or intentions, what?"

Banks remained unmoved; Popham had enough emotion for them both.

"You see, Sir Richard, there is insurrection in the *Río de la Plata,*" he continued, his eyes darkening. "The natives are unhappy under Spanish rule and it is ripe for the picking – now what do you say to that?" The man sat back in his chair and eyed Banks expectantly.

"An interesting observation indeed," Banks agreed, temporising. "Though surely beyond our concern?"

"Beyond our concern?" It was very nearly a shriek. "But my dear sir, we are on hand, and with a force that would otherwise be idle. Do I need to emphasise the resources the country has to offer? Why there is flour in great abundance, and beef cattle – both items we feel the lack of hereabouts and will be welcomed by the London market if nowhere else. And even a complete fool must be aware of the rich mineral deposits to be expected..."

Banks shuffled awkwardly in his chair.

"Those in high places shall certainly appreciate an inroad into such a rich resource," Popham continued. "Even if some less enlightened may not..."

"But the Spanish must surely be maintaining a garrison?" Banks questioned.

"Oh indeed," Popham agreed, though with a dismissive wave of his hand. "Less than a thousand and those mainly colonial troops or hired labour. Captain Waine estimates Buenos Aries could be taken with less than five hundred trained Englishmen, and I have asked General Baird for three times that number."

"And has he agreed?" Banks asked, wondering how far the opinion of a foreign merchant captain could be trusted.

"He is considering it," Popham conceded, "though we have worked together long enough and know each other well."

"It is no short trip," Banks continued. "Buenos Aries must be three thousand miles off, yet you speak as if it were but across the Channel."

"I say again, we have the only troops capable of striking at such an opportune time. Why, there is the 71st – a fine regiment and with me at St Vincent. You cannot imagine warriors such as they being satisfied with a simple garrison posting. And I might take the Chinese artillerists," Popham muttered, his mind apparently wandering off at a tangent as he fingered a small silver pencil thoughtfully.

"Forgive me, sir," Banks began. "I know nothing of any Chinese..."

"Artillerists," the Commodore interrupted sharply. "My Marine Battalion faced them at Blaauwberg. Came over to our side as soon as they saw how the wind fared."

"Indeed? And can they be relied upon?"

"I see no reason why not," Popham declared.

Banks raised his eyebrows questioningly although the effect was wasted.

"The Spanish will not know we are even at the Cape," Sir Home continued. "We shall have the entire country before anyone in Madrid, or London, is aware. And do I also have to point out that all trade with the Philippines will then be ours?"

"You might inform London before you move," Banks suggested, but Popham was resolute.

"It takes three months to extract a reply – why, I have yet to receive confirmation that the government even know we are in place."

"And the French?" Banks persisted.

"The French?" Popham questioned, momentarily confused. "What of the French?"

"Linois is off the *Île-de-France* and rumoured to have at least one liner within his force. Then there is Leissègues with five warships and the Hamburg brig that came in on Tuesday reports Willaumez to be nearby."

"Willaumez is heading for the 'Indies," Popham replied with what was close to a sulk. "Besides, I intend to take my own squadron, as well as any transports needed from the original invasion force."

"And if you meet with one of the enemy flotillas, will you have enough?"

"With three liners I can deal with any of them," the Commodore confirmed.

"And if two of the enemy's groups were to meet up, what then?"

"Then I shall face such a situation should it occur, Sir Richard," Popham declared, dropping the pencil on his desk with a clatter. "Though frankly do not think it will, and have to regard such a degree of pessimism to be particularly unbecoming."

"Then I apologise, Sir Home," Banks announced with a complete absence of sincerity. "Though I should not be doing my duty if I did not point out the obvious flaws in your plan."

"There are no flaws in my plan, Sir Richard." Both men were now angry and the atmosphere had grown tense.

"Then tell me who shall be protecting Cape Town?" Banks countered. "With all capital ships absent as well as a fair proportion of the garrison the place will be in danger of recapture. Why, there may be an invasion flotilla on its way here even as we speak, yet you will be leaving no one to defend from any attack from the sea."

"Why, you shall defend us," Popham told him simply.

"Me, sir?" Banks was amazed. "I am under Admiralty orders to make for the *Île-de-France* and see what is about."

"Well you shall just have to postpone your little cruise,"

Popham sniffed. “Far greater matters require your attention at Cape Town; I am surprised you should treat such an important outpost with such scant regard.”

Banks drew breath. “Sir, I have but four frigates,” he protested.

“Vessels which you will no doubt find to be ideal,” Popham agreed. “Remember we are about to enter winter and Table Bay suffers from extreme winds. If the enemy are coming, which I frankly doubt, they may choose to land in False Bay instead, so speed and communication will be essential.”

“But I cannot protect both areas,” Banks protested. “Even defending one will be a stiff call. Why, you are asking frigates to take on ships-of-the-line and such a thing is impossible!”

“Not as I gather,” Popham replied primly. “From what Captain King relates, Sir Richard Strachan achieved just such a feat in his recent action – well Sir Richard Banks must simply prepare to do the same.”

* * *

Adams stepped from the gig and began to make his way along Strand Street. It had not been particularly hard to swing some time ashore, not with commissioned officers being allowed a fair degree of latitude in such matters. But there had still been the inevitable delay while small and apparently trifling commitments needed to be attended to. These included consulting with Williams, the gunner, to calculate the total amount of powder and shot used in the recent action and ensuring that supplies of the latter would be available in the slightly larger bore that *Mistral*'s French guns required. Then there were his division's requirements: checking the small number of wounded were recovering and that hospital space could be provided for any that did not, as well as all the regular demands that plagued the most junior lieutenant. These were all new responsibilities for Adams although he found little attraction in the novelty; with untold riches almost within his grasp, his days as a sea officer must surely be numbered. That, and knowing Anne was less than fifteen minutes away, had made him a very preoccupied young man indeed.

But now he was finally ashore and with the sun high, warmth in the air and nothing more to curb his enthusiasm, he fairly bounded along the road. In his pockets were two golden guineas that had been borrowed from the purser. The loan had been secured at an exorbitant rate of interest, although Adams would hardly have cared were it doubled. Soon he would have enough to pay back both Foil and Summers, then open his own ledger in whatever bank he chose to patronise. If his calculations were correct, and since capturing the merchants he was not alone in working such things out, there should be more than enough to keep him and Anne in comfort at least until a position with the East India Company came his way. Or any other business enterprise; he was not dead set on the HEIC; there would be several others pleased to benefit from the services of one such as him. Unless he decided to start a private venture for himself, of course.

But before then he was relishing the prospect of announcing his good fortune to Anne. She would be delighted, and such wealth must surely raise his profile with her considerably. They had already calculated that she was no more than five years, eleven months and three days older than him, which was nothing for a man in his early twenties. Besides, the older they became, the less the difference would seem and he had long ago decided that he and Anne should grow old together.

Before leaving for St Helena he had moved her to a better room within Johnston's and left sufficient funds to cover all expenses; with the additional two guineas he was bringing now she should have more than enough to last the three months or so that Mr Brehaut recommended a prize agent would need before advancing funds. Of course, the government would not pay out so quickly; it might take far longer – years even – before *Mistral*'s crew were fully reimbursed for their actions. But that was the job of an agent, and why they would receive such a healthy portion of his money.

He was at the head of the Keizersgracht now and turned to cross the road, narrowly missing a horse and carriage as he did. It felt good that matters such as interest rates and monies outstanding were starting to lose importance, giving him the freedom to concentrate fully on his future. But as he grew closer to his goal, all he could truly think of was seeing Anne once more, that and informing her they never need to be parted again.

The entrance to Johnston's seemed unnaturally quiet: Adams had not expected her to be waiting outside, indeed she might be unaware *Mistral* had even come in the day before, although still he felt a measure of disappointment. But were that the case, Anne would be equally oblivious to the prizes currently lying at anchor or the wealth they contained. The realisation made his anticipation almost impossible to contain and he fairly skipped through the front door and into the hallway.

After the brightness of the noonday sun the parlour was uncommonly dark and there was no one to see him in – respectable houses like this did not encourage single men to call on women's rooms without some sort of announcement being made. But when Greta, one of the owner's daughters, did appear she hardly seemed pleased to see him.

"Is Michael with you?" she demanded curtly by way of greeting.

"Michael?" Adams asked in mild confusion. "Michael Summers? No he is aboard ship, though will doubtless be given leave in time. Why do you mention him?"

The girl considered this for a moment, then shook her head. "It is of no matter," she replied, although her manner was still cold and she viewed Adams with mild disdain. "But you are here," she observed pointedly.

"I am a lieutenant and so permitted certain privileges," Adams answered stiffly. "And I have come to see one of your guests, a Mrs Callaghan."

"Well you cannot," Greta snorted adding, "she ain't here," in a strange fusion of Teutonic accent with London slang.

"Not here?" Adams repeated softly as his world began to crumble into small pieces.

"Left about three weeks ago," Greta confirmed, "on the convoy, as far as anyone knows."

"But she can't have," Adams protested. "She simply must be in Cape Town."

"Well we can all agree on that," the girl huffed. "And so should our money – she left with her account unpaid; Papa is not pleased."

Adams shook his head; there must be some mistake, there had to be. Anne promised to wait for his return and here he was – Adams had kept his side of the bargain.

"Owes for eighteen nights' board, and fare," Greta told him stoically while consulting a small piece of paper. "Then there was laundry and other additions. Some clothes remained, otherwise we would not have extended credit to begin with, though they turned out to be worthless. When all is considered, one pound nineteen shillings and five pence three farthings is outstanding."

Adams' eyed widened. "That much?" he gasped.

"She also bought from half the shops in Shortmarket Street," the girl elaborated. "Ran up accounts and had them sent here, the pullet."

Adams reached into his pocket and found the two guineas; he had intended them for Anne, but not quite in this manner. He passed the golden coins across the counter; Greta collected them with the snap of a practised hand and a few copper pieces were thrust back in exchange. Adams pocketed the money without even the momentary pleasure of having provided for Anne this one last time.

"Will you tell Michael that I asked after him?" the girl enquired with the first sign of softening. Adams nodded, turned, then stepped out through the front door. Outside the sun still shone and the day remained every bit as warm, but he noticed none of this; all he could feel was a cold pit of emptiness inside.

* * *

"The man is mad," Banks stated bluntly when he had recounted his conversation with Popham to King. The pair were perched on a wooden bench in the anonymity of Cape Town's Heerengracht which, although busy, was probably a safer and more confidential place to talk than either of their ships.

"I had heard him to be a mite eccentric," King agreed cautiously while trying to ignore the fact that he owed his latest promotion to the officer in question.

"Mad I said, and shall stand by it," Banks maintained.

King glanced at him. "You're thinking of taking this to a court of enquiry?" he asked.

Banks sniffed. "I am," he confirmed. "Though wonder if we shall live to see one. It is the best that might be hoped for, should we meet with Linois or his ilk."

"But there is always the chance of reinforcement from England," King reminded him.

"My dear Tom, that is exactly what we were supposed to be!"

"But by now the Admiralty will know Cape Town is definitely ours..."

Banks shook his head. "Perhaps, though I cannot see it myself. With what we have already provided, the station can be set up as before. Goodness knows the natives are on our side; within months all should have been as it was in the last war, with the Eastern trade secured. Then we might have been able to start feathering our own nests."

King nodded; although the idea of a cruise and making even more prize money hardly held the attraction it once did. "But what if Sir Home were to take Buenos Aries?" he asked. "Surely that must also be to England's benefit."

"If he could hold it, yes, though I don't judge such a thing viable," Banks replied. "The local population may be eager for capitulation, but there is Montevideo not so very far away; they have considerably more troops stationed there and it is a fortified town. I cannot see the Spanish sitting back and accepting the loss of one of their major assets, not when they have the capability to take it back." He paused and added a wry smile. "But then I so evidently lack Sir Home's optimistic outlook."

King pursed his lips; it was a rum situation indeed. With the bulk of the original force gone, Banks' ships could post a guard over Cape Town itself, but little more, and if one of the French battle squadrons were to appear it would be a tall order for four frigates to fight them off. Should they fail, the French might not have the troops to mount an invasion but Cape Town would be extremely vulnerable and, with enemy warships forming a blockade, must surely cease to be of any use as a re-victualling station.

"Oh, and there was another thing," Banks snorted. "He wants to speak with you."

"Me?" King questioned. He had barely exchanged more than a dozen sentences with Commodore Popham and, after what he had just heard, was in no rush for more. "In what connection?"

Banks shook his head. "I cannot tell," he admitted. "Though do not suspect it will be to your liking."

* * *

"Intricate piece of ropework," Greenwood remarked. His mess was off watch and he had just returned from a private matter forward so was surprised to see Russell still seated and working at their table. Before him were several lengths of cordage together with a deadeye which he was trying against the line.

"It's a bobstay collar," Russell explained. Then, taking his eyes off his work, grinned. "Though I expects you knew that."

Greenwood nodded and took a seat opposite. "So what are you about?"

Russell placed the deadeye back on the table. "We need a replacement," he said. "Old one is worn and Pipes said I might try for it, though not while on watch – there's too much what needs doing quickly."

"So, can you set one up?" Greenwood asked and Russell nodded.

"Reckon so, it's just a matter of splicing and seizing and I'm no stranger to either."

The topman watched while Russell collected the wooden deadeye again then, placing it in the bight of the line, proceeded to clap on yarn with quick, neat turns. In no time the elm block had been secured and Russell turned his attention to the line itself. Measuring against the old piece of tackle, he made a straight cut with his clasp knife, and Greenwood was quick to notice how sharp the blade must have been to sever the fibres so cleanly.

"You're coming along nicely," he commented gruffly.

"Like I say, I done all the bits before," Russell shrugged. He had flipped the fid out from his knife and, after turning the line back on itself, was now splicing in an eye. It was a procedure Greenwood had done himself on many occasions and witnessed countless times more but, in the hands of a man who had been a lubber and a crook not six months ago, there was still something strangely fascinating in the procedure. Russell spliced well and without obvious effort, the stiff line being twisted and teased in what were clearly capable fingers. Soon there were eyes to both ends of the line and he placed the piece down apparently satisfied.

"Harridge will use that, sure as a gun," Greenwood told him.

Russell shrugged. "Needs to be wormed, parcelled and served first, of course," he muttered.

"Maybe so," Greenwood agreed. "Though I don't reckon you'll be doing the next in your own time."

* * *

It would be strange meeting Croft here, in the anonymous dining room of their former lodging house, but King had his reasons. For a start there was little confidentiality in the great cabin; he trusted McNamara of course, as he did the other stewards, but tonight they were to discuss something more sensitive than shipboard routine or even a plan of attack. This was undoubtedly a personal matter so needed to be treated with the greatest sensitivity.

And King was early; he settled himself in a corner seat at least half an hour before they were due to meet and was pleased to note no other diners in the plain little room. But then he was reasonably sure Croft would not be late and it would have been awkward to arrive together, while King also knew he needed time to compose his thoughts before they talked.

Actually Croft arrived shortly afterwards, which made King wonder if he had the same idea but, after a brief handshake and the ordering of that day's made meal, the two settled quickly. In the neutral location it was easier to ignore differences in age or rank and a conversation soon began; the pleasant talk of colleagues who had once been wary of the other yet now were undoubtedly friends.

"So three days at the most?" King asked as he clumsily broke into his bread roll.

"I might even say two," Croft chanced. "It all depends on the dockyard."

"Depends on the dockyard," King grinned. "How often have we heard that?"

"I think they will not let us down," Croft conceded.

"No, you are probably right," King agreed. "After all, we have sent a fair bit of trade their way of late."

The two laughed easily for a moment, then King grew more serious.

"Actually, James, that was what I wished to discuss with you."

Croft nodded; he had expected something aside from talk of the current repair although quite what still concerned him.

"I met with Sir Home today," the younger man continued, "he is pleased with our recent action." King paused, now that Croft was before him this was not as easy as he had thought. "Very pleased," he continued, "and wishes to show his appreciation formally."

Croft bit into his own bread and remained silent; there was little a Commodore could do in the way of honours to a simple lieutenant. Perhaps in Sir Home's case there might be promotion as he seemed to enjoy the act, but he had only recently taken up his post aboard *Mistral*, so that was out of the question.

"Yes," King continued uncertainly. "He was talking of the corvette we took. Murray saw her in and reports her to be basically sound, though there is much to do to her tophamper, as well as the hull."

Croft nodded cautiously, he had heard as much.

"Of course, nothing can be carried out for some while," King added. "As we know, the dockyard here is filled to capacity. But there is urgent need for such a ship and exceptions can be made. To be realistic it is still unlikely she will be ready for sea in anything less than six months and throughout that time will need a man to look after her, see her through the dockyard repairs and then on to fitting out, raising a crew and working up."

"You are talking of a commander's post," Croft remarked sharply, and it was almost an interruption.

"I am," King agreed, "and you are not being offered that." For a moment the two eyed each other like rivals, then King softened. "Not at first anyway. If agreeable, you will be allowed to transfer to the prize and take her as your own. Be in overall charge with a carpenter, boatswain and gunner as support; the standing officers can be decided upon later and obviously you will be consulted."

It had been easier thinking this through in the privacy of his cabin. With Croft sitting opposite, the process was almost painful, especially as an inner voice kept telling him it was the wrong move and he did not want to lose his first lieutenant.

"It may take weeks before she is even properly assessed," King continued. "Though months is not unlikely..."

"I understand," Croft declared, despite the doubt in his eyes.

"When she is ready to be taken into the service, and providing you have seen to your part effectively, Sir Home has agreed to promote you to commander, with the prize as your first ship."

There was a pause as King had expected, although it was one he found impossible to maintain.

"It is meant as a compliment to me," he persisted. "And quite customary; I understand every first officer at Trafalgar was treated similarly."

"That is so, sir," Croft agreed before a rare smile appeared. "Though our action was hardly such a battle."

"No indeed." Both men laughed once more, then King continued, "So what think you?"

The meal arrived at that moment and they were quiet as portions of a beef and kidney pie were placed before them along with two dishes of vegetables. For a moment the pair stared at the food as if it was something quite unknown, then Croft began to speak.

"It may be a compliment to you, though I am indeed honoured," he confessed. "And this is not a move I had cause to expect." That was true, he had been fearing something far worse. "But may I ask, do I have choice in the matter?"

"Choice?" King had collected his combined knife and fork from his pocket but was making no attempt to use it. "To be frank, I have no idea," he admitted.

Since speaking with Sir Home that afternoon King had been thinking of little else. An initial annoyance at losing his second in command had soon been displaced by far more personal regret. Rather than lacking the services of an executive officer he would be missing Croft as a friend, something that almost came as a revelation. "I should say so," he finally decided. "Though wonder why you ask."

Croft, who had collected his own knife and fork, now placed them on the table once more. "Because I have no wish to go," he said.

"Not go?" Now King had heard everything. "But it is

promotion," he insisted. "A man of your mettle could see a ship that size through the dockyard with his eyes shut. Just attend your duties and you will come out a commander and captain of your own vessel."

"I am aware," Croft replied almost primly. "Though it is not what I wish."

"Is it the prize money?" King asked. "Do you intend to retire?"

"Retire?" Again the smile. "A while ago I might," the older man confessed. "Though much has happened since. But if I am honest the money has no bearing, for I have little use for the stuff." Now he was playing idly with his napkin ring and King found himself waiting intently. "There is no one for me in England, no home as such, and neither has there been for many years. My salary is spent on mess bills, uniform and the occasional stay ashore when needs require, I truly have no need for more."

King supposed that was understandable and was strangely sorry.

"Oh, I should like promotion, I cannot deny," Croft continued, "though had long since discounted ever being in charge of my own ship, and surely would not refuse a swab were it offered. But then neither did I aspire to becoming first luff of a frigate," he added with a twinkle. "At least I had not for many years."

"One comes with the other," King told him in a level voice, despite his thoughts being in turmoil. "If you stay with me you will remain a lieutenant and likely never be given such a chance again."

"Then so be it," Croft responded with unexpected force. "My time aboard *Mistral* has been short but satisfying and I do not want for it to end."

"But promotion to commander," King reminded him. "It is all but promised..."

"As it will be when I do retire," Croft replied more lightly. "It is customary now for oldster lieutenants to be made up a rank when they finally go ashore."

"So I understand," King agreed. "But not the same as commanding your own ship."

"Possibly not, though I am content as second in command," Croft answered, almost sadly. "And, as I have said, feel you and I work well together: I do not wish for more."

2.

Due to her importance on the station, *Mistral*'s repairs were completed in good time: by the beginning of April she was at sea once more and heading north to patrol the waters off the western coast of Africa. The work carried out had mainly been to her spars and rigging so there was no need to evacuate the people, something Croft regarded as fortunate as all had been through enough changes of late. It might be an unconventional theory, and one he would hesitate to share with other officers, but still he felt the main workforce of a ship was something more than an anonymous body of faceless men. Each were individuals, with unique personalities and skills and it was by assessing and valuing their traits that the best could be achieved from them.

Those that currently inhabited the lower deck had not got off to the finest of starts and he was more conscious than most that their temperament at the beginning of *Mistral*'s commission had been poor. But that was not to be surprised at, with all having to get used to a new and recently captured ship as well as a fresh set of faces. Then there had been the recent action and the prospect of imminent wealth – something the hands had been quick to pick up on even without official announcement. However encouraging such rumours might appear, the argument and discussion they provoked hardly made for a good corporate feeling.

Things were continuing to improve however, and Croft hoped he had been instrumental in the change. Even while she was at anchor, he had continued the programme of continual drills; exercises that not only trained the hands but also revealed their qualities and allowed changes to be made to the station bill. Anyone not actively involved in the repairs was set to tasks that ranged from small boat work to yet more dumb show practice with the great guns. Not all had taken readily to the extra duties, especially as there was the absurd seaman's notion that any period at anchor was automatically a time to rest, but Croft had persevered. Minor disputes between *Hare*'s original crew and the new draft were still common but close supervision, backed by consistent minor punishments and one official flogging was also bearing fruit and he was quietly pleased with the result.

And the ship herself had improved far beyond the physical attention they had paid her; for a start their time in harbour had allowed the opportunity to give their new home a thorough clean. Sadly the decks were not paper white – none of the sand available had been sharp enough – but the strakes were now properly burnished and provided a far better surface for those accustomed to going barefoot. And below, fresh gravel lined their bilges and gave a clean base for her casks, while the scent of vinegar permeated everywhere and all brassware shone like gold.

Changes had also been made to her officers; Murray was gone, with all silently agreeing that the gunroom was a better place without him. The young man was offered the same chance Croft had so determinedly refused and, with the assurance of his type, had snatched at it. Since then, and for all the time *Mistral* remained at anchor, hardly a day passed without his being rowed about his new command, ostentatiously inspecting her from every angle and making sure all aboard his old ship were aware of his new importance. But Croft hardly noticed; at the time he had known what he truly wanted and there were no regrets.

For he already had a good ship and, though only second in command, wanted no other. And *Mistral* was in prime condition; she had three, probably four years' normal service before the first refit would be due, with a similar spell to follow before she was relegated to home waters. If spared, he should like to spend that time with her. Or longer, if King remained captain.

But that was the future, and it was a delight to realise there was almost as much pleasure in considering the present. *Mistral* had finally been able to provision properly, and that was something else that gave him immense satisfaction. Cape Colony was now several months into British ownership and efficiency ashore had improved to the extent that victuals could be supplied with reasonable reliability. These were still being provided by the East India Company but were of a comparable if not better quality than any normally received through government contractors and, with her holds finally cleared of French stores, they could now offer a traditional seaman's diet of salt beef or pork on four days out of seven, with an agreeably hard Suffolk cheese and British baked hard tack at all other times. There were the inevitable substitutions;

currently sweet oil was being issued in lieu of butter but the people appeared generally content, as they were with the short period of shore leave allowed before the ship sailed.

Despite the prospect of riches to come, none of *Hare*'s former crew had received any pay for over a year. Those of the fresh draft were slightly better off, but even some of them would have had difficulty raising the statuary two shillings that regulations stated every man must have in his pocket before being allowed ashore. It was the captain who finally came to the rescue; Croft had never figured King to have access to funds though somehow he had managed to produce enough coin to present each man with a guinea on account; an act that was universally appreciated and had also contributed to the general improvement in morale.

Several had not returned immediately, of course – that was always the risk, even on a foreign station and, though they would be giving up a considerable sum in prize money, a few took the opportunity for a more permanent departure. But the deserters were no great loss and mainly consisted of the blonde, heavily boned local men who had caused nothing but problems since their arrival, so Croft was delighted to see them go.

Once the remainder's money was spent in Cape Town's less salubrious quarters and *Mistral* put to sea once more it was as if a page had been turned. All major evolutions aloft could now be carried out in truly respectable times while both the speed and accuracy of their gunners was something to be proud of. And proud they were; since leaving harbour no day had ended without the hands being totally exhausted yet the satisfaction and confidence they exuded was almost tangible. Given the choice, Croft would be content for the exercises to continue until the ship finally paid off, but such things must come to an end. And now they had reached such a high standard he supposed it only reasonable that a make-and-mend should have been called for the rest of that day.

And so with the early dinner still being cleared away, some of the hands had already begun assembling for what looked like becoming another swelteringly hot afternoon. In no time the decks were filled with men once more but, rather than the shrieking of pipes or rumble of gun trucks, there was a snick-snick-snick of scissors as fresh cloth were cut, or the scraping of knives on bone for scrimshaw. And all the while the gentle murmur of conversation made a far softer alternative to the bellowing of orders, or curses, from implacable petty officers. But though the sounds of the half holiday might be alien, Croft was content; as he paused at the break of the quarterdeck he could see several groups of men and noted with satisfaction that nearly all contained some from both drafts. Not so long ago this casual socialising between the two would have been unheard of, and that it was occurring now confirmed Croft's personal belief in another, more subtle, benefit from regular exercise. Men who worked together – who had learned to cooperate to the extent that each depended totally on one another – also found it easier to live together. There was no reference to this in any training manual, but he had noticed the effect before and was pleased to see it demonstrated again now.

The bell rang out seven times just as a figure appeared at the mouth of the companionway. Croft recognised Adams, the third lieutenant. He would be taking the afternoon watch but was not due to relieve Hall and Dilson, the master's mate and midshipman who currently shared the conn, for a half an hour. Croft regarded the young man as he inspected the traverse board and decided there was one more area that might deserve a little attention.

As an officer, Adams was performing adequately enough while, on a more personal level, he seemed to be working well with Cooper, their newly appointed second lieutenant. But though Croft had never credited himself with any form of insight, there was definitely something about the lad that cried out for attention.

He appeared detached – isolated almost – which, in a crowded gunroom set amid an equally congested warship, was something of an achievement in itself. Moreover, though there was nothing to actually criticize in his performance, Croft suspected not all the lad's attention was being given to his duties.

It was hardly something that could be addressed now, not on an open deck and with a make-and-mend in full swing, but he would be keeping an eye on him. For there was no doubt in the older man's mind that Adams was in sore need of support.

* * *

All about their fellow seamen were involved in various activities although none of the four gathered together on the forecastle were particularly interested in practising any craft, and neither did they have clothing to make or mend; they were simply sitting in the early afternoon sunshine and enjoying not having to work for a spell.

"I'd like a tattoo," Swain announced after some consideration.

"Sure of that are you?" Greenwood enquired. "'Cause there's no going back."

"Stewart's having one," the holder pointed out as if it were a reason. They all turned to look and, sure enough, the dark-haired ordinary seaman was leaning back on the forebitts while two of his messmates worked on him. One held his shoulders against the wooden support while the other, a foretop man, repeatedly pressed a short piece of metal into the skin of his chest. Stewart's contribution to the affair was to stay reasonably quiet, although the look of pain and anguish on his face spoke volumes.

"Yes," Parker remarked after a moment. "I can see the attraction."

"Fellow's just been made up to ordinary," Greenwood explained. "A lot of Jacks take their first tat. then."

"Are you ordinary?" Russell asked and Swain shook his head.

"Not me," he declared with an element of pride. "Too much knot tying and fussin' about aloft for that."

Russell made no comment but Greenwood could read his thoughts.

"You could be," he told him seriously. "I told you before."

"Never been aloft," Russell shrugged.

"We could takes you," Parker offered.

"Time was when every raw hand had to touch the maintop cap afore they was fed," Greenwood recalled.

"Aye, chased them up with a ropes end, they did," Parker agreed casually.

"But they had to put a stop to it," Greenwood added.

"Oh yes, it had to end," the second topman nodded wisely.

Russell looked from one to the other, then Greenwood took pity on him.

"You see they soon got to realise that fallin' from the mast brought nothing but bad luck," he told him.

"And you know how superstitious your regular Jack can be," Parker agreed with a sigh.

There were times when Russell was still not sure when he was being teased, and this was one. But he had long since discovered there to be nothing unkind in the ribbing his messmates doled out; besides, the more he learned of his craft, the less likely he was to be made fun of.

"Well I ain't going aloft, an' I ain't ordinary," Swain maintained in an attempt to steer the conversation back to himself. "But I'd still like a tattoo."

"Why don't you ask Robins, then?" Parker suggested. "Though he seems to be making a right dog's dinner out of Stewart's chest."

The seaman had broken out in a sweat now; drops were running freely down his face, with some mingling with the fresh blood collecting on his belly.

"Don't fancy Robins getting' a hold of me," Swain announced.

"Jackson will do it," Parker advised.

"Jackson?" Swain questioned.

"Him what used to be a barber," Greenwood confirmed.

"Still is," Swain added brushing back his locks. "As you'd both know if you got rid of them benish pigtails."

"Well there you go," Parker retorted. "You want a tattoo, speak to Jackson."

"Aye, he'll tat. you for sure," Greenwood agreed. "An' he's a gun captain, so can get as much powder as he needs."

"Gunpowder?" Swain asked in alarm.

"Aye, it's what the best uses. A powder tat. will last longer than Robins' cheap ink."

"But ain't that..." the holder began doubtfully.

"You do want it to last?" Greenwood questioned.

"Oh yes, it must be permanent," Swain confirmed.

"So what you gonna have?" Parker asked.

"And where?" Russell added.

"You'd be entitled to a turtle," Greenwood told him. "Means you've been across the equator."

"Aye, anyone can have a turtle if they go south enough," Parker confirmed. "Even those who ain't ordinary."

"I don't want no turtle," Swain told them; then his eyes grew round. "I want a wild animal. A big one: face on and right across me back."

"A wild animal, eh?" Greenwood repeated thoughtfully.

"Right!" Swain assured him, warming to the theme. " A lion, or a tiger, somethin' you don't mess with."

"Well, I'm sure Jackson could organise that for you," Parker agreed. "What say we seeks him out?"

* * *

"So you were a Company man?" Brehaut remarked. Their main meal had long since been served and the first dogwatch begun but, as the make-and-mend remained in force, some of *Mistral*'s officers were still at the gunroom table and were now enjoying a dish of tea. "Good to work for, are they?"

Cooper, the new lieutenant, considered this for a moment as he sat back in his chair. He was a large, yet mild man with gentle eyes and a thoughtful expression. "I'd not say good, though the rewards were substantial," he replied eventually. "I only rose to fourth mate before transferring to the RN," he added, "so really didn't get the full benefit. But even as a cadet there were a pile to be made."

"A pile?" Foil, the purser, asked with sudden urgency. "In what manner may I ask?"

"You are given an allowance for cargo," Cooper explained, "and permitted a measure of private trade. There are rules, of course, though even a fool can make a decent profit, providing they have the funds to finance their purchases."

Manning, the surgeon, was also listening intently. He had once shipped with the Honourable East India Company, though it had been for such a short time it was hardly worth the mention. "So why did you leave?" he asked now, and Cooper shrugged.

"It was the same trip over and again," the lieutenant explained. "Admittedly the journey was long enough to give some variation: the Indian Ocean is nothing like the Atlantic, as some will be aware. But after four Eastern voyages I began to tire of it. And I did not care for some of the Honourable Company's practices."

"How so?" Brehaut asked.

"I shall not hide it from you, gentlemen, the ships are a free trader's dream. Not content with sums earned legitimately, many of their officers and most of the men make a deal more from smuggling. It is a trade I deplore and one that accounted for my father's life; I will have nothing to do with such business."

"He were a revenue man, I suppose," Brehaut sighed, adding, "A thankless task, to be sure."

Cooper went to reply but Foil had more urgent concerns. "But it would have been a lucrative career!" he insisted. "Would you not have made more by staying, even if it meant keeping your nose clean?"

"Oh for sure," Cooper confirmed. "But I did not choose to." He looked about the small assembly with a genial smile. "I have long since discovered that money has its uses, but only to a point. Can any of you tell me that, should you suddenly discover a fortune to your credit, it would truly change your lives significantly?"

"'Tis strange you should mention it," Brehaut grinned, "but some of us are hoping to be close to that position before long."

"Of course, I was forgetting the earlier prizes," Cooper agreed. "But that surely proves my point. You have riches in sight, yet still serve at sea when a more comfortable life is so readily available ashore."

"Well I shall retire as soon as my funds arrive," Foil snorted. "And was tempted to before, though not if it meant paying that robber who acts as my agent such a fee for an advance."

"But forgive me, sir, you are more a man of business than a seaman," Cooper countered. "What of you, Mr Brehaut?"

"Oh, I shall stay afloat, riches or not," the sailing master confirmed. "It is the only life I know and sincerely wish for no other."

"And Mr Manning?"

"I also," Manning agreed. "I have a wife and family in England who will doubtless find the money of considerable use, though should be happy to spend a little more time at sea before I finally joins them."

"Then I think you can understand my motives," Cooper concluded. "The Dear knows my current salary is less than I might expect as a Company mate, but there is always the chance of significant prize money, as you yourselves have proved. And, despite the common belief, I find serving His Majesty to be a more honourable vocation."

"And did you not come from Commodore Popham's ship?" Foil this time. The purser enjoyed a jape and was clearly working up to one.

"*Diadem*?" Cooper asked in innocence. "I did indeed."

"So there would have been a clash of majesties I have no doubt!"

The others acknowledged this with a round of polite laughter, although Brehaut was more interested to see how Cooper reacted to the joke.

"No, I shall not allow that," the new man declared genially. "Sir Home was not the easiest to serve at times and is indeed one of the reasons I requested a transfer, but he does not hold himself quite so high."

Again the laughter and Brehaut felt relief; Cooper had been presented with the perfect opportunity to disparage his former master, yet chose not to, even though some resentment clearly remained. After having to endure Murray, such an attitude came as a relief and he felt they had a worthy addition to the gunroom. "So, what think you of *Mistral*?" he asked at a break in the conversation.

"I like her fine," Cooper declared. "She is a sound ship and well commanded. There are a few changes I should like, though mainly to her rig, but I suppose we all have our individual preferences."

"The people are coming together well," Manning agreed. "There is always a danger of illness when two groups are merged and I had feared a bout of fever but it never materialised."

"Yes, the people are another matter," Cooper agreed, although he had a wry look on his face.

"How so?" Brehaut asked.

"It was something I observed earlier," Cooper explained. "In the midst of the make-and-mend. A large man, built like a bear and with almost as much fur."

"Sounds like Marshal – did he have a queue?" Foil asked.

Cooper shook his head. "Cut in the modern manner," he said.

"Then it were Swain, a holder," Manning again. "What of him?"

"He was having a tattoo cut across his back."

"Yes, that would be Swain," Brehaut confirmed.

"But what a subject!" Cooper remarked, resting back once more.

"Your Jack chooses any manner of designs for their tattoos," Foil grunted. "I do not care for the practice myself."

"Nor I," Manning agreed. "It is simply asking for mortification."

"What was he having?" Brehaut asked, intrigued. "The design, I am meaning."

Cooper shrugged. "The thing were barely half done and there was little more than a chalked plan for the rest. But it looked like the head of a large animal."

"Not unusual," Foil commented nonchalantly. "I seen leopards, tigers, eagles... one fellow had a snake what coiled about his body; claimed it kept him warm of a night."

"So what was it with Swain?" Brehaut persisted.

Cooper looked bemused. "Well that's just it, it looked like the head of a giant pig; now why would anyone want that?"

* * *

Mistral ended the northernmost leg of her patrol the following noon and as soon as Brehaut confirmed their position King ordered her about. For the nine days they had been away from Cape Town nothing of note had been sighted; they had spoken with five neutrals, including a Portuguese brig that might have spotted a collection of warships to the west. But her master had understandably kept them at arm's length and, despite diverting for two days to check, nothing was revealed. Apart from that, and the occasional swarm of native fishing craft – frail looking things to be so far from land – the journey had been fruitless. However, no sooner had they made their turn and were steering south once more, they caught their first sight of what appeared to be a considerable force heading in their general direction. And it was not long before some were revealed be to warships, although most aboard *Mistral* remained unconcerned.

"My guess is we've found Popham's squadron," Brehaut chanced when the sighting was still little more than a collection of topmasts. "They were due to leave for South America shortly after us, and might be expected hereabouts."

King made no comment, although he was a little concerned that the Commodore's plans were so widely known. The sailing master was proved correct shortly afterwards when their colours came into sight and *Mistral* began to bear down on the eclectic mixture of shipping. They would be heading for their first stop at St Helena and, even as he considered them, King could still not believe such a plan had come about.

It would be several hours before verbal messages could be exchanged but the fine weather was holding out and King was reluctant to quit the deck. Instead he decided to wait out the time in relative peace by the taffrail and was not displeased to find the first lieutenant already there.

"I shall take my leave if you wish for some privacy, sir," Croft offered.

"No, James, stay do," King told him. The pair had not begun on the best of terms but much had happened since and the older man's decision to refuse a command and so remain with *Mistral* had meant a great deal to King. He had also come to like his second in command far more than he could have expected and valued their occasional private conversations.

"So, Commodore Popham is bound for St Helena," the first lieutenant remarked.

"Indeed," King confirmed, "though I am surprised such matters are common knowledge. Not that you should not know, or the sailing master if it comes to it, but surely there is a limit?"

"Oh, I think you will find it general knowledge," Croft replied in his usual level manner. "Cape Town is not Portsmouth; many there have several occupations so the gossip is always more virulent."

"I had not considered that," King confessed, "but suppose there is little chance of the enemy discovering the mission?"

"Not at so great a distance," Croft agreed. "And truly it is a great distance."

"But if they are calling at St Helena first..." King reminded him.

"Ah yes," Croft agreed, "where he hopes to collect more troops – how many did he take from the Cape?"

"I know not the exact figure, but he was hoping for the entire Seventy-First," King answered. "General Baird estimated he should take more than a thousand as a bare minimum, and that was not counting artillery."

"Will the General be accompanying him?"

King shook his head. "He has matters to keep him at the Cape. Besides, I have the impression Sir David was not entirely in favour of the expedition."

Croft said no more and King was secretly glad. It was one thing to discuss Popham's plans in the vaguest of terms but, were they to dig too deeply, criticism would be hard to avoid, and that was a very different matter. For there could be no disguising the recklessness of what Sir Home intended.

Even after Trafalgar and the relative stability the action had brought, there was still no sight of an end to the war, in fact never had the country relied more on imported goods from the East to maintain its economy. The Cape Colony provided a vital link in that maritime trade and had only just been retaken; to risk losing it on the chance of securing another station, one smaller, more vulnerable and less important, was rash in the extreme.

"Flag is answering," Dilson, the signal midshipman, announced from further forward. *Mistral* had been flying that day's private signal for some time and now, it seemed, it could be read. "She's *Diadem*," the lad confirmed.

"Steer to pass her close," King ordered without moving. Much may have happened since they left Table Bay – the Commodore would have had time to think up many more schemes to extend Britain's presence in the Southern hemisphere, although he sincerely hoped not.

"And what when we return?" Croft chanced after a minute or so had passed.

"Then we continue regular patrols, though nearer to the Colony," King replied in a lower tone. "Sir Richard will have to cover the area from False Bay as far north as Cape St. Martin."

"A wide field," the first lieutenant remarked.

"He believes four frigates will manage it, though not simultaneously, of course. I understand a series of sweeps is proposed, with each ship remaining within signalling distance of one another."

"Even then..." Croft began, but did not continue. It seemed redundant to point out the obvious flaws to a fellow professional. Nothing could be blamed on Commodore Banks, of course; Cape Colony was simply too large an area to be properly monitored by the force he commanded. And if it came to action – if he were fortunate enough to bring all together to face either a French invasion force or a battle squadron similar to that already encountered – the British would still be facing poor odds indeed. With no solid battleships to fall back on, the enemy would be able to take them by strength alone. Then there would be nothing left to see off further attack and a vital station must inevitably fall.

"Well, we should make the Cape within four days," King remarked, finally breaking the silence.

"Indeed sir," Croft agreed, "and may find the situation changed when we do. And even if not," he continued, "it might only mean holding out a short while, for reinforcements could already be on their way."

King nodded, that was probably true; perhaps a month, maybe six weeks and further supply vessels may indeed arrive. Such a force would be escorted by light warships which would be a godsend, for frigates could certainly fight frigates. But if the enemy possessed anything larger the solid bulk of at least one line-of-battleship would be needed. So it made matters that much worse when three such ships – two-deckers that had been provided to give just such support – were heading away, even as they watched.

3.

There was no important news from either side and, after King had exchanged the briefest of very public words across the water with Hugh Downman, *Diadem*'s captain, *Mistral* was free to continue her return journey to Cape Town. But feelings of disappointment remained with many aboard her and were not confined to the officers. The lower deck may have been unaware of the overall situation, but they could deduce much from watching Popham's ships sailing away and sensed they were being betrayed. And when nothing significant happened for the next few days, King began to worry about the general lowering in morale. It seemed that, despite the effort put into forming them into an efficient unit, they were starting to grow truculent. Since sighting Popham's ships there had been two instances of fighting during mealtimes and a petty officer reported an able seaman for insolence; something that saw the man instantly reduced to an ordinary hand, although King feared they had not heard the last of the incident.

But all was soon to alter, although not in the manner any would have wished. Three days after seeing the departing fleet, and as dawn broke on what promised to be yet another fine morning, a call came from *Mistral*'s main lookout. The topmasts of another flotilla had been spotted; they were as yet undefined but the news was surely enough to banish any lingering resentment and even dreams of impending riches. At first some, mainly the new men, assumed them to be another India convoy even though the sighting's position and heading should have been enough to quash such fancies, while those of *Hare*'s original crew had reason to be more cynical. *Mistral* was a more powerful ship than their old brig and boasted a crew almost three times larger but, if what they now faced turned out to be another enemy battle squadron, a single frigate would be no match for her.

King had been in the process of shaving when the call came through and appeared on the quarterdeck still wiping the soap from his face.

"Where away?" he demanded of Cooper who had the watch.

"Off our larboard bow, sir," the new lieutenant replied. "Lookout believes them to be steering sou'-east."

King handed his towel to McNamara and reached for the traverse board. *Mistral* had been travelling south in broad sweeps to maximise her chances of sighting an enemy and it was no accident that the extreme end of the westbound leg, when the ship was close-hauled and on the starboard tack, had coincided with first light. With Cape Town still over a day's sail away, this was likely to be the last opportunity to spot anything significant before rejoining the rest of the squadron and they might finally have struck lucky.

The wind was a few degrees north of west and *Mistral* was sailing under topsails, topgallants, forecourse and staysails, which was comfortable canvas for the gentle weather. They could add more, close with the mystery sighting and have it identified in no time but, with the rest of the day ahead, that might not be the best of moves. Besides, whatever they had smoked had the windward gauge, and was creeping ever nearer of their own accord.

"Keep her as she is," he ordered, replacing the board. Then he felt at his chin, half of which still carried the last day's stubble. Brehaut and Croft had also heard the call and were just appearing on deck, closely followed by Adams. For a moment King considered returning to his quarters and continuing his shaving; whatever they were facing was too far off to be of immediate danger and a dramatic exit might impress his officers and show him as a captain with ice cold nerves. But most on the quarterdeck knew and, he hoped, respected him enough not to need such cheap tricks while he in turn had no wish to spoil the trust that had built up between them all.

"French do you think, sir?" Croft asked as he approached.

"It is possible – probable even," King answered nonchalantly. "Though we shall know for sure in time. And, be they enemy or friend, we lie to the east; with the sun still rising, they will have been aware of us for far longer than we them."

"Too far south for it to be Commodore Popham's force returning," Brehaut reported after studying the log and traverse board. "Only a major storm would have made them approach so, and the glass has been steady for more than a week."

"I have them!" It was the voice of Summers, the senior midshipman; Cooper must have sent him to the masthead as soon as the sighting was reported. "Five for certain; and I'd say making sou'-east by south."

"What size are they?" Croft bellowed.

"All are still hull down, sir," Summers called out in reply. "Though would judge them large; frigates at least, maybe bigger."

"And we can all agree they are unlikely to be Indiamen," King added more softly.

"Not from that direction, sir," Brehaut confirmed.

"Then I think we may assume them to be an enemy battle squadron."

King's words were greeted with stunned silence, even though all present had been thinking along similar lines. There were at least three such small fleets known to be in the immediate area not to mention the one that had captured their prize further to the north and to which *Mistral* originally belonged. King pursed his lips; Summers had mentioned five ships, which probably ruled out the last possibility but, whatever their identity, it looked as if they would be facing them on their own.

Banks had sent *Taurus* further south to patrol as far as the Eastern Cape, but *Relentless* and *Athena* should not have strayed farther than Table Bay. How close to port they were was another matter but, as *Mistral* and *Taurus* were expected back at any time, he doubted Banks would be so very far away.

"Take her south," King directed, breaking what he realised must have been an expectant silence.

"Starboard your helm," Brehaut ordered crisply and the ship began a gentle turn to larboard. King noticed how the braces were trimmed equally smoothly and held the wind at all times; it was truly gratifying to see those hours of exercise bearing fruit. Of course, some of the hands would not approve of his action; to effectively turn from an enemy was rarely a popular option amongst the lower deck, although King was hardly doing that. By heading south the enemy would still be closing on them and he could see little point in doing anything else. If the mystery squadron truly were hostile, the fact would be revealed soon enough; all he had done was reduce the speed at which they would meet and the alternative, sending *Mistral* in to gain a positive sighting, was far more dangerous. Venturing too close to an enemy force that had both strength and the wind in their favour was a fool's game; if frigates were included – as they undoubtedly would be – *Mistral* must then retreat for all she was worth, while relying on every spar, line and stitch of canvas holding to keep her safe. And it was still barely first light: the entire day lay before them. Holding back meant they may meet up with one or another of Banks' ships or possibly even raise Cape Town before they were overtaken.

And then he remembered exactly what support he could expect there and, yet again, it seemed the height of stupidity for the station to have been left so unprotected. Had so much as a single British two-decker been on hand, King felt they could have dealt with anything the French cared to throw at them. As it was, should all Banks' frigates be available, they would still be outnumbered while, if the French possessed even one liner, defeat seemed inevitable. But bitter thoughts would get them nowhere; far better to react to the present danger, and that was something King had no intention of courting closer than was necessary.

* * *

Summers held on tightly to the main topgallant mast as the ship manoeuvred. He was now reasonably competent aloft and prided himself in being able to do anything and go anywhere a topman could, although privately never felt entirely happy above the level of the fighting tops. And his present duty on the main crosstrees was not his favourite, neither was the responsibility it carried when an incorrect bearing or the simple act of mistaking a ship-of-the-line for an Indiaman could cost his ship dear.

"We're turning from them," Grover, the official masthead lookout commented. "And no bad thing, in my view."

Normally an able seaman would never have thought of addressing an officer directly although being aloft encouraged a degree of informality and many of the minor rules could be ignored.

"You think them the enemy then?" Summers questioned.

"Ain't no doubt about it," Grover replied before adding with a grin, "They're certainly where the enemy ought to be. Though you wouldn't find me sticking my neck out and saying so, not until I sees their colours."

Summers nodded and looked back at the faint grey shapes that seemed unmoving on the horizon.

"So, what would you say they were?" he asked.

"You mean French or Spanish?" Grover asked. "No way of tellin', not at this distance. But my guess would be French and, if there are five, some at least will be heavies."

"You mean fifth rates?" Summers asked.

"In the main," the seaman agreed. "Might have a liner or two amongst them an' all, but we won't know that till they're hull up."

Summers scratched at his nose before raising the glass to the sighting once more. Even ignoring what Grover said, it could hardly be an invasion fleet. For a start the direction was wrong, they would have had to come from South America, which seemed unlikely. "So the Colony won't be at risk," Summers remarked, more to himself.

"Na, the Cape'll stay safe," Grover confirmed with feeling. "It's us, the ships what've been sent to protect the place – we're the ones who look like being in for it."

* * *

They had yet to beat to quarters or even clear for action and whether there was a potential enemy on the horizon or not, the normal routine of the ship must continue. And being a washing day, most of the lower deck had been sent to scrubbing their second set of clothes so Greenwood's mess was one of many gathered about a row of tubs.

"Fine porker you're sporting there, Swain," Henderson, a boatswain's mate, remarked as he passed by.

"It ain't a pig, it's a boar," the holder maintained solidly. He had removed his shirt to keep it dry and, being totally involved in the washing, did not turn around.

"Never said it were a pig," the warrant officer sniffed as he paused to consider the image, "Though they're all very much of the same ilk."

"Now that's where you're wrong." Swain's tone had the air of one who had repeated the same thing on several occasions. "Boars are wild, with tusks that can kill as soon as look at you."

"Don't see no tusks on yours," Henderson replied. "Looks more like a pig to me."

"Tusks is coming," Swain assured him, still without turning."

"I has to wait a while afore they're added," Jackson, who had created the tattoo, told the warrant officer solicitously from the opposite side of the group.

"Otherwise the colours might run," Parker added with a straight face.

"Then for now it's a pig," Henderson concluded.

"Then you're wrong again, see?" Swain looked up angrily from his work and, finally realising who he was addressing, added,

“They're totally different, Mr Henderson, sir.”

“Get chitterlings from both,” the boatswain's mate replied airily, before moving on. “Get chitterlings from any kind of pig. And brawn.”

“It ain't a pig,” Swain stated sulkily. “It's a wild boar. They're totally different.”

* * *

Adams was not on duty for a good two hours yet he, like most of those officially off watch, had come on deck and, again like the others, was currently considering the enemy squadron. King had ordered no additional sail to be set and the light grey smudge of masts and topsails could now be seen by all aboard the frigate as the enemy grew steadily closer. But it would be some time, probably several hours, before they were properly in view and any action would have to wait a good while after that.

The young lieutenant was well aware of the situation although remained untroubled by it. Five enemy ships – the last part was still officially in doubt although most were privately sure – five enemy ships could play havoc with their four, and that was assuming *Mistral* were able to meet up with Commodore Banks' entire force. Even if the French lacked a two-decker they built powerful frigates; any of their new big forty-gunners would be capable of taking on even the mighty *Relentless* while smaller concerns, like themselves, would be easy meat. But still Adams was not impressed, and neither did he show any particular concern or worry. Since discovering Anne to have fled, his life had altered dramatically and so had something of his character.

Gone was much of the foolishness of youth: his previous guileless and at times juvenile outlook had been replaced by something more mature and worldly. To counter that he was now far less able to tolerate fools, and trivialities that had previously amused now seemed an unnecessary distraction.

The strange thing was, the change had not been immediate but had come on slowly and almost without his noticing. When he walked away from that boarding house on the Keizersgracht it was as if his whole life had been reduced to tatters and for several days he remained in deep mourning, both for his lost future as well as a past that now seemed somehow tainted. But time and the current voyage had helped him rebuild; a phoenix had risen from the ashes of his old life and it was a stronger, more deadly creature than any that had been before.

* * *

"I can see colours." The call was from Dilson at the masthead; the lad had replaced
Summers some while ago and as his adolescent shout rang out, all aboard *Mistral* paused to listen. "And they appears to be French," he continued.

The news caused a stir in the waist although those on the quarterdeck were less impressed.

"Believe?" questioned Croft from the mizzen fife rails. "What are you saying, Mr Dilson? Are they or are they not?"

"I-I believe so, sir," Dilson maintained.

"French without a doubt," Greenwood, who now had the masthead, added in a fatherly voice and there was another mumble of discussion from further forward.

"Well that only confirms what we have all been suspecting," King decided. "How far to the Cape, Master?"

"Brehaut scratched at his chin. "I doubt we'll raise it in daylight, sir," the Jerseyman replied. "Not unless the wind picks up and it shows no sign of doing so."

"Very well, then it is going to be a long haul and we have already postponed the midday meal. Pipe 'up spirits' and send the hands to dinner, then see the watch below are properly stood down. "And gentlemen," he added to the officers surrounding him, "may I suggest that those not on duty also go below? With the enemy at such a distance there is nothing to be gained by remaining on deck and I shall not clear for action in the foreseeable future. Take what comfort you can find and come back refreshed, for I think it will turn out a busy night."

* * *

Despite his own advice, King had no intention of leaving the deck for there would be little point; once stuck in the confines of even such palatial quarters he would soon become fretful as he imagined the size of his enemy and the speed with which they were overhauling *Mistral*. Far better to remain in the sunshine and open air of the quarterdeck where he could at least keep an eye on the approaching squadron and deny them any chance of deception.

Besides, he had other things to think about and, though the possibility of considering anything other than the impending combat might have sounded absurd to most, it was King's personal avenue to relaxation and he took it gratefully.

When they had left Table Bay there had still been no official assessment of the prizes recently taken, but even an initial inspection was enough to assure all interested parties of the wealth that would be coming their way. The first of the merchants had been carrying a cargo of silk which alone was in sufficient quantity to make all the commanding officers comfortable. If the other four proved as lucrative they would receive a substantial sum indeed and that was without considering the value of the corvette. For the first time in his life King could see a future where he was not dependent on earning a living and that inevitably meant the coming action, whether successful or not, would be the last he need fight.

Such a conclusion left him with mixed feelings; almost all his adult life had been spent at sea with only the briefest of times as a land animal, first as a beached lieutenant on Malta and then an escaping prisoner of war in France. But even they had been directly connected with his vocation, so how would he adjust to a permanently shore-bound existence?

The answer was clear: Aimée. She remained the one thing that made any sense of his life and, though the concept of spending the rest of it with her might not have been directly in his thoughts, there was something remarkably similar. For she had made a difference to him that was far greater than simply becoming his partner. King had never lacked ambition, but she promised something different from a rise in rank or prestige. With her he would have a home, a future: life in its fullest terms. And though he might dream of grand manors or country estates, all he truly required was enough land for privacy, a house that kept them warm and dry and financial security. With the amount he was in line to receive all were pretty much guaranteed, but without the essential element Aimée provided, would be worth nothing. And there was a corollary to that: Aimée gave him something no amount of money could ever buy.

They need not stay in England; there were plenty of places throughout the world that would welcome a gentleman of his measure and it might not even mean saying goodbye to the sea. He could set up in trade; nothing large, for that would inevitably separate him from his love, but enough to keep him in touch with the element that also held part of his affection. And there would be funds aplenty to finally settle the problem of his wife; lawyers could be employed to negotiate with her, possibly a settlement, or even an act of parliament – he had no idea how much either would cost but remained confident that, whatever the price, he would be able, and willing, to meet it. And he was not unaware of the luck that had followed him so far; the loss of his arm had been devastating but could have been so much worse. No more than a single step to one side, or Robert Manning not detecting the infection in time, and he would have ceased to exist long ago. All he needed was for that luck to hold out a while longer and a life better than he had ever imagined awaited.

The bell rang twice and he realised such purposeless dreaming had kept him occupied for all of half an hour. He ceased his pacing and looked again towards the enemy. They had grown marginally closer and he knew he must now forget all thoughts of the distant future and focus on matters more immediate. For this may well be the eve of an action and an important one. But as he waited for the hourly log to be run he was not as anxious as he might have been, which was doubtless all to the good and something else that Aimée could be thanked for.

* * *

By the end of the first dogwatch the enemy had closed to the extent that they could be more accurately identified.

"Three frigates for sure," Summers, who was back at the main masthead reported. "And there is definitely a liner, though the fifth is further off and I cannot be certain."

King glanced at Croft. Having a two-decker strengthened the

enemy's hand significantly; if their final ship turned out as powerful it would make the French virtually impregnable. In Strachan's recent action frigates had fared well against ships-of-the line, but they had been well supported and at any time could have retreated behind the bulk of British battleships; even if all Banks' force were raised, they would have no such refuge and, though *Relentless* was about as heavy as fifth rates came, she remained a frigate.

"No, the fifth is another single-decker," the lad finally announced and there was an audible sigh of relief from several on the quarterdeck.

"So at least we know what we are dealing with," Croft muttered softly. Quite unconsciously, he and the captain had retired to the taffrail once more. This was in no way to exclude others from their conversation although both men were aware that, in such a delicate situation, anything negative they said was liable to spread despondency.

Mr Brehaut reckons at least another fifty miles to the Cape," King mused. "We may yet raise it in daylight, though it is doubtful."

"And if we fail to spot another British ship before, shall be in a quandary indeed," Croft added.

"How so?" King questioned and Croft shrugged.

"We must stay in contact with the enemy, so will be forced to close," he replied. "And with the wind as it is, there is always the danger of a lee shore."

"But do you truly think them likely to approach so?" King persisted. "They can hardly be aware Popham and his liners have fled; indeed I should be surprised if they know our entire force with any degree of accuracy. So to broach the shore in the dark is the last thing they will attempt."

Croft acknowledged this with a nod, although he was still clearly troubled.

"We must remain in contact, however," he insisted. "And, though there has been a splendid moon of late, that will undoubtedly mean drawing closer."

"Then we shall," King declared. "I know nothing of the French ships but would still wager *Mistral* to be faster and a deal more manoeuvrable. It may be a memorable night, though I think we might still hold them off until dawn, and daylight should reveal at least one other British cruiser in sight."

"Sail ho, sail off the larboard bow!" the voice of Grover, the current masthead lookout, roared out."

"If not before," King added with a wry grin.

"Sir Richard, do you think?" Croft questioned.

"Let us hope so; it is certainly where I would expect him to be." King looked forward once more. "Mr Brehaut, steer directly for the sighting and raise the royals if you please."

With the enemy so near they could afford to stand away a little, especially when there was barely an hour in which to close with the fresh sighting. The additional canvas was set and drawing in good time and soon *Mistral* began cutting a fine plume of spray as she powered through the darkening ocean.

"Sighting is steering north, though I think she has smoked us," Summers reported. "Yes, she is tacking," he added and all on deck waited. "Coming round now and heading for us close-hauled. And she's adding her own royals!"

That was good news indeed; were Banks to have been patrolling off Cape Town he would have been looking out for *Mistral*, and if his lookouts were as sharp, may even have noticed her increasing sail. Summers had yet to make a positive identification, although King was already certain that *Relentless* was bearing down on them.

He was proved correct within half an hour; by then *Mistral* had added her studding sails and was fairly skimming over the water. But the light was failing fast and, though the two ships were closing rapidly, it would still be some time before signals could be exchanged. King could have instantly communicated the approach of an enemy fleet in a number of ways with some methods, such as the use of lights or by releasing *Mistral*'s sheets, being visible from a far greater distance. But he had more to convey than simply the presence of an enemy and needed to converse properly with Sir Richard.

He strode forward and singled out Dilson, who was standing with his signals party.

"You have today's code ready to hoist?" he asked.

"Indeed, sir," the lad replied. "And our number."

"Very good. I wish to tell Sir Richard of the enemy."

Dilson flipped open his signal book and began to leaf through the pages. They were using the latest code that allowed for quite complex signals that used fewer flags and it was ironic that the system had been devised by Home Popham, the very man who had made their current situation so very desperate.

"I can signal their bearing with one lift and strength with another," Dilson reported.

"Have that bent and ready at the fore," King directed and Dilson touched his hat before making for the larboard gangway. There would be a deal more to say if they could only get into range before dark, but at least Dilson was on top of matters.

"Enemy are spilling their wind!" This was Grover at the masthead again, and his message was almost to be expected. *Relentless* probably still lay out of sight, but the French would have noticed *Mistral*'s change of course and sudden increase in speed.

"Must have guessed we've spotted something," Brehaut commented to Croft who had joined them at the binnacle.

"Aye," the first lieutenant agreed. "And probably not sure what; 'tis pity *Relentless* is no longer a liner."

King could feel the ship move beneath his feet as *Mistral* encountered a patch of rougher water while the hum of the wind through her lines had risen slightly. He looked up at the canvas; every stitch was tight and there was little sign of strain, although he sensed he would soon have to order a reduction. Then, peering past the forecourse, he considered *Relentless* again. She was still hull down but they must be close to the time when messages could be read.

"*Relentless* is signalling!" It was Summers at the main who also had the benefit of the deck glass. "Four, seven, nine!"

"That's today's code, sir!" Dilson reported from the forecastle.

"Make the response and our number," King ordered, and the balls of bunting shot up to *Mistral*'s foreyard.

"Interrogative," Summers reported, when the signal had been acknowledged.

"The first signal, Mr Dilson," King directed from the quarterdeck.

"I don't like the feel of this wind, sir," Brehaut remarked, and King's attention returned to the canvas.

"Very well, bring her round and strike the stuns'ls," he ordered. The sky was darkening visibly now, but they were close enough to *Relentless* for a few minutes' conversation and it would be foolish to lose contact with the French.

"Flag acknowledges, sir," Summers reported as *Mistral* staggered into the turn. "And she's sending." The lad's voice had risen an octave; any movement on deck would be magnified many times over by the height of the main mast and it was clear Summers was having difficulty maintaining his position whilst keeping Banks' ship in sight.

"Bring her further to starboard, and heave to," King directed.

"Seven, one, six," Summers cried out.

Dilson had been sensible enough to realise what King had in mind, and was leading his signals team back as he flipped through his book.

"From *Relentless*, sir: 'Remain'," the lad reported formally as he reached the quarterdeck.

"Very good; acknowledge," King ordered. If his theory was correct, Banks would have the rest of the night to find his other two ships and be ready to meet the enemy at first light. He glanced across; the French had returned to the wind but under reduced sail and were approaching once more although far more cautiously.

"It will soon be dark, sir," Croft remarked and King glanced up at the sky.

"Indeed, though we shall have light at first," he replied. And that was true; the moon had been full and gloriously bright for the past few nights. But it was due to set at two; then there would be several hours with only the stars to reveal the enemy.

"With luck, Sir Richard will be able to raise *Taurus* and *Athena*," Croft continued more softly. That was also correct; were it not for the presence of a French two-decker, King felt they could have made a fight out of it. With roughly equal sides it might turn into a slogging match and none would come off undamaged, although he would still be confident of victory. But that extra battleship made all the difference; even if she had been another frigate there might still have been a chance, but a ship of at least seventy-four guns and potentially something larger – once that were added to the mix all was changed. The enemy frigates would have a stalwart to shelter behind, while a battery of thirty-two pound cannon would make short work of any fifth rate's fragile hull. Yes, it was the inclusion of that liner that tipped the odds decidedly in favour of the French and seemed likely to turn what might have been a hard-won victory into total and humiliating defeat.

4.

By the time darkness fell, *Relentless* had been out of sight for some while leaving *Mistral* as the only obstacle between five powerful warships and the Cape of Good Hope. But still King was in no rush to clear for action; once the bulkheads were down and *Mistral* had been turned into a true ship of war, there would be little comfort for those below and, with action promised for the morrow, it was better for all to get what rest they could. In the light from the early moon the French were plainly visible as they lay hove to, roughly five miles to windward; should anything be attempted he would have more than enough time to react.

But, yet again, his concern did not stretch as far as his own needs and as Cooper came on deck to stand the middle watch, King was still next to the taffrail and contemplating the line of enemy shipping that faced him.

Mistral had her main backed and, as with the French, was making barely perceivable progress crabwise as wind and stream gently nudged her towards the coast of Africa. If Brehaut's predictions were correct, this still lay some forty miles off, though close enough to be a consideration when it came to action. For now, though, he could see no sign of life from the enemy. They lay in line abreast with roughly half a mile between each; in the centre was the liner. The big ship looked far less ferocious with moonlight picking out her sails while the frigates to either side might have been courtiers paying attendance. Were he to have a squadron at his back, one that was powerful enough to meet such an enemy and his to command, King had no doubt how he would attack.

To career head on would be a mistake: the French held the windward gauge and their central ship lay right in its eye. Better to make for one of the outer markers and focus his force on that, leaving the enemy to reform and make what counter attack they could. Such thoughts were futile, however; there was no such squadron: when Banks finally did appear, the best they could hope for would be far inferior to what faced them. And, in any case, King had no experience of handling a group of shipping – in truth, he was still getting used to commanding a frigate.

The bell rang eight times and he stood to one side as the midshipman of the watch appeared with two seamen in tow to heave the log. It was a senseless procedure; *Mistral* was making no noticeable way: the small triangle of wood simply floated next to the hull and, after the lack of progress had been duly noted, King was able to return to his equally futile deliberations.

However, the diversion had served one purpose by emphasising the time he had spent on deck; really a spell in his quarters was called for. And then a compromise appeared; Cooper had the watch; what King had seen of the new man had been relatively impressive so, with little happening on deck, he decided to make a closer acquaintance.

* * *

" So is that it, then?" Swain questioned. "The Frogs are just going to sit there watching us?"

Greenwood's mess were on watch but, with little likelihood of anything needed from them, most had collected on the forecastle and were staring out at the silent enemy across the water.

"What would you prefer?" Parker enquired.

"Force like that could take us without even tryin'," Jackson sniffed.

"So why don't they then?" the holder grumbled. "There's light enough to see by."

"They probably will, come daybreak," Greenwood said. "But for now they can't be sure what we're hiding."

"Hiding?" Swain again. "We ain't hiding nothing."

"We know that, but the French don't," Parker explained. "All they can see is us, but they know we were speaking with someone a while back."

"So they're worried there might be a fleet they can't sees?" Swain asked as realisation dawned.

"That's about it," Greenwood confirmed. "They've probably heard of Popham's ships and that there're two-deckers amongst them; for all they know a couple could be just over the horizon waiting."

"Come daylight they'll come close and see for themselves," Jackson added. "Then they'll be in for a surprise."

"But there ain't any liners waiting for them," Swain protested.

"Aye," Greenwood agreed laconically. "That'll be the surprise."

* * *

"We're expecting Commodore Banks at any moment," King told Cooper.

"So I understand, sir," the lieutenant agreed. "I've warned the lookouts to be aware and young Cole is at the main masthead with a glass to be on the safe side."

"With luck Sir Richard won't be long, or alone," King continued. "But we shall lose this light in a couple of hours."

At his word, both men looked across; the moon was well on its way to the horizon and now marked out the French ships more in silhouette.

"If he comes in darkness, we will have to alert him to the current situation," Cooper pointed out. "Should I warn signals?"

Banks would definitely have to be kept informed, although King's mind rebelled against the idea of night communication. No complex messages or subtle instructions could be sent and all methods relied on coloured lamps or flares which were hardly private.

"No, I'll not have the enemy aware," he replied. "We shall have to wait for daylight."

"That's a long time, sir," Cooper pointed out. "Can we not at least indicate our position? In the time the Commodore's been gone the French must have crept up a fair way. Once the moon sets, there'll be nothing to guide him; he might pass us and run straight into trouble."

In all the hours he had spent in private debate by the taffrail, that single scenario had caused King the most worry. If Banks had been successful in raising other ships, they would be heading back at all speed, and it would only need an error of a few miles to see them blundering in to the French line unprepared. King might counter that by burning a lamp at *Mistral*'s masthead, although that would mean abandoning any hope of manoeuvring without the enemy's knowledge and he would prefer to change position as soon as they lost the moon.

"Any open light we show will be obvious to the French," King sighed. "And a masked lantern may not be strong enough for the Commodore to notice."

"Then why not a spout lamp, sir?" Cooper asked.

King raised an eyebrow. "Explain, if you please."

Cooper took a deep breath. "It's basically a large lanthorn, sir – the bigger the better – and fully enclosed apart from a funnel to one side. The whole thing appears like a gigantic kettle but, when lit, sends a beam of light in one direction only."

"Through the spout?" King suggested.

"Indeed, sir. And when that is blocked – as it might be easily – the light is shut off instantly."

"Ingenious." King was genuinely impressed and not just by the idea; evidently Cooper had a ready brain and was keen to use it.

"A properly set spout lantern can send simple signals," the lieutenant continued. "Or guide a boat through shoal waters with no light spilled to either side; you have to be directly in front of the beam or nothing is seen at all."

"So, you are suggesting we make up one of these spout lanterns and shine it out roughly where the Commodore should appear?" King asked.

"Yes, sir; one of the lads can sweep it back and forth across that sector. With luck Sir Richard will see it and so get a bearing on us, and all the while the French will know nothing of his arrival, or our position if it comes to it."

King scratched at his chin where the stubble was just starting to become noticeable. "I'd say it worth a shot," he said after a moment's thought. "Send for the armourer."

* * *

Though an idler, and accustomed to working only during the daytime, McPherson, *Mistral*'s blacksmith and armourer, appeared promptly and seemed to understand the concept of Cooper's light.

"If it ain't for permanent use, I reckons I can knock something up within a couple of hours, y'r honour," he claimed. The man carried an aroma of metal filings and old sweat but his eyes shone bright from within a greasy face and it was clear the project appealed.

"The sooner the better," King replied and McPherson touched a bruised knuckle to his temple before hurrying away. True to his word, he reappeared just as the moon was preparing to set and this time carried with him a large bundle.

"We'll take it to my quarters," King announced. Mr Cooper, you may leave Mr Harridge with the conn for a few minutes and join us."

The great cabin was dimly lit but still bright enough to blind those accustomed only to stars and a dying moon. McPherson went to place his package on the dining table only to be stopped by an anxious McNamara determined to preserve the furniture's surface with a piece of waxed cloth. But, once in place, the armourer finally revealed his creation with an element of pride.

The lamp was very much as Cooper had described; McPherson had taken a standard issue lanthorn and blanked out three of the faces with metal plates while riveting what looked like a horizontal smokestack to the lantern's hinged door. The result was lopsided and oddly elephantine in appearance but undeniably workmanlike; the new metal trunk stretched out a good nine inches and tapered to a squared-off spout about three inches across.

"The examples I have seen in the past had round spouts, but apart from that, I'd say there is little difference," Cooper announced on examining it.

"I took the liberty of adding some extra vents beneath the burner," McPherson explained, "for fear the flame won't stay alight, or the thing grows too hot. They are in the base so," he added, indicating a series of holes with a nailless finger.

"They will not show any light?"

"No, sir. We tested it in the workshop and there's nothing to speak of."

"Then I am sure it will be fine," King announced. "And you

have done a first rate job, McPherson; we will prepare it for use without delay."

"I'll arrange for the signals officer to become accustomed with it," Cooper said, leaning forward to collect the lantern. But the armourer was there before him and scooped his creation up in its cloth.

"If you'll forgive me, sirs, I'd like to explain what care is needed to the young gentleman me-self," he said. "I've fitted an oversize wick, which should burn brighter, though it needs a finer oil an' more of it." McPherson paused and rubbed at the lantern with apparent affection. "Though in truth an extra burner would be favourite, as one could be filled and its wick trimmed while the other is in use."

"Very good," King agreed. "Indent for another burner by all means and perhaps you would remain on hand to assist?"

"I should be glad to, y'r honour," the armourer replied with a toothless smile.

"Then present it to Mr Dilson, we shall be out presently."

McPherson knuckled his forehead briefly before leaving with the bundle tucked protectively under one arm, although something of his scent remained even after he had gone.

"That is good work," Cooper commented.

"Indeed so; McPherson seems to have taken to the task well, although all the enthusiasm in the world is of little use without a solid plan to follow." King turned to consider the new man. "And we have you to thank for that, Mr Cooper," he told him. "Tell me, you seem to know a deal about smugglers and their tools; might I ask, was it ever your concern?"

"In a manner of speaking," Cooper answered cautiously. "My father was connected with the trade."

* * *

An hour later the moon had gone completely but at the main masthead the enemy could just be made out by the light of innumerable stars. Sennett, formally of Greenwood's mess but now acting as midshipman, was at the crosstrees regularly sweeping the horizon with his telescope.

"You're wasting your time, Mr Sennett," his former mess captain told him with no hint of irony. "Glasses are only good when you know what you're looking at. It takes a trained eye to make a sightin' in the first place."

"Maybe so," Sennett allowed. He was considerably younger than Greenwood and found it harder to accept the change in seniority than the more jaded seaman. "To be honest, Greenie, I needs the practice."

"Then practice on the Frogs," Greenwood suggested, indicating the French that were barely visible to the north west. "They makes any changes in their rig, and the deck'll want to know about it. Even something subtle may tell them a lot. I'll keep a watch for *Relentless*."

It seemed a reasonable proposition and Sennett duly turned his attention to the enemy squadron. He was using a night glass which was sharper than most instruments although the extra clarity was only gained by missing one of the lenses and so presented an inverted image. But with practice he was becoming accustomed to viewing the enemy so, and set himself to systematically studying each ship in turn. Despite Greenwood's warning, all was quiet; there were no suspicious movements aloft and neither, as far as he could see, were any other preparations being made. The French ships seemed content to wallow in the slight swell with their mains backed to give an element of stability, while the wind and a mild current wafted them imperceptibly closer to the Cape. After examining each for the second time he was about to break the silence when he noticed Greenwood had grown tense.

"What do you see?" he asked after a spell.

"Can't be sure..." the seaman replied. "Might be imagining it, but I thought there were something to the sou'-east."

Sennett looked: the horizon was barely perceptible and appeared empty.

"I don't see nothing..." he began, but was stopped for the second time.

"There!" Greenwood insisted, pointing out into the blackness. "Those are topmasts, I'm sure of it."

Sennett gave the seaman a sidelong glance, the horizon was blank with not even a cloud to notice.

"Set your glass so!" Greenwood directed, and Sennett obediently focussed the instrument.

"Nothing," he reported. "Just like I – no wait..."

"Well?" Greenwood demanded.

"It's a ship alright," the lad finally agreed. "Just as you said."

"Then you'd better report in to the deck, Mr Sennett," the seaman suggested.

* * *

The dark waters appeared as empty to King as they had to Sennett; if *Relentless* truly were out there, she must be a good way off. For a moment he considered squaring away; the wind was holding firm and, with royals set, they should discover if Banks was approaching in no time. Of course that would mean abandoning the French, who might also see them go and, if he were in charge of a fleet being stalked, King would move as soon as his shadow departed. Then they would be left with the problem of seeking out the enemy with every chance the French might slip past and begin a bombardment on Cape Town. So no, he would remain in position; if Banks were coming he would show himself eventually, even if it took the rest of the night.

But now the gods were definitely on his side, for no sooner had King resigned himself to yet another interminable wait, Sennett, at the masthead, sang out once more.

"I have the sighting more clearly now," the lad cried. "She's close-hauled and making good speed under royals, bearing sou'-east."

"Can you identify?" King bellowed.

"Not for sure, sir," Sennett replied. "Though, I'd say she were *Relentless*."

King smiled to himself; the lad wanted to have Banks' ship in sight as much as any of them.

"She's certainly where *Relentless* should be," Sennett added, to a round of muted laughter from others on deck.

"What course, Mr Sennett?" Cooper this time.

"Heading west I reckons, though it is difficult to be certain.

She's on the starboard tack at least."

King well remembered the perils of masthead duty and how hard it was to judge the course of a distant sighting but, with the ship close-hauled, knowing the tack was as clear an indication as any. Banks must be heading several points away from them; if allowed to continue, he might easily pass by the enemy and *Mistral* completely. This was where Cooper's lamp would come into its own, although they would have to wait until *Relentless* drew a little closer.

"Deck there!" Sennett called out once more. "I have another, close on behind; she's on the same course, though I think the leading ship might be preparing to tack – yes, there she goes – and the other's following!"

Better and better; if that truly were Banks, he had met up with at least one other. And the fact they were turning meant that, for a while at least, both ships would be heading directly for *Mistral*.

"Mr Cooper, we'll have the spout lantern at the maintop, if you please."

"Maintop, sir," Cooper repeated automatically. "Very good."

It was not uncommon to hoist lamps aloft and the burning of coloured fires was customary in night signals. But the spout lantern was very much untested and a fire in the tophamper was the last thing anyone wanted.

"Mr McPherson, are you comfortable aloft?" King asked the armourer.

"Me sir? Go aloft? Yes, sir I can do that," the man declared and King drew the impression that McPherson would have followed his handiwork anywhere.

"Mr Cooper, would you also accompany the lamp, along with Mr Dilson?"

"Of course, sir," Cooper responded instantly.

"I don't have to tell you to be careful," King added more softly. "Take sand and water; if there is any danger of the lantern catching fire, douse the flame immediately, though I would rather it thrown over the side than a fire started."

"I understand, sir," Cooper replied and there was just enough light to show the sincerity in his expression.

"You are happy with its use?"

"Yes, sir. And there will be Mr McPherson to assist me. He

would appear to have high hopes for his contraption," the lieutenant added with a grin.

Both glanced across to where the armourer was already taking great care in attaching a halyard to the lantern.

"Well, I think we're about to find out just how effective it is," King grunted.

* * *

By the time the spout lamp, its carers and associated equipment was in position the oncoming ships should have been in plain view from the maintop. But as Cooper stared out, all he could see was dark ocean.

"Masthead there, do you have the sighting still?"

"It comes and goes, sir," Sennett called down. "You got to know where to look."

Cooper sighed: he could see nothing.

"Caught a glimpse just then," Sennett added. "They're still on the larboard tack, though I'd expect them to change shortly."

"Very good," Cooper replied, adding, "Hurry up with that lantern, you two."

"Just have to set the burner, sir," Dilson explained.

Cooper sighed again. Once *Relentless* and whatever followed tacked she would be heading away from *Mistral*, and the chances of either seeing a distant light would be reduced.

"Nearly ready now, Mr Cooper, sir," McPherson confirmed. The lantern was resting in the lee of the top's low bulwark with McPherson kneeling by it while Dilson made ready with a flint and steel. The first strike failed but on the second a small flame flared up with what seemed incredible brightness.

"Get it in the lantern!" Cooper snapped, even though much of the light was shielded by the men's bodies. But soon the burner was in place, the spout had been closed, and there was total darkness once more.

"It soon gets hot," Dilson commented and Cooper realised the lad had his hand clasped over the end of the spout.

"Stuff some tow in place, then hoist the thing onto the bulwark; we have no time to lose."

McPherson and Dilson dutifully heaved the lantern up and

rested it on the ledge.

"What bearing, Mr Sennett?" Cooper called up to the masthead.

"Still sou'-east, sir, though I caught a glance then an' I think she's preparing to tack!"

"Sweep east-sou'-east to sou'-sou'-east and be quick about it," Cooper ordered.

Dilson dutifully removed the rag and the light was revealed.

"Yes, tacking for sure," Sennett at the masthead announced. "We might catch them on the next leg."

Cooper suppressed a further sigh; by the time *Relentless* returned to the larboard tack, she would be further off with dawn almost breaking; by then it was quite possible both ships would have passed *Mistral*. He glared down at Dilson and McPherson; both were dutifully swinging the lamp across the arc and it was anyone's guess how far off the light could be seen.

"Anything?" Cooper called once more.

"Can't say, sir," Sennett reported miserably. "I've lost them again, but the last I seen, they were settling on the starboard tack."

Cooper swore quietly to himself; this was the end of his brilliant idea, the one his new captain had championed yet now seemed destined to make them both look foolish. It was utterly maddening to have come so far only to fail. For a moment he was even tempted to remove the spout and let the light shine out. Surely the enemy would miss such a pinprick from so far off. But though they might, the captain would not, and it was probably more than his commission was worth to do so.

"Shall we continue, sir?" Dilson asked.

Cooper glanced at the pair; the lamp was clearly hot and both were sweating freely while an overwhelming scent came from McPherson.

"Yes, continue," Cooper replied, then opened his mouth to add more when a cry came from Sennett at the masthead.

"I have them again!" he cried. "And they seem to be tacking!"

"Turning back do you mean?" Cooper demanded.

"Yes, sir. They're returning to the larboard tack. I think they must have seen us."

5.

By dawn, the situation had moved on apace; *Relentless* had indeed spotted Cooper's lamp and, encouraged by this, King squared away shortly afterwards and began steering for the northern end of the enemy's line. The move was bound to be noticed by the French, although they would not know the reason for it, and must be equally unaware of the two ships to the south east that were still barely visible to those aboard *Mistral*. But by observing the lantern, Banks had known they were underway once more and soon altered his own course to follow. There still only appeared to be one ship behind *Relentless* but, with the confidence gained from the success of the spout lamp, King felt even three well found frigates would make an impact on the enemy's force. They might not deal with the two-decker, but some of the smaller ships could be taken, and there was always a chance the liner would be wounded enough to turn away.

The first light of true dawn appeared just as *Mistral* was drawing level with the northernmost Frenchman. King knew the sun would be rising almost directly behind him, which was to the enemy's advantage, although he remained hopeful that a strong move from his side might distract them long enough and allow Banks and the other vessel to close without being spotted immediately.

He was taking a lot upon himself of course; nothing had been arranged with Banks and many would say that for the most junior captain in the squadron to blithely lead his Commodore into action was at the very least arrogant. But then he had known and served with Sir Richard for many years and felt he understood the man as well as any, while there were instances a plenty where junior men had taken the initiative in just such a situation.

At The Nile, Foley had seen the opportunity to squeeze between an anchored enemy and the shore and all but guaranteed the British victory, while King had personally witnessed Nelson's ship break out of line at St Vincent and so ensure the capture of two Spanish liners. Besides, whether Banks and the world in general gave approval later was purely academic as far as he was concerned; King now felt more certain than ever that this would be his final action. Whether they won or lost, all he had to do was survive and a life of pleasant indulgence lay before him.

But first he had to get through this final encounter and, as *Mistral* and all aboard her were likely to be in the thick of things before long, knew the preparations should begin immediately.

"Mr Croft, I should be obliged if the hands were sent to breakfast as soon as Mr Falmer can accommodate them."

"Very good, sir," Croft replied, touching his hat. "I had anticipated such a thing and seen the cauldrons were heated early."

King accepted this without comment although it was gratifying to note that, yet again, his second in command was on top of things. During his brief spell as a commanding officer, King had regarded himself generally fortunate in his lieutenants, although he had found a truly excellent deputy in Croft; it was almost a pity they would not have the chance to work together for much longer.

"And, if you will forgive me, sir, you should take a bite yourself." This was Croft again and, because it came from him, King found he did not resent the advice.

"We all should," he replied, coming to a decision. "Summon my servant, will you?"

McNamara appeared almost instantly and King was ready with his requirements when he did.

"I want a table set on the quarterdeck," he directed. "Take mine or use a spare from one of the messes, but lay it aft of the binnacle. And do we have cabin stores remaining?"

"Yes, sir," the Irishman responded, quickly catching on to his master's train of thought. "There's gammon and eggs, some mutton chops and soft tack that will toast up."

"Then prepare enough for the gunroom and cockpit," King ordered. "Spare nothing; there will be an action later and I want none of my officers to face it with an empty stomach."

* * *

By nine, when the sun was clear of the horizon, all hands had been fed and with the last vestiges of what had been a memorable meal cleared from the quarterdeck, *Mistral* finally became a true ship of war. With her galley fire quenched, bulkheads removed and guns readied for immediate use, she surged through the lightening seas with the growing light shining through her canvas. The wind was holding strong in the north west and she clung as near to it as the quartermaster dared; there remained several miles to cover before closing with the northernmost enemy but the weeks of training were paying off and both ship and crew were ready for action.

The French had also come to life; still in line abreast, all were back on the wind and, under topsails alone, running down towards the coast of Africa and, specifically, Cape Town. It was certain that even the farthermost ship could see *Mistral* as she clawed towards them although doubtful if *Relentless* were equally visible. For Banks was playing a wily hand.

Whether he had guessed where King was leading him was impossible to say, but he obviously knew his former lieutenant had the enemy in sight and seemed content for the junior man to bring the squadron in. Consequently Sir Richard, though steadily forereaching, was obediently following a good five miles in *Mistral*'s wake. Behind him another British frigate, the masthead could still not be sure which, was keeping pace and must also be invisible to the enemy.

King felt his ship would be within range of the first Frenchman within the hour; Banks and his follower would probably take that time again to draw level and, though more of the enemy squadron would doubtless become engaged by then, at least one of them should have been taken before a more general combat began. One of them, or *Mistral*.

* * *

In the waist, Adams and Summers were at the forward batteries. Though cleared for action, the ship had yet to beat to quarters, although most hands were already at their battle stations and eager for the forthcoming fight.

"Must say, it makes a change to have a man you can trust further aft," Adams muttered to the midshipman with a pointed look at Cooper who was inspecting one of the larboard cannon.

"And to know the people are in better practice," Summers agreed in equally low tones. Adams nodded, there was no doubting every hand was more familiar with his particular task and all had learned to work as a team, but there was also a more subtle improvement. As he glanced around at the faces he realised there was no longer two factions: those who had come from *Hare* and the new intake. The men were now one crew, with a common aim and shared understanding. Such a corporate feeling was important in any vessel and vital when it came to bringing her to action; whatever happened in the next few hours he was now far more confident of both the ship and the men who sailed her.

But not of himself; that was one area that had shown no improvement. The numbness that had descended after Anne left remained; if anything the sensation, or lack of it, had grown worse and now Adams had difficulty in showing any form of emotion. Consequently, he had no fear of battle but rather the opposite. The next few hours were bound to be an overload for all his senses and one he almost welcomed if only because it might shock his feelings back to something like normality. But for now he had no anxiety over what might happen and a total absence of interest regarding death or injury: such concerns could barely be considered when a far greater pain occupied all other available space.

* * *

At the starboard cannon that seemed to have become their own, Greenwood's mess were also preparing themselves in their own peculiar way. Swain had previously christened the weapon Thumper, and Russell, who knew his letters better than any, was chalking the name on one side of the cold iron barrel. All had been in action before with the last occasion proving extremely profitable; the current battle could promise nothing like the same financial reward although each was privately sure a far greater glory remained for the taking. And they would be fighting together – that was also generally accepted – for all their petty grievances against their country, the Navy or each other, no one could doubt their inherent loyalty and neither was there any question of defeat.

For the British were superior at sea; such had been proven over many actions during the last two wars. They won far more often than they lost and the few regrettable instances that fell into the latter category were almost certainly the result of deceitful work by a perfidious opponent. Some of them may fall, but they would be outnumbered by the enemy's casualties and certain to be soundly remembered by their shipmates when the guns finally cooled. And every one was equally convinced that what they did was right; hatred for any country that dared to threaten their own had been instilled in them since birth, while the French, the old and original enemy, received a greater measure than all others put together.

There was nothing personal in this; when faced with a Frenchman in neutral circumstances none would have resorted to anything other than curiosity and probably a measure of courtesy. But encountering them in one group, at sea and aboard a warship carrying guns which were pointed in their direction there was no question in any of their minds. The day would be long, hard and bloody but it would end with those that survived glorifying in their victory. For such was their right, and so convinced was each in this that it almost cancelled out any trace of arrogance.

* * *

"One of the French is turning."

King looked up at Croft's comment. The nearest frigate was holding her course and still creeping steadily closer under topsails alone, but the next in line had added topgallants and forecourse and was bearing down upon them with the wind more on her beam.

"And they'll probably arrive at about the same time," King murmured in reply. It was no accident that the two officers were standing by the taffrail once more.

"I doubt they have spotted the Commodore yet," Croft added and King nodded in response. The French liner lay just in sight off their larboard bow and was maintaining the same course as the frigates beyond her. Clearly *Mistral* was assumed to be alone, so two ships of roughly equal force were considered sufficient to deal with her while the other three maintained their steady progress towards the Cape.

It would be another half an hour at least before the first shots were exchanged, and King had yet to formalise any plan of attack other that taking the outermost ship and working inwards. If all went well he hoped to have dealt with the first before Banks' arrival, although that was assuming much. King was confident of his ship and felt he had a crew to be relied upon, but he was still realistic enough to know things could go wrong. A gun might explode or some fortunate shot from the enemy account for a particularly vital piece of equipment. Should such a disaster occur, *Relentless* would arrive to find *Mistral* a wreck, with a pair of stout frigates on hand to meet her and a further two, along with a seventy-four gun line-of-battleship, equally ready to finish her off.

But such was the stuff of nightmares and King had no wish to aid the enemy with negative thoughts. *Mistral* was on the top line; the most powerful ship he had commanded and, though she faced a vastly superior force, there was still no need for concern. They had both surprise and spirit on their side, while Cape Town was close by should it turn into a chase. But it would not come to that; he had already decided this would be his last action and reminded himself yet again that all he need do was survive. Even if they lost, they could not hold him prisoner forever; there would eventually be a secure future with Aimée – he only had to wait for it.

And so they went into battle.

6.

The breeze stayed in the north west and, even as the sun rose further, remained firm. *Mistral* was taking it on the starboard bow as she clawed her way towards the first of the enemy who, as with the second following less than a mile behind, was sailing with more sail set and the wind on her quarter. Both stood out plainly in the morning light and appeared well set up and ready for action. King paused for a moment then turned back to consider *Relentless*. The yellow orb of early sun cast her into stark silhouette, but it was still clear Banks' ship was gradually forereaching and must surely be visible from the nearest Frenchman. Providing she continued to gain, and with another frigate following close behind, the British should take the first two by force alone. Then King turned back and noticed bunting breaking out on the leading enemy frigate and shortly afterwards the signal had been answered by the more stately liner some miles off *Mistral*'s larboard bow.

"Penny to a pound, the leader's telling his flag about

Relentless," Brehaut grunted to the quarterdeck in general.

No one seemed inclined to accept the sailing master's odds although King felt *Mistral* had already been especially fortunate in guiding Sir Richard so far. And it appeared the luck was to stay with them a while longer; the enemy two-decker, along with her remaining frigates, was sailing large for the distant station and, though messages continued to be exchanged between her and the ships closer to *Mistral*, the liner did not alter her course. King was inwardly certain no French Admiral would stand by and allow three English ships to take on two of his, so either the frigate following Banks had not been spotted, or the enemy commander in question was unusually slow in coming to a decision. Either way, the delay served the British well; every second the main body remained heading for the Cape was one that could be used to their advantage. The British would need a few more breaks on a similar level if they were to avoid defeat, but knowing one had been delivered, and so early into the combat, was at least encouraging.

"Commodore's signalling!" the masthead reported, although Dilson had already noticed and was shouting out numbers to one of his party.

"Flag acknowledges, sir," the midshipman reported – *Mistral* had been flying the enemy's position and strength from her mizzen for some while; clearly the two British ships were now able to read the other's signals. "And there is a message: '*Taurus* has joined the chase,'" the lad added.

Banks must mean Bruce's ship was the one following, which was another piece of luck. *Taurus* was a mite heavier than *Athena*; she also carried a larger number of guns and was captained by a more experienced commander.

"Make, 'what of *Athena*?'" King ordered. Were Granger to also make an appearance they would have a battle indeed although Banks' reply was not hopeful.

"No knowledge," Dilson reported dolefully.

"Then we shall just have to make do with those we have," King replied lightly.

"There's another signal from the Frog," Brehaut again, and all eyes turned forward.

"*Taurus* must be coming into sight," Croft muttered and, sure enough, the flagship had no sooner acknowledged than she turned to larboard and began to make for them on a beam reach.

Mistral should have engaged both frigates long before the liner arrived, but it was still anyone's guess how soon Banks would join him. *Relentless* and *Taurus* were showing all sail up to the royals, and King knew Banks and Bruce were making what progress they could. But before they came into range he would have to face at least one enemy frigate on his own, and he may as well get used to the idea.

* * *

This was going to be a new experience for Russell. He had been in action before, of course – on the first occasion memorably so – and, even after such a short time aboard warships, considered himself relatively hardened to the butchery of combat. But it was one thing to fight merchantmen or an undermanned privateer, quite another a crack French man-of-war like the one currently powering towards them. A second and equally large frigate followed close behind while a two-decked battle wagon – something that would have been a challenge for all three British had they faced her alone – was also close by. But he had no room for doubts; the spirit of the mess remained high and, as he stood with the rest of his fellows, their general good humour was infectious.

"Ship like that won't give so much trouble," Swain stated with no authority whatsoever. "All we have to do is wing her about a bit, then leave the remains for Tricky Dick to sort out while we goes and sees about the rest of 'em."

Greenwood, standing closer to the enemy by the starboard bulwark, was not so sure but, as the holder's comments were generally positive, felt no need to dispute them. And he was generally confident; all *Mistral*'s carronades were loaded with bar shot and had been ordered to target the masts. But the great guns, such as the monster those of his mess would be serving, were carrying round shot and would be firing straight at the enemy's hull; a mode of attack he found both satisfying and somehow more honourable. It would not be easy though: unless the captain called for some fancy sailing, the French should keep the windward gauge and be a hard nut to crack. Nevertheless, all *Mistral*'s gunners were now used to their weapons and, in practice, could despatch three broadsides in five minutes, a reasonable rate for any ship of their size. If there was to be manoeuvring, some of the servers would be needed for other duties: Swain and Brown to join the afterguard, Frant and Collins to fight fires while, if canvas had to be set or struck, he and Parker must go aloft. Several would also join the larboard piece if that battery came into use and, should both broadsides be required at once, there would be further changes. But still he felt they would put up a decent fight and he wasn't as apprehensive as some.

Swain, for a start; despite his bellicose ways, Greenwood knew the holder was not as aggressive as he made out and that somewhere deep within that thick skull a degree of sensitivity lurked. In a pitched fight there were few better to be alongside, but Swain had already revealed that waiting for action was not his strong point.

And then Brown, the former tin miner and another who could handle himself in a ruck. As he took a discrete glance, Greenwood noticed the man was definitely showing signs of strain and even Jackson, their gun captain was putting on a brave face. But he would pull through, they all would; determination and spirit came naturally to men who lived the life they did. The waiting was definitely not easy but would not last forever. And Greenwood was not ashamed to admit even a part of him would feel better once battle commenced.

* * *

Closer and closer. The nearest Frenchman was now less than a mile off their prow and still coming at them hell for leather. King resisted the temptation to look back at *Relentless*; the heavier ship would not be in range for at least another half an hour. Instead he concentrated entirely on the enemy that would meet them far sooner.

The oncoming frigate remained under all plain sail, with no attempt being made to strike any canvas. That must surely mean she was intending to hit and run – literally fire one, or perhaps two broadsides, then leave any further destruction to her companion following behind. That made sense; if the Frenchman's gunnery was anything like efficient, *Mistral* could easily be slowed long enough to enable further damage to be wreaked by the second ship. Meanwhile, the stately liner was making steady progress and would doubtless arrive in time to finish them off. Of course, King could also cause damage and, even though unable to call upon the might of a two-decker, was determined to do so.

But determination was about all he had: apart from his opening gambit, King lacked any set plan. This absence of forethought did not trouble him greatly, however; he had been in action before and knew how easily ideas flowed once the guns began firing. Besides, even if he could think of nothing else, there were few better ways of attack than disrupting whatever the enemy had in mind.

"We shall close as much as we are able, then steer to larboard and initially engage with our starboard battery," he announced at last and, so quiet had he been while the tension mounted, his voice sounded unnaturally loud. "I intend to fire into the enemy's prow, then come back – tacking if need be – and repeat the process on her stern."

His senior officers accepted this with formal acknowledgements. All knew King would once more be asking much from the starboard gunners; they were to be used twice and should expect to receive at least one enemy broadside in return, while the larboard cannon remained redundant. But King would save the fresh men and carefully loaded guns of the opposite battery for the second frigate and felt they would be better spent dealing with that.

The decision made, he finally allowed himself to turn back and look at *Relentless*. The sun was fully up now and both Banks' ship, and *Taurus* close behind, were in plain view and sailing for all they were worth. Neither had set studding sails, but King could not blame them for that – the extra canvas would be an unnecessary obstruction when it came to fighting – yet still they would not be within even long range inside twenty minutes. It was a period he would have to spend on his own, and in the company of two French frigates. And that time was to begin very shortly.

"Enemy's opened fire!"

The call came from the foremast lookout although all on the quarterdeck caught the two jets of flame that were soon hidden by grey cloud as the smoke rolled down towards them. King only noticed one splash, and it was a good seventy feet off their beam. The other shot could have gone anywhere but now all knew the space between the two ships could be covered.

Croft was looking at him inquisitively and he shook his head. He had no wish to reply with his own bow mounted guns; the damage they might cause would be negligible. Far better to save the first shots for a time when more harm could be done.

Minutes passed, and all the while the two ships drew steadily closer. King eyed the two enemy vessels in silence. He had to gauge it right: make his move when there was range enough to cause true damage to the first, yet still be able to react to anything the second had planned. Then, just as the French chasers were due to fire once more, King reacted.

"Ready on my word," he warned before stepping forward and adding, "take her to larboard!"

"Starboard your helm – meet her, braces!" Brehaut roared.

"Chasers, Mr Adams!"

Forward, Adams touched his hat briefly, before calling out to the gun crews mounted on the forecastle and, just as *Mistral* was starting to turn, both cannon gave out with simultaneous reports.

The smoke rolled back over *Mistral*'s main deck, although few were concerned with where the shots had landed, they had more important matters to consider. Brehaut was watching the ship as she turned, ensuring their canvas retained what wind it could and the manoeuvre went as smoothly as possible, if only for the sake of those laying the guns. Meanwhile, Adams and Cooper in the waist were calling out to the servers to stand to and even Hopkins, the marine lieutenant, appeared properly attentive as he organised his men. The enemy remained beyond the accurate reach of their muskets but the ridged walls of red and white were an inspiring sight as they formed up behind the hammock-stuffed nettings. Only King and Croft seemed without a task, although both were concentrating hard, watching for the first sign that the enemy might be planning to turn also.

It came as *Mistral* had settled on her new course, and was too late; by then the British frigate was running straight with her slight list to larboard regular enough to allow for accurate shooting. And, even though it was still relatively long range, King had no hesitation in ordering the first broadside despatched.

With a rumble like the worst thunder, *Mistral*'s carriage guns spoke as one while her quarterdeck carronades added their own particular note of savagery a fraction later. King's ears began to ring while the shot was still in flight although the sensation was barely noticed as he set his mind totally on the target.

And it was good shooting; the enemy had just begun her turn to starboard, yet still found herself neatly bracketed, although few shots actually landed to either side. Most struck her firmly in the hull, while *Mistral*'s carronades, whose load was slightly later in arriving, produced even more spectacular results. The leading frigate's fore and main sails were instantly torn to ribbons and more damage was revealed seconds later. Either significant shrouds had parted or a round shot from the main battery had struck lucky, but the Frenchman's foremast definitely began to hang at a slight angle, suggesting any fresh sail would take it down completely.

The hands were bellowing hearty cheers from all about and King allowed himself one deep sigh of satisfaction, but that was all; her recent turn meant *Mistral* was now heading directly for the main French force – he had to bring her back and as close to the wind as she would lie, then hopefully fire another broadside into the first frigate, while preparing for the imminent arrival of the second. And all the while the knowledge that the nearest enemy had yet to fire her own opening broadside lay at the back of his mind. They might do so at any moment, and with similarly devastating results.

* * *

The first shots actually arrived less than a minute later, and it was a reasonable delay, considering the French had received appreciable damage while in the midst of a turn. Yet on the main deck where Greenwood and his men were struggling to reload the warm barrel of cannon number six, the results were certainly noticed.

The enemy's broadside was decidedly irregular but, as it thundered down upon her, *Mistral* was also caught mid-manoeuvre. And the iron rain battered against her starboard beam, rather than targeting her tophamper; the French had aimed uncharacteristically low and almost all their heavy metal dug deep into the British ship's tender hull.

Several struck the forecastle hammock netting and, though much of their impetus was absorbed, the barrier exploded under the impact, sending small, tightly-packed canvas packages flying about the waist. Two struck men, winding one and knocking the other senseless, but soon there were far worse casualties. Though the force of the round shot had been lessened by such a range, they retained enough momentum to account for Marine Privates Oats and Long, who died in a mess of blood and bone by the quarterdeck bulwark. Further forward, the main hull fared as badly; the frigate's eggshell sides were penetrated in several places with the resultant splinters tearing through the sweating gun crews, indiscriminately ripping flesh and muscle from any suitable target. Cole, the youngster only recently promoted to midshipman, fell to one, while Sayer, Russell's former accomplice, received a belly wound that was instantly fatal.

And the ship herself suffered; in addition to the damaged hull and some minor fittings that were smashed beyond recognition, the starboard cathead disintegrated allowing the best bower anchor to be sent on one last plunge through countless fathoms of clear water. Further aft, both cutters placed high on the spar deck disintegrated under the force of a single round shot. The boats were intended to act as reservoirs in case of fire and had been filled to the gunwales with sea water; the sudden deluge drenched those directly beneath, though at least the blood-streaked deck was washed clean.

But through the smoke, dust, screams and stench of the onslaught, order began to be re-established. The ship had been in the midst of being guided back towards the wind, and the manoeuvre continued with men trained to such a pitch that, only when *Mistral* was as close as they could take her, did they turn from their duties and attend to the bedlam that raged about. Those who were wounded but could still work continued to do so, only pausing to staunch cuts and minor abrasions from the ready-use packs of lint and canvas that were stored between every cannon. Any more seriously injured were dragged below to meet with Manning and his team on the orlop, while the dead were unceremoniously eased over the side with barely a thought. And soon – not instantly yet still with remarkable speed – *Mistral* was brought to order and quite shortly afterwards the first of her starboard pieces was signalled as being ready.

King had watched it all from his position on the quarterdeck; much of the damage had been received further forward, but that had not altered his stance, which remained upright and as exposed as any man in the ship. And, even in the midst of the chaos, he had time to consider the nearest Frenchman, as well as the second frigate that was still undamaged and now drawing closer.

"Starboard broadside's ready," Croft's report coincided with a sudden scream from one of the wounded but King guessed the meaning and a brief nod was sufficient reply. Seconds later, *Mistral* struck once more at the hull of the first enemy and, despite being so recently damaged, the second broadside was a true ship killer. The range had shortened considerably and King could see some shots arrive in detail. The Frenchman's fore topmast was the first to fall, with the main topgallant following it shortly afterwards. And there was obvious damage to the hull; the beakhead and surrounding area dissolved in a cloud of dust and splinters and holes appeared at random places along the frigate's sides. More to the point, only three guns protruded through the enemy's ports, the rest were presumably still being served, and King suspected those that could be seen had been abandoned. Then the main topsail yard sagged as if suddenly robbed of support, and a tangle of spars, canvas and cordage drooped down over the forecastle while the battered hull began to roll unhindered in the swell. The ship was by no means beaten, but he could leave what remained for Banks to finish off.

Yet though their first opponent might be disregarded, fine on the larboard bow the second was already rushing to take up the fight. Even as King watched, her topgallants were shed and, as her way began to slow, he sensed she was being commanded by a far more calculating captain.

He considered the new threat; the second ship was slightly to larboard allowing a tighter rake across her bows should he attempt the same trick. But the French would expect such a move, whereas that small margin to windward had given him another idea. King turned and caught the eye of the sailing master; he would be asking much, even to explain his plan would not be easy, but still he drew in a lungful of sulphurous fumes and began.

"Mr Brehaut, I intend to close further with the enemy, then turn to larboard, although will revert to my original course when we are half-way through the manoeuvre; do you understand?"

"Aye sir," Brehaut replied, quickly picking up on the plan. "And I can add t'gallants if you wish."

"No," King said firmly. "Keep her as she is, and kindly inform the hands." The extra canvas would give more speed but might also signal his intention and possibly negate the ruse he was planning.

King waited while the sailing master relayed his orders, then stepped forward and addressed the gunners in the waist. "Ready larboard battery!" Forward, Cooper and Adams acknowledged the warning with a touch of their hats, then the forecastle lookout's cry alerted all to further movement from the enemy.

A cloud of smoke from her prow showed how she had released her chasers and the subsequent whine of shot passing low overhead marked their passage; the guns had been laid more accurately than the previous frigate's. A quick look confirmed no damage had been caused although King's previous suspicions about his opponent's competence were confirmed.

"You may reply, Mr Adams!"

Now that *Mistral* had already demonstrated her power on the first frigate it would do no harm to discharge the forward facing guns. Considerably less than half a mile separated the two adversaries, and one at least should make a move before long.

"Start the turn, Mr Brehaut, but make it gradual." Again, he may as well signal his apparent intention if only to deter the Frenchman from trying anything different. Creaking slightly, *Mistral* began a graceful sweep to larboard, her speed increasing as the wind crept further onto her beam. And all the while King kept his eyes set firmly on the enemy; if they believed him, they should also turn, so presenting their larboard broadside to the threat and reducing the chance of being raked. But the frigate continued towards them without deviation, and King felt the first cold dread of doubt.

He chanced a look at Croft – the lieutenant sensed his captain's eyes upon him and tore his own gaze from the enemy.

"They're calling our bluff, sir," the older man grunted and King gave a nod of agreement. *Mistral* was now partially through her turn and just about where he expected to revert to his earlier course if the enemy had been encouraged round. But now he was not so sure. He could continue; make a true intention from the ruse, and fire into the frigate with his starboard guns, or still turn back, though he would be passing close to an enemy that should be expecting just such a move.

"Bring her back, Mr Brehaut!" King snapped, suddenly coming to a decision. "Sharp as you can!"

Mistral baulked as she was wrenched round and even luffed slightly when taken a fraction too far, but soon she had returned to her original course and was now far closer to the enemy. But the Frenchman had more in store for them. With a speed and grace that took all by surprise, the frigate finally swerved to larboard and King watched in horror as her starboard broadside began to be revealed.

He now had two options, turn back to larboard himself and present his own starboard broadside, or tack and continue with the unused larboard battery. But one thing was certain, if he remained as he was, *Mistral* would be raked from very close range and that might alter everything.

7.

"Port your helm, prepare to tack!" King waited while Brehaut stoically repeated his orders. It had not been such a hard decision; inwardly he sensed the Frenchman expected him to turn the other way and was pleased to be doing the unexpected. Tacking the ship in the face of an enemy might not be the best policy, but he was more certain of his men now and the prospect of finally gaining the windward gauge had been the final clincher.

Mistral swept into her manoeuvre and hung in irons for the least possible time. But all the while the Frenchman continued to turn, her broadside rounding on them at roughly the same speed. With a final flap of canvas, the wind began to be received on her larboard side, *Mistral* settled and picked up speed.

Now it was a race for the other's prow and one King was determined to win. Despite carrying less sail, *Mistral* had the advantage of a slight lead and, as her way slowly increased, he willed her further in front of the enemy. Then, as if conceding defeat, the French frigate released her starboard broadside; the guns must have been trained far forward and cast a wide spread, with no serious damage received. And then it seemed the way had been made clear; every larboard gun captain had their hand raised in readiness and, at an order from King, *Mistral*'s head was turned back on the Frenchman. Clinging as close to the wind as the quartermaster dared and throwing up a cloud of spray and spindrift, she swept across the frigate's bows.

"As your guns bear, lads!" Cooper roared. Clearly the second lieutenant intended firing almost directly at the enemy's stem, although *Mistral* was moving fast for such a ploy. But as the broadside finally rolled out in a stagger of shots that raised visible splinters from the Frenchman's prow, King was more than satisfied.

"An' now we gets ours!" a hand from one of the quarterdeck carronades grumbled, but King was already ordering *Mistral* round.

"Hard a starboard!"

For several telling seconds the British frigate would have her stern to the Frenchman but the enemy's broadside would not be directly facing them. Besides, a ship that had just suffered such a telling hit herself could not expect to be the epitome of efficiency. As it was, *Mistral* had almost completed her manoeuvre when the first shots of the second enemy broadside rang out. She was hit many times; several round shot blasted down much of her hull and the starboard quarter gallery in King's own quarters was all but demolished. But none went high and all on the quarterdeck remained untouched.

Though only by cannon fire; some fell to sharpshooters from the Frenchman's tops despite Hopkins and Bates organising snipers to return the compliment. And then, as *Mistral* finally finished her turn, and the Frenchman came into the firing arc of her starboard broadside, it was clear the British frigate was more than able to strike again.

* * *

"Our turn, lads," Greenwood announced as the dark mass of the French frigate came into view. "Any orders, Mr Summers?" he added to the midshipman standing nearby.

"Target the hull as before and continue to load with round," the lad told them crisply.

"Shall we double shot?" another server asked.

"No, single," Summers responded without hesitation. They had received no orders for increasing the load and it was quite possible subsequent broadsides would be delivered at a longer range.

Greenwood nodded; it was good to be under competent control. The lad had come a long way in a short time. As its captain, the starboard cannon was officially commanded by Jackson, but as most of the men serving it came from his mess, Greenwood privately considered it his own.

Subconsciously he checked all was prepared: powder for the next charge had already been received and now rested safely in the salt box. Round shot was also to hand in the garlands and bar or canister could be raised as easily. The fire buckets were filled and there was sand aplenty on the deck. Swain, standing by the side tackle, waited only for the gun to be fired; his back was bare and Greenwood could see sweat running freely down the unfinished tattoo that all had temporarily forgotten. The others were similarly poised including Russell, now properly equipped with a flexible rammer, Brown, and Gordon who would be helping Swain, Frant and the freckled-faced Parker, who gave a friendly grin. Slowly his eyes swept round the rest of the group, all were ready – some might say primed – with Jackson, who had set the elevation and was now only longing for the chance to shoot, the most attentive of all.

"Take your time lads," Adams ordered from further forward. "You don't come this close to a Frenchman every day."

Steadily the already scarred side of the enemy frigate crept closer and then it seemed as if *Mistral* was about to wear.

"Fire!" Cooper yelled just as the frigate's sails began to shiver. On every great gun the firing lines were pulled as one, while the main battery of carronades further aft followed in a close echo. *Mistral* heeled to the recoil and her canvas flapped further as the wind, stunned by the sudden explosions, quickly died. For a moment smoke hung over the entire ship causing men with lungs already fried by caustic fumes to cough and retch. And then the breeze returned, softly at first but enough to disperse the cloud and allow those aboard to see what damage they had caused.

All of the Frenchman's masts were intact, although a number of yards had fallen and much of the canvas had either been shot away or, in the case of the foremast, burnt up in a sudden flash of fire, the remains of which was still being fought. And the hull itself had come off badly, one wale was pockmarked with neat round shot holes and two gun ports had been knocked into one, while the fore chains were almost demolished. But the enemy was fighting back and, even as they watched, their great guns were being run out and trained directly upon the impudent British.

"Prepare to wear ship!"

The cry came from the quarterdeck and Swain and Brown silently left their work at the gun to attend the braces.

"Russell, lend a hand there!" Jackson yelled and the loader temporarily discarded his rammer and took Swain's place on the side tackle. Greenwood also piled in as the warm monster was heaved back into position. It was clear they would be firing again and soon, although at any time the enemy was likely to reply with their own broadside.

"Left – left!" Jackson roared as his crew angled the great beast round with their handspikes. "Right a bit – stand clear!"

Jackson leaped to one side as he raised his hand but, before the weapon could be despatched, the French had responded with an erratic broadside. Only part of the British ship's hull was within their arc but, as the shots began to rumble out, *Mistral* took her worst pounding so far.

The general aim was higher and caused destruction to the gun deck itself, although mercifully the French had fired ball; had grape or canister been used there would have been far greater injuries. As it was, several men fell as one by a starboard carronade and Henderson, the boatswain's mate that teased Swain about his tattoo, took the full force of an eighteen-pound ball in his chest. But far more harm was caused by splinters; several of the French round shot punctured holes in the frigate's bulwarks before going on to rip chunks from the pine strakes of the deck, slivers that silently embedded themselves in any available flesh. Others fell to shots from the enemy's marksmen aloft and, in one case, a fiddle block knocked free from one of the halyards. Less personal damage was also caused; the binnacle was struck to one side, scattering most of its contents across the quarterdeck, and the mizzen fife rail hit, although mercifully held. But the ship herself survived and, when order was once more achieved, Jackson was not the only one to be signalling his piece ready.

"Good work, lads," Adams muttered under his breath – despite each losing two men to the afterguard, his cannon had been served in record time. He glanced across to where Cooper's crews were proving equally swift.

"Starboard battery ready!" Cooper bellowed. The ship was deep into her turn and the Frenchman lay well within their grasp; there was a brief pause while all drew breath, then: "Fire!"

The order was greeted by yet another collective roar of heavy artillery although most were now too deafened to fully appreciate it. And even before the smoking monsters had come to a halt, their servers were crowding about, quenching the barrels with water-soaked mops before adding yet another load of devilment.

Jackson, at the rear of number six, looked about; Brown had returned to the gun yet Russell was still doubling on the train tackle – there was no sign of Swain. But the charge was now being rammed into the cannon's mouth; he could break the flannel cartridge with the pricker while the shot was being added so there was no time to wonder about one man not returning to duty.

"We'll catch her stern!"

The cry came from one of the lieutenants – no one could be sure which – but all were encouraged by it. *Mistral* must be creeping up on the enemy again and preparing to deliver the *coup de grâce*. After quickly dosing the priming pan, Jackson eagerly peered down the sights of his cannon and, sure enough, the enemy's counter was steadily creeping into view.

"It'll do, lads," he told them gruffly as he signalled the piece ready. Accurate aiming was not necessary; Captain King had done a wonderful job in presenting them with an unmissable target. For there, less than a pistol shot off, lay the Frenchman's rump and it was simply begging for a slap.

8.

Adams had moved up to the break of the forecastle and saw the broadside strike in vivid detail. The Frenchman's stern gallery went the same way as *Mistral*'s had minutes before and, though the neat round holes made by other shots seemed less dramatic, he could guess at the carnage they would wreak deeper inside the ship. And there was more; one of their last guns to fire had sent its load smashing into the frigate's rudder, crushing it and the sternpost into one and leaving what remained hanging drunkenly from a lower pintle. Whatever the damage caused by others, that shot alone had truly told for the Frenchman. Without time or space to rig a jury rudder, the frigate would be almost impossible to control – something Adams knew better than most – and in a single ship engagement must strike within minutes.

"Go aft to the quarterdeck," he snapped at a nearby lad who had just delivered powder to number two cannon. "Tell them the enemy's rudder is taken."

The boy obediently dropped his cartridge carrier and sped off along the starboard gangway, dodging the line of marines that were stoically picking off any Frenchman foolish enough to show above the taffrail. *Mistral*'s main topsail had been backed and another broadside, equally effective, could be expected shortly. The lad arrived and Adams could see him explaining to Brehaut through the thinning smoke. The sailing master turned to King and soon the shrill note of a whistle cut through the madness. Adams was the nearest commissioned man and had a reasonable command of the French language. He drew breath:

"*Vous rendez-vous?*"

There was a pause and he repeated the question. Then a head appeared cautiously above the Frenchman's taffrail. It was an officer; Adams was close enough to see the decoration on his cocked hat that sat above a look of utter desolation. *Mistral*'s starboard battery had finished reloading and the line of gun captains waiting with hands raised was both evident and ominous. The man considered them for a moment before turning towards Adams and meeting his eyes. Then, so slowly, he raised his hat high and nodded.

* * *

Well that's one we shouldn't have to deal with again," Brehaut grunted as *Mistral* picked up speed. Standing nearby, King was not so certain; there were instances aplenty of ships striking only to resume the fight when an opportunity presented. But he could not spare the time, or men, to send a boarding party. Besides, while he had been involved with the second frigate, *Relentless* had closed up and would shortly be engaging the first. With her close by, *Taurus* following, and his rudder smashed, the enemy captain would be a fool to break his word.

"We make for the liner."

It was the only option and King took it almost unconsciously. The two-decker was still over a mile off and bearing down on them with the wind almost on her beam. Once more, he would be meeting the enemy ship alone, but Banks could not take so very long in dealing with the first Frenchman and *Taurus* must surely be undamaged.

"Starboard the helm?" Brehaut asked, but King shook his head.

"No, Master, keep her as she is. In fact edge her closer to the wind."

Brehaut touched his hat. "Very good, sir."

King was in no rush to close with the enemy, and a point or two to starboard would secure the all important windward gauge.

"Deck there, I've a ship coming up on the larboard beam!"

King glanced across. The two undamaged enemy frigates were in plain sight though a good way off as they followed their liner into battle; the masthead could not be referring to either of them.

"Royals and topsails set and beating up on the larboard tack," the lookout continued. "She's a warship for certain, though I could not chance her size."

"*Athena*?" Croft suggested, and King nodded. For the final contingent of Banks' squadron to appear from the south west was entirely logical. The Commodore may well have put in to Cape Town when collecting *Taurus* and would have left word for Granger's ship to follow; that or she might have spoken with a neutral. But if the fifth rate were truly joining the fray it put a different perspective on things. She would be a good match for one of the French frigates and might even entertain both for a spell, leaving King, Banks and Bruce free to deal with the liner.

Anderson, the carpenter, had appeared nearby and was waiting to report; behind him the boatswain also had something to say; either might carry bad news about the state of the ship but King was strangely optimistic. Even if it were dire and *Mistral* could take no further part in the action, she had more or less dealt with two of the enemy. It was a reasonable haul for what had appeared a hopeless situation and, for his last battle, good enough to retire on.

* * *

But neither warrant officer had anything too dreadful to report. *Mistral*'s hull was holed in several places and taking in water, though not to an alarming extent. Anderson's mates were already addressing the leaks and hoped to have the hull sound by nightfall. Harridge was equally optimistic: his team were in the process of rigging additional preventer stays from the mizzen chains to support weakened main channels while most important lines had already being spliced or were in the process of being replaced. Once more, King felt grateful for the support of good standing officers; by attending to their duties so diligently they had taken a good deal of responsibility from his shoulders, enabling him to turn his attention elsewhere.

Astern, the beaten frigate was playing by the rules; there was no sign of her returning to the fight. All remaining canvas had been struck, she was rolling gently in the swell and presumably waiting to be boarded. But that must surely wait; beyond her, Banks would have no time for such niceties. After one long-range broadside he had abandoned the first frigate; presumably she had also struck or was considered unworthy of further attention, and now *Relentless* and *Taurus* were clawing to windward in an effort to join with *Mistral*. Both had reset their royals and were closing fast although there would still be a delay before all three could launch a concerted attack.

King considered the situation; he would have every reason to hold off and wait for support from his colleagues or, more to the point, allow Banks to take charge. Under Sir Richard's direction, the three should be able to run the proverbial rings around the two-decker. It would be like dogs baiting a bull; they might snap at the enemy's heels in the hope of bringing it down, but one carefully placed charge from the Frenchman would tear the life from either light frigate, and even *Relentless* would not fare well were a fully fledged liner to get to grips with her. But the idea of holding off did not sit well and King was also aware of how the situation must appear to the enemy.

Whoever commanded the French squadron must surely be in the two-decker; they would have already witnessed two of their force being soundly beaten and now the victors were making for him. To King's mind it was better to continue the action without a break, keep at long range of course but if *Mistral* could maintain the momentum already created it would place far more pressure on the French Admiral.

But what of the new arrival? King must not lose track of the entire picture.

"Masthead, what do you see of the fresh sighting?"

"Making good speed, sir," the lookout replied. "And I'd say she were *Athena*."

"Are the French changing course?" King persisted. He could make out the dim shapes of the distant frigates, but so much more might be seen in the clear air of a higher vantage point.

"They've been signalling to each other for some while, though they seems to be keeping the same heading, sir." This time it was Sennett's voice, the young hand recently promoted from the lower deck. "No, wait – the farthermost ship is turning, she's making for *Athena* – if that's who she is. An' yes, the other's making to follow."

King pursed his lips; that was bad news for Granger in *Athena* but could only be good for the rest of the squadron. Presumably the liner's captain felt confident of beating off *Mistral* and the other two British frigates, as well he might.

"Commodore's signalling now, sir!" Dilson reported, and King looked back to *Relentless*. Banks' ship was approaching the second Frenchman and, as he predicted, had not bothered to take possession. Instead, a line of bunting was showing from her fore.

"Our number sir. Then two, five, one – eight, six, four – two, four, nine..." The lad flipped through his book then looked up in surprise. "That's simply 'engage the enemy' – though it is strange that he should send in the Popham code."

"How so?" King enquired.

"Well, sir," Dilson began hesitantly. "We are still using the old book for some messages and there's a far easier hoist using Lord Howe's system: number sixteen, 'engage the enemy more closely'. It's what Nelson flew both at Trafalgar and the Nile and one of the first I learned."

"And your point, Mr Dilson?"

"Well, that only needs two flags, sir," the boy explained. "Whereas what the Commodore sent took nine."

King supposed it might appear strange although he quickly understood. Banks obviously agreed that pressure should be maintained but, by issuing a less precise order, was giving King room to organise his own attack with no supplementary directions as to how he should behave. That was freedom indeed and showed a degree of trust although for some while *Mistral* would still be facing the full force of an enemy two-decker on her own.

From across the quarterdeck he noticed Croft and Brehaut eyeing him with interest, and gave what he hoped would be a confident grin in reply.

"Very well, gentlemen," he said, speaking as lightly as he could. "It seems we have a battleship to fight."

* * *

On the gun deck it was apparent they were making for the French liner and Adams could not have been happier. Since the start of the action it was as if fresh energy were flowing through him; a sensation he was eager to maintain. For some while he had given no more than a passing thought to Anne, his finances or the future in general and it was only then, in a rare moment of reflection, that he discovered he cared little about any of them. For him the current action was all and, even if it cost his life, there would be few regrets.

And at cannon number six, Russell was very much of the same opinion. A year ago he had been nothing more than a petty thief; another parasite on society whose only satisfaction came from what could be swindled from honest men. Now he was a changed being, one who drew positive pleasure from his new found skills and the company of those he served with. And there was further gratification in working as a team, both in serving the cannon with others of his mess and generally being part of a crew. Those men, and the ship, were currently being put to the test and he was proud to stand alongside them; should he have to give everything then so be it, for at least he now had a life worth losing.

Further aft, on the quarterdeck, Croft also welcomed closing with the two-decker but for different reasons and with far more reservations. Despite a promising start, his naval career had become a disappointment. Matters only began to look up when his present captain took command of *Hare*, and improved further with the pair of them moving to *Mistral*. And that was how he looked upon it; they were a team. Before serving under King, Croft had found it hard to respect any man of a higher rank who was also his junior in age. Such situations could only grow more common with time and were one of the main reasons for considering retirement. But with his current captain it was different; whatever his age, King had become someone Croft could both relate to and respect, while the two of them having made so much from the current ship was in itself a testimony to their relationship. And as far as testing their creation against the might of an enemy liner; he had few qualms, indeed most of him relished the prospect, although another part was also conscious that something might be lost. *Mistral* could be taken or destroyed; either outcome appeared likely, although neither was the worst scenario. For a ship could be rebuilt, but the relationship between himself and the younger, one-armed officer he served was unique. And as for being replaceable, Croft knew that to be quite impossible.

* * *

"Bring her two points to larboard," King murmured and Brehaut duly ordered the helm across. They had drawn level with, and were now making directly for, the liner; the enemy vessel was on a close reach about a mile off their larboard bow and the two were closing fast.

"Coming into range now," Croft murmured softly and for the life of him King could not tell if this should be taken as a hint. But then neither did it matter; he knew exactly what he had to do, as well as when to do it. And that time was now.

"Prepare to turn," he ordered, almost conversationally. Then, far louder, "Ready starboard battery!"

The two lieutenants in the waist looked back at him and Cooper, the nearest, touched his hat in acknowledgement. At any moment the French liner would open up with her chasers but King preferred not to wait for that; not when a chance hit might ruin everything.

"Now, Mr Brehaut – starboard your helm!"

The turn was sharp enough to make all on the quarterdeck stagger slightly, even though they had expected it. But *Mistral* took the savage handling well; her braces came round as one and soon she had recovered balance and was heading to cross the bows of the more stately liner.

"Very good, Mr Cooper!"

His call came a fraction of a second before the second lieutenant's order to open fire, making King wonder if the young man would have despatched the broadside without his prompting. But *Mistral*'s broadside was heading for the enemy; that was the only thing which really mattered and King was not alone in holding his breath as they waited for the shots to strike.

"Nicely bracketed," Croft commented as the enemy flagship's hull was partially concealed amid a wall of water. King made no reply; Croft was right, the pieces had been well laid but it was extreme range and the spread still wide. Some may have hit and an eighteen-pound ball could still punish at such a distance, although much of its force would have been spent and, against the solidity of a liner, King could not hope for significant damage.

"Continue the turn!" he ordered, and Brehaut wore the ship round until she was on the same heading as the enemy. And then the small measure of superiority the British held was fully demonstrated: the French liner was sailing under all plain sail, whereas *Mistral* carried only topsails and forecourse, yet the two were soon maintaining a similar speed.

"She'll turn," Croft again, and once more he was correct. For the Frenchman to allow herself to be lured closer to *Relentless* and *Taurus* was too much to ask. Besides, *Mistral* was just about in range, as King had already proved.

"There she goes!" Brehaut confirmed as the flagship swept

closer to the wind and presented her starboard beam towards them.

The turn, which looked likely to develop into a tack, was carried out surprisingly well, King decided; the enemy's crew were on top form, something he should have expected in a ship so far from home.

"And now will come the broadside," Croft added.

Sure enough, the Frenchman's starboard side was momentarily concealed by the fire and smoke of a simultaneous discharge and, once more, all aboard *Mistral* waited.

This time those on the quarterdeck were directly in the firing line, so it was something of a relief when the first column of water erupted a good fifty feet off their counter. Other shot travelled further; there were splashes to either side while one all but spent round shot passed safely through the crowd of officers to land firmly on a skylight, crashing through the frame and sending splinters of glass all about. But apart from that, there was no material damage and neither were there any casualties.

"Starboard the helm," King ordered softly. The ship tacked easily and soon began to run parallel with the liner, both ships were now close-hauled on roughly the same northerly heading as the two British frigates that were still trying desperately to catch up. King glanced over the larboard quarter to where a pall of smoke told how Granger, in *Athena*, had engaged the more distant of the remaining frigates. If *Mistral* and the Frenchman continued as they were there was the very real danger of leaving the rest of the combat behind, while all the liner had to do was steadily edge closer to cause them real problems. No, he had to force the enemy to turn back, and there was one certain way that could be achieved.

"Ready starboard battery, Mr Cooper. Mr Brehaut bring her about to starboard once more!"

Mistral swept round gracefully in the steady wind and, for a moment was actually facing the oncoming British ships. But the turn continued, she wore, and was soon coming up on the stern of the French liner. This was far more dangerous; the frigate now benefited from having the wind closer to her beam, although to creep near enough to make a broadside worthwhile would place her in a vulnerable position when it came to avoiding the Frenchman's reply. But for the enemy to respond meant they would have to turn and forcing them to do so was worth the risk, to say nothing of what might be achieved with their own guns.

"She's coming round!" Brehaut's announcement came almost as a relief, even if it meant they were to face a two-decker's broadside once more, and at far closer range.

"Fire as you will, Mr Cooper!" King bellowed as the French ship continued to turn. If *Mistral* were to be punished it made sense to deliver her own shot first.

"Fire!"

The lieutenant's order came just as the Frenchman completed her turn and signalled as neat a broadside as King could have wished for. But even as the shot still hung in the air, he was working to get *Mistral* out of the danger area.

"Starboard your helm, Mr Brehaut!"

Already a moving target, the sudden turn to larboard would disconcert the enemy's gunners further – or so he hoped.

And he was partially right; the French broadside followed almost immediately, and mainly centred on the area where *Mistral* would have been had she not turned. But there were still some that found her and the closer range meant they made a greater impact.

One heavy round shot smashed into the main fife rail, sending line, belaying pins and splinters in all directions, while another was pitched slightly higher and hit the main topsail yard. Canvas billowed out in the wind and there was the clatter of blocks falling from above that mingled oddly with screams from the wounded. Some of these came from the crew of number ten cannon, the barrel of which had been struck fair on the muzzle, spinning the beast about like a child's toy and knocking down three servers as it did. And there was other, less obvious, damage; the spare bower was struck and sent the same way as its former partner while two further openings were torn into the frigate's upper hull. But, despite the loss of power from the main, King felt they could have fared worse.

"Is the mast damaged?" he asked vaguely but fortunately Harridge was at hand.

"Yard is split, sir," the boatswain called back from the break of the quarterdeck. "An' cannot be fished – I can see that from 'ere."

"But the mast?" King repeated impatiently.

"Don't look good, sir, an' we've lost the use of the fife rail."

So be it, but they still had a working foremast.

"Set the fore t'gallant," he ordered. *Mistral* had completed her turn and was now almost running before the breeze: once the extra canvas was added, not much speed would be lost. But turning again, and bringing the wind more on the beam, would be another matter; the intricate balance of rig that had made her so handy must surely have gone, while beating, or even a close reach, would be that much harder.

He glanced across to where *Relentless* and *Taurus* were still a fair distance off; he felt he had done enough but it remained vitally important to keep the liner's attention on him, and so allow Banks to coordinate his own attack.

"Starboard your helm," King ordered at last. "Take her three points to larboard."

Brehaut repeated his captain's order and added his own without comment. All knew it was a compromise. *Mistral* was not declining action – anything but; the turn would decrease her speed considerably while making her liable for at least one further broadside from the Frenchman and probably several more. But for the enemy to continue the fight meant they would have to draw close, and any distance covered would naturally bring them nearer to the oncoming British.

But there were some to whom the subtlety would not be obvious and, as King stood on the quarterdeck, he sensed how the change in tactics had affected those hands nearest to him. The recent damage had changed *Mistral* from an insolent, yet spirited, predator to little more than a wounded beast; one whose weaknesses had been fully revealed and only hope of survival lay in rescue from others of her kind. Those at a nearby carronade were decidedly less easy and there was none of the banter expected from fighting men during a lull in the action. They had fought hard and done much but, now the enemy had the upper hand, could expect to deal out far less than they received. And very possibly they might have to give their all.

9.

It seemed the French were determined to finish *Mistral* off. While the deck about him swarmed with various teams making running repairs, King stood aloof, his attention solely on the distant liner. She had turned to larboard once more and was now bearing down on their quarter; still a good distance off – long range for a full broadside – though the gap was narrowing visibly and the enemy seemed to have every intention of closing it further.

Which was strange: the liner's captain would have been far better to remain on his previous heading. Then he might meet up with his other two frigates, see off or destroy *Athena* and form an impregnable group that the two remaining and relatively undamaged British ships would find impossible to counter. But no, she was making for *Mistral*, the impertinent little gnat that had already caused such pain and finally looked ripe for swatting. King guessed an element of spite might be involved and a chill ran down his spine; to have riled a line-of-battleship's anger had been a bold move indeed.

Of course, he might still run and would have every reason to do so. Turning back to the east and taking the wind on the quarter would use *Mistral*'s foremast to the full and almost guarantee her safety. On the other hand, *Relentless* and *Taurus* were in plain sight and steadily creeping up. If he could only delay the Frenchman long enough, the Commodore would be able to launch an attack on the liner's vulnerable stern and that would place a different aspect on matters. Yet the only way he could hold the enemy's attention was to effectively offer his own ship up for sacrifice.

Which was naturally out of the question; trading a frigate for a two-decker might seem the bargain of the century to any dispassionate observer but was not one King could contemplate. However much it might benefit Banks and Bruce to keep the liner both occupied and from her compatriots, it could never be worth the total destruction of his own precious ship, to say nothing of the lives that must also be lost. And he was not indifferent to the fact that one of those lives might be his own.

No, there had to be another solution, and one he would no

doubt find in time. But one thing was certain: this would not be the honourable retirement from action – and effectively the Navy – he had envisaged. If that truly were his aim he would simply have to wait longer, work a little harder and risk slightly more.

* * *

"So what happens now?" Russell asked and Greenwood shrugged. The enemy ship was beyond their arc of fire; this was the first time the men of number six cannon had had time to talk since the action began and even then all were aware they might be called back to duty at any moment.

"Blowed if I knows," the seaman replied.

"Caught a tiger by the tail, or so it seems," Jackson supposed. "Anyone seen Swain?"

"He were injured earlier," Georgie, the boy, answered. "Saw him being sent down to the orlop."

"Bad was it?" Greenwood asked.

"No idea," the lad confessed.

"I suspect we'll hear the details in time," Brown grunted.

"And where's Parker?" Jackson again.

"Aloft," Greenwood this time. "With Harridge's lot trying to make sense of the main topmast."

"Didn't want you then, Greenie?" Gordon, one of the new men, asked.

"'Apparently not," Greenwood snorted in apparent disgust, although he privately accepted Parker to be the more capable topman.

"Hey up, here comes trouble," Jackson called as Swain made a cautious approach, his left arm heavily bandaged.

"Welcome stranger," Russell told him. "What's about then?"

"Splinter," Swain announced. "Nasty one, but the sawbones stitched it right enough."

Where'd you catch it?" Georgie asked as the seaman lowered himself delicately onto the deck next to the warm gun.

"Where do you think?" Swain snorted, adding, "In the arm," in case any were in doubt.

"Nasty," Jackson told him. "Though I take it you can still work."

"Surgeon said light duties," Swain told them importantly.

"Light duties?" Jackson repeated and considered for a moment. "Well that's alright then."

* * *

The French liner was maintaining her course and coming dangerously close to the time when her main broadside cannon could make merry with *Mistral*'s vulnerable stern. King considered the situation afresh; with their greater speed, *Relentless* and *Taurus* were also closing although it would still be some time before they might open fire. The French commander must know of the British ships' presence and it was possibly an indication of his determination to finish *Mistral* off that made him remain on the current heading.

King swallowed dryly with the realisation; it was an uncomfortable thought indeed and the inference that the enemy felt able to deal with him and still have time to turn back to be ready for Banks and Bruce, was no more pleasant. Yet again he was at a loss to know what to do and, yet again, decided where no plan existed he could do little wrong in disrupting the enemy's.

"Mr Brehaut, we shall shortly be turning to starboard," he said.

"Very good, sir," the sailing master responded. "Might I suggest we add the royals to the fore? With the wind so far aft she will carry them well enough, even without support from the main."

"Thank you, Mr Brehaut, but I do not intend to run. We are to turn and present our broadside to the enemy. And shall be aiming at her tophamper, so will be adding bar to the current charges and reloading with that alone – Mr Croft, kindly make Mr Cooper and those at the guns aware."

Both officers touched their hats in acknowledgement though made no comment and King felt a momentary wave of doubt. There was no denying what he intended was foolhardy in the extreme and equally senseless justifying it by claiming *Mistral* was less vulnerable receiving fire on her broadside. The enemy liner was powering towards them with the impetus of a charging bull;

even the loss of a major spar would hardly slow her and she might still alter course and treat them to a severe raking. But even that would delay her to some extent and provide the measure of space Banks needed to close upon her own counter.

He took a pace about the quarterdeck, less crowded now as many running repairs had been made, although the main still lacked a serviceable fife rail. Croft was bellowing down to the gunners in the waist, while Brehaut kept his own counsel next to the binnacle. And the doubts remained – King supposed he could consult either officer; get their opinion and, if need be, still order the ship about and head as far from the enemy as she could manage. He might even address the crew and gauge their reaction – after all, it was their lives he would be gambling with. Then a feeling of revulsion welled up that more than coped with any misgivings. Such a decision was totally his concern: to beg an opinion now would be an admission of defeat and could have no place in this, his final action. For a moment he briefly recalled resolving not to sacrifice his ship, although the memory only made him more determined. To surrender would be the true sacrifice, and that was something which might easily come about were he to simply run. This way he was fighting back; not with any hope of success, perhaps – some might judge it more a signal of defiance – and in no way would it guarantee a pleasant retirement with Aimée. But still King knew it to be the right course, and one he felt driven to take.

* * *

"Turning to starboard," Summers mused when Croft had finished his bellowed briefing and was returning to the binnacle. "That's quite a thing."

"It is," Adams agreed, though his eyes were bright and he clearly did not share the younger man's concern. To him it was a bold move for sure but the right one, and a chance to use his precious guns to the full. He reckoned they should get two, possibly three broadsides in before the oncoming Frenchman was able to respond and in that time would do a deal of damage.

Of course that was assuming the liner continued on her present course; more than likely she would turn at the same time as

Mistral, then it would become an outright and vastly unequal slugging match which no fifth rate could hope to win. But even that thought did not dissuade him greatly. For almost an entire day he had barely considered Anne, or her treatment of him and even if the subject were suddenly brought up, it would hardly have concerned him greatly. A residue of hurt remained, however, and served to make him resolute in all else. And there could be no doubting that he was spoiling for a fight.

* * *

"Right, we're going to have some work to do," Cooper was saying as he strode aft along the main deck behind the waiting gunners. "You heard Mr Croft, it will be bar on ball, then bar only and set your aim high."

"Like a Frenchman!" one of the servers grumbled.

"Yes, like a Frenchman," Cooper agreed, turning sharply in an attempt to identify the culprit. "And like a Frenchman, we won't have the windward gauge, so that will make it the easier for you. But that's where all similarity ends; if we can stop that liner for even a few minutes it will allow our companions to catch up. Between the three of us, she won't stand a chance and, also like a Frenchman, will surely strike – you see if she don't."

* * *

The shots had been signalled by twin jets of smoke from the liner's prow, but still the whine as they passed overhead made several on the quarterdeck uneasy.

"No damage," Brehaut muttered, although the tension remained high. To King, it was a very clear signal; if the enemy's bow chasers could reach them then his own broadside guns must also be in range. In which case the sooner they turned the better, but still he paused for just a second longer before issuing the order. For doubts remained and he longed to discuss his plans with Croft and Brehaut. Both were men he had come to respect and might be totally behind him in his actions. But equally they could be against, and that would present a dilemma he knew himself unable to solve.

"Very good, Mr Brehaut, you may bring her round!"

"Stations for wearing ship – up spanker!" the sailing master began. "Clear away the head bowlines, lay the headyards square!"

King felt a lump form in his throat; this was likely to be her last manoeuvrer but, despite the damage, *Mistral* turned as impeccably as ever and was soon coming up on the starboard tack with the Frenchman, now so much nearer, on her beam. Even though they must have anticipated such a move there was no change in the enemy and neither had Banks in *Relentless* reacted, nor Bruce in *Taurus*; the two British frigates were still bearing down and must be in range before long. But whether it had been for right or wrong, King had made his move and, now that *Mistral* was settled to her new heading, the business should begin as soon as possible.

"Very well, Mr Cooper," he bellowed. "You may open fire when ready."

10.

Many of the first shots fell rather wide, although that was to be expected as the guns had been double shotted, bar on ball. And the stately liner showed no major damage; her fore topsail was holed twice but the sail continued to draw and neither did she deviate from her course. The officers on the quarterdeck greeted the lack of visible result in silence, although both Croft and Brehaut had drawn closer to King, which might have been a demonstration of support. But *Mistral*'s second broadside was from slightly closer range and, now the gunners were firing with bar alone, they made better practice.

The holed topsail fell from sight as its yard was shot away, and the fore topgallant directly above flapped boisterously in the wind. King thought he could see further damage to the canvas on the main mast, although he may have been mistaken. But there was still nothing of any great importance to report and no one on the quarterdeck felt inclined to comment. The enemy began to show signs of life, however; two more shots from the bow chasers passed by overhead and her bows dipped slightly as the helm was put across.

"She's steering to starboard," Croft exclaimed as the liner

began to turn.

"And making a bad job of it," Brehaut added. "Are they ever going to take in that t'gallant?"

King held back a curse. The liner was indeed behaving appallingly; in his eagerness to return fire the French captain had abandoned any consideration to seamanship and the big vessel was being wrenched over with no regard for her braces. The damaged foresail had been left to fly uncontrolled and the hull immediately began to roll. But there was no mistaking the look of purpose in the double row of heavy cannon that had already been run out and were now bearing on them.

"With a sound tophamper, we might turn," Brehaut muttered. That was true, though if the main had been solid they would hardly have been in such a position in the first place. As it was, little could be done; King supposed he might yaw to larboard but that would only present their stern, while denying the use of their own great guns. No, he had known what must happen when placing the ship in such a position; there was a broadside coming, and *Mistral* would just have to take it.

A few seconds later the enemy guns opened up with a credible ripple of fire that ran down both gun decks from bow to stern. And such was the range that the British frigate felt the effect almost immediately.

Her main was weakened further, this time by a thirty-two pound ball striking the main chains squarely and dissolving the complex arrangement of deadeyes, lanyards and shrouds into a thousand splinters of wood and fibre. And a further round shot entered by Jackson's cannon, cutting down Russell and Parker and rolling the barrel sideways to the deck as the carriage beneath it disintegrated. Aloft, the foretop was struck, sending a master's mate and three members of the boatswain's party plunging to their deaths while the capstan was hit in two places. But apart from taking out one of their number, the main broadside pieces continued to be served and, just as the dust was starting to settle, the first gun captain's hand was being raised.

"Fire as you will!" Cooper's order rang out loud and was not disputed by the quarterdeck. With damage already received and more likely to follow, only a fool would insist on simultaneous broadsides. Three guns were despatched on his word, another followed shortly after, before an almost constant barrage of heavy artillery began with the deep booming of the broadside long guns interspersed by sharper snaps from the cannonades.

On the quarterdeck, King had noted Cooper's order and not interfered. Even ignoring the fact the new man was undeniably correct, Cooper had already demonstrated his good sense and earned the trust necessary to take such decisions, leaving King to study the enemy. And *Mistral*'s shots were beginning to tell; the Frenchman's mainyard was hit and, robbed of its support, the main topsail had been left to join the fore topgallant in flying free. Slowing the liner had ceased to be an objective, however; with the wind all but killed by their gunfire, neither she, nor *Mistral*, were moving perceivably. For a moment he wondered about altering the gunners' aim; they were close enough to fire a double load of round shot at the hull, and two eighteen-pound balls would have a decided impact on even a battleship's timbers. But he was forgetting the true purpose of the engagement; he needed to see she remained where she was, to disable her permanently so making it possible for Banks to take her apart with *Relentless*' greater manoeuvrability and heavier cannon.

Then another French broadside erupted. Once more it rippled from bow to stern and again seemed horribly measured. The deep thud of shots striking low sent shudders throughout *Mistral*'s frame while, further forward, her bell along with its belfry exploded noisily. And higher still her tophamper was hit yet again; the fore topmast, already weakened by earlier shot, now disintegrated, sending a tangle of line, spars and canvas tumbling onto the men below while a lighter ball from the Frenchman's upper deck buried itself with relatively little effect in the solid base of the frigate's bowsprit. But *Mistral*'s guns continued to fire; some from the forward battery were constricted by the remains of the fallen topmast, but that was soon dealt with and the aft cannon, together with all quarterdeck carronades, maintained their unrelenting bombardment.

Looking down upon the gun deck, King was amazed any could live in such conditions, let alone perform feats of intense physically activity. With almost clockwork regularity the hot weapons were being cleared, loaded, aimed and finally despatched, only for the process to begin once more without a break. The gun's crews were mainly stripped to the waist and sweat ran freely down tanned backs made darker still by random deposits of soot, sawdust and more gruesome organic matter.

"Any sign of *Relentless*?" Brehaut was almost screaming at him from a few feet away yet King still had difficulty making out the words. Banks must surely be up with them by now but all he could see in that direction was the greasy black cloud of combat as it rolled away with the wind. And the Frenchman could be expected to fire again at any moment; King indistinctively switched his glance to the huge smoking monster now slightly less than a cable off their beam which, even as he watched, despatched yet another broadside.

And then Brehaut was dead; a thirty-two pound ball effortlessly wiping the Jerseyman from the deck and leaving nothing but a pile of steaming filth in his place. King turned away from the sight and had to hold back the instinctive gag that owed as much to shock as revulsion. But that shot was only one of many sent and other damage soon took his mind from the loss of his friend.

Mistral's main was struck yet again, and this time the entire mast tumbled; heavy lengths of pine crashed down on those below, killing and maiming without distinction while pieces of tackle as heavy as enemy shot and every bit as dangerous, accounted for others. A tangle of line – surely more than could ever be needed for a single mast – slithered to the deck in clumps, tripping those still serving guns or trying to clear wreckage and suddenly it seemed the dead and injured outnumbered those still living. Standing nearby, Croft grabbed at a boarding axe and began to hack intensely at the heavy cords that pinned down the quartermaster and his timoneers while, in the absence of gunfire, the bellowing of orders contrasted oddly with screams from the wounded.

"Heave her over, lads!" This was Cooper, who must have abandoned his guns and was organising a party to remove the giant trunk that had so recently been the lower mainmast. Without thinking, Croft dropped his axe and became one of the helpers. Together, and under the junior man's direction, they manhandled the great lump to larboard then all cheered as one when it was finally tossed into the stagnant water below.

That single expression of victory set a precedent; with the bulk of the wreckage gone, movement became easier and as all set to flinging further wreckage over the side a positive chorus of defiant bellows followed from officers and men alike. Then a cannon sounded. It was nearby; one of *Mistral*'s heavy carriage pieces that must have been primed before the damage. The deep-throated call to arms was irresistible and soon another joined it. Slowly at first, and then with a rush, men began to return to their pieces. The guns were soon being served as before and despatched with the same regularity until it became clear that, though sorely wounded, *Mistral* was yet unbeaten.

* * *

The next French broadside came shortly afterwards and took away the rest of her fore. The mast was hit at roughly the same level as the main, but fell more conveniently over their larboard side, and was cast loose with the minimum of fuss. Returning from the task, Adams discarded the axe he had been using and drew his hanger. The starboard battery of the guns he commanded had fallen silent but soon came to life as he called for the servers to return and shortly afterwards their irregular bombardment resumed. With dry mouth and flaring anger he found himself bellowing pointless obscenities at the enemy, yet for all his exertions little seemed to be changing aboard the French ship. She still lay broadside on and almost undamaged by their fire whereas *Mistral* was fast approaching a wreck. He gripped his sword tightly; if only they could pull alongside. Memories of his last boarding action were fresh in his mind; it was just the type of combat he yearned for – intimate and personal – a chance to show exactly what he was made of, even if it meant dying in the process.

But though the liner was at point blank range, too much water lay between for such a jaunt and, with only one mast still standing, *Mistral* was in no condition to close the gap. Then, even as he watched, the enemy's mizzen fell, bathing her quarterdeck in canvas and forcing her stern around.

And Adams was not the only one to notice; the cheering that had become as constant as *Mistral*'s gunfire now rose to new levels. He glanced back; no man had ceased to work, every functional gun was in use with servers from the redundant larboard battery either assisting their colleagues, clearing wreckage, or tending to the wounded. And even many of the latter had forgotten their predicament and were joining in the general ovation, their shouts being more of defiance than pain.

For a moment Adams was mildly humbled at this display of bravado, one that came from an inner energy that needed no support from foolish notions, wronged love or supposedly broken hearts. And then he noticed Summers.

The lad was pacing back and forth behind the guns showing all the *sangfroid* of a seasoned officer twice his age. For a moment their eyes met and the midshipman seemed to acknowledge him, before adding a word of encouragement to the nearest team and continuing to walk with little regard for the death and destruction being wreaked about him.

And it was a sobering sight; Adams felt his anger abate further as the lad calmly ordered a member of the afterguard to assist with the train tackle of number four cannon. The midshipman had every wish to live, yet carried himself well and was an encouragement to his men. Once more the natural valour contrasted strongly with Adams' own, selfish, variety; a boy with his whole life before him was being silently brave while he, who supposedly had little left to live for, did nothing other than fluster and fume.

"Powder – powder here!" Adams looked round to see one of the nearby servers crying out in desperation. *Mistral*'s casualties must have included some of the boys and now the supply of cartridges was slowing.

"Greenwood, Swain, Brown – join the powder team!"

The men had been serving number six cannon before the weapon was disabled. Now the smoking barrel lay amid the remains of its carriage whilst others of its crew had mysteriously disappeared. The three instantly responded to Adams' call and, abandoning the wreckage they had been in the midst of clearing, headed for the main hatch and joined the group of powder monkeys in their work. Adams turned away a calmer man, and began to check others still serving the cannon.

"No gun, Jackson?" he asked, noticing number six's former captain.

The man shook his head and appeared stunned, but Adams

could spare no time for finer feelings.

"Go to number two; their captain's just been taken."

Slowly, but with increasing purpose, Jackson made for the fresh weapon; Adams watched as the tackle man who had been fingering the gunlock cautiously, moved away and allowed him to prime the pan. Then, at a word from their new captain, all stood to one side, and Jackson tugged firmly on the firing line. The cannon erupted with yet another guttural roar; its crew added a cheer to the cacophony before continuing to serve the beast with no attempt at gauging the result of their action.

Adams moved on, his anger now contained, then paused to consider the Frenchman again; the loss of her mizzen had caused her to drift slightly and more of her bows were being revealed. And then he took a sharp intake of breath as the shadow of another ship passed by. He spun round, hardly daring to believe what he saw; but there – to his right and beyond doubt – was the ghostly form of another frigate.

It was *Relentless*; under full sail as she passed *Mistral*'s stern and made for the Frenchman. She was clawing into the wind and clearly being pressed hard, but making good way as she stood towards the liner. Her sails were battered, with the fore topgallant little more than ribbons, but still she remained very much under control. As if to demonstrate the fact, the heavy frigate then bore hard to starboard, sending her main guns round to face the enemy and, even before the evolution was complete, her broadside was despatched.

Then there came true carnage; Adams had the rare chance of watching a ship receive another's broadside and his lateral vantage point made the action appear particularly devastating. *Relentless*' main battery was made up of twenty-four pounder carriage pieces that had targetted the Frenchman's hull. Adams could see the result of their work by what was blown up from the enemy's upper decks. All manner of detritus was hurled clear of her bulwark and into the ocean beyond while the liner visibly rolled from the impact. For a moment her tattered tophamper could be seen waving as if in desperation amid the smoke and then, almost as an afterthought, her main came down.

Even from such a splendid viewpoint, Adams had no idea if the hit had come from *Relentless*' cannon or one of their own, but the huge spar seemed to fold and, rather than falling to one side, collapsed in a tangle of canvas and cordage.

Now the enthusiasm on *Mistral*'s deck knew no bounds. News of *Relentless* joining them, combined with the very visual demonstration of their enemy's vulnerability, had stirred all to a fever pitch. Adams instinctively bellowed for order and was glad to note Summers also taking up the cry. The guns were undeniably hot, so it was more important than ever to see they were adequately sponged while, with *Relentless* potentially in the firing line, it might also become necessary to order a first reduction in powder. But as the Commodore's ship fired yet again, it was clear that not only were the British seizing control, they might also be gaining the upper hand.

* * *

On the quarterdeck, Croft was as elated as any although, as first lieutenant, could not appear so. But when he met his captain's eyes it was still hard for both of them not to crumble into what might become laughter or tears.

"We cannot withdraw," he finally bellowed.

"No, have to continue firing," King yelled in agreement. "But the enemy will be distracted!"

That was certainly true except, as Banks had been able to position himself just off the Frenchman's stern, it was doubtful if many of the liner's guns could actually bear on *Relentless*. *Mistral* remained a target however and, though several French guns were firing out of sequence, she was by no means beaten.

The enemy were keeping to broadsides, but these had become unregulated to the point where they were verging on individual fire. Halfway through the latest barrage, Croft noticed only one shot actually striking and that caused no casualties, yet fountains aplenty were being raised as much as fifty feet from *Mistral*'s hull. Such random shooting was surely the sign of a flagging crew and the feeling of relief was like warm water added to a cold bath.

The danger had not passed, of course, but compared to what they had endured, seemed almost negligible. So it was more with interest than despair that Croft noticed a heavy ball strike *Mistral*'s mizzen chains near to where he and King stood. Alone, the damage was slight but, when taken in conjunction with another French shot that slammed into the frigate's mizzen top, it brought disastrous results.

"Mast's going – secure yourselves!" Harridge's frantic call was correct, if the warning redundant; on a crowded quarterdeck already strewn with wreckage there were few places to hide. Croft glanced up at the tottering tower of pine and cordage, then noticed his captain had sensibly dropped to a crouch, with his one hand futilely guarding his scalp from the coming impact. Without a thought, Croft hurled his body over King's while his two hands did a far better job of protecting his own head.

The world turned dark as remains of the mizzen topsail blanketed much and the clatter of falling debris sounded loud, even to ears already numbed by cannon fire. Those caught beneath struggled under the cloying canvas while chunks of wood and tackle continued to rain about them. Croft was one of the first to free himself, and turned back to rescue his captain who still lay prone on the deck.

And then it happened; one moment Croft was stretching forward to drag King up, the next a thrill ran down the older man's back. There was no pain – he was only dimly aware of the deck as it rose up to meet him. Then, even before it made contact, he lost consciousness.

11.

If this truly were hell, all Russell's expectations had been met. It was dark for sure; despite several spears of flame that burned with an intensity that hurt his tender eyes, areas of dense blackness remained that might easily hold untold terrors. What air there was could have come straight from a furnace and had been further enhanced by a charnel house stench that constantly threatened to make him gag. His tongue felt dry, swollen and oddly placed within a mouth filled with another man's teeth while the ache in his leg reminded him of a recent pain that had been so very much greater. All about, other souls lay in similar torment while strange faces floated above that seemed indifferent to their misery and might even be viewing it with contempt. But at least the melancholy chorus of groans and appeals to long lost mothers was being stifled by a more regular rasping noise that was far less disturbing, and it was only when he came to consider the sound further that Russell realised it came from his own lungs.

But the discovery at least brought a measure of normality to his situation; as well as hearing, seeing and smelling, if he could also make a sound then presumably life remained and he might do more. Then, greatly daring, he moved his head sideways. A myriad of lights exploded like all-enveloping suns but, once they had set, he found he could see more clearly. And then the pain returned in force.

It came from his left leg, just below the knee to be exact and, though Russell was sure he had never experienced anything quite so bad, an element of familiarity remained. He reached down to the spot, feeling at it with hands too large for such a delicate task. The limb was bandaged, he could tell that much, and the space below felt strangely empty.

"Back with us, are you?" a voice asked. It came from one of the faces staring down and Russell brought his hands up to keep the thing at bay. "Steady there, you're amongst friends," the vision told him. "An' you've got a mess mate next to you – Parker, he's one of your lot, ain't he?"

Russell glanced cautiously to one side where a grey form could indeed be seen, but quickly brought his eyes back to the figure above him.

"Caught the same ball you did, though he came off worse – twice as bad you might say."

"So I'm wounded?" Russell asked in a voice loud enough to echo, yet the question still had to be repeated before it was understood.

"Aye, that you are," the face had lowered itself to catch Russell's words and now took on the features of Driver, one of *Mistral*'s loblolly boys. "Frog round shot made a nasty mess of your pin; Mr Manning cut the rest off so it wouldn't give no more trouble." The lad considered him with interest. "You don't remember, do you?"

The seaman shook his head then wished he hadn't as the lights returned.

"Surgeon's given you laudanum," Driver continued. "Probably

still with you."

Russell went to nod then changed his mind. "Yes," he whispered weakly.

"That's as it should be," Driver assured him. "We weren't expectin' you to wake again this watch. You'll get another dose at eight bells – think you can wait that long?"

Russell said nothing; he was already exhausted by the brief exchange and felt in no need of any strange concoctions. Besides, that was in the future, for now his only wish was to return to the deep forgiving sleep that made all things right and, by the time Driver had moved on to his next patient, was already snoring deeply.

* * *

At roughly the same time King was waking, but from a sleep that was anything but soothing. Rather than Russell's drug-induced coma, his had been all too active and filled with strange images and worrying scenes that left him more tired than before he turned in. And there was so much he didn't understand – why he should be on the quarterdeck and lying in a grimy scupper rather than his usual cot? And what had McNamara been thinking of letting him retire fully dressed in the first place? Then sense and the memories began to return as he realised his recent nightmares were only too real and had followed him into consciousness.

Levering himself up, he rested for a moment against the bulwark and felt at his head. There was surprisingly little pain; the solid lump to the right side, just above the temple, was tender but when he brought the hand down and examined it he could see no trace of blood. Reassured, he rose further and, still gripping tightly to the bulwark, cautiously looked about.

It was just as he suspected; rather than a dream, *Mistral* had indeed been in combat and was now decidedly the worse for wear. Her guns were at rest but smoke still hung above them and even in the ringing silence King sensed the battle was not long ended. He raised his head further; one of the biggest concerns for any seaman was the state of the masts and, rather than an intricate and finely balanced tophamper, the sight that met his eyes was truly the stuff of nightmares. Little more than stumps remained of all three while even the bowsprit was battered and lacking its jib boom.

Lowering his gaze, King then took in his more immediate surroundings. The quarterdeck was indeed a shambles but much was being put to rights even as he watched. Several gangs of men had been set to clear wreckage, something they were doing with unbounded enthusiasm. Some cheered as the splintered remains of fittings and equipment were recklessly tossed over the side and every so often a pair would break away to shake another's hand or hug a particular friend in greeting or celebration.

King took all in but understood little. There were no senior officers present and those of warrant rank – he could see two boatswain's mates and the quartermaster – were behaving just as foolishly as any of the hands while from further forward came the sound of *Nancy Dawson* being scraped out on a fiddle.

Still confused, King shifted his attention to the Frenchman lying ominously close across a stretch of darkened water. Was it possible that *Mistral* had survived even one broadside from those grinning monsters? The French guns were silent now, though the liner also wore a pall of smoke over her main deck. Hers was far darker however, and King soon realised much of it stemmed from a small fire that had broken out on the forecastle.

Beyond the Frenchman he could see *Relentless*; the frigate was keeping her distance, presumably cautious of a smouldering enemy. But Banks' ship was in the process of launching a boat, which would take possession of the liner. And then he noticed another vessel, crisp in the afternoon sunlight and closing on the liner's prow – it took several seconds for him to identify *Taurus*. Bruce's frigate lacked much of her fore topmast but still remained a viable entity and would have been ideally placed to rake the enemy's bows.

At the sight of this last section of jigsaw everything fell into place. *Mistral* must have endured the liner's broadsides long enough to allow Banks and Bruce to catch the larger vessel in their crossfire. Even when doled out by single-deckers, such punishment must have been truly devastating; King could easily imagine the scenes of carnage and butchery as heavy shot raked the battleship from both bow and stern. However hard his own crew were now celebrating, there was no doubt about the final clincher in their victory.

The realisation of what must have happened awoke more immediate recollections: *Mistral*'s mizzen mast falling, seeing Croft being struck by a piece of stray tackle and the sudden and terrible loss of Brehaut. The last memory hit him with all the power of fresh news and he felt himself buckle slightly as he gripped the top rail. The sailing master had been no distance from him and the pair had served together for many years, yet now he was gone, and King remained. Much the same could be said for Croft; they might not have been shipmates for as long, but what had started as a wary relationship had grown into something far more valuable. For a moment King wondered at the strange logic that decided he should survive and the others be taken, before the remorse began and came in waves until he knew himself to be awash.

His knuckles whitened and tears were close by as he gripped the brass rail. For a moment he considered sending for his servant, but McNamara assisted the surgeon when in action and must have work to do elsewhere. King's own quarters would offer a degree of privacy however and were not so far off; he really should go there unless he wished to disgrace himself entirely. And then he saw Cooper.

"Are you hurt, sir?" The young man was flushed and slightly out of breath as he made his way aft through the chaos of the quarterdeck.

"A little stunned," King replied thickly as he hurriedly released the top rail and rubbed at his face.

"You were beneath the mizzen when it fell," Cooper reminded him. "It must have shaken you; I had to attend to Mr Croft first but you should also be with the surgeon."

King stared back blankly.

"Mr Croft was injured; I have sent him below," the lieutenant explained, adding, "and the Frenchman has struck, though you'll be a knowing that I'm sure."

"James?" King exclaimed weakly. "Is he alive?"

"He is, sir," Cooper assured him. "Mr Manning has him in his care. He were badly cut so I had to attend to him first."

"Of course," King agreed.

"Do you have orders for me, sir?"

King brought his hand down and looked about. It was strange

but knowing Croft to be amongst the living had almost given him new life.

"We must secure the ship," he said while his mind cleared further.

"Very good, sir," Cooper answered. "I have spoken to the carpenter who is currently sorting the damage for'ard, though he reports there to be little in the well. Mr Adams is securing the guns as we speak. Mr Harridge was also wounded when the mizzen fell but is at work and not judged to be in danger; his party are seeing what can be done in terms of a jury rig."

"Very good," King told him as strength slowly returned.

"The Commodore is taking possession of the Frenchman," the lieutenant continued. Might I suggest we send our marines across to assist? And if you will forgive me, sir, I think you should be below."

"All in good time," King almost snapped; what was Cooper thinking of? With so much to do there would be little chance of rest for anyone and he had no intention of sulking off into his cabin. "You may certainly ask Mr Hopkins to organise his marines; they can bear a message from me to Sir Richard that I will prepare forthwith. And we must see to the men," he continued as more ideas formed. "As soon as the guns are secure send for Mr Falmer."

"The cook, sir?"

"Yes, have him fire up the stove and set some meat a boiling. Beef, pork – whatever was in steep, but see it is served up without delay." The idea of food was actually quite repugnant to him, but King knew the appetite of the regular Jack; none had eaten since breakfast and a deal had happened since. "He may issue hard tack and cheese along with any soft fruits we may have before then."

"Very good, sir. And can I suggest grog?" Cooper chanced. "It ain't every day frigates take a third rate – I could speak to the purser."

"Do that," King agreed. "See every man is given a tot with the promise of another at eight bells." He glanced once more at the smoking liner that still seemed daunting, even in defeat. "I should say they deserve it."

* * *

"It will help with the pain," Driver insisted as he extended the small metal cup in Parker's direction.

"Don't feel no pain," the topman lied.

"No pain?" Driver questioned.

"Not much," Parker grunted, adding, "Maybe a little, but I can handle it."

The loblolly boy considered the cup for a moment. "Most Jacks hound me for the stuff, 'specially those with wounds such as yours. What say I set it down here – then if you changes your mind you can help yourself?"

"As you will," Parker agreed although both knew the cup would go untouched. In truth, what was left of his legs throbbed with a dull yet persistent ache that made both limbs feel as if crushed under some huge and immovable rock. But Parker had already learned laudanum would do little to truly ease the pain; the best he could hope for was sleep and even the deepest could not last long enough to cure him. Besides, he had spent a lifetime controlling both emotions and feelings and preferred to fight them head on with a clear mind.

"What about you, Russell?" Driver asked Parker's neighbour.

"I'll take some," the seaman answered more readily. "An' another tot of rum if you've the spare."

"That were only for the one time," Driver told him sternly as he measured out a dose from the ribbed glass bottle.

"How long'll we be staying here?" Parker enquired while his friend was heaved up and given the drug.

"What, in the cockpit?" Driver grunted as he returned Russell to the deck. "Can't rightly say; like as not most of you'll be transferred to sick quarters ashore as soon as we makes Cape Town."

"And when'll that be?" Parker persisted.

"Can't say that neither," Driver made to stand. "Though we ain't so very far off. Probably take us a day once we gets going; that's if there's something available to take us in tow."

"Sick quarters?" Russell repeated doubtfully when the loblolly boy had moved on. "Would that be a hospital?"

"Like as not."

"Never did like the sound of them places," Russell confessed.

"They varies," Parker tried to move then winced as the pain in both stumps rose up. "Though none is good."

"But we'll be sent back eventually," Russell insisted.

"Doubt it. What use will they have for folk like us aboard ship? You might get by on shore – a one-legged man can at least move about a bit."

Russell shrugged. "We can both still splice," he said. "And sew – we can surely sew – maybe join the sailmaker's crew if the bosun won't have us?"

"Oh aye," Parker agreed. "And drink grog, carve scrimshaw or play a hand of Crown and Anchor like any sound Jack Tar. But you won't find either of us dancing no hornpipes." He paused and added in a softer tone. "And neither will we be going aloft, so you can say goodbye to that as well."

"Then we goes ashore together," Russell stated firmly, as his voice began to thicken. "Look after each other, like we was aboard ship."

"Aye, maybe we shall," Parker agreed without conviction. "And Cape Town's as good a place as any."

"You mean they won't be taking us back to England?" the thought shocked Russell back to sensibility, but only for a moment.

"Told you, we're no longer needed," Parker repeated sadly. Then, as the deep rumble of his friend's snores began, added, "Not on land, nor aboard ship, and certainly not aloft. So you might as well get used to it."

* * *

"I have just returned from speaking with the Commodore," King announced to the room in general. "He is arranging for *Taurus* to take us in tow when her repairs are complete."

They were in *Mistral's* great cabin although the title bore little relevance to the battered space that still bore scars from the previous day's combat. Only the table and chairs, furniture McNamara had rescued from the ship's hold, bore any sign of respectability. And those gathered about it, men who were mainly dressed in clothes first donned the morning before, looked far from pristine.

"Very good, sir," Croft replied in his customary level tone, although the bandage that covered most of his forehead did much to conceal any surprise. “But might I ask of the liner?”

“Sir Richard believes she can be made to sail,” King announced. “Not far perhaps, but if the weather remains clement she should fetch the Cape without trouble.”

“I understand it to be barely over the horizon,” Adams added and there was a significant pause; in the past Brehaut would have confirmed their position and noticing his absence in such small matters only made the loss more obvious.

“The first Frenchman we met is all but done for,” King continued hurriedly. “And as much may be said for the other two, though the Commodore hopes they might still be saved. As most of you will know, work is in hand to set jury rigs though one at least might yet have to be abandoned.”

“And what of the last, sir?” Cooper asked. “The frigate which made off?” Of them all, the new lieutenant seemed the least affected by their recent action and was definitely the most alert present. Even Adams who was several years younger seemed exhausted in comparison.

“Of her we know little,” King replied. “Last seen she were steering sou'-west under every stitch of canvas that could be raised; *Athena* tried to pursue, but had already been badly mauled and could only watch her go. The journey home should be short, however, and she should not bother us.”

“And in the future, sir?” Cooper again. “Do you see her posing a threat to the colony?”

“I think not.” King's answer was immediate. “*Mistral* is without doubt the worst damaged of any British ship, yet Cape Town's yard will set her to rights in time. The same can be said for *Athena* but even before long distance cruises can be established, *Taurus* and *Relentless* remain relatively undamaged and will see off a single fifth rate.”

“And when can we start for the Cape?” Croft this time.

“Not today, nor probably tomorrow,” for a moment King's mind went back to the organised chaos he had just witnessed aboard *Relentless*. With his own ship damaged and a captured enemy liner along with several hundred prisoners to organise, Sir Richard had been more than occupied. “There is much needing to be done aboard those taken before then and I am sure you gentlemen will not be bored in *Mistral*.”

The remark brought a smattering of laughter, as King had hoped.

"Mr Hopkins, you and your entire marine force shall transfer to the captured liner and remain with her until we make harbour."

"Very good, sir," the officer replied. Hopkins had already been informed of the arrangement yet his prior knowledge had not been revealed in any clever remark or smart rejoinder and King wondered briefly if the recent action had altered the young man for the better.

"When the order comes to square away we shall be travelling in convoy and, despite the short distance, it may not be an easy passage. But I think we can all be confident of dining together at Johnston's come Saturday night.

Once more the brief laughter was proof that all were not quite as spent as they appeared. Only Adams might have been less than enthusiastic, but then King had long since given up trying to understand that particular young man. Besides, soon it would not be necessary, for there was one more point on which he had personally decided and it was not something he cared to share with anyone.

"Then, if we are all clear on what is intended, perhaps we should return to our duties?"

His guests rose to leave but it only needed a look from King for one, the first lieutenant, to remain and, as soon as the room was otherwise emptied, the pair seated themselves once more.

"I have not had the chance to speak before," King began, "and now it has come, find the words hard to find. Though I am obliged to you, James, and not just for your actions in the recent combat."

"If you will excuse me, sir, it is I who should be thanking you," Croft replied evenly. "Being appointed executive officer of *Mistral* was beyond my expectations and, I will admit, has changed my life – for the better, of course."

"Few could have done a finer job," King told him. "In fact I would venture none; I shall always be grateful to you."

"There is no need," the older man smiled. "For this has been the best time in my career and my only wish is for it to continue."

"Continue?" King repeated, absent mindedly.

"Indeed, sir. The ship will have to be brought back to service order, and dockyards are the same the world over; there will be a deal to do in seeing no corners are cut. And we may even make some improvements; I have a number of suggestions you may wish to consider when the time is appropriate."

"Yes, of course," King agreed, while ignoring the pang of guilt. For his own plans were very different, and did not involve *Mistral*, or the elderly officer who now sat before him.

* * *

Parker had been quiet for some while, although Russell sensed he also was wide awake.

"Is the pain worse?" he asked.

"It's there," the topman confirmed softly.

In the eternal dark of the orlop, time could only be judged by the arrival of food and, as none had been offered for some while, it must be night. Besides, all else was quiet, only the random moan from a fitful sleeper conflicted with the sounds of far off hammering or an occasional bellowing of orders from the decks above. Russell and Parker were barely inches apart and had already become used to communicating in a gentle whisper that was as intimate and private as the confessional.

"You should be taking the laudanum," Russell told him yet again. "There's still a draught there, I can reach it if you wants."

"Kind of you to offer," Parker told him. "I remembers a time when you wouldn't have."

"That were a while back," Russell replied defensively. "I didn't know you then."

"You thought you did," Parker persisted. "Thought I were just another Molly, and one you could make money from."

"Like I says, it were a while back; I've come a long way since."

"That you have," Parker agreed. "And don't think you have to stop, just 'cause you've lost a leg."

"Can't stay a sailor," Russell reminded him.

"Maybe not, but there'll be other things."

Other things; Russell could not imagine what, for he already seemed to have tried most. But nothing compared to the comradeship he had found in the last few months. This might be down to *Mistral* or the Navy in general but, now that he had sampled such a life, he wanted no other.

"What about you?" Russell asked.

"Me?" Parker gave a brief snort of laughter. "I ain't got to worry; we old Molls look after one another. Probably end up with a beggar's pitch on a prime Cape Town street and earn myself a fortune."

Russell turned away knowing this was pure bravado. "It ain't going to happen, is it?" he asked bluntly.

"No," Parker agreed after a pause. "It ain't."

"You could find yourself a life," Russell persisted.

"Not one I want," Parker replied. "If I can't be at sea, nothing else will do."

12.

King would have preferred to end the voyage, and his career, with a dramatic flourish: to have anchored his last command man-of-war fashion: charging in under full sail only to run up into the wind at the last moment and take all in while releasing the best bower and firing off her saluting guns. When the smoke cleared *Mistral* should have been revealed lying innocently at rest with booms out and boats in the water. In the present circumstances that was not to be, however; her battered hull needed to be towed to the spot and, in the absence of suitable ground tackle, secured to a fixed mooring until she might finally be warped into the dockyard's understanding embrace.

"All sound, sir," the coxswain reported touching his hat.

"Very good," King acknowledged turning away. They were now safe in the small roadstead just off the dockyard entrance and, if what he intended came about, he had just issued his last order as her captain. And possibly as a sea officer, he reminded himself, although the concept remained every bit as hard to accept. But, however alien the act might feel, it was surely better to make the break now and leave a way clear for another man – his replacement – to oversee the frigate's repairs.

Not that one would be needed straight away; Croft had been as good as his word and was currently assembling copious notes and observations on every aspect of the ship. If even half his ideas were turned into reality, *Mistral* should come back as one of the finest fifth rates in the service.

And King could not deny that part of him wanted nothing more than to retain her command and take the frigate to sea once more. With Banks as his Commodore, Croft his first lieutenant, Manning for surgeon and Cooper, Adams and Summers as supporting officers, he would be truly set. They needed a replacement for Brehaut of course, but competent sailing masters were common enough and one more familiar with local waters might be found. They would lack the charm and understanding of his old friend, although King had once considered Adam Fraiser to be irreplaceable. And then he remembered his own situation and once more decided the change was for the best.

For he had surely done enough. A one-armed officer was hardly a rarity in the service – indeed one notable example had achieved more than most – but then neither was such a disability an asset. Admittedly the only area where he was truly limited was physical combat and the older he became the less such an activity appealed. Yet still he felt retaining his position as a serving post captain would be an uphill path and one likely to end with the indignity of forcible retirement as a yellowed Admiral. He had been lucky with all his promotions, and in being given such a game little craft as *Mistral* to end on. If he were to continue he might count on three, possibly four years with her, working alongside men he had come to know, like and respect and on a station that positively guaranteed action and prize money. But then he had already accumulated funds that would see him settled for life, and when the time came to be ordered home, it must surely be the end of his career.

So it was better to finish now and on his own terms; go while the cheers for a battle well fought still rang in his ears, and look forward to a life of placid contentment in the Hampshire countryside with Aimée.

Or so he told himself.

* * *

Mistral's bruised hull seemed even worse for wear when her crew began to leave. By noon there were barely a dozen regular hands still aboard and the first of the dockyard workers had started to appear. However, Adams felt no inclination to move and, in a gunroom stripped of much of its furniture, remained seated alone at the vast table, sipping miserably from a cup half-filled with cold tea.

For there was nothing for him on shore and he definitely had no desire to join the other officers in transferring to Johnston's, the boarding house that was now their regular haunt when in harbour. Anne was long gone, of course, but the place still held memories which had yet to be exorcised.

Movement from outside caught his attention and he looked up to see Harvey, the gunroom steward, at the doorway.

"Beggin' your pardon, sir, but I've been ordered to clear these quarters."

"Clear?" Adams questioned absent-mindedly.

"Yes, sir. The fellows from the dockyard want to start striking bulkheads – they're all coming down, even the one between 'ere and my pantry."

"And they are starting already?"

The steward nodded. "Gonna make a clean sweep of the entire ship, they are – like we was clearing for action only worse. What with Mr Croft's plans for reorganising, I can't see them being set up again any time soon, though I expect you are aware of all that, sir."

"Indeed, I shall be assisting Mr Croft," Adams agreed as he finally stood.

"There's still some dunnage in your cabin, sir," Harvey persisted. "Shall I have it sent ashore?"

"If you would," Adams replied as he made for the door.

"Are you staying with the other officers, sir?" the steward enquired.

"No," Adams paused. "Not at Johnston's, I need somewhere closer by – so I might be on hand for the refit, you understand. I shall send word in due course."

* * *

Russell stared listlessly at the flaking ceiling. His bed was one of ten in the shabby little hospital room which was an improvement on the sick berth aboard *Mistral*, but only just. Apart from light and air from two grubby windows, about the only thing that could be said for the place was it had space and even then he could have reached out and touched the beds on either side. But there was also a decent sized alleyway down the middle; twice a day a trolley would appear bringing food and, on the same journey, take away their waste. He had actually been wondering when the next visit was due when something else at the foot of the bed caught his attention and Russell was surprised to see his former messmate standing before him.

"Feelin' better are you?" Greenwood enquired awkwardly.

"I reckons," Russell replied as he elbowed himself upright. "Kind of you to visit; given shore leave have they?"

"Permanent," the seaman told him. "We've been moved into barracks at the castle. Snug little billet and most of the lads are there; them what survived," he added.

"Must be good," Russell pondered. "Being together, I mean. There are a couple from *Mistral* in the next room, though no one I knows well."

"It's a shame Parker didn't make it," Greenwood remarked. "The two of you would have been company for each other."

"He didn't want to," Russell replied softly. "Without his ship, his mess and his precious tophamper he didn't have a lot and weren't the kind that takes readily to change."

"You could say the same for most of us," Greenwood chanced and Russell nodded sadly.

"The barky will be in dock I suppose?" he asked.

"Aye, they reckons six months though dockyard mateys are the same wherever you go. It'll probably end up more like nine, and then they won't have finished. But how is it with you?"

Russell shrugged. "Sawbones says the stump's healing nicely and they'll fix me up with a peg afore long."

"That'll be useful," Greenwood remarked as he settled himself on the bed, casually taking up the space allowed by Russell's missing limb. "Get that in place an' you won't know yourself. I seen men with jury spars get about lovely."

"Maybe so," Russell agreed doubtfully. "Though not aboard

ship I'm thinking."

"So what'll you do then?" Greenwood asked quickly.

"Oh, there are one or two tricks up me sleeve," Russell answered less certainly.

"Tricks?" Greenwood questioned. "Would they be like the old ones: those you used to play?"

"Similar, I suppose," Russell agreed, mildly abashed. "Got a couple of ideas an' havin' a peg might even come in handy."

"Well that's alright then," Greenwood told him although there was something in his manner that suggested otherwise.

"You got a better idea?"

"Not for now, but maybe the future," his friend continued cautiously. "And I'm not making any promises like..."

"Come on, Greenie, spill."

"Like I said, no promises," Greenwood repeated. "But Matt Falmer was one of them taken."

"Falmer?" Russell repeated in surprise. "The slushy? He should have been in the magazine where no harm could come to him."

"It weren't in the action, this were later," Greenwood explained. "Just last week, when we was put ashore. First spell of leave and the cove fills his-self up with shellfish. Some were not so ripe and the next you know we're planting the poor bugger. But the fact remains, when *Mistral* does come back, she'll be needin' a cook."

"No good to me," Russell told him. "I know little of such things."

"Neither did Falmer," Greenwood sniffed. "Else he'd have been more careful what he ate. Besides, I can remember a time when you weren't so clever. Worse than that – you thought you knew it all and that's a place few come back from."

"But I were never a seaman," Russell protested. "Never got rated ordinary, even with two sound pins."

"Would have, it were just a question of time; 'sides, there's more to being a Jack than knowing the ropes. Attitude means a lot on the lower deck and you've got that in spades."

Greenwood paused to allow Russell to consider this, then continued more cautiously.

"Slushies are a bit like officers," he pondered. "All they do is stand about and let others do the work. You'll have to check your mates are up to the mark and make a bit from what you can scrape from off the coppers, but nothing a man like you can't handle. And there'll be time to bone up on your duties while the barky's in dock."

"You offering me the post?" Russell asked.

The seaman shook his head. "Not down to me," he replied, "but there's no one else more suited an' I know Mr Croft would take a suggestion. As I say, fellow with your inclination would make a go of it, and couldn't do much worse than poor old Falmer."

"I'd be back aboard ship..." Russell mused.

"Aye, and it'd be *Mistral*," Greenwood agreed. "Same mess if you wanted it, though you might be too good for us. Most cooks berth in the cockpit."

"Mess would suit me fine," Russell said after a pause. "And I'd be interested – if the chance came along that is."

* * *

Never had the anonymity of Cape Town's Heerengracht – the long, straight street known locally as Gentleman's Walk – seemed so welcome. Manning and King sat on a stone bench in silence as they considered the far off groups of gentry enjoying both the cool of a late summer's afternoon and the chance to show off their fine clothes. The air carried a hint of landed fish from the nearby market yet still seemed clean enough to men accustomed to ocean winds, while the distant murmur of friendly conversation gave a homely, civilised feel to the place.

"Will you miss this?" Manning chanced after they had been quiet for some while.

"Cape Town? I suppose I shall," King murmured. "The place has settled of late and seems agreeable to our rule."

"I was meaning more the foreign travel," Manning persisted. "You have spoken of venturing into trade but that can never have the same freedom you now enjoy."

"As an unemployed sea officer?" King laughed. "No, I should think not. Though since *Mistral* were taken into dock, I must confess the time has rather dragged."

"James Croft appears busy enough. He came by the boarding house this morn' and enquired after you."

"Did he indeed?" King gave a sheepish grin.

"You will have told him of your decision – to resign your command, I mean?"

"Not yet," King replied. "It is a question of judging the time."

" *Espoir* leaves on Friday," Manning reminded him.

"And my passage is booked aboard her," King confirmed. "I must speak to Sir Richard once more, then all will be made public."

"You have no doubts? No last minute concerns that what you do is right?" King knew Manning was now regarding him intensely and could not be certain if it were with the eyes of a friend or a surgeon. "You have been a sea officer most of your life and nearly always a Navy man," he continued. "In all the years I've known you the prospect of life ashore has never appealed."

"I shall adjust," King declared, "and will have Aimée beside me which shall certainly help."

"Oh, undoubtedly," Manning agreed. "But will it be enough?"

King went to reply but Manning had more to say.

"I felt very much the same, and not so long ago." The surgeon had looked away now and was staring into the distance. "Returning to the land and living with Kate seemed the answer to everything. I had dreams of establishing a practice ashore and perhaps writing of my experiences, though a few weeks of family life were enough to convince me otherwise."

"For now, maybe," King suggested. "Though you shall return."

"Oh undoubtedly – if she will have me," Manning laughed. "But we are talking a long a way into the future; I know now there is more I must do before we finally settle together and believe Kate feels the same." Manning turned back and considered King once more. "As I think you and Aimée will as well."

King shook his head. "We were happy while in France and during our spell in England."

"But for most of that you were either avoiding recapture or preparing for your court martial; how long have you actually spent together in one house? And – dare I mention it – was it so very long before you and Juliana tired of one another?"

"Aimée is not Juliana," King remarked sharply.

"No, of course she isn't; the two are very different. But you are the same, Tom, and were born for the sea. Are you truly prepared to give it up for one woman?"

"It isn't just Aimée," King protested. "I've had my fill of a captain's responsibilities and am only too pleased that James is caring so well for *Mistral*."

"Yet you said yourself, life is dull without a ship to fuss over."

"Perhaps, but it is a dullness I welcome. A week from now I shall be at sea once more with nothing of note to consider until I reach England."

"And you shall have plenty to occupy you then," Manning supposed.

"Oh indeed," King agreed. "Much to be done; a whole new life to plan."

"Two lives," Manning reminded him, "though doubtless all will be accomplished in time. And then?"

"Then I – we – shall simply live it," King replied.

"But, let us consider yourself for a moment," Manning suggested with no hint of irony. "You have been made post and are what many consider a made man. Such a rank must surely have been an ambition and one you have achieved despite a number of setbacks. Have you truly come this far in order to turn aside now?"

"It isn't as easy at that..." King began, but Manning was no longer in the mood to listen.

"I need not remind you of the recent successes; *Mistral*'s commission, though brief, has been naught but victory and she is about to be rebuilt into as fine a frigate as any could wish for."

"Ah, but what after that?" King questioned.

"After that you shall surely be found something larger. I may know little of the Admiralty but understand this much – it is not run by fools as many suppose. For as long as this war lasts, a fellow such as yourself shall be found employment; there will be time enough later to turn from the sea and tend your garden."

King grinned. "You make the choice sound easy," he said. "And for me it is; for I shall be with Aimée and truly want nothing more."

"And I hope you will be happy," Manning told him seriously. "But if not, if you find the dust of land palls, you will be anything but and can only make Aimée miserable also."

The last point was one King had not considered. "Maybe you are right, Bob," he said after a moment's thought. "And if you are, I shall doubtless admit it."

"So what are you to do?" Manning asked after a while.

"I – I am not certain," King confessed. "But do know this: when *Espoir* sails on Friday, I shall be aboard her. And nothing you or anyone can say will change that."

* * *

Adams had thought it to be Anne from some way off but did not react. Twice already in the short walk down Strand Street he had caught sight of someone looking remarkably like her so assumed his mind was playing more tricks. But as the figure drew closer his doubts began to fade and disappeared completely when she so clearly recognised him.

He stopped, still wondering if it might be some form of dream even though the vision was now running towards him, its smile – her smile – so open and familiar. His mouth twitched but no answering expression could be summoned and neither was he able to move. But when she reached him and he felt her body, smelt her scent and heard the deep purr of her greeting, there could be no doubt: Anne was back and, more than that, she was back with him.

"Whatever happened?" he asked when her long embrace finally relented. "Where did you go?"

"Further inland," she told him breathlessly. "There are some of my former countrymen's forces there, along with a few Cape Town residents who did not wish to meet with the English. I heard my brother was among them and found him and his wife. John, don't you see – Wieb is alive. Alive and well, as are his family!"

"But the money!" Adams exclaimed, without feeling even vaguely embarrassed about mentioning something so basic. "You took all I had and left nothing but debt – not even a note!"

"Oh yes, and I am so sorry – it was a mistake. I thought the lodging house would retain my room and shall surely pay for all you spent. I have discovered my husband's bankers and now have enough for us both; we can continue as we had planned!"

"Continue?" he questioned vaguely.

"Yes, you can be rid of this foolish uniform," she said, tugging at the lapels of his stained tunic. "And find yourself a proper position ashore. My brother may help; with the British in command he can be free of the army and intends to stay and raise his children. As we might too," she added coyly. "Oh, do you really not see? Everything can be the same as it was."

Adams drew breath; his brain still reeled from their meeting while the wonderful feeling of holding her was only enhanced by the story, which was so easy to believe. Whether they could continue was another matter though, for something of his old self had definitely altered. It might have been caused by the shock of her leaving, the recent action, or any one of the many more subtle changes that had come about in the last few months. But of one thing he was certain; things could never be the same again.

* * *

"So you've changed your mind, yet still wish to go?" Banks asked with a look of amused confusion. "Tom, you're not making sense."

"I realise that, sir," King agreed sheepishly. "And I am sorry; sorry to have caused so many problems."

"It is of no matter," the older man assured him. "Tell me what you have in mind and do not concern yourself; so far the whole thing has remained between you and me, no one else is involved. So what exactly is the concern?"

"It is mainly Aimée," King replied, blushing slightly. "I want her for my wife and nothing else will do."

"And now you have the funds to see such a thing to fruition," Banks agreed. "But I already know that – it's why you originally chose to go."

"So I realise, sir." King paused and seemed to be searching for more words.

"You obviously have a problem," Banks continued. "I shall help if I can but need to know what it is. If you are short of ready coin I might advance a little though the Admiralty cannot prevaricate too long over our recent captures. And you should be due a pretty penny," he added with obvious satisfaction. "I should say the liner will be bought into the service, along with at least one of the frigates. With head money for the rest and what you are due for those Indiamen you will be comfortably warm for the rest of your life."

"Indeed, sir," King agreed, "though I am quickly learning that money is not all. I need time more than anything; time to be with Aimée, to see us through whatever hurdles we have to jump, then start our lives together."

"All this I know," Banks repeated. "It was why you were resigning your command and commission. Are you saying you have changed your mind and wish to remain in the service?"

"I suppose so, sir." King drew breath. "I wanted to request a leave of absence."

The older man smiled, nodded wisely and actually went to speak, although King was now into his stride.

"I've a good man in James Croft; he is an excellent premier and admirably suited to see *Mistral* through the dockyard. And *Espoir* is heading for England at the end of the week; I might still take passage in her and be home for the rest of the British summer. That should be long enough to put all to rights there, and hopefully see us wed or at the least amicably settled."

Banks closed his eyes but made no comment.

"Then back with the first convoy south in time for *Mistral* to be released from her refit," King continued more hesitantly.

"And the start of the new trading season?" Banks questioned.

"Yes, sir," King barely whispered.

"Well, you seem to have thought of everything," Sir Richard sighed, before the grin returned.

"Surely such a thing is not unheard of?" King asked quickly as his doubts rose further.

"No, no not at all," the senior man confirmed. "Even on foreign stations there are those who must return for commitments ashore, though these are usually connected with parliamentary responsibilities or business matters; in truth I have never heard of anyone leaving to achieve a divorce."

"But are you agreeable, sir?" King asked.

"Agreeable?" Banks questioned. "Given the choice of losing you completely or merely for a matter of months, do I have to choose? There is much to do in this station and I had been rather looking forward to having you in my squadron. So frankly, Tom, I could not be more pleased."

Author's Note

Of all the historical figures featured in my Fighting Sail series, **Sir Home Riggs Popham (1762-1820)** is probably one of the lesser known, although I found him hard to include for a different reason.

In introducing any character there are certain parameters that should be observed; they must be recognisable without becoming clichéd, individual but not too extreme, but most of all, they have to be believable. If any break this rule or stand out as being overly surreal or avant-garde in any way, the entire story can fall apart. Those drawn from history usually comply, the vast majority being well rounded and presentable (or, if not, have been made so by the passage of time), but in the case of Home Popham I was left with a dilemma. However extreme the man's personality may have been, and only so much can be drawn from even the most detailed biography, his actions alone are enough to reveal a brilliant mind, yet one that was not without faults, together with a personality that can only be described as eccentric. I had intended to feature him more prominently but the closer I researched the more unconventional he appeared and I was forced to draw back for fear of including a character that many would consider implausible.

He was, however, real and, I believe, every bit as bizarre as his brief appearance here suggests. Even a cursory inspection reveals an attitude and temperament that would attract classification today, while his ability to make enemies verged on the pathological. And his career was every bit as singular; in the forty or so years he was active, Popham organised and led operations on both land and sea, carried out extensive scientific surveying in India and the Far East (he was responsible for discovering a passage that ultimately established modern day Penang), involved himself in commercial activities that undoubtedly included smuggling, established the Sea Fencibles and carried out delicate diplomatic roles in India, the Middle East and Russia. He also narrowly avoided bankruptcy on at least one occasion, fought a major legal action that went as far as the House of Commons and was not backward in accepting honours as well as blatant financial inducements from foreign powers. But though his failures could be truly massive, and despite the many instances of him being recalled, reprimanded or, on one occasion, removed from the Navy list, Popham continued to attract important positions and was finally made Commander-in-Chief of Jamaica before retiring due to ill health in 1817.

Today he is probably best remembered for his *Telegraphic Signals or Marine Vocabulary*; a remarkable work that truly reflects his intense and often obsessive nature. Though initially introduced in 1803 it was not universally adopted by the Admiralty until the end of the French Wars, when most of his opponents had either died or ceased to take an active interest, and the system continued to be of service to the Royal Navy until well into the twentieth century.

If fictional, the character of Popham would probably have been rejected on the grounds of being too radical but, though my depiction of him in *Sealed Orders* is not extensive, I believe it to be typical of the man. And though he might not have been the archetypal naval hero, I was particularly pleased to have included him, even in such a limited way.

The Battle of Cape Ortegal (also known as **Strachan's Action**) took place on the 4th of November 1805 off southern Spain and is generally regarded as the last chapter in the Trafalgar Campaign. Although evenly matched in line-of-battleships, the addition of four fifth rate frigates made the British force far superior to that commanded by *Contre-Amiral* Dumanoir Le Pelley. Dumanoir was a veteran of the earlier battle off Cape Trafalgar where he commanded *Formidable* (80) in the vanguard squadron which was cut off from most of the fighting by Nelson's masterful tactics. He escaped with the battleships that were later met off Cape Ortegal. During the action Strachan sent his frigates in to chase and partially disable the heavier French and so allow his liners to catch them; hardly a radical step in itself although the single-deckers were then allowed to remain in action and actually exchanged broadsides with the larger ships. Ultimately all four French two-deckers were captured and saw service in the British fleet with Dumanoir being held prisoner in Tiverton until his return to France in 1809. There he faced two courts of enquiry and a court martial but, after finally being acquitted of all charges, he was promoted to *Vice-Amiral* in 1819.

The **attack on Buenos Aries** was launched by Popham in very much the way I have described although in reality there was no battle squadron conveniently on hand to defend Cape Town and the recently captured station was left with limited naval protection. Though the campaign was initially successful, Buenos Aries being captured on June 27th 1806, Popham's forces were not generally welcomed by the inhabitants and it was clear from the outset their tenure would be brief. The Spanish subsequently counter-attacked and Buenos Aries was retaken less than two months later. Popham's naval squadron bombarded the recaptured city but, when news of his exploits reached England, he was recalled and censured for leaving his original post.

Alaric Bond
Herstmonceux 2018

Principal Characters

(ranks and positions shown are those at the start of the book)

HMS *Hare* (16) Cruizer class brig-sloop

Tom King	Commander
James Croft	First Lieutenant
Brehaut	Sailing Master
Jones	Surgeon
Foil	Purser
Williams	Gunner
Anderson	Carpenter
Harridge	Boatswain (Pipes)
Bryant	Coxswain
John Adams	Midshipman
Michael Summers	Midshipman
Dilson	Volunteer
Cole	Volunteer
Henderson	Boatswain's Mate
Newton	Carpenter's Mate
Bates	Sergeant of Marines
McNamara	Captain's Steward
Harvey	Gunroom Steward
Greenwood	Topman and Head of Mess
Parker	Topman
Jackson	Gun Captain
Swain	Holder
Sennett	Ordinary Seaman
Brown	Ordinary Seaman
Daines	Gun Captain

HMS *Mistral* (36)

Murray	Lieutenant
Cooper	Lieutenant
Hopkins	Marine Lieutenant
McPherson	Armourer
Falmer	Cook

HMS *Relentless* (38)
Sir Richard Banks
Commodore

HMS *Athena* (32)
Granger Captain

HMS *Taurus* (36)
Bruce Captain

HMS *Diadem* (64)
Sir Home Riggs Popham
Commodore
Hugh Downman Captain

HMS *Narcissus* (32)
Ross Donnelly Captain

Spartiate (privateer)
Savarez Captain

Also

Robert Manning	Surgeon
Seth Driver	Loblolly Boy
Russell	Sharper
Sayer	Sharper
Aimée Silva	King's companion
Sir Ralph Faulks	HEIC Commodore
Sir David Baird	Lieutenant-General
David Callahan	American passenger
Anne Callahan	American passenger
Wieb	Anne Callahan's brother

Selected Glossary

Able Seaman	One who can hand, reef and steer and is well-acquainted with the duties of a seaman.
Academy	*(Slang)* A brothel, also Nanny House and Pushing School.
Back	Wind change; anticlockwise.
Backed sail	One set in the direction for the opposite tack to slow a ship.
Backstays	Similar to shrouds in function, except that they run from the hounds of the topmast, or topgallant, all the way to the deck. (Also a useful/spectacular way to return to deck for a topman.)
Backstays, Running	A less permanent backstay, rigged with a tackle to allow it to be slacked to clear a gaff or boom.
Barky	*(Slang)* Seamen's affectionate name for their vessel.
Belaying Pins	Wooden pins set into racks at the side of a ship. Lines are secured about these, allowing instant release by their removal.
Binnacle	Cabinet on the quarterdeck that houses compasses, the deck log, traverse board, lead lines, telescope, speaking trumpet, etc.
Bitts	Stout horizontal pieces of timber, supported by strong verticals, that extend deep into the ship. These hold the anchor cable when the ship is at anchor.

Block Article of rigging that allows pressure to be diverted or, when used with others, increased. Consists of a pulley wheel, made of *lignum vitae*, encased in a wooden shell. Blocks can be single, double (fiddle block), triple or quadruple. The main suppliers were Taylors, of Southampton.

Board Before being promoted to lieutenant, midshipmen would be tested for competence by a board of post captains. Should they prove able they are then known as passed midshipmen, but could not assume the rank of lieutenant until appointed as such.

Boatswain *(Pronounced Bosun)* The warrant officer superintending sails, rigging, canvas, colours, anchors, cables and cordage etc., committed to his charge.

Boom Lower spar to which the bottom of a gaff sail is attached.

Braces Lines used to adjust the angle between the yards, and the fore and aft line of the ship. Mizzen braces and braces of a brig lead forward.

Brawn Potted meat, usually pig and drawn from the head.

Brig Two-masted vessel, square-rigged on both masts.

Bumboat *(Slang)* Small vessel that carries supplies to ships at anchor. These usual consist of small luxuries, fresh bread, illicit drink and cheap novelties etc. which are offered at an exorbitant price.

Bulkhead A partition within the hull of a ship.

Bulwark	The planking or woodwork about a vessel above her deck.
Canister	Type of shot, also known as case. Small iron balls packed into a cylindrical case.
Carronade	Short cannon firing a heavy shot. Invented by Melville, Gascoigne and Miller in late 1770's and adopted from 1779. Often used on the upper deck of larger ships, or as the main armament of smaller.
Cascabel	Part of the breech of a cannon.
Caulk	*(Slang)* To sleep. Also caulking, a process that sealed the seams between strakes.
Channel	*(When part of a ship)* Projecting ledge that holds deadeyes from shrouds and backstays. Originally chain-wales.
Chink	*(Slang)* Money.
Chips /Chippy	*(Slang)* Traditional name for the carpenter. Originally from the ship builders who were allowed to carry out small lumps of wood, or chips, at the end of their shift.
Chitterlings	Basic meal made from the small intestines of a pig.
Close-Hauled	Sailing as near as possible into the wind.
Coaming	A ridged frame about hatches to prevent water on deck from getting below.
Companionway	A staircase or passageway.
Counter	The lower part of a vessel's stern.
Course	A large square lower sail, hung from a yard, with sheets controlling and securing it.
Cove	*(Slang)* A man, usually a rogue.
Cull	*(Slang)* As above.

Cutter	Fast, small, single-masted vessel with a sloop rig. Also a seaworthy ship's boat.
Dale	Drain aboard ship, larger than a scupper.
Deadeyes	A round, flattish wooden block with three holes, through which a lanyard is reeved. Used to tension shrouds and backstays.
Ditty Bag	*(Slang)* A seaman's bag. Derives its name from the dittis or 'Manchester stuff' of which it was once made.
Double Tides	*(Slang)* Working alternate watches (also watch and watch about).
Dunnage	Officially the packaging around cargo. Also *(Slang)* baggage or possessions.
Fall	The free end of a lifting tackle on which the men haul.
Fetch	To arrive at, or reach, a destination. Also the distance the wind blows across the water. The longer the fetch the bigger the waves.
Forereach	To gain upon, or pass by another ship when sailing in a similar direction.
Forestay	Stay supporting the masts running forward, serving the opposite function of the backstay. Runs from each mast at an angle of about 45 degrees to meet another mast, the deck or the bowsprit.
Friday Face	*(Slang)* A dismal countenance. Before, and even long after the Reformation, Friday was a day of abstinence, or *jour maigre*.
Frizzen	The striking plate that encourages the spark in a flintlock mechanism. Also known as a steel.

Futtock A lower frame in the hull of a ship (similar to a rib). Futtock shrouds run down from the edge of a top to the mast.

Gentleman's Walk *(Slang)* Cape Town's Heerengracht (now Adderley Street) a road that led to the fortress and was a popular promenade for senior officers and the gentry.

Glass Telescope. Also, hourglass: an instrument for measuring time (and hence, as slang, a period of time). Also a barometer.

Gingerbread *(Slang)* The ornate carvings common on larger ship's sterns.

Grimaldi (Joey) (1778 – 1837) English comic actor and comedian.

Gun Room In a third rate and above, a mess for junior officers. For lower rates the gun room is the equivalent of the wardroom.

Go About To alter course, changing from one tack to the other.

Halyards Lines which raise yards, sails, signals etc.

Hanger A fighting sword similar to a cutlass.

Hard Tack Ship's biscuit.

Hawse Area in the bows where holes are cut to allow the anchor cables to pass through. Also used as general term for bows.

Hawser Heavy cable used for hauling, towing or mooring.

Headway The amount a vessel is moved forward (rather than leeway: the amount a vessel is moved sideways) when the wind is not directly behind.

Heave To Keeping a ship relatively stationary by backing certain sails in a seaway.

HEIC	Honourable East India Company.
Holder	One aboard ship employed to move stores below deck.
Idler	A man who, through his duty or position, does not stand a watch, but (usually) works during the day and can sleep throughout the night.
Île-de-France	Modern day Mauritius.
Interest	Backing from a superior officer or one in authority, useful when looking for promotion.
Jib Boom	Boom run out from the extremity of the bowsprit, braced by means of a martingale stay, which passes through the dolphin striker.
John Company	*(Slang)* The Honourable East India Company.
Junk	Old line used to make wads etc.
Jury Mast/Rig	Temporary measure used to restore a vessel's sailing ability.
Lagged	*(Slang)* To be transported.
Landsman	The rating of one with no experience at sea.
Lanthorn	Large lantern.
Larboard	Left side of the ship when facing forward. Later replaced by 'port', which had previously been used for helm orders.
Leaguer	A long cask with a capacity of 127 imperial gallons, normally used to hold water.
Leeward	The downwind side of a vessel.
Leeway	The amount a vessel is moved sideways by the wind (as opposed to headway, the forward movement, when the wind is directly behind).
Liner	*(Slang)* Ship of the line (of battle). A third rate or above.

Linstock	A forked staff to hold a lighted slowmatch. Using a linstock enables a gun captain to fire his weapon from a distance, without the aid of a gunlock.
Loblolly Boy	*(Slang)* Medical assistant.
Lubber/Lubberly	*(Slang)* Unseamanlike behaviour; as a landsman.
Luff	Intentionally sail closer to the wind, perhaps to allow work aloft. Also the flapping of sails when brought too close to the wind. The side of a fore and aft sail laced to the mast.
Martingale Stay	Line that braces the jib boom, passing from the end through the dolphin striker to the ship.
Molly	*(Slang)* Male homosexual (or female prostitute).
Mother Midnight	*(Slang)* Midwife.
Nanny House	*(Slang)* A brothel, also Academy and Pushing School.
Oldster	*(Slang)* One considered old for their current rank. Usually used in connection with midshipmen or lieutenants.
Orlop	The lowest deck in a ship.
Ordinary Seaman	A reasonably experienced hand who has usually served at sea for between one and two years.
Peter (Blue)	Introduced in the 1750's as a blue flag with six white balls. The later version, which replaced the balls with a white square, became the signal to recall everyone to the ship.
Penny Gaff	*(Slang)* Popular lower class entertainment, the forerunner to music hall.

Point Blank	The range of a cannon when fired flat. (For a 32 pounder this would be roughly 1000 feet.)
Pushing School	*(Slang)* A brothel, also Nanny House and Academy.
Pusser	*(Slang)* Purser.
Quarterdeck	In larger ships the deck forward of the poop, but at a lower level. The preserve of officers.
Queue	A pigtail. Often tied by a seaman's best friend (his tie mate).
Quoin	Triangular wooden block placed under the cascabel of a long gun to adjust the elevation.
Ratlines	Lighter lines, untarred and tied horizontally across the shrouds at regular intervals, to act as rungs and allow men to climb aloft.
Razee	A frigate created from the hull of a ship-of-the-line; the top deck is effectively removed.
Reef	A portion of sail that can be taken in to reduce the size of the whole.
Reefing points	Light line on large sails which can be tied up to reduce the sail area in heavy weather.
Reefing Tackle	Line that leads from the end of the yard to the reefing cringles set in the edges of the sail. It is used to haul up the upper part of the sail when reefing.
Rigging	Tophamper; made up of standing (static) and running (moveable) rigging, blocks etc. Also *(slang)* clothes.
Running	Sailing before the wind.
Schooner	Small craft with two or three masts.
Scran	*(Slang)* Food.
Scupper	Waterway that allows deck drainage.

Sharper — *(Slang)* A cheat; one who lives nefariously by his wits.

Sheet — A line that controls the foot of a sail.

Shrouds — Lines supporting the masts athwart ship (from side to side) which run from the hounds (just below the top) to the channels on the side of the hull.

Smoke — *(Slang)* To discover, or reveal something hidden.

Soft Tack — Bread.

Spirketting — The interior lining or panelling of a ship.

Spring — Hawser attached to a fixed object that can be tensioned to move the position of a ship fore and aft along a dock, often when setting out to sea. Breast lines control position perpendicular to the dock.

Stay Sail — A quadrilateral or triangular sail with parallel lines hung from under a stay. Usually pronounced stays'l.

Stern Sheets — Part of a ship's boat between the stern and the first rowing thwart and used for passengers.

Stingo — *(Slang)* Beer.

Strake — A plank.

Tack — To turn a ship, moving her bows through the wind. Also a leg of a journey relating to the direction of the wind. If from starboard, a ship is on the starboard tack. Also the part of a fore and aft loose-footed sail where the sheet is attached, or a line leading forward on a square course to hold the lower part of the sail forward.

Taffrail — Rail around the stern of a vessel.

Thumper — *(Slang)* A third rate or above.

Ticket Men — Hands employed aboard a pressing tender to replace those crew seized, and see the vessel safely to harbour.

Timoneer — One who steers a ship.

Tophamper — Literally any weight either on a ship's decks or about her tops and rigging, but often used loosely to refer to spars and rigging.

Tow — Cotton waste.

Trick — *(Slang)* A period of duty.

Veer — Wind change, clockwise.

VOC — *Vereenigde Oost-Indische Compagnie*. The Dutch East India Company that was formed in 1602 and officially became defunct in 1799 although the title, and much of the ethos, remained for some while.

Waist — Area of main deck between the quarterdeck and forecastle.

Wale — A reinforced section of hull that runs from bow to stern.

Watch — Period of four (or in case of a dogwatch, two) hours of duty. Also describes the two or three divisions of a crew.

Watch List — List of men and their stations, usually carried by lieutenants and divisional officers.

Wearing — To change the direction of a square-rigged ship across the wind by putting its stern through the eye of the wind. Also jibe – more common in a fore and aft rig.

Wedding Garland An actual garland that would be raised when a ship was expected to remain at anchor for some while. It signified the vessel was not on active duty and women were allowed aboard. This was considered a preferable alternative to granting shore leave, a concession that was bound to be abused.

Windward The side of a ship exposed to the wind.

Wool Gathering *(Slang)* Daydreaming.

Yellow (Admiral) The rank of Admiral was achieved solely through seniority. Following a man being made post (captain) he gradually rose on the captains' list as those above him died, retired, or were promoted. On attaining flag rank he would normally be appointed Rear Admiral of the Blue Squadron, the lowest level of flag officer other than Commodore. But should the man be considered unsuitable for such a position, he would effectively be appointed to an unspecified and non existent squadron and forcibly retired from the sea.

About the author

Alaric Bond has had a varied career, writing for various periodicals, television, radio comedy as well as the stage. He now focuses on historical nautical fiction with thirteen published novels, eleven of which are in his acclaimed 'Fighting Sail' series.

Set during the Revolutionary and Napoleonic wars, these have no central hero but feature characters from all ranks and stations; an innovative approach that gives an exciting and realistic impression of life aboard a warship of the period.

Apart from writing, Alaric enjoys sailing, cycling and playing an assortment of musical instruments rather badly. Until recently he ran a successful restaurant with his wife; they have two children and live in Sussex.

www.alaricbond.com

About Old Salt Press

Old Salt Press is an independent press catering to those who love books about ships and the sea. We are an association of writers working together to produce the very best of nautical and maritime fiction and non-fiction. We invite you to join us as we go down to the sea in books.

More Great Reading from Old Salt Press

Honour Bound by Alaric Bond
Satisfied that he has forged HMS Kestrel into a formidable weapon, Commander King is keen to take her to sea once more. But the war is not progressing well for Britain, and his hopes of remaining in Malta are shattered as Kestrel is moved closer to the action. And so begins a story that covers two seas and one ocean, as well as a cross-country trek through enemy territory, a closer look at the French prison system and a reunion with several familiar faces. Containing breathtaking sea battles, tense personal drama and an insight into the social etiquette of both Britain and France, Honour Bound is a story brim-filled with action and historical detail.
ISBN 978-1-943404-14-8 e.book 978-1-943404-15-5 paperback

The Elephant Voyage by Joan Druett
In the icy sub-Antarctic, six marooned seamen survive against unbelievable odds. Their rescue from remote, inhospitable, uninhabited Campbell Island is a sensation that rocks the world. But no one could have expected that the court hearings that follow would lead not just to the founding of modern search and rescue operations, but to the fall of a colonial government.
ISBN 978-0-9922588-4-9

Evening Grey Morning by Red Rick Spilman

In *Evening Gray Morning Red,* a young American sailor must escape his past and the clutches of the Royal Navy, in the turbulent years just before the American Revolutionary War.

In the spring of 1768, Thom Larkin, a 17-year-old sailor newly arrived in Boston, is caught by Royal Navy press gang and dragged off to HMS *Romney*, where he runs afoul of the cruel and corrupt First Lieutenant. Years later, after escaping the *Romney*, Thom again crosses paths with his old foe, now in command HMS *Gaspee*, cruising in Narragansett Bay. Thom must finally face his nemesis and the guns of the *Gaspee*, armed only with his wits, an unarmed packet boat, and a sand bar.

ISBN: 978-1-943404-19-3 978-1-943404-20-9

Finale by Joan Druett

This cross-continental journey had proved very pleasant, particularly considering that he was dead. Or so Timothy ironically mused…

The year is 1905, and the heyday of Thames, in the goldfields of New Zealand. Back in 1867, Captain Jake Dexter, a flamboyant adventurer and pirate, and his mistress, the actress Harriet Gray, invested the fortune they made during the gold rushes of California and Australia in a theatre and hotel called the Golden Goose, which has become an internationally acclaimed tourist venue, famous for its Murder Mystery Weekends. Guests gather, and a fake murder is staged, and it is up to them to find the killer. But this hugely successful venture is now at great risk. Timothy Dexter, an American of dubious ancestry, threatens the inheritance of the Golden Goose Hotel, and the Gray family gathers to hold a council of war, interrupted when a real murder intervenes. And a young tourist, Cissy Miller, entrusted with a Harlequin costume and a very strange mission, may be the only one to hold the key to the mystery.

B07C6627YW e.book 978-0994124661 Paperback

Rhode Island Rendezvous
Book Three, The Patricia MacPherson Nautical Adventures
by Linda Collison
Newport Rhode Island: 1765. The Seven Years War is over but unrest in the American colonies is just heating up…
Maintaining her disguise as a young man, Patricia is finding success as Patrick MacPherson. Formerly a surgeon's mate in His Majesty's Navy, Patrick has lately been employed aboard the colonial merchant schooner *Andromeda*, smuggling foreign molasses into Rhode Island. Late October, amidst riots against the newly imposed Stamp Act, she leaves Newport bound for the West Indies on her first run as *Andromeda's* master. In Havana a chance meeting with a former enemy presents unexpected opportunities while an encounter with a British frigate and an old lover threatens her liberty – and her life.
ISBN: 978-1-943404-12-4 978-1-943404-13-1

Blackwell's Paradise by V E Ulett
The repercussions of a court martial and the ill-will of powerful men at the Admiralty pursue Royal Navy Captain James Blackwell into the Pacific, where danger lurks around every coral reef. Even if Captain Blackwell and Mercedes survive the venture into the world of early nineteenth century exploration, can they emerge unchanged with their love intact. The mission to the Great South Sea will test their loyalties and strength, and define the characters of Captain Blackwell and his lady in *Blackwell's Paradise.*
ISBN 978-0-9882360-5-9

The Beckoning Ice by Joan Druett
The Beckoning Ice finds the U. S. Exploring Expedition off Cape Horn, a grim outpost made still more threatening by the report of a corpse on a drifting iceberg, closely followed by a gruesome death on board. Was it suicide, or a particularly brutal murder? Wiki investigates, only to find himself fighting desperately for his own life.
ISBN 978-0-9922588-3-2

The Shantyman by Rick Spilman
In 1870, on the clipper ship *Alahambra* in Sydney, the new crew comes aboard more or less sober, except for the last man, who is hoisted aboard in a cargo sling, paralytic drunk. The drunken sailor, Jack Barlow, will prove to be an able shantyman. On a ship with a dying captain and a murderous mate, Barlow will literally keep the crew pulling together. As he struggles with a tragic past, a troubled present and an uncertain future, Barlow will guide the *Alahambra* through Southern Ocean ice and the horror of an Atlantic hurricane. His one goal is bringing the ship and crew safely back to New York, where he hopes to start anew. Based on a true story, *The Shantyman* is a gripping tale of survival against all odds at sea and ashore, and the challenge of facing a past that can never be wholly left behind.
ISBN978-0-9941152-2-5

The Money Ship by Joan Druett
Oriental adventurer Captain Rochester spun an entrancing tale to Jerusha, seafaring daughter of Captain Michael Gardiner — a story of a money ship, hidden in the turquoise waters of the South China Sea, which was nothing less than the lost trove of the pirate Hochman. As Jerusha was to find, though, the clues that pointed the way to fabled riches were strange indeed — a haunted islet on an estuary in Borneo, an obelisk with a carving of a rampant dragon, a legend of kings and native priests at war, and of magically triggered tempests that swept warriors upriver. And even if the clues were solved, the route to riches was tortuous, involving treachery, adultery, murder, labyrinthine Malayan politics … and, ultimately, Jerusha's own arranged marriage.
An epic drama of fortune-hunting in the South China Sea during the first two decades of the nineteenth century, The Money Ship is a fast-moving novel on a sprawling canvas that spans three oceans and a myriad of exotic ports. As the pages turn, Jerusha voyages from the smuggling and fishing port of Lewes, Sussex to Boston in its glittering heyday, then back to newly settled Singapore, until her quest for love and pirate treasure comes to a spine-chilling climax in the benighted lands of Borneo.
ISBN 978-0994124647

Blackwell's Homecoming by V E Ulett

In a multigenerational saga of love, war and betrayal, Captain Blackwell and Mercedes continue their voyage in Volume III of Blackwell's Adventures. The Blackwell family's eventful journey from England to Hawaii, by way of the new and tempestuous nations of Brazil and Chile, provides an intimate portrait of family conflicts and loyalties in the late Georgian Age. Blackwell's Homecoming is an evocation of the dangers and rewards of desire.

ISBN 978-0-9882360-7-3

Britannia's Gamble by Antoine Vanner

The Dawlish Chronicles: March 1884 – February 1885

1884 - a fanatical Islamist revolt is sweeping all before it in the vast wastes of the Sudan and establishing a rule of persecution and terror. Only the city of Khartoum holds out, its defence masterminded by a British national hero, General Charles Gordon. His position is weakening by the day and a relief force, crawling up the Nile from Egypt, may not reach him in time to avert disaster.

But there is one other way of reaching Gordon…

A boyhood memory leaves the ambitious Royal Navy officer Nicholas Dawlish no option but to attempt it. The obstacles are daunting – barren mountains and parched deserts, tribal rivalries and merciless enemies – and this even before reaching the river that is key to the mission. Dawlish knows that every mile will be contested and that the siege at Khartoum is quickly moving towards its bloody climax.

Outnumbered and isolated, with only ingenuity, courage and fierce allies to sustain them, with safety in Egypt far beyond the Nile's raging cataracts, Dawlish and his mixed force face brutal conflict on land and water as the Sudan descends into ever-worsening savagery.

And for Dawlish himself, one unexpected and tragic event will change his life forever.

Britannia's Gamble is a desperate one. The stakes are high, the odds heavily loaded against success. Has Dawlish accepted a mission that can only end in failure – and worse?

ISBN 978-1-943404-17-9 978-1-943404-18-6

HMS Prometheus by Alaric Bond

With Britain under the threat of invasion, HMS *Prometheus* is needed to reinforce Nelson's ships blockading the French off Toulon. But a major action has left her severely damaged and the Mediterranean fleet outnumbered. *Prometheus* must be brought back to fighting order without delay, yet the work required proves more complex than a simple refit.

Barbary pirates, shore batteries and the powerful French Navy are conventional opponents, although the men of *Prometheus* encounter additional enemies, within their own ranks. A story that combines vivid action with sensitive character portrayal.

ISBN 978-1943404063

Britannia's Spartan by Antoine Vanner

It's 1882 and Captain Nicholas Dawlish has taken command of the Royal Navy's newest cruiser, HMS *Leonidas*. Her voyage to the Far East is to be peaceful, a test of innovative engines and boilers. But a new balance of power is emerging there. Imperial China, weak and corrupt, is challenged by a rapidly modernising Japan, while Russia threatens from the north. They all need to control Korea, a kingdom frozen in time and reluctant to emerge from centuries of isolation. Dawlish has no forewarning of the nightmare of riot, treachery, massacre and battle that lies ahead and in this, the fourth of the Dawlish Chronicles, he will find himself stretched to his limits – and perhaps beyond.

ISBN 978-1943404049

The Blackstrap Station by Alaric Bond

Christmas 1803, although the group of shipwrecked Royal Navy seamen have anything but festivities in mind as they pitch their wits against a French force sent to catch them. And all the while rescue, in the shape of a British frigate, lies temptingly close, yet just beyond their reach… Encompassing vicious sea battles, spirited land action and treachery from friend as much as foe, *The Blackstrap Station* tells a stirring tale of courage, honour and loyalty, set against the backdrop of what becomes a broiling Mediterranean summer.

ISBN 978-1-943404-10-0 e.book 978-1-943404-11-7 paperback

Water Ghosts by Linda Collison

Fifteen-year-old James McCafferty is an unwilling sailor aboard a traditional Chinese junk, operated as adventure-therapy for troubled teens. Once at sea, the ship is gradually taken over by the spirits of courtiers who fled the Imperial court during the Ming Dynasty, more than 600 years ago. One particular ghost wants what James has and is intent on trading places with him. But the teens themselves are their own worst enemies in the struggle for life in the middle of the Pacific Ocean. A psychological story set at sea, with historical and paranormal elements.

ISBN 978-1943404001

Eleanor's Odyssey by Joan Druett

It was 1799, and French privateers lurked in the Atlantic and the Bay of Bengal. Yet Eleanor Reid, newly married and just twenty-one years old, made up her mind to sail with her husband, Captain Hugh Reid, to the penal colony of New South Wales, the Spice Islands and India. Danger threatened not just from the barely charted seas they would be sailing, yet, confident in her love and her husband's seamanship, Eleanor insisted on going along. Joan Druett, writer of many books about the sea, including the bestseller Island of the Lost and the groundbreaking story of women under sail, Hen Frigates, embellishes Eleanor's journal with a commentary that illuminates the strange story of a remarkable young woman.

ISBN 978-0-9941152-1-8

Captain Blackwell's Prize by V E Ulett

A small, audacious British frigate does battle against a large but ungainly Spanish ship. British Captain James Blackwell intercepts the Spanish *La Trinidad*, outmaneuvers and outguns the treasure ship and boards her. Fighting alongside the Spanish captain, sword in hand, is a beautiful woman. The battle is quickly over. The Spanish captain is killed in the fray and his ship damaged beyond repair. Its survivors and treasure are taken aboard the British ship, *Inconstant*.

ISBN 978-0-9882360-6-6

Hell Around the Horn by Rick Spilman

In 1905, a young ship's captain and his family set sail on the windjammer, *Lady Rebecca*, from Cardiff, Wales with a cargo of coal bound for Chile, by way of Cape Horn. Before they reach the Southern Ocean, the cargo catches fire, the mate threatens mutiny and one of the crew may be going mad. The greatest challenge, however, will prove to be surviving the vicious westerly winds and mountainous seas of the worst Cape Horn winter in memory. Told from the perspective of the Captain, his wife, a first year apprentice and an American sailor before the mast, *Hell Around the Horn* is a story of survival and the human spirit in the last days of the great age of sail. ISBN 978-0-9882360-1-1

Lady Castaways by Joan Druett

It was not just the men who lived on the brink of peril when under sail at sea. Lucretia Jansz, who was enslaved as a concubine in 1629, was just one woman who endured a castaway experience. Award-winning historian Joan Druett (*Island of the Lost, The Elephant Voyage)*, relates the stories of women who survived remarkable challenges, from heroines like Mary Ann Jewell, the "governess" of Auckland Island in the icy sub-Antarctic, to Millie Jenkins, whose ship was sunk by a whale.
ISBN 978-0994115270

Britannia's Shark by Antione Vanner

"Britannia's Shark" is the third of the Dawlish Chronicles novels. It's 1881 and a daring act of piracy draws the ambitious British naval officer, Nicholas Dawlish, into a deadly maelstrom of intrigue and revolution. Drawn in too is his wife Florence, for whom the glimpse of a half-forgotten face evokes memories of earlier tragedy. For both a nightmare lies ahead, amid the wealth and squalor of America's Gilded Age and on a fever-ridden island ruled by savage tyranny. Manipulated ruthlessly from London by the shadowy Admiral Topcliffe, Nicholas and Florence Dawlish must make some very strange alliances if they are to survive – and prevail.
ISBN 978-0992263690

The Guinea Boat by Alaric Bond
Set in Hastings, Sussex during the early part of 1803, *Guinea Boat* tells the story of two young lads, and the diverse paths they take to make a living on the water. Britain is still at an uneasy peace with France, but there is action and intrigue a plenty along the south-east coast. Private fights and family feuds abound; a hot press threatens the livelihoods of many, while the newly re-formed Sea Fencibles begin a careful watch on Bonaparte's ever growing invasion fleet. And to top it all, free trading has grown to the extent that it is now a major industry, and one barely kept in check by the efforts of the preventive men. Alaric Bond's eighth novel.
ISBN 978-0994115294

The Scent of Corruption by Alaric Bond
Summer, 1803: the uneasy peace with France is over, and Britain has once more been plunged into the turmoil of war. After a spell on the beach, Sir Richard Banks is appointed to HMS *Prometheus*, a seventy-four gun line-of-battleship which an eager Admiralty loses no time in ordering to sea. The ship is fresh from a major re-fit, but Banks has spent the last year with his family: will he prove worthy of such a powerful vessel, and can he rely on his officers to support him?
With excitement both aboard ship and ashore, gripping sea battles, a daring rescue and intense personal intrigue, *The Scent of Corruption* is a non-stop nautical thriller in the best traditions of the genre. Number seven in the Fighting Sail series.
ISBN 978-1943404025

Turn a Blind Eye by Alaric Bond
Newly appointed to the local revenue cutter, Commander Griffin is determined to make his mark, and defeat a major gang of smugglers. But the country is still at war with France and it is an unequal struggle; can he depend on support from the local community, or are they yet another enemy for him to fight? With dramatic action on land and at sea, *Turn a Blind Eye* exposes the private war against the treasury with gripping fact and fascinating detail.
ISBN 978-0-9882360-3-5

The Torrid Zone by Alaric Bond

A tired ship with a worn out crew, but *HMS Scylla* has one more trip to make before her much postponed re-fit. Bound for St Helena, she is to deliver the island's next governor; a simple enough mission and, as peace looks likely to be declared, no one is expecting difficulties. Except, perhaps, the commander of a powerful French battle squadron, who has other ideas.

With conflict and intrigue at sea and ashore, *The Torrid Zone* is filled to the gunnels with action, excitement and fascinating historical detail; a truly engaging read.

ISBN 978-0988236097

Made in the USA
Middletown, DE
13 May 2020